Romance at Stonegate

Ellen M. Levy

(Author of *My First 65 Years*)

The characters in this book are fictional. The places, weather, newsworthy events (Sinking of The Titanic, The Big Wind, etc.) and times (for train schedules, Shabbos candle lighting, etc.) are historically accurate.

ISBN: 9781986345248

Dedication

To the brave women of the early 1900's,
who laid the foundation for our freedom as lesbians.

And to my wife and friends,
who have endured my obsession
with Deborah and Miriam.

TABLE OF CONTENTS

Preface i
Acknowledgements iii
The Family Trees vi

I. STEPS TO ROMANCE

Step One . . . . Quest 1
Step Two . . . . Sparks 6
Step Three . . . . Foundation 9
Step Four . . . . Intrigue 13
Step Five . . . . Awareness 16
Step Six . . . . Correspondence 20
Step Seven . . . . Re-acquaintance 26
Step Eight . . . . Intrigue 33
Step Nine . . . . Shabbos 35
Step Ten . . . . Kisses 37
Step Eleven . . . . Awakening 39
Step Twelve . . . . Desire 41
Step Thirteen . . . . Excitement 44
Step Fourteen . . . . Adventure 47
Step Fifteen . . . . Judgment 50
Step Sixteen . . . . Ecstasy 53
Step Seventeen . . . . . . Passion 55
Step Eighteen . . . . Separation 59
Step Nineteen . . . . Anticipation 63
Step Twenty . . . . Syncopation 66
Step Twenty-One . . . . . Lost 69
Step Twenty-Two . . . . . Jealousy 73
Step Twenty-Three . . . . Opportunity 76
Step Twenty-Four . . . . . Paradise 78
Step Twenty-Five . . . . . Declaration 82
Step Twenty-Six . . . . . . Commitment 85
Step Twenty-Seven . . . . Intimacy 89
Step Twenty-Eight . . . . . Celebration 92
Step Twenty-Nine . . . . . Transitions 95
Step Thirty . . . . Comfort 98
Step Thirty-One . . . . . . Arrangements 101
Step Thirty-Two . . . . . . Reflections 104

II. STAGES IN ROMANCE

Stage I . . . . Introduction to Boston 109
Stage II . . . . Cohen Family 112
Stage III . . . . Privacy 115
Stage IV . . . . Adjustment 117
Stage V . . . . Museum 119
Stage VI . . . . Intolerance 122
Stage VII . . . . Exploring Boston 124

Stage VIII . . . . Discovered 130
Stage IX . . . . Discord 132
Stage X . . . . Jewish Practices 135
Stage XI . . . . Boston History Lesson 139
Stage XII . . . . Birthday Celebration 142
Stage XIII. . . . . Lesbian Connections 145
Stage XIV . . . . Ruth's News. 151
Stage XV . . . . Exploring New York 153
Stage XVI. . . . . Christian Holiday Season 162
Stage XVII . . . . The Letter. 165
Stage XVIII. . . . . Wedding 169
Stage XIX. . . . . Explanations 175

III. ROMANCE TO RELATIONSHIP

Peyrek (Yiddish for "Chapter")

Peyrek A . . . . New York Adjustment 181
Peyrek B . . . . First Steps 183
Peyrek C . . . . New Endeavors 186
Peyrek D . . . . Bubbie 190
Peyrek E . . . . Friends 196
Peyrek F . . . . Reconnection 199
Peyrek G . . . . Next Steps 201
Peyrek H . . . . College 206
Peyrek I. . . . . Henry Street Settlement. 207
Peyrek J. . . . . Governess Duties 209
Peyrek K . . . . Extra! Extra! 210
Peyrek L . . . . Baby Sylvia 213
Peyrek M . . . . Crisis in Boston 215
Peyrek N . . . . Suffrage Parade. 217
Peyrek O . . . . Baby Love. 220
Peyrek P . . . . Return to the Berkshires 224
Peyrek Q . . . . Ruth's Choice. 227
Peyrek R . . . . Sylvia's Fate 229
Peyrek S . . . . Family. 238
Peyrek T . . . . Heartache. 241
Peyrek U . . . . Reunion. 243
Peyrek V . . . . Publishing Shop 248
Peyrek W. . . . . Readjustment. 251
Peyrek X . . . . Boston. 253
Peyrek Y . . . . The Move 256
Peyrek Z . . . . Success 257

IV. LOVE

Part 1 . . . . Valentine's Day. 263
Part 2 . . . . Shanda/Shame 264
Part 3 . . . . Wedding Preparation 266
Part 4 . . . . Nuptials. 272
Glossary . . . . Hebrew/Yiddish 280

Preface

What a joy it has been to write this book! What began as a short story while staying at my timeshare, a romantic turn-of-the-century "cottage" named Stonegate, in Great Barrington, Massachusetts, took on a life of its own. My girls (an appropriate term for 17 and 18 year olds in 1910) became a rich part of my everyday life. My perspective on the world changed as I imagined each place I visited as it might have been during the early part of the last century.

The historical research was fascinating. What was the actual weather on the days mentioned in the book, the right time for sundown on each Shabbos, the correct train schedule, or the accurate days of religious observance, etc.? I had to take a few liberties, such as:

The Boston Symphony Orchestra performed Bruch's Kol Nidre concert two evenings earlier in Northampton, Massachusetts, rather than at Symphony Hall.

The actual ice cream shop in Great Barrington in 1910 was owned by a gentleman named "Foote", but the only photograph I could find was from Cassidy's, a shop that opened on Main Street in 1914.

The photograph of Squaw Peak, at Monument Mountain Reservation, was taken from the southern view, though they would have traveled north to get there from Great Barrington. There were too many electrical wires in the photographs from the correct direction, so I took it heading south and reversed the picture!

The photographs from Henry Street Settlement House are current. The original entrance has been blocked and the signs are from this century but I thought it better to have photos of the actual building.

I also took present day photographs of many of the buildings I mentioned in the book. I tried to avoid anything modern, though some of the photos may not accurately represent what things looked like in the 1910's. For example, the sign for the "Aspinwall Equestrian Stables" was still standing, but it presently looks like it is over 100 years old. I assume the paint would not be as faded as it appears in the photo. (But imagine my excitement to find the original sign still standing!)

One of the other interesting aspects to writing a book set in 1910 was to imagine what it was like to be a lesbian in that era. Today, we take many privileges for granted. How lonely it must have been then, before lesbian bars and events, before books on alternative lifestyles, before the internet! It was a challenge for my girls to find other young women to understand their issues.

I feel grateful for those courageous souls who dared to be true to their sexual identity in a time short on openness and acceptance of differences. I hope this book helps make LGBT young adults aware of the struggles that faced the women who came before us.

Ellen Levy at Stonegate

Acknowledgements

Had I realized the intensity of research required to make this project historically accurate, or that it would take 46 edits to get to the finish line, or how many wonderful people I needed to assist me in producing a well-written book, I would have shied away from the task. But I am grateful for the experience and for the patience of my loving wife, Pauline Albrecht, who endured my daily communion with my characters, Deborah and Miriam. She reminded me periodically that they were not real people, something I occasionally forgot.

The first group I need to thank regarding my blossoming writing skills, are the wonderful women of my Writer's Circle, at my winter home, The Resort on Carefree Boulevard. Led by Dana Finnegan, my first mentor in this process, I was gently guided to make significant changes to my a very rough draft, thinking it my final copy. Many hours and about 30 edits later, I am astounded by their encouragement, given the confusing and poorly written material I initially presented.

I then approached my friends Cindy Empey and Phyllis Guiliano, to read the book and give me feedback. They said I had written a wonderful story, not curbing my enthusiasm by telling me how much work there was left to do.

I then joined a small group of fiction writers, where I was gracefully led to writing better prose by my next mentor, Kate Barteletti. Kate, along with Cookie Gibbs and Nancy Carlson, gave me concrete assistance that helped me craft my story into an easier-to-read and possible-to-follow tale. Once, I even caught my neighbor Maureen Coughlan on her way to Dublin in one of my many attempts to get her assistance in making my Irish governess character, Bridget, more authentic.

The next step in my journey was to gather historically accurate information about the times and the places. The librarians in Great Barrington, Lenox, and Pittsfield, Massachusetts were great guides. Gary Levelle, the archivist of the Great Barrington Historical Society provided me with information about the town, Stonegate's history, and the picture of the Cassidy Ice Cream Parlor. A trip to the Yiddish Book Center in Amherst, Massachusetts, changed my storyline, when I discovered several actual printing presses from 1910 behind the book displays. On the spot, I changed Mr. Cohen's printing press to one that exclusively published Yiddish literature. It was then necessary for Bubbie, his mother, to be primarily Yiddish speaking, so I got assistance from Phil Schwartz, a friend's 95-year-old father, whose mother-tongue was Yiddish.

Phil taught me that Bubbie would never say "Come sit down", but rather, "Come sit down and eat something".

Next were those who helped me gather historically accurate information for the Boston locations. An architectural tour of the Boston Public library and tours at Isabella Stewart Garner Museum and the Museum of Fine Arts added to my data and to my ever-growing collection of photographs. My experience of all these familiar locations took on a whole new 1910 perspective.

My visit to Manhattan was thrilling. Finding the Knickerbocker Hotel was amazing because, despite its complete modernization, the outside façade remained untouched. Inside I discovered a historical book about the hotel and a manager, Hank Serreno graciously gave me a copy. Standing at the gate of Barnard College, imagining my girls as they took their first steps into this campus made my heart thump. Next, I combed the streets of the Upper West side until I found the perfect home for the Levines. The Tenement Museum bought reality of the times to light, since the buildings were restored to the early 1900's. The most overwhelming experience was standing outside the still operational Henry Street Settlement House and being told stories of its founder, Lillian Wald, by an older woman who grew up across the street and knew the local folklore.

Back in Boston, I wanted to gather more information about what it would be like to be a lesbian in 1910's. I met with Libby Bouvier at The History Project, the group chronicling Boston's LGBT history. Libby added information that enabled me to enrich the characters and she provided details that will guide my sequel!

I reached out to several people to assist me with my writing skills. At about the 35th edit, I read the entire book out-loud to my friend, Sara Fleming, during a road trip and she provided a needed perspective. I also read it to my wife, Pauline Albrecht, who had been waiting anxiously to hear my story, my sister, Nancy Levy, and my college roommate, Vicki Kaplan. Nancy and Vicki were my Jewish guides, helping enrich cultural and religious details. I then read part to Ed Drucker, who helped me tremendously with my writing skills; I could hear his comments in my head as I completed additional edits on my own. Lois Johnson and Lois McGuiness both listened to parts and gave me valuable feedback.

I had selected a photograph to represent Deborah, but it's copyright was held through Duke University. I would like to credit "Hugh Mangum Photographs, David M. Rubenstein Rare book & Manuscript Library, Duke University," for the photograph of Deborah Levine.

Then my third beloved mentor, Fay Jacobs entered my life. A writer herself, she offered me incredible guidance, both in grammar and in developing the story arc. Fay helped me turn a good story into well-written prose, something for which I will be forever grateful.

As the book neared completion, I still had to face the numerous typographical errors I had created while editing, punctuation (my greatest weakness), and the necessity of tightening the book, which had reached over 100,000 words. I read it out-loud again to Vicki Kaplan, who read along and helped me tremendously with an initial copy edit and with detailed content changes. Phyllis Guiliano graciously agreed to do a final copy edit, reading it for third and fourth times and offering exceptional commentary regarding inconsistencies.

The final step was to compile historically accurate photographs to transport you into the era in which I have been living for the past two years. I took many photos of still existing structures and searched the internet to fill in the gaps. Then I turned to Sara Yager, a friend and graphic designer, to work her magic with my grainy pictures from the early 1900's. She expertly and precisely prepared this project for publication, enhancing the photographs and designing the layout. Sara was a gift to this book.

My hard work was supported by a huge cadre of friends who supported me through this process. I cannot thank each individually yet I could not have managed without their guidance. They made this project a pleasure, rather than a task, making it so enjoyable that I have almost completed the first draft of the sequel!

One final acknowledgement is to my Aunt Sylvia, my father's special needs sister, who lent her name to the baby in this book. She lived a short life in the early 1900's and she would be a forgotten soul, except for this testament to her existence.

Family Tree
(Age in 1910)

LEVINE

Mr. Levine
(40) ——— Mrs. Levine
(38)

Deborah
(18)

Milton
(14)

Anna
(11)

45 West Street, Great Barrington, Mass.

410 Riverside Drive, New York City

The Levines are a warm, loving family with an affluent New York City life. They are excited with their new country home, where they can be closer to nature and can get away from the hectic pace of the city.

Family Tree
(Age in 1910)

COHEN

Bubbie
(68)

Mr. Cohen ——————— Mrs. Cohen
(50)   (39)

Miriam
(17)

Hannah
(21)

22 Homestead Street, Roxbury, Mass.

Soon after immigrating to the United States, the Cohens moved to Roxbury, Mass.
Mr. Cohen's successful Yiddish publishing company on Boston's Newspaper Row
has allowed them to purchase a single-family home near their temple. Mr. Cohen's
mother, Bubbie, moved in with them after her husband, Zadie, died.

Family Tree
(Age in 1910)

GOLD

Mr. Gold
(46)

Mrs. Gold
(35)

Ruth
(18)

David
(15)

Beth
(13)

94 West Street, Great Barrington, MA

353 Riverside Drive, NYC

The Gold's are a successful, cosmopolitan New York family. They have a great interest in accumulating anything that will showcase their material wealth, such as high fashion, a particular passion of both their daughters.

Family Tree
(Age in 1910)

BERKOWITZ

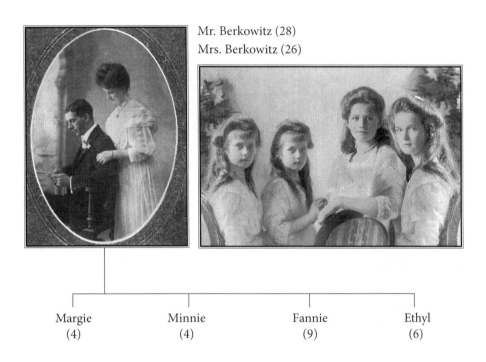

Mr. Berkowitz (28)
Mrs. Berkowitz (26)

Margie	Minnie	Fannie	Ethyl
(4)	(4)	(9)	(6)

11 Old Stockbridge Road, Lenox, MA   *410 Riverside Drive, NYC*

This young family moved into the same building as the Levines in New York City, and they quickly became close friends. The Levines were quickly drawn to the sweet parents and their four adorable daughters. The Berkowitzes later purchased a large cottage in Lenox, MA.

Deborah Levine

Miriam Cohen

Steps to Romance

Step One ❧ Quest
Tuesday, July 5, 1910

"Oh, Deborah, why are you crying?"

"I have cried myself to sleep every night since you told me of your plans for our extravagant new summer home, Mother. You are wildly enthusiastic, but I am dismayed with your endless adventure in rural living," Deborah said, surprised her mother had entered her bedroom without knocking.

After Deborah admitted her distress, Mrs. Levine lovingly embraced her eighteen-year-old daughter.

"Deborah, I hope that in time you will view this experience with enthusiasm. Many families of New York and Boston have built summer cottages in the Berkshire Mountains, so we will not be the only city people in the western corner of Massachusetts. After a harsh winter, the area becomes a world-class cultural center, with museums to explore, concerts to attend, and even some noteworthy theater. I believe we will all learn to appreciate the beauty of this mountainous area and to love our new country life."

It was 1910, and the Levines of Manhattan had searched all the Berkshire hill towns and chose Great Barrington for their luxurious vacation home. This was an ideal village, with small shops, a theater, and local farms to provide for everyone's needs. The Levines found an exceptional plot of land on a large hilly area on the edge of town. They set about designing their dream home and named it "Stonegate". None of them imagined this would be the perfect setting for unexpected romance.

"Oh, Mother, I know you want me to be pleased," Deborah said with tears running down her cheeks and a raised voice, "But I am not happy with this decision. I would rather be with my friends in the city than be stuck in some remote country village. Maybe I should stay here and let you go without me." She slumped in her chair and became quiet.

Mother took a step back, unused to being yelled at by her daughter. "Please give this a chance, Deborah. You just might find it to your liking, once you are there."

"Well, I doubt that!"

Even after Mrs. Levine's gallant effort to entice her eldest daughter with her romantic notions, Deborah remained leery about ever finding happiness in Great Barrington. She imagined sitting on the veranda of her new home for hours on end, reading and re-reading the books she brought from New York.

After a few moments of restless thought, Deborah blurted out, with surprising hostility in her voice, "You are taking me away from everything I am accustomed to. It is painful to think of my friends exploring the latest exhibit at the Metropolitan Museum or attending "Ziegfeld's Follies" at the Jardin de Paris Theater, which I will certainly miss. While my friends enjoy the stimulation of New York City, I will be in isolation: bored, lonely, and counting the days until fall. You clearly do not understand how difficult it will be for me, as for any girl my age, to be isolated from my friends and everything which brings me comfort."

Mrs. Levine hoped Deborah's concerns would dissipate when she said, "I have one piece of information that might change your mind. I recently learned our closest neighbor will be another Jewish family from New York, the Golds, and they have an 18-year-old daughter, Ruth, just your age!"

"I am pleased to hear that, but I am still distressed," said Deborah with her right hand on her hip.

"I hope you will change your mind." The discussion ended abruptly as Deborah got up and left her mother sitting alone in the room.

In the months leading up to the move and her long train-ride to Great Barrington, Deborah anticipated making Ruth's acquaintance. Despite her determination to dislike everything about this move, she was slightly hopeful about Ruth. Yet, she presumed they would not have any shared interests or values.

At their first meeting, soon after she arrived, Deborah felt disappointed. Their potential as friends dissipated as it became clear that Ruth cared more about fostering her social popularity than serious relationships, including those with her own family. Deborah had learned from her mother, a beautiful, fashionable, wealthy woman who could have anything she wanted in the world, that it was the merits of strong relationships, especially with one's family, that provided worth.

Ruth, on the other hand, made sport of leaving family behind and assembling everyone about her age into her social circle. She quickly included Deborah in her daily gathering at the ice cream parlor, though Deborah wondered if she and Ruth had anything at all in common. Not only did Ruth seem superficial, Deborah found her obsession with the young boys in town quite tiresome. Ruth's companions seemed frivolous, though Deborah imagined that their company would be somewhat better than loneliness. From Deborah's perspective, these young folks lacked the richness of spirit of her New York friends, yet Deborah knew there were no other choices for her summer activities other than re-reading her books.

Since summer began, Ruth tracked the arrival of the young people to their vacation homes, declaring that enough had arrived to have a festive party at her home. Ruth claimed her party was to introduce everyone to her friend from overnight camp, Miriam Cohen from Boston, who was to stay for almost three weeks. Deborah surmised Miriam was just an excuse for Ruth to have the first party of the season. Because of Deborah's apprehension about the young people she had met so far, she had little faith that she would like Miriam any better than the others. She was very wrong.

Deborah's Journal, July 6, 1910

I am still not pleased with this countryside venture, and meeting Ruth and her friends has not helped my mood. Now I have to go to a boring party, with people I don't like, and I have to be nice to Ruth's camp friend, Miriam.

Maybe I am being too pessimistic, my usual approach. I need to remember my mother's words, 'You'll never know unless you try.' She tells me to view everything with a positive attitude; it is the way to make something good of a difficult situation. Mother is so wise. So, keeping her philosophy in mind, I will walk into this party with a new outlook.

After all, I live my life as if I am the same as other girls, but I know in my heart that I am different. I long for a female companion as in my dreams, but I must live my truth in secret. Might I ever find a person like myself? Might there be a girl of my dreams?

In the house next door, Ruth's friend, Miriam, was equally apprehensive about this party, but for different reasons. She was usually optimistic, and she had great hopes that her 17th summer would bring richness to her life. When her camp friend, Ruth Gold, graciously invited her to spend almost three weeks in the Berkshire Mountains, Miriam was excited. Ruth promised the weather to be temperate, and each day filled with fascinating young people. But now that Miriam was here, she was uncomfortable about many aspects of the adventure.

She worried over her personal insecurities and lack of experience at parties. In her own Boston neighborhood, she attended family celebrations, Bar Mitzvahs and weddings. She had never attended an un-chaperoned party with her peers. What should she wear? How to behave? Would she embarrass her hostess? Miriam was not used to being around boys, except those with whom she had grown up. In fact, her social life revolved around her sister, Hannah, her neighbor, Marjorie, and several girls from the synagogue.

Miriam's nervousness extended beyond this party. Most significantly, she realized that, for the first time in her life, she would not be eating kosher meats, since there were no kosher butchers in the area. Miriam decided she could manage because the Golds ate in a kosher style: no milk with meat, and no pork or shellfish at any time.

Also, there was no synagogue to attend for Sabbath. While Miriam appreciated the adventure away from her parents, being away from her older sister, Hannah, made her uneasy. They had never been apart for long and Miriam worried Hannah would be isolated in her absence. Hannah had no friends other than her sister.

Hannah seemed happy with a life centered on the temple and her family, not seeming to need friends. She never expressed thoughts of a richer life ahead nor talked of marriage or children. She filled her days with reading, living her life through the characters in her books. Hannah studied art books for hours on end, appearing content, though it was difficult to know because Hannah rarely spoke of her feelings. Yet Miriam valued her sister's opinions; they turned to each other to discuss everything of importance in their lives.

College was never a financial option for either Cohen sister, and their father deemed it inappropriate for them to find work. Without a husband or children to attend to, their weeks were all the same. Weekdays had little predictable activity other than playing board games in the evenings. Weekends focused on attending temple, and honoring Shabbos, the Sabbath, with a period of rest.

During her first couple of days in Great Barrington, Ruth's family troubled Miriam. Ruth's parents, though pleasant, were unlike her own parents. Instead of hovering over Ruth and providing for all her needs, they remained uninvolved in their children's lives. Ruth's brother, David, a soft-faced, brooding 15-year-old, did not interact with anyone. Beth, her perky, 13-year-old sister, spent much of her days primping in front of the mirror. None of these people interested Miriam, but she knew she would adapt.

Miriam was also unsure about Ruth, an especially pretty girl, with small features, lovely skin, a delicate mouth, and mounds of dark, shiny hair. When Ruth directed her gaze at people, her piercing almond-shaped eyes made people notice. Her fashion sensibility and an endless clothing budget assured that she was always dressed in up-to-date finery. But these characteristics never attracted Miriam. Instead, Miriam was drawn toward people who displayed compassion and had a gentle demeanor.

Ruth and Miriam had been wonderful camp bunkmates, always whispering late into the night after the lights went out, talking about the other girls, the camp activities, and planning what they would do together the next day. Miriam was grateful to be included in Ruth's social activities. However, during Miriam's first days in the countryside, Ruth seemed to be the one doing all the chatting. She prattled on about mutual friends in what felt like gossip rather than shared recollections. Ruth asked very little about Miriam's family, her friends, her interests. Miriam hoped that would change.

Despite her discomfort, Miriam retained great hopes for the summer. She daydreamed that she would walk into the party and find someone with whom to fall in love. Then her thoughts turned sour, imagining spilling her drink all over her new dress. Her father always said, "Look at each new experience for its potential." Miriam decided to try her best to remain open to adventure.

Miriam's Diary, July 6, 1910

I have felt ill at ease since arriving in Great Barrington. In comparison with Ruth's exuberance, my life seems dull and unimportant. I am grateful to have pleasing friends, wonderful parents, and a sister who adores me, yet I am unsatisfied. Something is missing. I don't want to spend my life living up to everyone's expectations and only being noticed as a good girl. I want to become better than my parents' dreams for me. Despite all the sweetness around me, I feel lonely and inconsequential.

My dreams are vague. Everyone expects that by my age I will marry and have children to fulfill my life. But no boy has ever captured my heart. And, although I love children, I want to create something or be part of something bigger than myself. I want purpose outside of motherhood. How does a girl who has finished school create anything new in her life? How can a life that is so predicable be gratifying or interesting? Will this visit be the beginning of a new life for me? Will I learn to be more self-assured? Could this be the adventure I am seeking? I hope so.

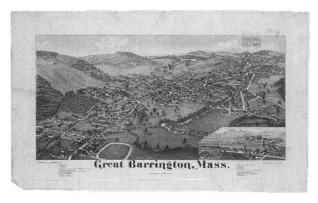

Great Barrington, Mass.

Step Two ✦ *Sparks*
Thursday, July 7, 1910

"It is time for a party!" exclaimed Ruth with a bright-eyed look beaming across her face.

She explained she had arranged a gathering to introduce Miriam to her friends. But Miriam winced. "Thank you for going out of your way to arrange this get-together but I am not used to parties. I hope I don't embarrass you."

Ruth waved her hands in dismissal, saying, "You'll have a good time. I wanted to have the first party of the season and your arrival gave me a good reason."

The only topic of discussion during Miriam's first two days in the country was this party. Ruth went through Miriam's clothes to choose what she should wear, selecting a simple light blue dress. Then Ruth went through her own wardrobe to find jewelry and a hat for Miriam since those she packed did not live up to Ruth's standards. Once Miriam's outfit was set, Ruth moved to concerns about her own clothing. She spent hours choosing what to wear, the food she would serve, who to invite, and other details of minor interest to Miriam.

Miriam was relieved the party would be on Sunday, because sundown on Saturday, the end of the Sabbath, was not until 8:32 pm. Neither Ruth nor Miriam would be able to attend a party during Shabbos.

For Miriam, this Shabbos would be the first in her life when she would not be in temple. The Gold family would observe a day of rest from Friday sundown to Saturday sundown in observance of the strict Sabbath rituals.

On the night of the party, Ruth appeared downstairs in her fashionable empire-style scarlet silk dress with a low-cut lace bodice. The dress had a huge deep scarlet bow under her breasts, with a matching sash atop the overskirt. A lace panel peaked through a slit in the front of her long gown. Ruth walked erectly, with her head raised and shoulders back, parading around the parlor to show off her costume. Once she had collected enough accolades from the family to please her, she was ready to welcome her guests.

Ruth and Miriam stood at the doorway as young people arrived; everyone dressed perfectly, in fashions suitable for a New York party. Ruth, distracted when they made a fuss about her dress, forgot to introduce Miriam. No one commented on Miriam's attire nor made any attempt to engage her, making Miriam aware of how Ruth was different than she was at camp. She was flirty with all the young men, something Miriam never expected, since Ruth spoke disinterestedly of boys during their late night talks at camp.

Miriam's awkwardness with unfamiliar people lessened when Ruth's new neighbor, Deborah Levine, arrived. Deborah, a tall, exceptionally attractive young lady with inquisitive eyes, wore a tailored white blouse and a simple beige linen skirt, a less fashionable ensemble than those worn by others. Deborah was quite awkward during her introduction to Miriam, her face noticeably flushed. Deborah was a little tongue-tied, an ungainliness which put Miriam at ease.

Instead of fussing over Ruth, Deborah turned to Miriam and asked her where the cold drinks were being served. Miriam pardoned herself and led Deborah to the dining room, where they noticed they could speak together without interruption.

The girls made pleasantries, sipping lemonade, conversing calmly and quietly, avoiding the bustling activity in the parlor. Miriam's outstanding beauty, her soft wavy dark hair, sweet face, lithe body, and deep, bright eyes mesmerized Deborah. Unlike Ruth, Miriam was reserved. Her soft blue dress trimmed in white eyelet lace made Miriam appear sweet.

Miriam noticed she was at ease for the first time since arriving in the Berkshires, partially because Deborah appeared more serene than the others. Miriam was happy to answer Deborah's many questions.

"Is there great theater in Boston?" Deborah said with wide-open eyes. "Do you go to parties like this one often? Do you have any sisters or brothers?"

As Miriam answered each query, Deborah always had another question ready. Suddenly Miriam ran out of things to say. Without any warning, she excused herself and joined the chattering young girls on the back porch. She left so suddenly, Deborah wondered if she had said something to offend her and followed a few minutes later. She found Miriam standing slightly behind Ruth and her circle of friends. Miriam seemed a little uncomfortable, yet Deborah noticed that Ruth did nothing to bring her into the conversation.

Deborah stood alone in a corner, gazing at Miriam but trying not to be too obvious. After a few minutes, Deborah noticed one of the boys enter the porch and head directly to Miriam. He stood quite close to her and tried to engage her in conversation. The boy reached out to touch Miriam's arm and Miriam automatically withdrew from him. Deborah thought, That is just as I would do. He tried again and again Miriam pulled her arm away. When he did this a third time, Deborah could not tolerate watching his misbehavior.

"Stop being disrespectful," Deborah called out to the boy, as she approached them and pulled his arm off her. "Leave her alone."

Deborah immediately realized this was none of her business. Miriam had not asked for assistance, yet Deborah could not stand to watch him make such a sweet girl uncomfortable. Luckily, no one else heard this interaction. Deborah did not know if Miriam was pleased or annoyed with the rescue. She was angry with herself for intervening.

Unsure of her next move, Deborah went into the other room to sulk. This attractive girl had captured her attention and she had just behaved badly. She thought, I have a bad habit of acting impulsively when my sensibilities are rattled. A moment later, when Miriam approached, Deborah averted her eyes and walked away. By now, she was fairly certain Miriam was aggravated.

Deborah recognized her interest in Miriam as similar to how she once felt about a girl in her school. She wanted to have a close friendship, and it did not end well. Mad at herself for her actions then and now, Deborah bid Ruth a quick goodbye and walked out the door.

Miriam was confused by Deborah's sudden departure, having found Deborah's somewhat forceful interruption a relief from the boy's unwanted advances. Miriam admired her assuredness and wished she possessed Deborah's confidence. Miriam was disappointed when she left abruptly, wanting to thank Deborah for helping with the boy. She also hoped to get better acquainted.

Ruth's party dress

Miriam's party dress

Step Three ✢ *Foundation*
Monday, July 11, 1910

The day after the party, Deborah, hoping to see Miriam, went to the ice cream shop as Ruth and her friends did every afternoon. As soon as she walked in, she noticed Miriam sitting silently next to Ruth. She bravely sat down in a chair on her other side, hoping Miriam would not notice her sweating palms. "I am sorry, Miriam," she said to her quietly. "It was wrong of me to interfere with you and that boy at the party last night."

"Oh no, I was glad you did. He was getting to be a problem. Why did you leave so suddenly?" Miriam asked with a directness that surprised Deborah.

"I was embarrassed about my behavior," Deborah admitted, with a flush crossing her cheeks. "I thought you were angry with me."

"I was not angry, but I did wonder why you departed without saying goodbye. I thought you had gotten bored with me."

Deborah smiled. "Miriam, we were both foolish, worrying each other was upset. I was having such a nice time getting to know you. Maybe we should start all over."

"I would like that," responded Miriam, now flushing as Deborah had.

"Let's take a walk," suggested Deborah as she stood up.

Deborah and Miriam excused themselves and left the ice cream shop, strolling along the nearby streets while they talked. It took them a few minutes to get settled into conversation, starting with one-word answers and silences.

Once they relaxed, they talked of things that were important to each of them. Deborah talked of valuing unique friendships and independent thought. She told Miriam about her friends, making them sound more interesting than she actually found them. Deborah described an exciting life, filled with outings to theaters and museums. Deborah feared that by trying to sound upbeat, she was beginning to sound like a fake.

Though Deborah did frequent cultural activities, she found her daily life unsatisfying. What Deborah did not say was, I often fill my days daydreaming and writing. She captured her expansive ideas and opinions on paper, though her writings only reached her desk, where the stacks grew towards the ceiling. She had dreams that someday one of her articles would appear in a magazine, but she knew, as a female, she was unlikely to be published.

"Tell me about things you like to do," said Deborah, turning the attention away from herself.

Miriam also wanted to sound interesting, so she discussed her favorite artists, "I love to go to the Museum of Fine Arts. I am a huge fan of the Impressionists, especially Monet, Degas, and Renoir. I love their use of loose brushstrokes. It is clear that they have moved outside of their studios into the outdoors, since they are able to capture true palates of the sky and water."

"You seem to know a great deal about art," responded Deborah. "I too enjoy museums. I go to the Metropolitan Museum with my friends quite often. Do you go with your friends?"

"No. I go with my sister, Hannah. She and I both have great admiration for painting, though neither of us has any talent with a paintbrush. Hannah has a brilliant mind and a fascinating view of artwork, so I love going with her. Hannah is my closest friend."

Deborah and Miriam continued talking as an especially beautiful stallion passed by. They discovered their mutual love of horses. After a bit of horse talk, Deborah suddenly changed the subject, "Miriam, I want to tell you something very personal I have never told anyone."

"I am honored that you want to tell me," shared Miriam.

Deborah became pale and turned her head downward. She sat on a large rock and motioned for Miriam to sit by her. Their close proximity made Miriam a bit uncomfortable, yet Deborah did not notice. She quietly explained, "There is another reason I got so upset when that boy grabbed your arm last night. Earlier this year, I had a troublesome experience with someone who grabbed me. I have not talked about it because it was so disturbing. I was thinking about my own experience when I stopped that boy."

When Deborah became silent, Miriam said, "It is okay to tell me."

After taking a deep breath, Deborah said, "It was one of my parent's friends. He arrived at our house when no one was home, other than me. While he waited for my parents to return, he helped himself to several glasses of brandy. He asked me to sit on the couch with him and I did so, innocently. Suddenly, he pulled me into his arms and started to grab at me. I pulled away but he held on tight, forcing one of his hands down my dress, touching my breast. I was able to pull away from him and rushed off to my room. I never told my parents and thankfully, I have not seen him since. I was quite upset by the experience."

"No wonder you reacted so strongly when that boy was being inappropriate. I am so sorry, Deborah. What a horrible experience."

"It already feels better, now that I have admitted what happened. Thank you for listening."

Initially, Deborah was glad she revealed this painful situation and pleased she had chosen Miriam to tell. Yet, soon she got quiet, had second thoughts, and looked away. They sat in silence for a short while, then Deborah announced she needed to go home. Again, she left Miriam suddenly, though this time she said goodbye.

Deborah's Journal, July 11, 1910

My mind is racing. Maybe I said too much to Miriam. Perhaps Miriam really was angry about last night and was just being polite. Once more, I am reminded of problems from my past: rejections and misunderstandings. Again, I have vowed to myself to think before I act. I need to stop being so reckless.

But my mind keeps returning to Miriam. I am intrigued with her sweetness, innocence, and beauty. She seems tentative at times. At other times, like when she directly questioned why I left the party so abruptly, she seemed forthright and balanced. I do not understand her bond to such a shallow person as Ruth. Miriam does not seem superficial at all.

We talked so easily together. I hope to see Miriam again. Her quiet charm rattled me.

Miriam's Diary, July 11, 1910

I was really pleased when Deborah talked to me but sorry she had such a terrible experience. I did not know what to say to comfort her. I got nervous, as if she expected me to say something brilliant. I often find myself feeling awkward with new people and I am no match to Deborah's intelligence. I fear I can be tiresome and I did not want her to have to endure my meaningless conversation. I do not feel equal to her, yet she intrigues me tremendously.

Something about Deborah has caught my attention. The soft, dark hairs that spill out of the twist that she piles on top of her head are as unruly as she seems to be. Her lips are full and her unblemished skin appears silky. She stands tall, with a stately, self-assured pose. It is not just her beauty that has me curious. Her dark eyes seem to look right through me, as if she can see beyond the surface of my face.

I am curious about her. She seems to be a contradiction, strong and forthright much of the time, yet also plagued with self-doubt. She was so bold and assertive when she pushed that boy away from me that I felt protected. Yet she worried I was angry with her. I find her fascinating.

I would like to share something personal with Deborah, as she shared with me, but I have had no traumas to share. My life is boring. Maybe someday I could talk with her of my discontent. I wonder if she would understand that it is the lack of anything important to discuss that bothers me the most.

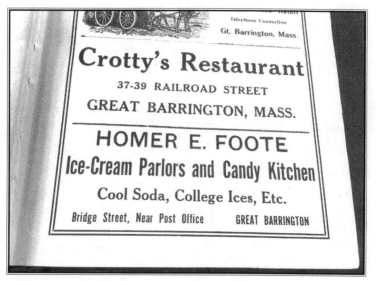

Advertisement for the Ice Cream Parlor

Great Barrington ice cream parlor

Step Four ✤ *Intrigue*
Tuesday, July 24, 1910

Every afternoon Miriam rode horseback with Ruth along a lane near Deborah's house. Deborah was pleased that after riding, Miriam stopped to visit her. She told Deborah that once she figured out that Ruth preferred to stay with the horses to flirt with the stable boy, she left directly after their ride.

For her part, Deborah knew exactly what time Miriam was likely to arrive and she waited by the place where the road took a small turn. Deborah loved to be greeted by Miriam's silly grin, as if Miriam had not anticipated Deborah's arrival. Deborah also loved Miriam's horsey aroma and the riding clothes she still wore. She looked forward to riding together someday.

Deborah thought of inviting Miriam for a walk in the country, just the two of them. She imagined them walking down a path, stopping at the edge of a stream, and picking wildflowers together. Deborah visualized grabbing Miriam's hand to help her across a small brook and sitting close by her on the grass. She dreamed of many lovely moments.

To their mutual delight, Deborah's and Ruth's families planned a day at nearby Lake Buel on the following Sunday. They climbed into their two carriages, following each other to the swimming hole. Each family had purchased a fancy buggy for the country, leaving their luxury cars in New York. Even though many families brought their city vehicles to Great Barrington, the Levines and Golds preferred the enchanting image of horse-drawn carriages for their country life. They found it easy to take the train from the city to the country, leaving their modern automobiles behind.

As soon as they arrived at the lake, Deborah's agreeable siblings, Milton, 14, and Anna 11, headed to the water's edge with Ruth's sister, Beth. Milton was a tall, lean boy with carefully parted dark hair and a wide-eyed expression of excitement. Anna's upturned mouth, which seemed in a permanent smile, gave a cheery impression, which matched the sparkle in her eyes. The three children got along easily, splashing and screaming excitedly. Ruth's brother, David, was somewhere out of view. The two mothers, dressed in city attire rather than bathing costumes, sat together in chairs that had somehow fit into the buggies. Ruth and Deborah's dads, both handsome, serious-minded men, went to the water's edge to board a boat. While boarding, talking distractedly about their temple's brotherhoods, they misjudged the muddy shallows and slipped into the water. Deborah and Miriam giggled and shook their heads as the fathers splashed in the lake.

"Look at Ruth," said Deborah. "She is parading around in her new bathing costume, gathering lots of attention from boys."

"I am pleased she is occupied, and we don't have to listen to her all afternoon," responded Miriam with a buoyant lilt in her voice.

"I feel the same way. Let's take a walk." As they strolled, Deborah asked delicately, "I was wondering how you and Ruth came to be such good friends. You seem so different from one another."

"Ruth and I were fine friends for many years at our Jewish overnight camp in upstate New York. She was always fun and sociable, including me in activities. I felt like one of the popular girls when I was with her, but Ruth seems so different now."

"How has she changed?"

"First, she is flirty with boys. Also, I find she is focused on her own needs all the time. Sometimes it seems Ruth does not notice me. She talks at me and asks nothing of my life. Oh, that sounds so ungrateful. I am appreciative she invited me to her country home."

"I am actually relieved to hear your view. I wondered what you saw in her, since I too find her self-absorbed. I am sorry you have to endure her."

"Oh no. It is not that bad. I am pleased to be here, and I am especially pleased to get to know you," Miriam said, blushing a bright shade of red.

"I am glad to get to know you as well," responded Deborah with a pounding heart that she hoped was not so loud that Miriam noticed. She was certain her face had turned as red as Miriam's, so she quickly turned the conversation to her love of horses. They chatted easily.

After a picnic lunch, Deborah, Miriam, and Ruth took a walk along the lake. Ruth, in her typical animated style, spoke of her own interests. "I thought my party was quite successful. Everyone told me they had a good time and they all liked the dress I wore. And there were hardly any leftovers of the little sandwiches I served."

Ruth asked little of Deborah or Miriam's opinions. When she went off to walk with a boy she had just met, Miriam turned to Deborah, giggling, and said, "I am so glad she found someone else to talk to. I hope he is a better listener than me."

Deborah responded, "She certainly can be tiring."

Deborah and Miriam wandered for a while, then sat on a cool rock overlooking the water. "I'd like to know more about you," said Miriam. "Can you tell me what you do when you are not going to theater, concerts, or museums? I am trying to picture what a full life entails."

"Oh Miriam. I think I mislead you a bit. I do attend all those events, but most of my life is quite boring. I spend a great deal of time in my room, writing."

"What do you write about?"

"Anything," answered Deborah. "I seem to have opinions about everything, so I write long articles, supporting my thoughts on any number of topics. My mind never settles down, but writing my opinions calms me. No one ever reads what I write, of course, but I like to imagine that someone would find my thoughts interesting."

Shyly but firmly, Miriam said, "I would love to read what you write. While I am in Boston, could you send samples of your writing to me?"

"Sure. But you might find it tedious."

"I am certain your ideas will be interesting. And your competition for my attention is needlework, which bores me to tears," Miriam said with a smile.

"Then I will send you some of my writings. The topics range from current news, to the plight of young women, to a book I just read, to something I saw out the window. Maybe you will disagree with me."

"I hope to disagree sometimes so we can have long-distance conversations."

"I look forward to that."

Walking quietly, the two of them observed the natural beauty of the setting. They spoke of the wild flowers, mushrooms growing on an old tree stump, and melodious bird songs, rather than of other people. They both noticed how happy they were together. Indeed, their friendship sparked a pleasant feeling for them both.

Lake Buel

Step Five ❧ Awareness
Thursday, July 26, 1910

Miriam was quite bored at the Gold's, so she was enthusiastic when Deborah's family invited her for an outing to the Berkshire Museum in Pittsfield, a journey of over 20 miles. It was sweet of Deborah to include Ruth in the invitation, Miriam thought, but when she declined the offer to come, both girls felt relieved.

"It was nice of you to invite me to join you on this trip, Mrs. Levine," said Miriam with a broad smile, as she climbed onto the Levine's luxurious buggy. Miriam pictured the Levine's horse and buggy, with its leather seats, gold embellishments, and extravagant façade on the cobbled streets of a city, rather than the countryside. The two padded benches fit the family plus an extra passenger comfortably. Luggage could be strapped to the back under the collapsible roof, which was ready to be raised in inclement weather.

"It is a pleasure to have you with us, Miriam. Deborah is always talking about you and we like to get to know her friends," replied Mrs. Levine. "It is a long ride but we have been looking forward to seeing this museum. On route, we will take you all to lunch at the Curtis Hotel in Lenox. There is speculation that Nathaniel Hawthorne and Herman Melville, both local celebrities, dined there together and exchanged advance copies of their upcoming books, *The Wonder Book* and *Moby Dick*.

"I loved *Moby Dick*, so that would be exciting for me," Miriam said with a wide grin.

"You might also be pleased to be in the same dining room that Hawthorne sat in. You might not know *The Wonder Years*, but you would certainly know him for *The Scarlet Letter* and *The House of Seven Gables*.

"I did read both of those in school, but I found *The Scarlet Letter* disturbing. I felt badly for the woman who was humiliated and publicly scorned by her whole village. And *The House of Seven Gables* was equally grim, so I prefer to think of Herman Melville as having sat in my seat."

Mrs. Levine smiled, pleased that her daughter's friend was well read and opinionated.

After a delightful lunch, they arrived at the museum. Milton and Anna, with permission from their parents, left to find exhibits to interest them. Deborah called out excitedly, "Come on Miriam. Let's go explore on our own. I want to start with the European art, which is my favorite, but then I would like to explore everything else."

Mr. Levine chimed in with, "Whoa, Deborah. Don't plan too much for one day. This museum has numerous collections. We can come back another time."

"Oh Father! You know me. I want it all. It is hard for me to focus on just one thing. Tell me what time we need to leave and I will be certain to fit in everything Miriam and I want to see in the time allotted."

Mrs. Levine, eyebrows raised, added, "Miriam. Don't be shy about asking for what you would like to see. My daughter's enthusiasm can be quite over-whelming. Don't let her drag you around, making you follow her whims."

"I will speak up for myself, Mrs. Levine," Miriam assured her with a quick nod. Miriam knew, however, she was likely to let Deborah lead their museum exploration, though she felt surprisingly strong with her.

Deborah and Miriam navigated much of the Berkshire Museum, which had been built in 1903 by Zenus Crane, heir to the paper manufacturing company located in Dalton, near Great Barrington. He wanted to bring art, science, and culture to western Massachusetts.

The girls stopped occasionally for a thorough look at special displays, such as the featured exhibit of William Stanley, who invented the new elec-trical system used to light the main streets of Great Barrington. He later formed Stanley Electric Company, rivaling the inventions of the electrical pioneer George Westinghouse. His company was eventually purchased by Edison General Electric Company. It was Deborah who was initially interested in this exhibit, though Miriam became fascinated as she learned about this local pioneer.

Mostly, as Mrs. Levine predicted, Deborah was a whirlwind, scurrying through almost every exhibit room. Miriam did ask to stop when she found something of interest. Deborah was very accommodating and seemed gen-uinely intrigued with the exhibits Miriam chose. After many hours in the museum, the girls knew each other a little better and liked learning from each other. Miriam loved Deborah's energy and Deborah liked Miriam's focus.

In fact, Miriam found Deborah remarkably stimulating and was pleased Deborah showed genuine interest in her tastes. As they wandered through the galleries, Miriam loved hearing of Deborah's life in New York City and of her unique friends. They both had a love of the arts, and they had marvelous discussions of their special discoveries at their favorite museums.

The family was happy, yet exhausted, when they climbed into the buggy for their ride home. They spoke about what they liked best, with Anna or Milton sometimes interrupting with their stories. When they got to the Gold's, Deborah and Miriam sat on the porch for a little time alone before going inside.

After having such a marvelous day at the Berkshire Museum, Deborah could hardly wait to invite Miriam to join her family again, "Tomorrow there is a sacred music concert at St. James Church. Would you like to go with us?"

"I have been taught that Jewish girls don't listen to Christian music nor enter a church, so I must decline your invitation. Your family is obviously more liberal than mine."

"Then instead, will you join us at a concert of more modern music on the town green the next night? We can ask Ruth to join us."

"I would be delighted, though I hope Ruth declines the invitation," Miriam admitted with a chuckle.

"Then," said Deborah with a smile, "We will not bother to invite her."

Softly, Miriam commented, "Sadly, that will be our last evening together."

Trying not to choke on her words, Deborah responded, "I will miss you."

"Likewise."

Deborah found their last evening together delightful. The weather was cool, so she and Miriam huddled together on a blanket on the lawn at the concert, right next to Anna and Milton. Once, Deborah reached over to brush a wisp of hair off Miriam's face and her fingers felt electric as they touched Miriam's skin. Miriam grabbed Deborah's hand at the end of the concert, as if in thanks, and that small gesture brought Deborah incredible pleasure.

Their parting at evening's end was sweet. After thanks to the whole family, Miriam turned to Deborah for a private goodbye, "Thank you for making my visit to the Berkshires so pleasing. I have thoroughly enjoyed getting to know you. I hope you will send me some of your writings, as you promised. I look forward to staying in touch."

Deborah started to choke up, so she said very little. She eked out, "I promise to write you. It was wonderful meeting you." Later she wished she had said more.

Miriam's Diary, July 31, 1910

I am now on the train ride home from my summer vacation. Deborah gave me a handful of posies on my last day, to add cheer to my journey. They lit up my heart and I plan to press them so I may keep them forever.

The depth of my feeling surprises me. I wonder if Deborah suspects how strong my reactions are towards her. I think about Deborah often when I am not with her. I wonder if she or anyone else suspects the joy she has brought into my summer. I have never had such a reaction to anyone, not even a boy. It feels odd to have these feelings for a girl.

Deborah's Journal, July 31, 1910

I wonder if Miriam has suspicions that my feelings have grown beyond those of a proper young lady. Did she ever notice me watching for a glimpse of her ankle as she boarded the buggy? Did she see rosiness in my complexion when she arrived or the disappointment in my face as she left? I know I react to her in the way other girls react to boys. Does she react this way also? Sometimes I fancy Miriam steals glimpses of me when she thinks I am looking away. Maybe I am imagining these occurrences or maybe they are just wishful thinking.

I am forlorn as I think of Miriam's return to Boston. I have grown quite enamored with her. My secret feelings have been stimulated, and I wonder what will come next. My desire is for Miriam to be part of my future. Is it possible for me to think of a way that may happen?

Transportation to The Berkshire Museum

Step Six ✤ *Correspondence*
Wednesday, August 3, 1910

Deborah moped around the house for the two days following Miriam's departure. Her mother noticed her distant mood and lack of activity. "What is wrong Deborah?" her mother asked with concern during Deborah's second pouty morning.

"I am feeling a bit lost, now that my new friend, Miriam, has left town. I am back to worrying about re-reading my old books again as my only form of entertainment."

"What about your other friends, those nice young people you visit regularly at the ice cream parlor?"

Deborah realized she needed to maintain the image of caring for the others so she would not arouse her mother's suspicion about her true feelings. "You are right mother. I need to reconnect with all of the others. I was so busy doing things with Miriam I have almost forgotten about the rest of them. I will go to the ice cream shop this afternoon."

"I hope that will lift your spirits."

"Mother, I have been wanting to tell you something. My attitude has changed since you found me crying in my room back in July. You were right that I would find some joy in this country-style living. It was not my next-door neighbor, Ruth, who took me out of my misery, but my friendship with Miriam." Deborah quickly added, "As usual, your words were wise. I apologize for being so contrary."

"I am just pleased that you have found some pleasure in our new summer retreat. Mothers often get the brunt of their children's frustration, but I must admit I never saw you quite so worked up before."

"I am sorry. I will try harder to control my anger by going to my room to write. That usually calms me down."

August 4, 1910

Dear Miriam;

I had a lovely time getting to know you. You added much joy to my summer. I don't know how I will manage with just Ruth and her friends as companions now that you are gone. These are not people I would usually befriend, but there are no other options for me here. I worried I would spend my days reading the books I brought with me. That might be what I end up doing for the rest of the summer!

I was pleased you agreed to stay in touch. I was especially thrilled when you said you were willing to read some of my ramblings. I am so excited to share my writing. Even after your reassurance, I am a bit worried you will find me too wordy, or contrite, or uninteresting.

At home, the pile of articles I have written is a foot tall! Since arriving here, I have just a few, and I searched through them carefully for something that might be of interest to you. I thought you might relate to my article, "How Can a Young Woman Find Fulfillment?" Maybe you can offer some insight into this common dilemma for girls like us. I assume that you and your friends face the same situation. There is not much industry for those of us out of school and unmarried.

I look forward to hearing from you, and continuing the discussion, as you suggested.

Fondly,
Deborah

How Can A Young Woman Find Fulfillment?

The role of a young girl is simple: to obey her parents and treat everyone with respect. The role of a girl in school is also clear: to study hard, to absorb the rules of social etiquette, and to learn the skills necessary to be an abiding wife and mother. The only role of a young woman who has finished school seems to be to find a young man to be her husband. If he is a good provider, she will want for nothing.

Life does not always work that way. What options are available for the young woman who does not want a husband or family? What will her tasks in life be? For a countrywoman, there are choices such as participating in the running of the farm, canning, baking bread, and sewing. For a city girl, the jobs include cleaning, ironing or factory work. Also, there are many great stores in cities, where girls can find employment.

For women with intelligence and breeding, the options are more limited. Stenography and teaching are two common choices. Nursing is another option, though women must have a special calling to choose that career. Other women are musicians, artists, or dancers, though success in these areas requires exceptional skill and perseverance. A few young women have found their way into the field of journalism, working for periodicals or newspapers.

How does a young woman make inroads to the career of her choice?....

August 12, 1910

Dear Deborah:

I was pleased to get your letter so soon after I arrived home. I enjoyed getting to know you too, and I look forward to our winter of correspondence.

I was happy to receive your writing sample – all five pages of it! I was impressed with your writing skills. It was well written and a clear description of your opinions. You are a talented girl!

In addition to liking your writing style, I was thrilled with the subject you chose. You have described my personal distress with more clarity than I could. I want to be more than a wife and mother, though those roles satisfy most young women. I have not selected a career and I don't like any of those you mentioned. I cannot picture myself in the arts, working in a store, or anything else useful. (Though I suspect you are heading towards that journalistic career you mentioned.)

My father owns a small Yiddish publishing company on Newspaper Row in Boston. There are few roles there for women but he won't let me help out anyway. Actually, that is one of my frustrations. My father does not believe that a girl should have a career. He has forbidden my sister, my mother, or me to work. Instead, my days are spent at home or occasionally visiting friends. I am bored and I feel useless.

Your article talks of girls having options. Until reading this, I believed I had no choices. I now see that my life is less constrained than I thought.

I have been thinking about what I might do to find satisfaction. Maybe bringing children into my life will help. I thought of one family of three youngsters, whose mother died this year. The dad is struggling to manage his 3, 5, and 7-year-old girls. He brings them to temple but they are disruptive. I wonder how I could help him. Maybe you have some ideas.

After I finished reading your paper, I kept thinking of all the girls who would benefit from reading what you have to say. There must be ways for you to get this article printed, though I know female authors are not usually published. Would you ever consider sending it off to a magazine with a male pen name? I know that is dishonest and probably against your morals, but your writing deserves to be in print.

I look forward to hearing back from you soon. I also look forward to reading more of the papers you have written. I think our correspondence will be a wonderful addition to the long winter ahead.

Miriam

August 15, 1910

Dear Miriam;

I was impressed that you suggested a dishonest tactic for getting published! I am certain it is a common practice for a female to publish as a man, though I have no idea whose pen names do not accurately represent the sex of the author. Do you know of this practice because of your father's publishing company? I will give your idea more thought.

I am really glad you found my writing helpful. I would be thrilled to write you further about my ideas on young women being independent and finding ways to be gratified with their lives. My friends and I discuss this issue frequently. Only one of my friends chose to go to college and she will fulfill her dream of being a teacher. None of us is looking for a young man to take care of us. That leaves us with a job as our only option. Journalism is certainly appealing to me, but I have no idea how I would get started. Who would want to listen to the ramblings of a young Jewish girl?

I was pleased that I stimulated some thoughts for you about something you could do to provide your life with meaning. I think you should approach that dad you mentioned and offer to watch his children during services. It would be a real mitzvah, a good deed. I assume he will welcome the offer with great relief. Would you be upset to miss services? Would your parents allow it?

What would you do with your life, if all options were available to girls? Are there other dreams you wish to fulfill?

I am sending you another sample of my writing. This article, "Parents of Young Women" is a testament to the admirable skills of my mother as a parent. She is loving, wise, and productive with her life. Mother works with several Jewish charities, giving lots of her time to benefit others. She volunteers with young mothers and organizes clothing drives for needy immigrant families.

I am certain you will have many opinions about these writings too. I wish to learn about your parents. Please write back soon. I look forward to receiving your letters.

Fondly,

Deborah

Parents of Young Women

When most people think of being parents, they think of having infants or young children, but those children grow up. When the child reaches the age of 18, the role of the parents changes significantly. Once the child is a young woman, her parents need to ease their control and let their child pursue her own beliefs. There is no guarantee that the young woman will have the identical values of her parents and, as long as her behavior is above reproach, the daughter should be honored for her opinions. Parents who are not able to accept their child as an individual will lose their child's respect. It is critical to support a daughter's skills, attitudes and principles, and assist them in their quest for a gratifying life. Parents can be helpful guides as long as they keep their own desires in check….

August 21, 1910

Dear Deborah;

Your letter arrived Friday, just before Shabbos. I read it quickly, before we left for services. I was not able to answer it until today, since I do not write on the Sabbath.

I was very excited with your encouragement regarding the young family at temple. I don't know why I had not come up with such a logical idea myself. On Saturday morning I approached the dad and offered to help with the children during services. There were tears in his eyes as he told me how much he would appreciate this. He was able to spend almost the entire morning praying, while I entertained the children. They seemed quite happy, despite just losing their mother. I promised him I would return next week to do the same. He said he would like to pay me, though he does not have a lot of money. I told him I was not doing this for money and again there were tears in his eyes. I got as much from doing this mitzvah as I would have gotten from being in the Sabbath service. Thank you so much for your article, since these ideas resulted from your suggestion.

After this worked out so well with the family at the temple, I had another idea. Just a few houses away on my street is another family in need. They have an eight-year-old girl who is not able to walk and cannot attend school. The only people in her life are her parents and her three brothers. What a lonely life she must lead! Knowing you would encourage me, I went to their home this morning and talked with this little girl's mother. Both the mother and little Leah were pleased she had a visitor.

I will go again next Wednesday and hopefully weekly. I have already started to think of things to do with Leah and I have begun to gather trinkets from our attic that Hannah and I outgrew long ago. It feels wonderful to help when I know I can benefit others. Thank you for your encouragement.

On another topic, I laughed when you wondered whether I knew of women using men's names because of my father's publishing company. He publishes only in Yiddish and there are no women writing Yiddish books! At least none that I know of!

I have read your second article. Again, you have chosen a subject that deeply touches my own concerns. I love my parents and I would never do anything to defy them, yet I do think differently from them. Their thinking is based on their definition of the laws of the Torah. There is room for independent interpretation of Jewish teachings, but there is no room for defiance or disbelief. My parents are very loving and they would sacrifice anything for Hannah and me. I do not mean to be ungrateful, yet I have recently realized they only offer us guidance in religious matters. My parents make the assumption that Hannah and I will make the right choices in every other area. It is wonderful they have such faith in my judgment, but sometimes I wish they would guide me, as your parents guide you. I was a bit envious of your parents' involvement in your activities. It was also lovely to hear about your mother's giving heart.

I have begun to think of places you could publish some of your articles. There are many women's magazines, but I do not think you should start with "Ladies Home Journal," "Good Housekeeping," "McCall's," or any of the other national magazines. Perhaps you should submit to local publications, where you might have more success. Your local newspapers might be a place to start, and I don't mean the "New York Times"!

I look forward to your response and for your next article.

Miriam

Step Seven ❧ *Re-acquaintance*
Wednesday, April 12, 1911

Deborah and Miriam wrote many long letters to each other over the winter. They discussed Deborah's writing, at times concurring, and at other times having lively discussions about their differing opinions. Miriam spent many hours penning her answers, knowing that Deborah would have a window into her thoughts through her words. She believed Deborah was far more articulate than she. Miriam had been right to look forward to this correspondence; they got to know each other better by sharing their thoughts.

Miriam was thrilled Deborah and her family had invited her to spend two weeks with them at their summer home, prior to her visit with the Golds this coming summer. Deborah's parents planned many adventures for the two girls, but Miriam hoped they would find time to ride horses and take long walks, just the two of them. Miriam was so excited about her return to the Berkshires, she could think of little else. Although she was a bit apprehensive about her time with Ruth, seeing Deborah again delighted her.

As summer approached, Deborah's days at Stonegate became filled with thoughts of Miriam. Deborah imagined Miriam disembarking from the train and she dreamed of throwing her arms around Miriam. She feared, however, it would be inappropriate. Deborah longed to be in her embrace, though she knew she must feign satisfaction if Miriam just gave her a simple kiss on her cheek.

Deborah's Journal, April 12, 1911

The winter of 1911 was the longest season in my memory. I was focused on Miriam. The more I heard from her, the more I yearned to be near her. Miriam regularly mentioned missing me, but my longing was desperate. My concentration was erratic and I was blind to making new friends. I missed Miriam's sweet laugh, her cheerful smile, and her occasional brief touch. Beneath her gentle demeanor and agreeable disposition, I sensed a depth of spirit. And through her letters I got to know her better; they taught me of both her inquisitive mind and her loving heart.

I am certain Miriam must remain unaware I want to steal away her heart. Oh my, I never admitted that before. My intentions are not honorable. It is affection, not just companionship that I seek. My desire for a girl to love is my heartfelt secret.

On July 10, when the moment finally came for Miriam to disembark from the train, Deborah ran to greet her, pleased her family had elected to stay home. They embraced with great fervor and held each other for just an extra moment longer than was standard. The flush on both girls' faces expressed mutual excitement. They were thrilled to be back in each other's company.

"I am so glad you are finally here. I have missed you," Deborah blurted, savoring every second of Miriam's touch.

Miriam answered loudly, "I have missed you, too," thinking Deborah had grown more beautiful during the past winter. Miriam saw a golden luster in Deborah's eyes.

"How was your trip, Miriam?"

"The trip was fine, with a lovely breeze coming through the windows. It was actually the most comfortable I have been in many days. We are experiencing extreme heat. Three people from my temple have already died."

"I am sorry to hear that. I was worried about your arrival during the worst heat wave ever recorded in this area. I heard it reached 106 degrees in New York City on July 4, where over 100 people and over 500 horses died during the past week. Luckily, it is about ten degrees cooler in the mountains, though it has still been unbearably warm; the heat broke a couple days ago."

"I am comfortable right now."

"I am glad. Let's hope the weather continues to improve so we can go on all the adventures my parents have planned for your stay," said Deborah wincing, wanting to discuss more than the weather.

Deborah motioned to the driver, a somber yet faithful older man with a ruddy complexion and clothes too tight for his large belly, who had been working with the Levines for many years. He hastily grabbed Miriam's bags and the two girls climbed into the buggy. As Deborah and Miriam sat down together, alone except for the driver, they touched each other with urgency. They kissed each other's cheeks repeatedly and sat with their bodies leaning against one another. Deborah's excitement drowned out her insecurities. She now trusted that Miriam had pined for her too.

As they headed up Deborah's street, Miriam caught a glimpse of the Levine's magnificent home. She had only seen Stonegate from the road last summer, but upon entering through the stone gate, she took in the enormity of the clapboard home with its expansive lawn. As she got closer to the house, she noticed colorful gardens and smelled fragrant flowers.

Deborah's parents waved from the front porch, sheltered under the stone portico. Mrs. Levine called out with a smile beaming across her face, "Welcome to our home. I am so pleased you have come." As they got out of the buggy and approached the porch, Mrs. Levine walked to meet them and cradled Miriam's hands in a very warm welcome.

The Levine's were a handsome couple. Miriam noticed that Mrs. Levine had the same dark eyes, silky skin, and soft mouth as Deborah. She could have easily been mistaken for Deborah's older sister, though she was approaching forty. Mr. Levine, a distinguished looking man, had a wide face and a thick, soft handlebar mustache. He was a formally attired man - even in his own home. His straight hair, parted slightly off-center, was a comment on his own sense of propriety.

Mr. Levine shook Miriam's hand and said, "Welcome. I hope your stay with us is pleasant."

Their young houseboy, a shy lad of about fourteen, took Miriam's luggage and disappeared inside. They all walked up the huge stone steps, onto the grand porch. As they passed through a heavy wooden door into the front parlor, Deborah noticed that Miriam unobtrusively reached up with her right hand and touched the mezuzah, a piece of parchment inscribed with Hebrew verses from the Torah inside a decorative case, mounted on the doorpost. She kissed her own hand where it touched the mezuzah. Miriam obviously did this as she entered each Jewish home, something Deborah had never done.

As they entered the parlor, brilliant light streamed in through four huge windows. Miriam glanced left, towards a rich mahogany fireplace with carved pillars and then right, toward a bay of three curved windows. Beneath the softly flowing off-white drapes were thickly cushioned window seats. The richly colored oriental rugs, the dark maroon patterned wallpaper, and heavy brocade furniture made this late-Victorian summer cottage a perfect place for relaxation. After reading extensively about decorating, Mrs. Levine had grace, practicality, and common sense in mind when designing Stonegate.

Deborah's sister Anna greeted Miriam. She was a delightful eleven-year old, small for her age, with a head full of dark curls, and an enormous smile. She still possessed the look of a child, with her frilly peach dress and matching bow, though soon she would blossom into a teenager.

Without a moment's hesitation, Anna exclaimed, "I have a new game to show you. I just learned it from my friends."

Anna wrapped yellow yarn around her fingers and then transferred it to Miriam's hand with several loops and twists. Once the yarn was wrapped successfully, Anna withdrew her own hands. She announced, "I did it!" obviously elated that she had performed this task correctly.

Deborah's charming brother Milton entered the room. Although a fifteen-year-old boy who probably had more interesting things to do than see his sister's friend, he was quite engaging. He made eye contact with everyone and told a joke he had learned.

"A young boy goes out for a walk. He comes to a river and sees another boy on the opposite bank. "Yoo hoo" he shouts, "How can I get to the other side?" The boy looks up the river and down the river and shouts back, "You are on the other side."

Although this was not a very funny joke, everyone congratulated him on his recitation.

When the two children left, Deborah grabbed Miriam's hat and parasol, dropped them casually on the closest chair, and exclaimed loudly," "Let's go on a tour of the house."

Deborah showed Miriam the back parlor first, with its alluring rounded corner, complete with another window seat and graceful curtains. In the corner was a circular wooden table, set with freshly cut pink roses and a pitcher of fresh-squeezed lemonade for their enjoyment. Miriam sat momentarily in one of the richly upholstered chairs, weary from her trip, but Deborah was anxious to show her more, so she arose before settling in too comfortably.

They scooted by the dining room, into the kitchen. Deborah said, "Let's see what the cook has for us." Deborah's eyes got large when she noticed the rotund woman with a reddish complexion preparing cookies for their afternoon snack. Miriam's nose twitched with the delicious aroma.

They headed up the long staircase with a warm cookie in each hand. Deborah was anxious to show Miriam the bedroom she would occupy. As promised, it was right next to hers. Miriam's face warmed as she noticed the doorway connecting the two rooms, with a small water-closet in-between.

Deborah left the bedroom so Miriam could freshen up. Miriam caught her breath and stilled her racing heart. She opened her valise and placed some clothing in the generous closet. This closet was distinctly different than the small armoire in her Boston bedroom. She thought of her family home, more modest, though just as welcoming. Miriam washed her face and headed back downstairs.

Following their afternoon snack of lemonade and more cookies, the girls excused themselves to walk in the gardens. Deborah headed towards the flowerbeds. "Come see my mother's collection of colorful rose bushes and wildflowers."

Deborah took Miriam's hand and they entered the garden through a small gate. Deborah could barely control her palpitating heart. She feared the pounding would reach Miriam's ears as they walked into her mothers' special space. Unlike the formal gardens surrounding the house, this garden was untamed. Deborah wondered if Miriam realized she had not released her hand. They strolled around, still attached, as Deborah pointed out the flowers that had taken over this lovely garden. She dropped Miriam's hand as they walked around the rest of the property.

After strolling for a while they sat on a log, quietly listening, watching, and enjoying one another's company. Time apart had emboldened Deborah, and she leaned against Miriam, who did not pull away. They nestled against each other for several minutes before heading back for dinner and an evening of song around the grand piano.

The air cooled as the sun went down. When the youngsters retreated to their bedrooms, Deborah's mother engaged Miriam in a conversation about her family. "Deborah tells us your parents are quite observant."

"My family centers their lives around our local conservative temple. We attend services regularly, keep Kosher, and observe Shabbos strictly. My grandmother speaks mostly Yiddish, so we have all learned and can converse with her. I have a wonderful sister Hannah, who has a brilliant mind and a gentle manner."

Deborah's parents asked several more questions before they bid one another goodnight. Miriam headed up the stairs with Deborah at her side. They hugged as they parted for the night, lingering a few extra few moments, as they had at the train station.

Miriam readied herself for the night with a smile on her face. Just as she approached the bed, weary from the long day of traveling, she heard a soft rapping at the door that connected the two rooms. Without waiting for a response, Deborah quietly pushed open the connecting door. Miriam's heart raced, not knowing if she would enter the chamber. She sweetly bid Miriam a final goodnight and then closed the door. It seemed a reminder that Deborah was close by. Miriam was disappointed the evening had ended. She hoped other nights might end differently.

Great Barrington train station

Stonegate front porch

Mezuzah

ABOVE: *Stonegate bedroom*   BELOW: *Longfellow house*

Step Eight ❖ *Intrigue*
Thursday, July 13, 1911

Deborah's Journal, July 13, 1911

I can hardly believe Miriam slept just beyond my door. From the moment we met, I experienced an exceptional interest. She is charming, sincere, and warm. I understand why Ruth befriended her during their summers at camp. I too would have latched onto her, taking her for my special friend. That is what I want now, for her to be my special companion.

I have known for many years that my interest lies with girls. The immature boys who try to show off have never charmed me. I have never responded to their attention, which made them try harder to impress me. I would rather spend my hours with my girlfriends, sharing stories and laughs together. Girls are more courageous, sensible, and better able to share feelings. I hope to share many sentiments with Miriam. Maybe my secret life can become real.

It is the time after we retire that I imagine most while dreaming. I envision we steal some extra time together when she lets me sneak into her room after everyone else is asleep. We whisper to one another in the dark. If I am really bold, I touch her arm or hold her hand as we share our deepest thoughts. Might this really happen?

Have I been too bold with Miriam? Was it acceptable that I took her hand in the garden? Did she notice how close I sat to her or mind that I opened the door to her room to say goodnight? Did she see it as an invitation? So many questions, so much fear, so much hope.

After a good night's sleep, Deborah and Miriam took an early morning walk through the neighborhood. They did not wander far, but Miriam found it enjoyable to peek at the huge houses of wealthy owners along Deborah's road.

Deborah described the bright yellow Garrison Colonial directly across the street from Stonegate, "The locals call this house The Longfellow House because it is a copy of the Cambridge, Massachusetts home of Henry Wadsworth Longfellow."

"He is one of my favorite poets," Miriam said with a shine in her eyes and a shrug of her shoulders. "I wonder who lives there."

Deborah answered, "I have no idea. But we both know who lives next door."

"Ruth," Miriam said with a sigh. "We really should visit her. She will be my hostess after I leave your home, so I owe it to her to be attentive. But I would rather not stop to see her right now."

"I agree. We can stop by later to say hello. Right now, I would just like to continue our walk together."

Delighted in their shared dismissal of Ruth, Deborah reached out for Miriam's hand. But Miriam pulled it away from her soft grip and said, "NO," quite emphatically.

Deborah's face blanched. She had offended Miriam. She had behaved the same as that boy at the party who had grabbed Miriam's arm. "I am sorry," Deborah said.

Miriam said nothing.

After walking silently for a few minutes, Miriam broke the painful silence. "I am sorry I withdrew your hand so abruptly. I did not mean to hurt your feelings. I was aware of being on a public road and it felt awkward." They continued to walk, attempting to talk as if nothing had happened.

Deborah was put at ease somewhat by Miriam's explanation of her reaction, but she was reminded that she too often reacts without thinking first.

Miriam's Diary, July 13, 1911

I have been grappling with my reaction to Deborah's holding my hand. Was it just the public nature of the touch? Girls often hold hands with one another. Could it have also been the intensity of my feelings for Deborah that caused me to react so strongly? I knew it upset her.

There was also something else going on in my head at the moment she grabbed my hand. Each corner we turned on our walk brought views of additional magnificent Victorian homes with turrets and large porches. It reminded me of the differences between our families. Does Deborah fully understand the contrast and would it matter to her if she did? It is clear that richness of possessions is not what I seek; it is the power of close friendship I crave.

Step Nine ❧ *Shabbos*
Friday, July 14, 1911

Miriam woke on Friday morning quite distraught. As Shabbos approached, she wondered what would happen. No one had mentioned anything about Friday night. There was no temple anywhere near Great Barrington and Deborah had already said her family was less observant. Miriam was used to her entire weekend being centered on her temple and the observance of all rituals. She did not want to place any demands on her host family, but she was anxious that they might have expectations for her to participate in another outing during Shabbos. She would need to refuse. She was preoccupied with these thoughts as she readied herself for the day. It soon became clear she need not have worried.

"Miriam," said Mrs. Levine after breakfast. "I would like to find a way to honor your observance of Shabbos. We will have Friday night dinner together, as we always do on Shabbos, but there is no synagogue nearby to attend services. Would you be willing to lead a small service for us?"

Miriam let the question sink in and smiled. "How very sweet of you. I will be happy to lead everyone in Shabbos blessings over the candles, the wine, and the bread. Maybe Anna and Milton could help me with songs that welcome the Sabbath bride. I can also lead the blessings before and after the meal."

"Is there anything else we could do to make you comfortable?"

"Thank you for asking. I would like to spend this evening and tomorrow quietly. I am used to a tranquil observance of Shabbos."

"Then it shall be so," responded Mrs. Levine, and she told her children of the plans.

Miriam was very pleased when Mrs. Levine promised, "We have planned a short day of adventures for today, but we will be certain to come home long before sundown, so that we can prepare for Shabbos."

"Thank you so much," said Miriam with relief and appreciation in her heart.

Miriam thought, what a sweet family this is. Miriam would rather have time alone with Deborah but she was happy to go along with their travel plans, knowing the Levines would respect her needs for the Sabbath.

Shortly after this conversation, they all piled into the buggy for a trip north, through Stockbridge. They drove by The Mission House, the Indian Monument, and Heaton Hall, places that had more interest for Deborah's parents than the rest of them. It was exciting for Miriam when they traveled west, crossing the New York border. Miriam had never before been outside of Massachusetts.

They stopped for a picnic lunch. The challenge came when Miriam needed to relieve herself. She had to learn the delicate art of gathering her long skirt in her arms, while squatting uncomfortably in the woods. Deborah explained the difficult technique to her and happily her clothes remained unstained in the process.

After a pretty, yet boring day with the family, Deborah and Miriam were both thrilled to be back home. They excused themselves to freshen up for the Shabbos meal. All went smoothly with the Sabbath prayers and rituals and Miriam was grateful for a peaceful evening.

Deborah was pleased her mother chose to honor Shabbos on Saturday for Miriam. It was lovely for the whole family to have a quiet day. Deborah and Miriam spent the day taking walks, strolling in the garden, and sitting on the front porch. Anna and Milton managed to be respectful, keeping their voices low and their games quiet. As evening arrived, Deborah's mother brought out the braided Havdalah candles, and they welcomed the first stars with all the traditions. Miriam was comfortable as they recited the familiar prayers and she began to anticipate the adventures awaiting them the next day.

Shabbos candles and challah

Step Ten ✤ *Kisses*
Sunday, July 16, 1911

After breakfast, Deborah suggested she and Miriam ride horses, something she had been planning since they first met. They agreed to change into their riding clothes and meet at the stable. Miriam, in borrowed breeches, stood by Deborah's mother's mare as Deborah approached the barn. The vision of Miriam dressed to ride took Deborah's breath away. After packing their picnic lunch in the saddlebags, they headed to Monument Mountain Reservation, five miles away. They rode easily, passing several other groups of riders on their own summer outings. From a distance Deborah spotted the knife-edge summit of Squaw Peak, so she knew they were getting close.

They rode until they found an isolated area to tie the horses. Selecting a soft floor of moss for their picnic, they skirted the huge boulders of pink quartz covering the mountainside. Deborah's heart fluttered, partially from the strenuous ride, but mostly from contemplating uninterrupted hours in this secluded setting with this beguiling girl. They carefully laid out their drinks and sat on the blanket, sitting closely, but not touching.

Taking off her riding hat, Miriam let down soft waves of hair. Her tresses spilled out of her usual chignon and Deborah marveled at her beauty. Deborah followed suit, freeing her lengthy hair from its twisted bun. They lay back on the blanket, letting the sun warm them. Deborah wanted to reach over and tenderly caress Miriam's hand, or better yet, put her arm around her, but thought it might frighten Miriam. She could not risk upsetting her on this perfect day. They lay side-by-side in silence.

Miriam spoke first, whispering as if they were in a secret world, "The ride was delightful. I am glad you brought me to this beautiful location."

Deborah responded quietly, requiring that they move closer together on the blanket to hear each other. "This is a special place that I have been wanting to share with someone. I am delighted you are that person."

They listened to the birds and the rustling of the trees as the wind rushed by. A grasshopper jumped onto their spread and they sat up, watching it. Deborah could smell Miriam's sweet scent. She was tempted to make a physical connection, the urge growing more desperate, but she did not want to repeat her error of yesterday. Deborah turned away, afraid she could not control herself.

To soothe herself Deborah asked, "Tell me about your girlfriends back home."

"I have many friends who go to temple with me in Boston. Besides my sister, Marjorie is my closest friend. She is a neighbor I have known my whole life. She and I stop over to each other's homes frequently."

Deborah talked of her girlfriends in New York, then took in a deep breath and added, "I always wanted a special friend. I am hoping you could be her."

Miriam blushed. As tears filled her eyes, she admitted, "I would like that too."

Miriam reached out and stroked Deborah's cheek, the boldest move of her life. They looked into each other's eyes with such deep emotion it scared them both. As they both lay back on the blanket, Deborah could hear Miriam's breath, which was as heavy as hers. Neither of them moved for several minutes.

With hesitation, Deborah asked, "May I touch you?"

Miriam nodded and almost silently said, "Yes."

Deborah gently touched Miriam's cheek, then caressed her entire face. When she brushed her fingertips against Miriam's lips, she heard a restrained gasp. She combed Miriam's hair away from her face and caressed it in long, slow strokes. Miriam smiled in pleasure as Deborah's fingers glided along her scalp. Miriam shifted her head slowly in rhythm with Deborah's movements.

Deborah gently traced Miriam's lips, as if in invitation, and her lips parted in response. When Deborah moved closer, she felt Miriam's breath. Deborah pulled Miriam into her embrace and they lay still on the blanket. Miriam could not resist as Deborah's lips softly brushed against hers. She never dreamed of excitement like she was feeling. She never imagined such sweetness.

Their kisses began in soft connection. As their arms encircled each other with more force, their lips locked with equal pressure. They stroked each other's hair, backs, arms, and faces and their tender kisses became more insistent. Their bond became surprisingly intense as Deborah's face flushed and she felt palpitations in her chest. They pushed hard against each other, and Miriam noticed she could feel Deborah's breasts against hers. All her sensations moved to her own tingling nipples. They clung to each other, kissing and exploring, making wishful moans and sighs.

Then birds around them began chirping loudly, disturbing their reverie. They backed off from each other slowly, Deborah trying to control the pounding in her chest. Miriam reached out and held Deborah's hand. Even this bit of touching became out-of-control, as they tangled their hands together, rubbing each other's fingers with the same exhilaration that had been on their lips moments before. Miriam encased Deborah's hands to still the growing excitement.

Both women knew, instinctively, it was time to leave. Parting silently, then packing to leave, they approached the horses, with joy on both their faces.

Step Eleven ❧ *Awakening*
Sunday, July 16, 1911

Miriam's Diary, July 16, 1911

Following our afternoon of riding, I came directly back to my room, supposedly to freshen up, but actually to revisit what just happened. It never occurred to me that Deborah and I would actually kiss. It was such a surprise. I have often imagined my first kiss, as all young girls do. I thought it would be with a boy, though boys never interested me the way they were supposed to. Despite all the romantic notions I was taught, I expected my first kiss to be awkward.

But my first kiss was thrilling. I had never felt excited like that before. My heart was pounding out of control and my face felt warm. I never imagined that lips touching could arouse such strong feelings throughout my body. I liked it more than anything.

Deborah has touched me deeply. She is both gentle and strong. She has a curious spirit and a boldness I have always longed to have. With her, I find myself being more daring than I would have ever thought possible. She is so very beautiful. I love her deep dark eyes, her pearl-like skin, and luscious lips, which felt as wonderful as they appeared. Her caress was tender, yet insistent. As she held me against her, I could feel her wonderful curves. I am filled with longing and anticipation.

I never considered two girls together. I wonder whether Deborah has. Is she scared of our behavior? I sensed no apprehension in her. I am surprised at myself. Instead of fear, she has aroused temptation and wakefulness in me. What will tomorrow bring?

Deborah's Journal, July 16, 1911

I will remember today forever. This was the day of my first kiss. It was as if my whole existence built towards the moment when Miriam and I connected. I never imagined the power of two lips touching, creating a language of their own. My lips told Miriam the secrets of my heart in ways my words could never express. It was not a peck but a deep connection. I am certain there will be more kisses.

As I write this very personal account of my feelings and behavior, I must make certain that no one ever finds my journal. I have never before hidden things from my parents, but it is important they never find this.

It has been in my head, but not in my body, that I desire girls. I had no idea what girls do together, but I now know what I want – to run my hands along Miriam's whole body and have her do the same to me. The most intense sensation focused on my women's place, which was awakened today.

I have relived every moment, imagining what might have occurred if we had not ceased touching. The feelings were almost too intense to stop, with a desperate excitement. Our connection was beyond anything I imagined. Was Miriam caught up in the same intense feelings? Will she be scared away? Does she understand the depth of affection I have for her?

It is hard to imagine that Miriam will return to her life in Boston and I will return to mine. Will she retreat to the world of being with boys? I cannot contemplate being without her yet I know we cannot be together forever. I feel certain nothing will ever be the same again. I think I am in love.

Monument Mountain

Step Twelve ❧ *Desire*
Sunday, July 16, 1911

That evening, Deborah wished her mother would continue to play the piano for a long while. Her concert gave Deborah time to recall the afternoon and contemplate afternoons to come. She glimpsed at Miriam sitting next to her, seemingly absorbed in the music. Perhaps Miriam was reliving their time together as well. Deborah pondered whether Miriam was visualizing tonight, once they close their doors and the whole family retires to their beds. Would Miriam be expecting Deborah to join her?

Once the music ended and everyone headed to bed, Deborah cautiously opened the door between their rooms, hoping she was not being too forward. Miriam timidly invited her in. Deborah knew they needed to be very careful, because sound travels easily through the house. Her young sister or brother would not understand sounds they heard in the night, yet her parents certainly would. Luckily, Mr. and Mrs. Levine's bedroom was at the other end of the house. Deborah remembered they were noisy enough this afternoon to awaken all the birds in the area. There were no birds to save them tonight.

Seeing Deborah in her doorway aroused Miriam. She was both scared and eager, and unsure how Deborah would view her slightly stiff pose. Miriam noticed a wonderful sensation under her nightdress and could hardly wait until they were in each other's arms.

Once Deborah was in her room, Miriam moved to Deborah and silenced her with a finger on her lips, equally aware of how sounds would carry. She caressed Deborah's back and she ran her fingers through her hair. Deborah felt courageous when she headed toward Miriam's bed and was surprised when Miriam followed eagerly. They lay on top of the comforter, wrapped in a warm embrace. Miriam found pleasure in lying with Deborah but worried what might happen next. She stiffened, almost unperceptively. Miriam could not deal with more intimacy than they experienced earlier in the field.

Deborah whispered, "May I sleep by your side? If we drift off, we must not sleep soundly. I need to return to my room before morning."

"Yes," responded Miriam shyly. She was mostly pleased, though a little disappointed, that sleeping was what Deborah had on her mind.

"My heart is pounding so loudly I hope it does not alert anyone that I am in your room!" chuckled Deborah. "I am afraid it will keep us both awake."

"Just a moment, Deborah, I need to say my bedtime *Shema* (the beginning of morning and evening prayers) before we fall asleep." She covered her eyes and began, "*Sh'ma Yisraeil, Adonai Eloheinu, Adonai Echad.*"

Deborah joined her, adding the English translation, "Hear, O Israel: The Lord our G d, the Lord is one."

Eventually, slumber took over and the girls slept nestled in each other's arms, hardly moving. Deborah awakened in the middle of the night, knowing she needed to go to her own room but she could not leave until she kissed Miriam one more time.

Deborah's soft kisses awakened Miriam and she responded with a sleepy, yet tender peck. They caressed each other quietly and soon Deborah felt delight, like this afternoon, returning. Their kisses became urgent. As Deborah caressed Miriam's back, arms, and down her hips, she heard a slight moan of pleasure, meant for her ears only. For Deborah, it was wonderful to feel Miriam's body responding to her touch. Miriam did the same and Deborah's whole body became warm and extremely sensitive too.

They pressed their bodies as closely together as they could. Deborah felt the beating of Miriam's heart and she could feel Miriam's nipples become hard. The elation Deborah felt led to courage. Miriam did not push her away as Deborah stroked her flat stomach; her hands slid upward slowly, stopping to make certain she had not passed some invisible boundary. Miriam grabbed Deborah's hand and Deborah feared she was going to make her stop. But instead, Miriam guided Deborah's fingers upward. She could hardly believe she was cupping Miriam's full, firm, scrumptious breasts in her palms. Miriam's breathing quickened. Tentatively, Miriam's hands circled one of Deborah's breasts in response. Through the fabric of their nightdresses, they created intense pleasure for one another, becoming lost in sensation. Deborah felt herself responding all the way down in her secret place.

"You need to go back to your room," whispered Miriam haltingly. "I am afraid we will make too much noise if we continue. I don't want to be caught."

"You make me so happy," Deborah responded, kissing Miriam gently on the forehead before reluctantly returning to her room for the rest of the night.

Miriam's Diary, July 16, 1911

Deborah just left my bedroom and I must write again. We moved quickly from a kiss to so much more. When Deborah stroked my body, I could not stop her. It was more pleasure than I ever imagined, especially when she dared to rub my breasts. My entire nether region became moist and began to throb. The pleasure was extreme. Now I understand the pull of physical pleasure that gets some people in trouble.

It felt right, though my head is spinning with the warnings I received from my parents. They told me not to be lured by impure thoughts. If they ever knew I was not just thinking those thoughts, but acting on them, they might disown me, especially if they knew it was with a girl.

But it feels so natural being with a girl. What could be more comforting than being with someone whose body and sensations are so like mine? Our connection is from our hearts, not just our bodies.

What comes next? I do not even know for sure what men and women do together. I cannot imagine what two girls do. It felt so good to have my breasts rubbed and so very thrilling to rub Deborah's. I hope whatever is next comes soon.

Deborah's Journal, July 16, 1911

My heart is so full. My mind is swirling with thoughts of Miriam. She must care as much for me as I care for her or she would not have allowed me to get so close to her! I am so happy with her.

My body was as excited as my heart. I was so daring tonight, not only kissing Miriam but also touching her breasts. I was shocked when she responded by fondling mine. The pleasure was powerful. I hardly dare to write about the other sensations I felt. My woman's parts felt swollen and wet. I now need to reach down and calm the excitement.

I look forward to more time alone with Miriam, tonight and every night while she is here.

Step Thirteen ✦ *Excitement*
Monday, July 17, 1911

The next morning, Deborah woke Miriam from a deep sleep. Miriam had been lost in dreams that were a retelling of the night's ardor. After a moment of confusion, Miriam understood as Deborah explained, "The family is awaiting your arrival at the breakfast table." One more kiss and she headed back downstairs, following the aroma of coffee.

Mr. Levine had taken two whole weeks off from work, so he could be with his family as they explored the area with Miriam. They planned an excursion for today to the Red Lion Inn in the nearby town of Stockbridge. Deborah could not imagine being by Miriam's side for the whole day without touching her and she worried their glances might give them away.

Following breakfast, Deborah and Miriam walked into town to collect provisions. Despite their desperate desire to touch one another, they walked quietly side by side. They had a quick reunion with Ruth, who was predictably sitting with her girlfriends at the soda shop. After finishing their errands, they headed back to Stonegate in time for their departure.

Miriam noticed their traveling party was just the right size for the buggy. Anna and Milton sat next to her, Deborah and her mother across from her, and Mr. Levine seated aloft, next to the driver. Deborah and Miriam were careful not to steal too many glances at each other.

They headed out of Great Barrington, amid bright green picturesque scenery. Everyone glanced over each other's shoulders and pointed to wildlife they noticed, as the buggy wound along the Housatonic River for the seven-mile trip. When they got to Stockbridge, Anna and Milton whined that they were hungry, so the whole group went directly to The Inn for lunch.

As soon as they climbed the stairs onto the huge porch, Mrs. Levine gathered everyone for a history lesson, "The Red Lion Inn has welcomed visitors for over a century. It was rebuilt a few years ago after a deadly fire. Then the roof had to be replaced just over a year ago, due to a second fire. Let's go see the beautiful new furnishings."

No one was disappointed. The alluring dining room décor was a tasteful contrast of rich mahogany furniture, off-white patterned wallpaper, and crisp table linens. The food was equally marvelous. After lunch, they wandered around the well-appointed side rooms, taking in the beauty of the refurbishment. Each room was filled with comfortable upholstered chairs, elegantly framed paintings, and bookcases of leather-bound volumes.

Deborah whispered to Miriam, "Let's sneak up the stairwell and find a cozy corner where I can steal a kiss."

But as the restless youngsters began to run up and down the long porch, Mrs. Levine called out, "What are you doing up there? We need to leave before Anna and Milton bother someone."

After lunch, they all wandered around the small town, stopping at the general store for penny candy for the ride home. After Milton insisted, they also visited the ice cream shop, where they each got a dish of creamy ice cream. By the time they climbed into the buggy, everyone was tired so the rocking lulled everyone to sleep. Miriam smiled at Deborah sleepily and leaned against her for her own nap. Deborah took much pleasure in having Miriam against her shoulder, knowing they could risk this small intimacy as everyone else napped. Dusk fell during their ride and cooled the tepid air.

They arrived home in time for a very light supper. After eating, Deborah, with an exaggerated yawn, asked "Do you mind if I go to bed early?"

Miriam politely said, "If no one minds, I will follow you. I am also tired."

"If my parents ever knew our plans, they would follow too!" giggled Deborah quietly on the way up the stairs.

Deborah quickly put on her nightdress and joined Miriam in her room, not waiting until everyone else was in bed. They locked both doors to keep out unwanted visitors. The others were still downstairs, so they felt safe heading directly to Miriam's bed, to caress each other comfortably. Soon after they began kissing, Deborah's tongue unexpectedly found its way into Miriam's open mouth. They both reacted by pulling back slightly.

Miriam said, "Let's try that again. I think it might be nice."

Soon their tongues explored while their hands groped each other's bodies. They pressed even closer, making it difficult to fondle each other's breasts, so they touched where they could reach. As they changed positions, Miriam felt Deborah's thigh nudging between her legs. It was unintentional that this would arouse her and she let out a soft moan. They smiled at this discovery and repositioned themselves to rub against one another. The pleasure mounted to heights neither of them ever imagined. Then suddenly, as the sensations reached a peak, they both gasped at the same time, held tight and sighed deeply. They lay back, panting, and rested in each other's arms.

In a raspy whisper, Miriam said, "Oh my! Thank you." Regaining her composure, she added, "I hope we have not been too noisy. I don't think anyone was disturbed. I feel safe and extremely content." Miriam said the *Shema* before they drifted off to sleep.

In the morning, memories of the night lingered as Miriam wiped sleep from her eyes. As she hurried to complete her toilette, she daydreamed. What was that sensation last night? The pleasure was so extreme, more than she had ever known. Then it was followed by such an amazing calm. The entire experience was more pleasurable than a thousand ice cream cones.

General store

Red Lion Inn

Step Fourteen ❖ *Adventure*
Tuesday, July 18, 1911

The sun shone brightly the next morning, and Deborah was afraid she had missed their early 6:00am breakfast. She hurriedly got ready for the day and rushed down the stairs to the breakfast room. The whole family was assembled, and she begged pardon for her her lateness. She could barely look at Miriam, certain that with one glance everyone would know their secrets. Anna giggled because Deborah was late.

On this day, the whole family planned to attend the 106th Columbia County Fair in Chatham, New York, a long 22 miles away. Deborah hoped she could sit next to Miriam, not across from her, to avoid looking longingly into her eyes. She also wanted to feel Miriam leaning against her, a small consolation.

Mrs. Levine explained, as she was prone to do with each new site, "The Barrington Fair is the regional agricultural fair which has been held for over 50 years in Great Barrington. But it will not open until after you return to Boston, Miriam. We think it is important for us city folks to see how the locals entertain themselves, so we decided to take you all to the Columbia Fair. Because Miriam and Deborah both have a great love of horses, we chose the fair day that features horse racing. It is a long trip in a buggy, but we hope it is a worthwhile adventure."

After several delays, they finally got started at 7:30am. The trip was very long, since their horse and buggy could only travel up to eight miles per hour, depending on the road conditions. Although their buggy was relatively comfortable, they were packed in tight, the road was bumpy, and the weather was quite warm. Anna and Milton took turns pointing out all these challenges. Although they were both usually agreeable, they both complained periodically, getting restless, and asking for several stops to stretch or relieve themselves. Mrs. Levine limited the amount of drinks they could have, to limit the number of required stops. What might have been a three-hour trip had they driven straight through, took close to four hours.

They finally arrived at the county fair, full of dust and excitement. After a quick trip to the privy, they all met at the lemonade stand to quench their collective thirst and to have popcorn fritters to hold them over until lunch.

"There are so many things I have never seen before," Miriam said, reviewing the program. "I want to see a chicken coop. And can we visit the cattle, sheep, and also the goats? I can't imagine what prize-winning vegetables look like."

Everyone giggled at her enthusiasm, as Mrs. Levine said, "Let's satisfy all of Miriam's wishes, if we can. First, let's watch the jugglers and listen to local school groups sing, since they are on route to the animal areas."

Reaching the animals, the family stopped first at the 4-H booth, a new youth group aimed at developing the skills of potential farmers. Miriam called out, "These youngsters know much more about farm life than I will ever know."

At the barns and paddocks for the farm animals, Miriam was as fascinated as a small child, calling out every few minutes, "Oh look."

Miriam caused quite a stir when reaching a very muddy pen, with large, squatty, pudgy animals she did not recognize. "What are these?" she asked.

"Pigs," answered Milton, pleased to know something Miriam did not know.

"I thought pigs were small and pink with curly tales, like in the picture books," said Miriam.

After another round of laughter, Miriam set out to find more unfamiliar animals. Deborah whispered in her ear, "I love your enthusiasm."

They feasted on a picnic lunch brought from home. Then Mr. Levine bought everyone large servings of fresh ice cream, made from the cream of local cows. Afterward, they were each given a few pennies to spend on carnival games, amusement rides, entertainment, or special snacks. Deborah and Miriam headed to watch the balloon rides.

When they passed the Tunnel of Love, Miriam whispered to Deborah, "I wish we were brave enough head into the dark passageway to steal a kiss. It is so sad we need to hide our feelings."

Deborah responded in understanding, "It would be wonderful to go into the Tunnel of Love together but that will never be possible for us. Our kisses will have to wait until we are home."

After watching balloons soar high into the air over the fairground, Deborah and Miriam spent some of their money on a ring toss game. When Deborah won a grand prize, a large stuffed bear, she offered it to Miriam.

"I think your family would think it odd for you to give away your prize," Miriam said, smiling but refusing the gift.

When everyone gathered a short while later, Deborah's mother said politely, "Deborah. You should turn the bear over to Miriam, since she is your guest."

Miriam took it happily, imagining the train trip home to Boston with this large pink bear on her lap. Anna looked at it jealously.

Mid-afternoon they claimed front row seats to await the horseracing. They smelled the familiar aroma of horses and heard the clip-clop of hoofs as they turned to watch the horses prance onto the field.

"I am going to enjoy this a great deal," Miriam said excitedly, her eyes wide with delight and curiosity.

A couple of times the two girls reached out and grabbed each other's hands as their favored horse crossed the finished line. Deborah hoped this gesture passed as friends excited with the win. The girls were anxious to move onto their next adventure, wanting to be outside the watchful eyes of the family.

Columbia County Fair

Columbia County Fair jugglers

Sheep at the Fair's animal pavilion

Step Fifteen ✤ *Judgment*
Tuesday, July 18, 1911

The girls walked around the Country Fair, discussing the difference between life in the country and the daily lives they led in their respective cities. At first it was pleasant chatter.

But when Miriam commented, "I wonder why anyone would choose to be a farmer? It is such a messy job and they have to work so hard to make any money. Maybe they could not do anything else," Deborah became angered.

Deborah announced angrily, "You are talking of the country-folk as if they were all simple, making disparaging comments about people just because their lives are different from ours. You are speaking of people who choose to use their hands instead of their heads to earn a living as if they are less than you. Why would you say something like that?"

Miriam responded, "Sorry," making Deborah more enraged, believing it was not a satisfactory answer. Miriam's only other response was to show stress on her face and tears in her eyes.

Deborah continued with a trembling voice, "I need to walk away before my anger makes me say things I will regret." Miriam did nothing to stop her.

Deborah wandered around on her own for about twenty minutes, upset by Miriam's shallow comments, hoping to calm down. As she pondered their one-sided argument, she wondered if Miriam possessed the depth of character she wanted in a companion. Maybe Miriam was just sweet and innocent and nothing more. She worried that Miriam's willingness to engage in the most wonderful physical connection Deborah could imagine had led her astray. That was not enough for her. Maybe Deborah had mistaken Miriam for the person she hoped to find. How could she say those things? Did she really mean them?

When Deborah returned to the spot where she left her, Miriam was not there. Deborah had expected that Miriam would still be sitting in the same place, with tears in her eyes and apologies in her heart. Deborah looked around frantically. Where had she wandered to? Had she run away? Deborah widened her circle, looking in all the nearby places, trying to find her. Within five minutes she shifted from angry to worried. Deborah wondered if she was too harsh with Miriam, then if Miriam was safe, if she was lost, or if she was upset. Where had she gone?

After searching for about ten more minutes, Deborah stopped to think about where Miriam might be. With the horses? Or at the midway? Then suddenly she remembered the most wonderful moment they shared earlier and she headed to the one place where Miriam might be waiting. As Deborah arrived at the Tunnel of Love, she spotted Miriam.

Deborah approached her with downward-turned eyes, not sure how she would respond. Miriam held out her hand, with no concern about who might see them. Deborah followed as Miriam purchased tickets for this ride and silently lead Deborah onto the awaiting car. Deborah was stunned. Who was this brave girl?

Miriam had been overwhelmed when Deborah began yelling, telling her she was being judgmental of others. No one had ever talked to Miriam that way. Nor had anyone ever told her she was disapproving. Miriam was shocked and angry. When Deborah walked away, she was pleased to see her leave and that scared her.

Miriam wandered around, thinking that Deborah was different than the sweet girl Miriam thought she was. Deborah was harsh in her criticism and quick to judge. Miriam did not expect to be treated that way. She felt her face flush and her fists clench.

But Miriam's thoughts started to change as she wondered whether she had been judgmental. Was she looking down on people as if their jobs were menial? Her comments had come quickly, without much thought. Her face flushed again, this time from embarrassment about her own behavior. There was so much that was new to her in this country life. She was still learning about these folks who were so unlike city people. Maybe she was saying critical things and needed to be corrected. But she was shocked by Deborah's loud and angry words. Deborah had behaved just as badly as Miriam had.

As she wandered the fairgrounds, Miriam thought about the Deborah who had awakened her to so many new feelings. She thought about the girl with strength of character that she so admired, who could open her mind to her new ways to look at the world. Miriam wanted to be strong like her. Miriam wanted Deborah. But now she had made a mess of things.

Miriam knew they needed to re-connect. She found herself at the Tunnel of Love, the place where they had spoken special words. She waited. She hoped Deborah would figure out where she was when she calmed down. Miriam was pleased when Deborah finally came into view. There was no immediate need for apologies. That could come later. They just needed a few minutes of peace. There was no bravery in Miriam's decision to buy tickets to the ride, just a clear sense that perhaps they viewed the world differently.

As the small, enclosed car entered the dark tunnel, they kissed one another. It was not a kiss of passion or desperation or anger or fear or any of the emotions Miriam thought it might be. It was just a sweet kiss, reminding them both of how much they cared for each other. This was, after all, the Tunnel of Love.

The Tunnel of Love

Step Sixteen ✣ *Ecstasy*
Tuesday, July 18, 1911

Deborah and Miriam arrived back at the appointed meeting place for the family exhausted, having been through a huge range of emotions that day. After leaving the Tunnel of Love they quietly apologized to one another, promising to discuss their differences of opinion later. They elected to enjoy the rest of the day together without conflict or disruption.

Everyone had stories to tell about what they had seen during the day, so the ride home was animated. They were so busy talking excitedly no one thought to complain about the trip or ask to stop a single time. They all chattered at the same time, with overlapping conversations about their favorite experiences.

Back at home, Deborah and Miriam went into Mother's garden to sit on a bench and talk about what had happened earlier.

"I am sorry I yelled at you," said Deborah bowing her head and looking at the ground.

"I am sorry I was belittling of people I do not understand," responded Miriam with a slight wince.

After a moment of silence, with tears in her eyes, Deborah continued, "I am also sorry I ran away. I know that is not the best way to respond but I was too surprised and angry to be reasonable."

"I was actually glad to see you go, which scared me," Miriam said, as huge tears fell down her face. "I was afraid of your anger and furious at you for yelling at me. You can tell me when I have done something you don't like, but you cannot yell at me harshly. Especially when it is about something I was unaware I was doing."

"I scare myself when I get angry. I often run away, like I did at Ruth's party. I need to learn to trust you, and I need to trust myself."

"You can trust me. I will not yell at you. Even if I disagree with you or feel anger, I will not be harsh." Miriam went on, "For me, the challenge is talking about how I feel. I got so overwhelmed that I could not find words to put to my feelings. You need to be patient with me."

"We both have things to learn." After a moment of silence and more tears, Deborah said, "I want to be better at controlling my feelings and responding to yours."

Miriam took a deep breath and dried her tears on her hanky. "I guess we both need practice. I am glad to have you to help me. I think we will both be better people as we assist each other."

"This was a satisfying ending to our first fight," Deborah whispered.

"Yes," agreed Miriam softly. "We have a newfound trust in one another. I am glad we talked."

As evening fell, Deborah and Miriam headed to their own rooms and lay in their beds until they could hear the sound of snores down the hall. Only then did Deborah dare to open the door to join Miriam for another night of pleasure.

Mother's rose garden

Step Seventeen ❋ *Passion*
Wednesday, July 19, 1911

It was a lovely morning. Deborah's family had no plans today, which thrilled both girls. Miriam realized that during her whole first week in Great Barrington they had not spent any time with Ruth, so they headed to her house for a visit. After an hour of listening to her prattle on about all the boys in the area, they were thrilled to have the excuse of heading home for lunch. Miriam eased her way back into Ruth's good graces by agreeing to join Ruth and her friends at the ice cream shop the following day.

After a wonderful lunch of salad greens picked right from the garden, Deborah hitched up the horses and led Miriam out of town. Miriam could see a sparkle in Deborah's eyes and knew she had plotted something special.

They rode silently along the river for a while before Deborah tied the horses. She took a small package from the saddlebags and guided Miriam down a path into the woods. When they reached a small clearing, Deborah opened her satchel and produced a blanket and a towel. She laid the blanket on the grass, on a soft bed of ferns.

As she beckoned Miriam towards her, Deborah said enticingly, "Come sit with me."

"It is so nice to be here without Anna, Milton, or your parents nearby. I am glad to have some time alone with you," said Miriam softly.

After talking quietly for a few minutes, Deborah surprised her, suggesting something more risqué than anything Miriam had ever imagined.

"We are both quite hot from our ride, so let's take a swim," said Deborah nonchalantly.

"But we have no bathing outfits."

"We can swim in our chemises."

Miriam responded with a tightening chest, wondering if this had been Deborah's plan all along. "Deborah! I am not used to undressing in front of anyone, not even you."

But Miriam delighted in this naughty and immensely exciting behavior, though she worried, "Do you think someone might come by?"

Deborah said with assurance, "I am certain no one will venture this way."

Leaving their clothing on the shore, they headed into the water hesitantly because it was icy cold. Once they had submerged, they moved into each other's embrace. It was satisfying to hold each other body-to-body, with their tingling skin protected only by the thin layer of summer undergarments. They both had firm nipples from the cold water, which made it even more invigorating. They warmed a bit as they shared body heat but the water was too cold to stay in for long. When they got out of the cool water, Miriam came to Deborah with the towel and dried her skin, a very sensuous feeling. It was so unlike Miriam to be the initiator of such luscious behavior. Deborah closed her eyes, enjoying the caresses.

Deborah wanted more intimacy and felt very daring. She pulled down the shoulder straps of Miriam's undergarment, as Miriam resisted only slightly. She seemed very shy as Deborah exposed her breasts and looked her over with great interest. Deborah wondered if she had gone too far. Miriam allayed her fears when she reached over to Deborah's wet underclothes and with a few quick moves she playfully exposed her upper body to the air. They gazed at each other with desire, then dared to move closer until their nipples touched. They embraced, with their naked breasts rubbing against each other.

When Deborah began pulling at Miriam's bloomers, Miriam's response surprised her, giving in rapidly to her insistent hands. Miriam stood in the sunshine, completely naked. She understood Deborah's pleasure, viewing her every curve. Deborah then pulled at her own clothes and flung her under-garments onto the rocks. She stood in front of Miriam fully undressed. They looked each over for a long time, marveling at the experience of feeling so very exposed.

Deborah motioned toward the blanket and they slid onto it timidly, slowly reaching over to one another. When Deborah touched her, it was unlike any-thing Miriam had ever experienced. The feel of Deborah's cool skin heated her. Their nights of embraces had been exciting but a caress on naked skin was ten times more special. Miriam wanted to savor every moment; she pulled herself against Deborah's nakedness. They remained still in each other's arms, afraid to move, yet unwilling to let go.

When Deborah boldly reached out to touch Miriam's full breasts, Miriam took in a sizable involuntary gulp of air. Deborah traced Miriam's curves and she inhaled again. Deborah's hands slid down her body, to her hips. "I like feeling your cool skin against my fingertips," Deborah purred. "I feel your soft hairs as I stroke your neck and arms, but when I reach your breasts, your skin is as smooth as silk," she continued. "I love how your body moves as I stroke you, letting me know that you are appreciating my touch."

Deborah wanted to savor every inch of her, so she tried to move slowly from part to part. Each new area she touched evoked reactions. Miriam wanted Deborah to feel similar sensations, but Deborah made her wait. She softly explained she wanted all the pleasure to be Miriam's at this moment. Once Miriam understood, she let Deborah's hands travel all along her body. Deborah touched her from her face to her torso and then her back to her buttocks. Their eyes locked.

Deborah could stand it no longer. She slid her hand down to Miriam's private area, surprised by Miriam's wetness, though her own body had responded in the identical way. She dared reach along Miriam's crevices and touched her, as she would wish to be touched. Deborah was delicate in her movements, caressing every secret place. It was both mysterious and familiar. Deborah slid her fingers along Miriam and felt her softness become firm. Miriam pushed against Deborah's fingers and Deborah understood what Miriam wanted. She quickened her movements to match Miriam's moans and Miriam uttered incredible sounds Deborah had not heard before. Deborah moved faster and harder. Miriam's excitement was obvious, so Deborah continued. Just when Deborah did not think Miriam could stand it any longer, Miriam arched her back and let out wonderful, long, guttural gasps. This went on for short while, until Miriam fell back in a heap of sweat and smiles.

Her breathing was still ragged but it gradually slowed to a soothing pace. Deborah held Miriam against her, Miriam's warm and wet body providing immense pleasure.

They kissed and cuddled, grins on their faces. As they continued to embrace, Deborah felt her own breath quickening and Miriam sensed that Deborah was ready for her turn. Miriam touched Deborah as she had been touched. She began slowly, finally reaching the sweet spot where Deborah awaited her. Her excitement rose more quickly than Miriam's, since her sensations began while she was giving Miriam pleasure. Miriam quickly increased the pace of her touches, since Deborah could not stand for her to hesitate. It was not long until Deborah became totally out of control, writhing beneath Miriam's fingertips. Miriam held on, despite Deborah's lurching, and it was a very short time before Deborah screamed out, as Miriam had. Surely, all the birds in the area could hear her cries, but they left the girls to their pleasures.

There was no sweeter feeling than what they had both experienced. They lay back on the blanket, curled in each other's embrace, falling asleep, folded into each other. After an afternoon nap under the sun they awakened and dressed with the undergarments that had dried in the warm afternoon. Unhitching the horses, they headed home with a sweet breeze cooling their skin. They smiled at each other, taking in the miracle of being together.

Miriam's Diary, July 19, 1911

I experienced enormous pleasure with Deborah today. As she touched me, I became lost in the sensations and stopped thinking, aware of the excitement in my body and in hers. I became wet down below and the pleasures became extreme. I thought I would explode and then I sort of did. The feelings peaked in pleasure more dramatic than I had ever felt. Then there was enormous peace throughout my body. It was all so unexpected.

I wonder why I am not feeling any guilt or remorse? I would not want anyone else to know what we did today, yet I feel no shame. I can hardly wait until we find more opportunities to pleasure each other again.

Deborah too seemed surprised by it all, so I feel certain she has never experienced such familiarity with anyone else. I feel closer to her than I have ever felt to anyone. I wonder if she feels the same and what will happen when we are living apart.

Now I must hide my diary. Though no one typically comes into my room other than the housekeeper, I should never risk anyone finding this.

The swimming hole

Step Eighteen ❀ *Separation*
Thursday, July 20, 1911

The Levines were invited to a teatime organ concert in the music room of Kellogg Terrace, a romantic castle in the center of Great Barrington. Miriam was pleased to join them at this ornate Renaissance-style building with spectacular grounds. She wished she could explore all 40 rooms and 36 fireplaces, but she had to be satisfied with quick peaks into areas she could see on route to the water closet.

Deborah and Miriam returned home in enough time to go to the ice cream shop for a short while. Ruth greeted them like long lost friends, even though they had just seen her. Miriam felt relieved to be back in good stead with Ruth.

Deborah's father had promised a return trip to the Berkshire Museum, keeping his word on Friday. Anna and Milton were not pleased, so Mother offered them a special treat while the rest explored the artwork. Deborah and Miriam knew each other much better now, so this trip differed significantly from their previous visit. Miriam led the way at least half of the day, and Deborah was happy to follow.

Back home, Deborah and Miriam headed to their favorite spot, Mother's garden, to discuss Miriam's upcoming move to Ruth's house on Tuesday. Deborah said, "I think my parents succeeded in their goal for your visit. They wanted to introduce you to the wonders of country living."

"I think they also wanted to prove to you that your life at Stonegate will be gratifying," Miriam said with a side-wards glance. "Your mother has been attentive to your needs as well as mine."

"My mother is always attentive to her children, and I am pleased that carried over to the way she treated you. I was also pleased with my father's reaction. He is always less effusive, but he tried to make your stay enjoyable. They both enjoyed your company."

"It has been a pleasure to get to know them both. I also enjoyed Anna and Milton. I have had a wonderful time with your family!"

Deborah smiled and said, "I have enjoyed your company more than you might realize. I am very sad you are leaving. You will be just one house away, but it will feel like you traveled many miles from my embrace."

"I really don't want to leave," said Miriam. "But I know Ruth will be waiting anxiously for me. She seems to have numerous acquaintances, yet I wonder if she has any real friends. It is no wonder she is excited I will be staying at her house."

"I think you are right," Deborah said, turning her head, changing the subject. "I requested that my parents plan no excursions for your last day with us, on Sunday. They assumed we would get together with our friends, but that is the last thing on my mind. You will get plenty of socializing when you are back at Ruth's house. For our last day, nothing would be sweeter than riding our horses, swimming naked in a stream, or engaging in passionate pleasures."

Miriam had an approving glint in her eyes, "Oh my, it sounds like you have another day of wonderful adventures planned."

Shabbos was especially sweet for the girls. On Saturday morning, Anna and Milton stuck by Miriam's side, while in the afternoon, Deborah and Miriam sat on the porch and exchanged their favorite books with one another. Miriam arrived with "Peter Pan" by J. M. Barrie and Deborah brought "Room with a View" by E. M. Forster. They sat on the porch all afternoon, reading each other's favored books.

On Miriam's last morning at the Levine's, she engaged Anna and Milton in a playful game of tag. After lunch with the family, Deborah and Miriam took the horses for a long jaunt through the countryside. They stopped at a secluded spot where they would not need to be quiet.

Deborah spread a blanket on the cool grass. When they kissed, Miriam responded with zeal, their hearts pounding in keeping with the rest of their bodies. Though they were comfortable in their riding outfits, they soon discarded their clothing completely. Deborah assured Miriam that no one would find them in this isolated location. Before becoming carried away with passion, they went for a swim in a deep pool nearby. Afterwards, they dried each other off and lay on the blanket, with the sun beating down. They held each other tightly, rubbing their bodies together in a dance of emotions.

Miriam, with tears glistening in her eyes, said, "I am deeply aware that I will be moving to Ruth's house, so today feels like a parting of sorts."

Deborah's eyes reflected her emotions, too. "I know our days will be separate and I will no longer be able to sneak into your bed at night. I am very sad."

After somber talk of their impending separation, they held each other for a long time and wept. Deborah regained her composure, suggesting, "Let's plan ways to meet daily while you are staying with Ruth. It will not be the same, but happily you are not heading back to Boston yet. Thinking of months apart is almost more than I can bear. We must focus on this time when you are nearby."

Understanding this would be their last opportunity for intimacy, they soon began grabbing at each other with the desperation they had felt many times before.

As Deborah stroked Miriam's body, Miriam squirmed a bit, then said "Ow."
Deborah laughed, "The sun has burned sections of your skin."

"Yours also," chuckled Miriam as she rubbed Deborah's red shoulder.

They found they both had sunburns in places that they should not, giggling
as they explored each other for patches of redness. Their burns were not severe,
so touching their tender flesh brought silliness, rather than pain. They shifted
from sadness to frolicking on the blanket. Within a short time, as they rubbed
the unburned parts of each other, they each reached frantic relief. They lay
back, panting and laughing. It was exhilarating to be in love.

Returning home with smiles on their faces, which everyone interpreted
as joy in their horseback ride, they knew no one would guess the wonders of
their afternoon.

After another wonderful meal, they all sat around the piano singing until
bedtime. Miriam enjoyed these evenings greatly. After changing into her nightclothes, Miriam wrote in her diary.

Miriam's Diary, July 23, 1911

*I am pleased to be part of this loving family and to be included in
their wonderful traditions. When I compare my evenings with the Levine
family to those at my home in Boston, I see many differences.*

*The Levine's evenings are active and noisy, with boisterous joke telling
or games of charades. Although her parents do not typically participate
in the games, they often encourage the progress of the winners or provide
guidance for the losing player. Her parents sing around the piano, as
they did this evening, or engage in lively conversations. I appreciate their
inclusion of me in everything.*

*My family is also loving but in such a different way. At home,
Mother sits quietly with her crocheting in her lap and a copy of the latest
Jewish Advocate, the local newspaper, by her side. Father studies the*
Talmud, *the record of the rabbinic teachings, until his eyes fall shut and
he snoozes in his chair. Although it is discouraged to study alone, he and
his study partner give each other assignments to prepare for their next
discussion of the sacred texts. My grandmother, Bubbie, retreats to her
room after she cleans up from dinner. She spends her evenings quietly
reading her treasured Yiddish stories. Hannah and I play card games
until we get sleepy. Conversation is minimal, yet there is a sweetness and
predictability to our family time. I love our evenings together as much as
I enjoy the interaction of the Levine household.*

When the household was silent, Deborah and Miriam climbed into bed together. They discovered that their afternoon pleasures had awakened their bodies, rather than satisfied them. Deborah caressed Miriam's womanly parts in circles around her most tender area. She soon heard the familiar squish of wetness. Deborah let one finger reach a tiny bit inside. Miriam encouraged her, as she thrust herself around Deborah's finger. Deborah reached in deeper. Miriam moved so that Deborah's finger glided in and out. Deborah whispered a quiet "shh", as Miriam made melodic sounds that matched her excitement. But Miriam was too lost in pleasure to quiet her sounds. Deborah's hand kept pace with Miriam's frantic moves and Deborah increased the back and forth and in and out movements. Deborah had to hold her other hand against Miriam's mouth as she called out loudly when caught in the frenzy of excitement. Deborah could feel rhythmic pulses inside Miriam as she squeezed Deborah's finger in a tight grip. With one last, loud gasp, Miriam fell onto her back, satisfied with the way Deborah had touched her.

In their excitement, they almost forgot the whole family was just down the hall. Happily, when Deborah became aware of anything other than Miriam's pleasure, she heard the familiar snores of her father and mother. They were safe!

Deborah and Miriam held each other closely. After a quick recitation of the bedtime Shema, they fell asleep together. When Deborah awoke to use the water closet, she headed back to her own room, to assure they would not be found together in the morning.

Kellogg Terrace

Step Nineteen ❧ *Anticipation*
Monday, July 24, 1911

The day Miriam left, Deborah spent the afternoon weeping. She told her parents she was not feeling well and they left her alone. The next day, she met Miriam at the ice cream parlor, but they were both desperate for time alone. Miriam excused herself from the afternoon activities, feigning a headache, and met Deborah behind the house. They scurried off to the wooded area nearby, hoping no one would notice their stealthy entrance into the woods.

Once in the woods, they were frantic for intimacy. They knew they had limited time and risked discovery, which added a bit of excitement to the encounter. It was barely five minutes before Deborah had her hands under Miriam's skirt, where she found her completely ready. Deborah barely started to caress her silky parts when Miriam let out a muffled groan. They chuckled and sat on the grass for Deborah's turn.

Finding their position awkward, it took Deborah longer to relax into the pleasure and be satisfied. Afterward, they were both disheveled, with twigs in their hair and wrinkled skirts. They fixed themselves the best they could and left their hiding spot separately to avoid discovery.

After leaving Deborah, Miriam headed to her sickbed, to get rid of her supposed headache. She passed Ruth's mother on the stairway. Mrs. Gold worried that Miriam was flushed. If she only knew why!

In her room, Miriam took off her dress and lay on the bed. She closed her eyes and daydreamed about the intense feelings of just a few moments before. She found she was again aroused and memories of Deborah's hands on her made her more excited. Miriam had never before given herself pleasure but she felt she needed it. Climbing under the covers, she brought her hand down to the very wet area that Deborah had just visited. Miriam imagined that her hand was Deborah's. She made circles with her fingers, intensifying the pressure of her touch gradually. She stroked, as Deborah had, though it felt different. Miriam soon felt the familiar quickening and shallow breath, rubbing herself until release came. Miriam was pleased to know she could now pleasure herself when Deborah was not around to do it for her. She drifted off to sleep.

When at home, Deborah was eager for more luxurious afternoons of loving play. She tried to fabricate a reason to get together, but could not come up with a creative solution. Luckily, Miriam took it into her own hands at the ice cream parlor the next afternoon.

Deborah and Miriam watched Ruth paying lots of attention to the handsome boy who was sitting near her. Miriam realized Ruth might be delighted to have a free afternoon to spend with this boy, who Ruth introduced as Michael.

She told Ruth, "I would like to spend tomorrow afternoon with Deborah, instead of going horseback riding with you. Would that be possible?"

Ruth excitedly replied, "What a great idea! Michael and I can ride together and my mother will assume I am with you and not ask questions. A perfect solution."

Michael agreed to the plan and Deborah casually said that would be fine with her too. Deborah and Miriam did not dare to look at each other directly because they knew they would break into huge grins.

Miriam spent the evening and next morning anticipating her time with Deborah. Right after lunch they departed for a long walk, traveling past all the houses to find a quiet spot where they would not risk being found. They reached a deserted area, following a path into a deeply wooded hideout. Deborah had packed a blanket and Miriam later discovered Deborah had put on her favorite underclothes in anticipation of their time together. They were a bit shy since this felt naughtier than when they were at Deborah's house, but once they locked their lips together, it felt familiar. They touched and teased each other until they reached their glorious peak together. They lay back in each other's arms, content and happy.

Miriam headed back to the Gold's but she was not looking forward to spending time at Ruth's house. Ruth's dad, a prominent New York lawyer who only came to Great Barrington for weekend visits, was disruptive due to his booming voice. A dapper but humorless gentleman significantly older than his wife, he had a sour expression permanently etched on his mustached face. Ruth's mother, who had the same almond-shaped eyes as her daughter, was a fashionable picture of confidence. She wore stylish clothing to accentuate her slim figure, and dramatic hats to bring attention to her lovely face and rich brown hair. Miriam had a hard time warming up to her, especially since Mrs. Gold barely talked to her. Also, Miriam sensed Mrs. Gold preferred the company of her friends to that of her children, something Miriam found distasteful. Ruth's sister, Beth, a pretty girl with long dark hair and attractive features, had one favorite activity: changing her clothes several times a day for no apparent reason. When she and her brother David were together, their sport was squabbling. Miriam found herself constantly making disparaging comparisons to her delightful time at Deborah's house.

Miriam also saw that Ruth consistently focused on her own needs and did not seem to notice Miriam's discomfort. Each day after breakfast Ruth brought Miriam to meet her girlfriends at the soda shop to gossip about the day before. After lunch and horseback riding, Ruth headed to the ice cream shop again, where all her friends gathered, and she expected Miriam to join her. When the young folks headed home for dinner and evenings with their families, Miriam followed Ruth. She spent the evenings listening to Ruth's chatter, since no other options were available.

Miriam thought, No wonder Ruth appears desperate for attention. She gets very little from her own family.

Michael

Step Twenty ❧ *Syncopation*
Wednesday, July 26, 1911

After Deborah and Miriam's afternoon of intimacy, they became deter-mined to get together more often. Miriam encouraged Ruth to get more serious about her new beau, Michael. As Ruth told tales of their kisses, Miriam listened to all the boring details and feigned interest in him. Michael was a good choice for Ruth because he was handsome, certainly Ruth's primary criteria. He seemed pleasant and he was the only new Jewish boy in town. With Miriam's encouragement, Ruth began to plot ways to be with him. As predicted, Ruth's plan involved Miriam providing an alibi while they snuck away. How perfect!

On their next afternoon together, Deborah and Miriam went back to the woods but this time they headed further into the forest, to assure more privacy. It did not take them long to find a soft spot to settle down and they wasted no time reaching inside each other's blouses.

They were sucking each other's breasts with great gusto when Miriam suddenly pulled away, putting a finger to her lips. As they quieted, Deborah heard the sound of voices quite nearby, her eyes opening widely as she rec-ognized Ruth's high-pitched squeal. Ruth and Michael had chosen the same place for their rendezvous!

While Deborah and Miriam listened to Ruth and Michael, they slowly pulled their clothing over their bodies, getting fully dressed and continuing to listen. At first, they heard lots of giggles but then the sounds quieted. Listening more intently, they heard the distinct sound of kisses. My, they were noisy kissers! When the sounds turned to soft moans, Deborah and Miriam found it exciting to imagine what was happening nearby.

Deborah mimicked what she imagined Michael was doing to Ruth and quietly narrated their actions. When they heard the rustling of leaves followed by whimpers, she whispered, "They laid down on the grass." Deborah and Miriam followed suit.

"Michael is feeling Ruth's breasts." She did the same to Miriam.

"He is moving his hands down the length of her torso. Now Michael is undoing Ruth's blouse and lifting it over her head."

As she imagined out loud, "He is undoing his trousers", she pulled off her pantaloons, exposing her naked bottom to the air.

"Ruth is stroking his nakedness," and she stroked Miriam's favorite body part.

Deborah and Miriam heard Ruth making louder noises yet they were careful to keep their own voices low as their passion increased. As the sounds intensified, they became immensely excited, grabbing at each other forcefully. Just as they heard Ruth and Michael call out in ecstasy, they reached their own explosions. All four of them seemed in syncopation.

Satisfied, Deborah and Miriam dressed quickly and positioned themselves innocently on their blanket. Luckily, the couple did not see them, but this close call made them talk of finding a new place next time.

On the way out of the woods, Miriam thought of her conversations with Ruth, who had talked of kissing this boy but not of the intimacies they obviously shared today. Was this their first time? Or had she withheld the real stories? Miriam was anxious to hear Ruth's stories tonight, to see if she was willing to share her experience.

Ruth did not share a word. But happily for Deborah and Miriam, Ruth had a great need to see her new boyfriend frequently. The next day, they watched Ruth as she and her young man walked towards the woods in the same direction they had headed the day before. Deborah and Miriam headed the opposite way.

Deborah and Miriam had both been stimulated with the events of the previous day and once they settled onto their blanket, they began retelling what they had heard. They touched gently as they talked, not letting themselves act out their activities as they had the day before. The withholding of their touch during the storytelling had an excitement of its own. And while they had not yet touched each other, they were soon both moist. They reached over and stroked each other intimately, making sloshing sounds that added to the excitement. They both narrated their loving play.

"It feels wonderful when you touch me," Deborah began. "Please move your fingers around in circles."

"I love to excite you."

"I am getting very close. Go faster."

The wetness and the words combined to make Deborah's final release fierce. Next it was Miriam's turn.

Deborah sucked on Miriam's breasts and soon Miriam begged, "Please stroke me." Then she added, "Inside please."

"Faster. Faster." Miriam implored. "More. More," she eked out, just before she exploded around Deborah's finger.

They held onto each other afterwards and both fell asleep for a short nap. Miriam awoke to the feeling of Deborah stroking her special place. She watched Deborah's fingers rub her lower lips and Deborah smiled when she noticed Miriam was awake. As Miriam started to move, Deborah stopped her and continued her strokes. She continued to watch as Miriam produced more fluid. She could hear the squishy sounds as Deborah rubbed her. Once Miriam was almost ready to explode, Deborah took her wet fingers and stroked her own wetness. Miriam assisted her, finding she was equally slippery. Slowly, but firmly they rubbed each other. As they reached the point of no return, rubbing faster and harder, they had one more explosion of simultaneous passion.

Step Twenty-One ❧ *Lost*
Friday, July 28, 1911

It was Shabbos. The one redeeming factor at the Gold's home was that Mr. Gold was much more observant of Shabbos than the Levines. He led the Friday night prayers much as Miriam's father did, and on Saturday morning, he led a complete Shabbos service, except for the Torah service. Everyone participated, and it was easier to tolerate David and Beth in this setting. They had a traditional Shabbos lunch and as tradition dictates, no one engaged in any activities all day other than reading or taking walks. Miriam spent most of the day alone, to her delight. Following the afternoon service, Havdalah, Ruth became quite chatty, but after a full day of calm, Miriam had much more patience.

Miriam next saw Deborah on Sunday at the ice cream parlor. Deborah arrived first, settling into a seat near the doorway to await Miriam's arrival. The sun shone and she was about to see her girlfriend, so her spirits were high.

After Miriam arrived, they became engaged in a lively conversation. Suddenly Deborah's face blanched and she stopped talking mid-sentence. Miriam followed her gaze and it settled on an unfamiliar girl who had just entered the ice cream shop. When the stranger noticed Deborah, she looked surprised.

"Judith," Deborah mumbled under her breath, as she darted for the door.

Baffled, with no idea who this girl was, Miriam rose quietly to go in search of Deborah. Glancing in all directions, she finally spotted her scurrying off towards the woods. Miriam set out in pursuit.

She hurried along the same wooded path they had taken the day before, though she was unfamiliar with these woods. Actually, Miriam possessed no skill in finding her way in any woods and after five minutes she was lost. She tried retracing her steps, only to find each group of bushes less familiar than the last. She headed down a different path, only to feel more confused. Trying to find her way back to the main road, she was ready to give up her search in favor of finding her way out of the forest, but the path eluded her. Miriam had no idea what to do, so she sat on a tree stump and cried.

She realized she was wasting time when she could be actively looking for a way out of this predicament. Miriam wandered aimlessly for about an hour before stopping again. Looking down, she noticed a rock formation she had seen before. She had been going in circles!

When Miriam's stomach began rumbling, she realized it was approaching dinnertime and everyone would soon be heading home. Dusk would hamper chances of finding her way out and for any rescue party to find her. As she stopped to think about what to do, tears glistened and her heart beat faster. Miriam was scared.

Suddenly there was a rustling near her. Her breath caught and she stood still, hearing the noise again, her body tensing even more. As a chipmunk scurried past her, Miriam exhaled. But it was not long before the original sound returned, closer than before. Miriam gasped again and waited. This time, a skinny green snake over a foot in length slithered out of the woods. Sweat broke out on her forehead, her palms became damp, and she did not move or regain her composure until the snake was out of sight. She hated snakes!

The sky started to darken, her hopes dimming. Miriam wondered if she would be lost in the woods all night. Would a wild animal attack her? Where would she sleep? Would they find her dead in the morning?

She started down a narrow path and caught her dress on a branch. As she heard it rip, she was distracted from watching her footing and scratched her ankle on a briar. She looked down and could see blood trickling down her leg where her stockings had torn.

Miriam sat on the ground, with limbs shaking. She tried to mop the blood on her ankle with a corner of her dress but it kept bleeding. She was exhausted, thirsty, and more scared than she had ever been. After all, she possessed no skills to assist in this situation. But she needed to find her way out of this scary place before darkness fell completely. Her mind wandered to her family. How would they react if they learned she had perished in the woods? Would Deborah feel guilty for running off? How was Deborah? What had happened to her? Why did the sight of that girl at the ice cream shop make her run away? Thoughts tumbled from her brain. Was she going to die? Would Deborah love again if Miriam died? This was all too terrible to be happening.

Then, in the midst of her jumble of feelings, Miriam heard voices in the distance. Real voices. And they were calling her name!

Miriam called back in the loudest voice she could manage, wondering why she had not thought to call out for help. "It is Miriam. I am here. I am here!"

Miriam heard a response to her screams and tears fell from her eyes in large droplets. She called back and wandered in the direction of the voices until they became louder.

Someone yelled, "Stay still."

A second voice said, "Yell loudly, so we can follow your voice."

"I am over here. Come find me. It is Miriam. Come rescue me," Miriam yelled into the void.

In just a few minutes, Miriam spotted a small group heading her way. She scurried in their direction, recognizing Ruth, Michael, and a boy who frequented the ice cream shop. But before they reached her, Miriam heard a sound to her left and turned to see if a large, dangerous animal had reached her before the rescuers had.

It was Deborah! Deborah approached her with her arms outstretched and Miriam ran into her embrace. All of Miriam's rescuers ran to her and individually hugged her. She was genuinely glad to see Ruth and her friends, but mostly, she was thrilled to have Deborah at her side.

Fearing what would happen to Miriam in the woods took Deborah's attention away from her own concerns. Deborah had been overwhelmed and distraught when she ran from the ice cream parlor. Returning an hour later, she learned Miriam had followed her out. She went in search of her, first at the Gold's and then at her own home, becoming increasingly worried when Miriam had not been seen at either place. Deborah became more distraught, realizing Miriam might have followed her into the woods. She knew Miriam had no experience navigating unfamiliar territory. She went back and called out her name. When there was no response, she gathered a small search party from those left at the ice cream shop and they went in pursuit. It was half an hour later when they finally heard Miriam's voice in the distance.

After a short reunion, Deborah brought Miriam to the Gold's house, where she found the family waiting with pale faces. Beth and David ran up to her and welcomed her with hugs, unusual behavior for anyone in this family. Deborah explained simply that Miriam had been lost in the woods.

While Deborah wanted to stay and explain her behavior at the ice cream shop, she headed home quickly. Her family was equally concerned. Miriam would have to wait to hear her explanation.

After Miriam cleaned up and changed her clothing, they all sat down to an animated dinner conversation, the first since she had been at this house. Everyone asked what had happened.

Miriam explained simply, "I attempted to take a walk in the woods but I quickly got lost."

David asked seriously, "How did you survive in the deep woods?" making the situation sound like a mystery he was reading.

Beth asked indelicately, "How did you manage for so many hours without a toilet?" Her mother quieted her query before Miriam had to offer details.

After their late dinner, Ruth asked in private, "Why did Deborah run from the ice cream shop?" Miriam was impressed that Ruth had noticed something outside herself.

"I do not know. I have not had an opportunity to ask her."

Ruth questioned Miriam in a style unlike her normal patter. "Miriam. Tell me what happened to you in the woods. You were missing for a long time. I was worried." Miriam shared tales of her misadventure for the rest of the evening.

Deborah's family was so concerned about Miriam's disappearance, that, when Deborah arrived home, four people were about to mount their steeds to go in pursuit.

During dinner, Anna and David asked endless questions. David made up tales of all the frightening things that could have happened to Miriam in the woods and everyone laughed at his creative stories. Anna chimed in with stories of her own, mostly about the animals that might have provided comfort to Miriam. Deborah appreciated being with her family, forgetting her own concerns until she headed to her bedroom. She would discuss everything with Miriam tomorrow, hoping she would understand.

Lost in the woods

Step Twenty-Two ❧ *Jealousy*
Monday, July 31, 1911

The next day, on a walk, Deborah began the conversation with the safer topic, Miriam's disappearance. She told her about her family's preparing a group to search. "I was frightened when I could not find you. I would not know what to do if you were hurt."

"I was more afraid than I had ever been," Miriam admitted. "I tried to find my way back, but I kept getting more confused. After what felt like hours, I gave up, lowered myself onto the ground and cried. Soon after I sat down, I heard all of you calling for me. I don't know why I had not thought of calling out for help."

"Don't berate yourself for what you did or did not do. All that matters is that we found you safe."

"I was so relieved to be rescued. I never thought I would be so glad to see Ruth. It was very sweet she and Michael searched for me. I also appreciate that your family was setting up a rescue party. Everyone has been so kind."

Miriam motioned to a bench along the river and sat. Deborah joined her. Without hesitation Miriam asked, "What caused you to run away from the ice cream parlor? Did it have anything to do with the new girl who came in?"

Deborah rose and paced in front of the bench. "I need to tell you the whole story but it is difficult for me to talk about it. I could not speak of it with anyone but you."

"You can tell me anything," said Miriam, not certain whether she could remain neutral if this had to do with another girl.

Deborah took a deep breath. "When I was in school, I was quite smitten with a girl in my class, Judith. She was bright, interesting, and very attractive. I made a fool of myself, following her everywhere. She was not interested in befriending me and she eventually became annoyed. In front of all my friends, she complained I was pestering her and should leave her alone. I was exceedingly embarrassed. The girl in the ice cream shop was Judith, that very same person."

Miriam was surprised; Deborah's explanation was certainly unexpected! She felt badly for Deborah's disgrace, but also worried that Judith might still have a special place in Deborah's heart. Miriam knew that Deborah was anxiously awaiting a response, so she answered Deborah's unasked questions.

"My first reaction," Miriam said, with more assurance than she felt, "is jealousy. Judith was the first to steal your heart and I do not like that anyone else has been special to you. Was this girl more important to you than I am?"

"NO!" Deborah responded quickly and firmly. You don't need to be jealous. I did not feel anything towards her like I feel towards you. It was more of a crush than love."

"It pleases me to know I have nothing to fear," said Miriam, letting out a deep breath. "Yet I am concerned this girl could cause another scene, recreating the horrible experience you had."

Deborah reacted immediately with wide opened eyes and a trembling voice, "I could not stand for that to happen again."

Miriam went on with some tension still in her voice, "I don't want to put people's eyes on us. It might make people wonder about our relationship if they learn you had these feelings for a girl in the past."

"I know. But what can I do to prevent that happening?" Deborah asked, shrugging her shoulders.

Miriam came up with a solution. "You could approach Judith the next time you see her and ask for her forgiveness. If I was her, and you approached me that way, I would listen."

"But she isn't you. You are sweet and she certainly is not."

"But she still might respond to your plea of forgiveness. It is worth a try."

"I will do my best and hope she has matured as much as I have since that time."

Miriam then took a deep breath and shared the hardest truth. "I have one more issue to discuss. I was surprised you reacted by running away, rather than facing Judith. I always think of you as strong and able to manage anything. Running away from your fear is something I might do but I am disappointed when you behave that way."

"I am embarrassed I did that."

"I hope both of us can learn to be braver when faced with our fears. Hopefully we can help each other through such challenges." Miriam said.

"I am so appreciative of having you in my life. I think we are both stronger because we have each other."

Miriam's Diary, July 31, 1911

Deborah and I had a meaningful conversation today, despite her emotions being raw. We talked openly about her behavior and our fears about what might come, should Judith react less graciously than we hope. She listened to my suggestions, which pleased me. My typical response is to withhold my ideas but with her I can be forthright. Our conversation warmed my heart.

The most thrilling moment in our talk was when Deborah told me her feelings towards Judith were a crush, not love. Does that mean what she feels towards me is love?

Judith

Step Twenty-Three ✤ *Opportunity*
Tuesday, August 1, 1911

Deborah was acutely aware that Miriam was a good influence. As Deborah explained her harassment by Judith, Miriam was sympathetic, which gave her courage. When Deborah saw Judith walking towards the ice cream shop the next day, her heart skipped a beat, but she stopped to talk, as Miriam had suggested.

After Deborah offered her apology, Judith remained calm and was neither dismissive nor understanding. When Judith mentioned her family would be leaving the Berkshires that afternoon, Deborah felt relieved and safe. And she credited her bravery to Miriam's encouragement. She could not wait to describe the meeting to Miriam and let her know Judith was leaving town immediately.

During the rest of their first week living apart, Deborah and Miriam found ways to rendezvous but they wanted desperately to spend more time together. Their separation was about to change thanks to an invitation the Levines received to visit their delightful Manhattan neighbors, the Berkowitz family.

Mr. and Mrs. Berkowitz recently purchased a summer cottage in Lenox, another Berkshire town, and they invited Deborah's whole family to visit for several days the following week. They suggested Deborah bring along a friend. She longed to invite Miriam, but would Ruth mind?

The Berkowitzes disclosed that Deborah's guest would have to share her bedroom, which they hoped would not be inconvenient. Inconvenient? It would be the most exciting situation Deborah could imagine. The thought of several days in the same bedroom as Miriam thrilled her. Ruth would probably be fine with Miriam accepting the invitation but would be displeased because it would be harder for her to see Michael. She could hardly wait to tell Miriam.

Deborah pulled Miriam aside at the ice cream parlor that afternoon. A huge smile crossed Miriam's face as Deborah explained, "You are invited to be my guest when we visit our friends, the Berkowitz family, in a nearby town next week."

When Deborah explained the sleeping arrangements, Miriam became as excited as Deborah. She was so thrilled her eyes moistened.

Before they left the ice cream parlor, Miriam told Ruth of her travel plans. Ruth had a devastated look on her face until Miriam promised a daily rendezvous for Ruth and Michael until they departed. Ruth had still not told Miriam of their personal encounters and Miriam did not admit she knew.

After leaving the others, Deborah and Miriam talked excitedly about every aspect of their upcoming adventure. They talked about Lenox, the family they would be visiting, and their visions for their nights together. They marveled at their good fortune. Not only were their bodies incredibly connected but also each day they felt more trusting of one another. Every day Miriam was sharing more and Deborah began to have hopes for their future together.

The Berkowitz home at 11 Old Stockbridge Road, Lenox, Mass.

Step Twenty-Four ❧ *Paradise*
Thursday, August 4, 1911

Miriam awoke slowly this morning, having fasted the day before to observe the sad holiday of *Tisha B'Av*, designated as a day of tragedy following multiple disasters for the Jewish people. Her mood was somber, so Deborah left Miriam on her own as she requested. By noon, Miriam's spirits changed.

Deborah's mood was quite jubilant. After lunch, Deborah's mother asked her why she was so excited about their upcoming trip. Deborah felt she needed an excuse and told her mother, "I would like to return to the millenary shop we visited on our last trip to Lenox. I saw a stunning hat. Maybe, you will buy it for my birthday."

Luckily, Deborah had admired a hat at this shop, though the details were vague. Hopefully her reddened face and faltering voice did not give away her fib.

As the day approached for their travels, Deborah packed and repacked several times, paying special attention to her nightclothes and undergarments. She wished she had told her mother of the lacy pantaloons she had seen, instead of the frivolous hat. Miriam would be more interested in her private apparel!

Prior to their departure for Lenox, Miriam made a special effort to be nice to Ruth. Ruth had been so focused on her daily liaisons, she hardly noticed Miriam was distracted. Miriam asked Ruth about her boyfriend and their afternoons together, trying to tease out the truth. Ruth talked about his kisses, keeping the full story to herself. Miriam could not chide her for her withholdings, since she had certainly not told Ruth of her own afternoon delights.

On Monday, the day of their departure, Ruth did not notice Miriam's excitement. What a self-centered girl she was! Of course, Miriam was grateful for Ruth's invitation to stay with her family and for the introduction to her neighbor Deborah. For these reasons alone, Miriam was willing to remain connected, though Ruth certainly did not live up to her new standards for friendship.

As the Levine's buggy drove next door to pick up Miriam, Deborah's heart began beating rapidly. Her whole family was excited about this trip, so her eagerness was not especially noticed. As they rounded the corner into the Gold's driveway, Miriam, waiting outside, was quite a vision, wearing the dress that Deborah most favored. The waistline accentuated Miriam's wonderful curves, the neckline dipped just enough to show her amble breasts, and the new style of full skirt exposed her ankles. A huge smile took over Deborah's face.

Mr. Levine helped Miriam aboard. Anna and Milton moved to one side, so Miriam could sit next to Deborah. They were excited to see Miriam since she always paid lots of attention to them. Deborah loved everything about her. Yes, it felt like love.

The trip to Lenox was long and uneventful. Mrs. Levine pointed out the Crane Paper Mill, where fine stationary was produced by the same family who built the Berkshire Museum, but other than that, it was hills and valleys most of the way. On arrival, the Berkowitz's summer cottage impressed Miriam with its size and beauty. She wondered why there would be no separate bedroom for the two of them in this huge home, until the Berkowitz's four pretty young daughters emerged from the side of the house. Mrs. Berkowitz introduced herself, the four-year-old twins, Margie and Minnie, six-year-old Ethel, and Fannie, the eldest at nine-years-old. She explained Mr. Berkowitz would arrive from New York the next day. Given the size of their brood, Miriam was impressed they found enough space to fit the six of them.

Miriam felt at ease with the Berkowitz family. They offered lemonade to quench everyone's thirst and passed popcorn they gotten from the horse-drawn wagon earlier that day. The girls entertained them with a sweet rendition of "Yankee Doodle" which they had been practicing for their guest's arrival. Miriam wished she could spend another month in Lenox with this lovely family.

While Miriam knew their intimacies would need to wait until after dark, she wanted to see the space she and Deborah would share. Her fantasies would seem real if she could see where they would enjoy their delights. Happily, her daydreams were realized as Deborah and Miriam were escorted to their room. They climbed up two flights of winding stairs to discover they would be in the turret! Windows surrounded this enchanting room at the top of the house.

The children all bounded up the stairs, with Fanny proclaiming, "This is our favorite room."

"How delightful!" squealed Miriam, with as much enthusiasm as the children.

"Come look out this window. I can see the mountains," exclaimed Ethel.

Minnie chimed in with, "Look at the pink garden." Pink was obviously her favorite color.

Not to be left out, Margie yelled out, "Look", pointing to a large expanse of grassy lawn out the third window. They all headed to her window, seeing nothing of significance.

"Birds," she explained. The girls then departed abruptly, in search of something else to catch their fancy.

As soon as they were alone, Deborah pronounced excitedly, "One bed. One large and comfortable looking bed! We are so fortunate!"

"No wonder the children love this special room. It is like a dollhouse at the top of the world."

Mrs. Berkowitz arrived upstairs and asked, "Is this adequate? I am sorry there is only one bed and no water closet on this floor," as she pointed to a small chamber pot for their use during the night.

"We love this space," Miriam assured her with a warm smile, which did not give away her overwhelming excitement.

While Mrs. Berkowitz was with them, Deborah tried to restrain her delight, but once they were alone she giggled unreservedly. They would have more privacy than they could have imagined and with one bed they could play and sleep together in comfort! Deborah and Miriam talked quietly together until they realized no one could hear them in their little hideaway.

Miriam said, with a twinkle in her eye, "There is a full hour before dinner. I thought we could take a short nap." It was clear they would use their time for activities other than napping!

Alone, with the door shut tightly, Deborah and Miriam took off the other's clothing, carefully placing everything in the cupboard. As they got down to their undergarments, they moved to the bed. Deborah tantalized Miriam, stimulating every inch of her skin. After many minutes of soft strokes, Deborah moved her fingers southward, stroking until the hardness beneath her fingertips encouraged a firmer touch. Deborah brought Miriam slowly to the brink of release. With a few quick, firm moves Miriam was satiated. After she recovered, she focused on Deborah. Deborah's turn was very swift. Once they were both satisfied, they fell asleep in each other's arms.

Deborah and Miriam dozed off but were suddenly awakened by many small feet on the stairs to the turret. They pulled on their underclothing and lifted the sheets just in time for the four small children to push open the door.

Fannie hurriedly told them, "It is time for dinner. They are waiting for you in the library." She and the other children scurried away, unconcerned they were sleeping together in the same bed. After all, one bed was all the family had provided. The benefits would remain a secret.

They had a delicious dinner, with everyone chattering happily. After they finished, Mrs. Berkowitz accompanied the children on the piano as they sang "Three Blind Mice", "Little Bo Beep" and "Ba Ba Black Sheep." Anna joined in but Milton seemed a bit lost with all these girls. Miriam sweetly engaged him in games of checkers. Once the young children went to bed, the rest of them sat around the fire and talked of their trip through the towns of Stockbridge and Lee.

After everyone retreated to their bedrooms, Deborah and Miriam entered the turret. They undressed and headed to their bed for a delicious night of loving. By habit, they kept their voices low and controlled their personal sounds, but for the first time they were not sneaking.

"I am so happy," said Miriam. We have each other, two lovely families with well-behaved children to entertain us, and more privacy than we ever imagined. I wish we could stay here forever."

Turret bedroom in Berkowitz home

Step Twenty-Five ❦ *Declaration*
Tuesday, August 8, 1911

Deborah and Miriam both awoke early, totally refreshed. They shyly availed themselves of the chamber pot, turning their backs to each other. Once relieved, they climbed back into bed. They must have each had delicious dreams, because they were both ready for a morning frolic. It was a very short time before their needs were appeased and they were ready to head to breakfast.

After they ate, Mrs. Berkowitz, Deborah, Miriam, Anna, and the four girls, walked into town. The little girls pointed to one thing after another, as excited young children do. Mrs. Levine stayed back to read a book. It was a treat for her to have time to relax, with no responsibilities.

As they got close to the town, Miriam requested, "Can we visit the Hotel Aspinwall?" She pulled a brochure out of her pocket and read, "The most fashionable, exclusive, and attractive resort in this country." She continued, "I found this brochure and it has intrigued me. I heard that many famous people visiting the Berkshires stay at this grand hotel and I would love to see it."

Mrs. Berkowitz led them to the north end of town to survey the European style hotel. She reminded the little girls, "You need to be well behaved. We want to see the marvelous furnishings, but we can only do this if you agree to be quiet."

Although there were many times the girls were tempted to let out a squeal or call to their mother, they remembered their promise. The girls tipped their heads to see the high decorative ceilings but kept their hands off the velvet settee. The twins peeked around the gilded panels leading to the dining room, watching waiters balance enormous silver trays of delicacies. The elegantly dressed women mesmerized Fanny, and Ethel watched the bellboys delicately balance multiple suitcases. As they left, Mrs. Berkowitz praised them with, "Thank you girls for behaving so nicely. Let's find a treat for each of you."

The search for their treats brought everyone into the bustling town. Deborah exclaimed, "There are so many fancy shops. It reminds me of Newport, Rhode Island, where we visited our cousins once. I want to search for a millenary store I visited before. I want to show my mother a hat, which she might buy me for my birthday, which is just a few days away."

The girls each got a special candy as their treat. Fannie chose a Tootsie Roll; Ethel wanted Necco Wafers; Minnie selected a Hershey Bar; and Margie got Hershey's Kisses. Anna chose Chiclets gum instead of candy and everyone else shared a large Toblerone bar, imported from Switzerland. They headed back delighted, despite not finding the store Deborah sought.

At home, the four young girls played hide and seek with Miriam for a long time. Milton stood by himself, with his hands in his pockets. When the game ended, Miriam paid special attention to him, understanding how out of place he felt. She became so incredibly bored with checkers she taught him how to play gin rummy. He was entranced with this new game.

In the evening, after the little ones had been tucked into their beds, Miriam found the family had recently obtained the popular new "Landlord's Game," a board game about economic privilege, buying properties, and creating monopolies. Anna, Milton, Fannie, and Miriam played, buying and trading railroads, utilities, and luxury apartments and occasionally going to jail. Deborah asked to be included the next time they played. Everyone stayed up past their typical bedtime, but at 10:00 Mr. Levine dampened the fire and said they would have to finish the game the next morning. Deborah and Miriam feigned tiredness and everyone said goodnight and headed to bed.

When Deborah and Miriam got upstairs, they washed their faces and put on their nightclothes. Sitting in the comfortable overstuffed chairs in their bedroom, they discussed their lives in their respective hometowns and their friendships. The discussion turned to their relationship with one another.

Deborah explained, "Being with a girl was something I always wanted. I had dreams about several girls in my school, though I never acted on my desires. I felt closer to girls than I could ever be with boys. My episode with Judith made me worry about my future. I knew then I was different from the other girls. However, I could not express my feelings. I worried about how I would ever find a fulfilling relationship. I had no idea about what females might do together intimately until I met you."

Miriam admitted she had no awareness of physical relationships between girls at all. "I had never looked at girls the way you had. I always had wonderful girlfriends but I never wanted to be closer. Until I met you, I never had any of these thoughts or desires."

Unexpectedly, Deborah took in a deep breath, pinched her lips tightly, and said assertively, "You must know, you would find it easier to be with a boy. You have not thought through all the consequences of being with me. You might face all kinds of rejection; from your family, friends, from everyone. I suspect this is a difficult path. Are you strong enough to deal with the pressures you will face? We both need to consider what we are doing. I need some time to think, as do you." Then she became silent and looked away.

Miriam was startled; Deborah had turned away from her. What should she do? Miriam wanted to run away and think about what Deborah had said and what she could say to Deborah. But they were here together, sharing a bed. Miriam had been so eager about spending the night with her, but now she wished she could retreat to another room. Instead, Miriam withdrew into her mind. She thought of Deborah's words and how hard they would have to fight to be together. Deborah was correct. Miriam had never acknowledged the consequences and losses they might face. She never knew this life was possible so how could she prepare for it? She had never imagined anything but happiness together.

After a long period of silence, Deborah approached Miriam, tenderly brushed her hair from her face, and looked into her eyes. For the first time, Deborah uttered the words "I love you."

Tears ran down Miriam's cheeks and she moved into Deborah's arms. Miriam responded with tear-chocked words, "I love you too." They both cried quietly and held each other very tight.

Deborah said, "I know we cannot work out these issues in one evening. Come lay with me on our bed. Tonight is all about love."

Deborah stroked Miriam's body slowly and sensually. She paid attention to the fact they had just declared their love to one another, rather than her fears about the future. They shared their love very sweetly and lovingly.

Hotel Aspinwall, Lenox, Mass.

Step Twenty-Six ❧ *Commitment*
Wednesday, August 9, 1911

After their intense evening, Miriam felt nervous. She wanted to prove her love and commitment to Deborah without upsetting her further. She decided to find an exceptional gift for Deborah's birthday, to make a public statement, giving Deborah something special in front of everyone.

The two mothers, the two oldest Berkowitz daughters, Deborah, and Miriam gathered after breakfast to go shopping. Deborah wanted to find a hat and Miriam wanted to find Deborah's birthday present. Anna and Fannie hoped their mothers would buy them each a trinket.

Mrs. Levine led the group directly to the millinery shop to find Deborah's birthday gift. While walking, Deborah told Miriam the hat was her excuse to her mother for her eagerness for this trip. Miriam understood and agreed not to be overly enthusiastic.

They arrived at the shop where Deborah's mother sought the hat of Deborah's dreams. When they entered the store, the younger girls pointed to every hat, asking if it was the one. The rest of them ogled the unique hats created by very talented milliners. It was hard for Deborah to settle on the one she supposedly had seen before and wished she was more excited.

Miriam pointed to a blue felt and lace hat, obviously the one she preferred, saying, "How about this one? Could this be the one you saw?"

Deborah nestled up close to her and whispered, "I think it would look beautiful on you, with your soft features and bright eyes, but it is not for me."

Deborah selected a white hat with a wide brim and a huge black and white striped ribbon and told her mother this was the one that had caught her eye last trip. Mrs. Levine had the clerk take it down from the top shelf for Deborah to try on. Her mother raved, as did Mrs. Berkowitz, but the only opinion she cared about was Miriam's. With a grin, Miriam pronounced it pleasing. It was soon packed into a decorative floral hatbox, which looked like a gift itself.

They walked down the street, window-shopping in all the elegant stores. When they passed a jeweler, Miriam asked, "May we go inside?"

They searched the gems, with Fannie and Anna again being the most vocal about their favorites. Miriam showed Deborah many bracelets and Deborah approved of all her choices. Miriam did not seem content with Deborah's response, so she moved to necklaces. Again, Deborah approved of most of them, to Miriam's dissatisfaction.

When Deborah noticed a black onyx cameo with small pearls and tiny diamonds, she turned to Miriam and said, "Look at this lovely pin. It would go perfectly with the hat I just selected."

Miriam had the brooch wrapped up and she handed it to Deborah with a broad smile, "It is an early birthday present."

"Thank you so much," was all that Deborah could say in front of everyone else, as she smiled sweetly at Miriam.

Both Mrs. Levine and Mrs. Berkowitz approved of the selection, neither questioning why Miriam bought Deborah such an expensive birthday gift.

Miriam hoped the magnificent pin was proof of her love for Deborah. She had never given such a distinctive gift to anyone.

A bit nervous about everyone else's reaction to her expensive purchase, Miriam steered the group into a general store, hoping to distract them. Many items charmed Fannie and Anna, asking first if they could each have a harmonica, then a game, then some candy. They finally settled on paper dolls, which Mrs. Levine happily bought for both of them. Anna got teenage paper dolls with fancy dresses and Fannie chose dolls of adorable children with pint-sized clothing. They begged their mothers to take them home, so they could examine the dolls' costumes more closely. Deborah was glad they tired of shopping because she was anxious to get back to the house to think further about their dilemma and talk with Miriam, as this was their last night in Lenox.

Back at the Berkowitz home, the four parents gathered for a short while, then announced they had decided to extend this vacation. Everyone had been having such a good time that the Berkowitzs had asked the whole family to stay until after Deborah's birthday, the following Sunday. The children shouted in joy and Mr. Levine offered to send a telegram to the Gold family in the morning, explaining their change of plans.

When they got upstairs, Deborah said she needed to write in her journal. Miriam was relieved to postpone their conversation, not having had enough time to think through all the issues. As it turned out, Deborah found writing agitated her, while Miriam found it helpful to put her thoughts on paper.

There was no loving tonight.

Deborah's hat

Deborah's Journal, August 9, 1911

Miriam was trying to prove her love for me by buying me the beautiful brooch. It was such a lovely gesture, but I remain worried. Miriam does not understand what we will face if we choose to be together for the rest of our lives. We risk losing our families. Where would we live? Would everyone hate us? Where could we find like-minded girls? I do not wish on her all the struggles we would face. It would be kinder to let her go and let her meet the boy her parents would want for her.

Last night brought up many issues that have been lurking in the back of my mind. As I fell in love with Miriam, I ignored thoughts about our future. I have been so caught up in loving her that I did not think about whether she would be able to commit to me. How silly to be blinded by my feelings. Now that I have voiced these hidden apprehensions, I realize how desperately true they are. I saw the concern, confusion, and ignorance on Miriam's face. She had truly never thought of the potential challenges that lie ahead for girls like us. She was naïve and unaware of the sacrifices it would take to make a life with a girl.

What now? I know she loves me, as she tried to prove by buying me such an extravagant gift in front of my mother and Mrs. Berkowitz. How will her mother react when she learns of this purchase? How would her parents react if they learn she has fallen for a girl? She talks of her parent's religious devotion and I wonder if she really understands that Jews do not accept girls like us. Will she be disowned? Discarded by her family?

What about my parents? How would they react? They have gotten to know sweet Miriam but would that be enough to earn their acceptance? They clearly approve of her as my friend and acknowledge the joy she has brought into my life. But what if they knew what we do beneath the covers and that we have declared our love to each other? Would Mother withhold her love from me? Would Father anger and dismiss me from his life?

I must be brave and get through each day with a smile on my face. I must look into Miriam's eyes and see the same girl I declared my love to last night. She is the one who stole my heart, bringing such joy to my soul and to my body. We need to find peace together, but that is difficult now that I have expressed my concerns openly. But I must remember, Miriam has not changed. She is the same beautiful girl I loved yesterday and the day before. She is my Miriam, bigger than her innocence or my concerns. But we are traveling a difficult path together, in choosing to love one another.

Miriam's Diary, August 9, 1911

It was wonderful that Deborah and I declared our love for each other last night. It added tenderness to our intimacy.

I tried to allay Deborah's fears, but there was truth to her concerns. I had not thought about how being in a relationship with a girl would be received by my family. Their disappointment at no marriage and no grandchildren would be devastating. They always expected I would marry and produce heirs.

Deborah's question of my strength to fight society's expectations is also valid. I have avoided conflicts throughout my life, never standing apart from my family or community. I have never taken a firm position on any political or social issues. I have always followed my parent's guidelines. So being with a girl, rather than a boy, would surely make me an outcast. Would my friends reject me? And what about Hannah? I have always loved her more than anyone. Would she tolerate this departure from normal society? There is so much to think about. I could not imagine leaving Deborah, but will the cost of our love be too great?

Here we are in this most beautiful of settings, with more privacy than we ever dreamed of. Why have I gone and ruined it all? Why have I been such a stupid girl, never realizing the consequences of my love? I have been as naive as everyone always claimed I was. Now I understand what they meant.

Deborah is the only person I trust to hear my deepest feelings. If I discuss this with her, will she become angry? Will she reject me? I cannot stand the thought. But if we don't talk, it will distance us. We must talk, as I want her more than I ever wanted anything in my life. I pray we can get through this.

The brooch

Step Twenty-Seven �֍ *Intimacy*
Friday, August 11, 1911

The heaviness between the girls remained palpable. For both of them, this new day was full of fleeting thoughts of their intense conversations of the day before. They got through the day without arousing suspicions, but neither of them had their usual spark.

They spent the morning at the house, entertained by Anna, Milton, and the four Berkowitz children. During the afternoon, Mrs. Levine suggested the adults take a special trip to the nearby Edith Wharton estate.

Mrs. Levine explained, "Edith Wharton is a famous novelist who wrote a book I treasured, The House of Mirth, which chronicled her life in New York. Mrs. Wharton is also a designer and crafted her magnificent home in Lenox on the principles of her first book, *The Decoration of Houses*. We used this book as a guide in designing Stonegate, including Mrs. Wharton's rules of 'scale, order, and harmony.' I heard that Mrs. Wharton and her husband, Edward, recently sold their home. I wonder if we could take a peak around it while the contractors are busy readying it for its new tenants."

Mr. Berkowitz offered to stay home with the children, to assist their governess, Bridget, while the others headed to the car, a 1911 Cadillac Model Thirty, a fancy four-cylinder, three-door model. The driver headed up the long entrance to the Wharton home, where they could view the vast lawns and extraordinary estate.

Mrs. Levine described the home, quoting Mrs. Wharton's friend and novelist, Henry James, as "a delicate French chateau mirrored in a Massachusetts pond." The home was as dramatic as they imagined, an elegant and massive two-story building set on a hilly slope, with formal gardens as impressive as the residence. They were not able to go inside, though they delighted in the view from the lawn.

They arrived home in plenty of time for Miriam to prepare for Shabbos. She has spoken to the cook about her rituals and she put the candles, wine, and challah (braided egg bread) at her place. Miriam led the family in the Shabbos prayers, followed by a lovely meal and an evening of quiet. The children were fascinated, since many of the traditions were unknown to them.

When the family retired for the night, Deborah and Miriam headed to their chamber, where Deborah pulled Miriam gently into her arms. They clung to each other silently for a long time. Miriam spoke first. "I love you, Deborah. I want things to work out forever between us. But I want to talk with you about the issues you brought up last night."

Deborah said, "I love you too. I hope I was not too harsh last night."

"You were right," admitted Miriam. "I was naïve. I had not thought one bit about the consequences of loving a girl. Now, each of your concerns is also mine. I am new at recognizing what I might have to deal with, but I am willing to face everything."

Tears trickled down Deborah's face and she held Miriam tight, speaking in a raspy, tear-soaked voice, "I always wanted a relationship like ours. I always desired a special girl in my life and now that I found you I do not want to risk losing you."

Miriam sighed deeply. "I am relieved I have not ruined the best thing I ever had."

Deborah wet her lips and responded, "You have not ruined anything. Until last night, I was very alone in the world. I never had anyone with whom to discuss the issues deep in my heart. Loving a girl was central to my being, but no one in the world knew of my desires. I did not mean to sound threatening, but years of worries came flooding out. We will face them together. Now that you showed me your strength, I love you more than ever. Now I feel safe."

"You are safe. I will listen to all your worries and offer comfort whenever I can. I hope you now trust I will never leave you for a boy, no matter how tough it becomes for us. I do not feel weak or naïve with you. I feel like half of a couple."

They talked about every area in their lives where their loving might bring them loss. They discussed parents, siblings, friendships, and religion. Though Miriam never had these thoughts before, she willingly explored all the terrible possibilities. Although they knew they would face many uncertainties, they could manage because they were truly a couple in love.

Exhausted from conversation, they removed their clothing, giggling a bit at how wrinkled everything had become. They would deal with their apparel after Shabbos ended. For now, they needed to lie naked in each other's embrace.

"I never wanted to connect physically as much as I do now," Miriam said. "But it needs it to be true loving, not passion. It is a mitzvah, a good deed, to have intimate relations on Shabbos."

"I feel the same way." Deborah said, "My touches will be gentle and my caresses will be healing."

They rubbed each other softly, letting their fingers speak of their love. Deborah stroked Miriam's body, with her eyes wide open. She looked at every pore of Miriam's skin, every soft spot, and every hair that rose when it was fondled. When Deborah got down to Miriam's woman's place, she explored it thoroughly, first with her fingers, and then with her eyes. They had never before looked at each other's private areas, but it seemed important to know everything. After tender loving, they fell asleep wrapped in a safe embrace.

Cadillac Model Thirty

"The Decoraton of Houses" cover

Edith Wharton estate

Step Twenty-Eight ⚜ *Celebration*
Sunday, August 13, 1911

It was Deborah's birthday, a time for celebration, made more special by Deborah and Miriam's newly opened hearts. The day began with sweet pancakes with strawberries and whipped cream, almost like having strawberry shortcake for breakfast! At lunch, they had sandwiches made with Deborah's favorite bread, challah, the traditional Shabbos bread. It had never been an option for a sandwich because the family always finished the whole loaf on Friday nights, but Mrs. Levine had asked the cook to bake a large loaf for Deborah's birthday. They had lemon cookies for dessert, another favorite, and leftover cookies in the afternoon. It was a delicious day.

For the afternoon, the Levines and the Berkowitzes took everyone to visit a nearby farm. Until they arrived, Deborah had no idea they would visit The Aspinwall Equestrian Center, a horse farm! The children kept the secret well, packing apples in the buggy, which Deborah assumed were for their snack, though they were to offer to the horses.

The barns had numerous stalls filled with exquisite horses and rows of saddles, stirrups, and bridles in the tack room. Outside, they visited the gated paddocks and watched horses being led through open pastures by experienced horsewomen. Getting ready for an upcoming horseshow, women rode sidesaddle, wearing the corsets, long dresses, and top hats fashionable among the equestrian crowd. In a separate arena two women wore billowy jodhpurs, topped with long fitted waistcoats. They looked sassy with their dark gloves, leather boots, and small hats cocked on their heads. These two women, who dared to straddle their horses in an unladylike manner, hypnotized Deborah and Miriam.

After a wonderful afternoon, they headed home for a special dinner of trout caught by the two fathers early that morning. For dessert, there was an especially rich chocolate cake with deep chocolate frosting, a perfect birthday treat.

As with any birthday, there were gifts. Mrs. Levine produced the hat Deborah had selected, along with a hatpin to match. Mr. Levine had shopped by himself and produced a small jewelry box. Inside was a small locket, with a "19" engraved on the front, to commemorate Deborah's age. She was surprised and pleased.

The children insisted Mrs. Berkowitz buy a lacy nightdress for Deborah, so her dream of having new underclothes had come true. The two dads looked away, hiding their embarrassment in viewing her underwear. Everyone teased them about this and all had a good laugh. Miriam smiled, imagining how much Deborah and she would appreciate this present.

The final gifts came from the children. With help from her mother, Anna had made an elegant peach hair bow. Peach was Anna's favorite color and she presented it with great fanfare. Milton, also with his mother's assistance, had picked out a decorative hairbrush for his sister.

The Berkowitz children ran into the other room to collect a box they had decorated. Each of the children had drawn pictures and glued flowers and bits of lace on the wrapping paper. The paper itself was a present and Deborah clearly treasured it. She took a great deal of time marveling at every scribble and adornment.

"Deborah. please remove the paper very carefully, to preserve the children's artwork," Mrs. Levine suggested.

They girls giggled excitedly when Deborah asked, "Can it be framed?"

Very carefully, Deborah unwrapped the gift, which, to her delight, was her own "Landlord's Game". Now she and her family could play it any time.

After the presents, the young children were sent to bed. The twins both wiped the sleep from their eyes as they kissed Deborah, wished one more "happy birthday", and departed with their mother. Anna and Milton headed to the kitchen for a late-night snack of cookies and milk, before heading upstairs. Deborah and Miriam talked with the two fathers for a while, reviewing the visit to the horses, the wonderful party, and the great food they had eaten all day long. Once Mrs. Berkowitz returned, they talked about leaving tomorrow, something no one wanted to face.

"Your visit was a gift to the whole family. Please come again. Miriam, the children adore you, so please be certain to come back," Mrs. Berkowitz said.

Would that be possible, thought Miriam? Would it? Every day with the Berkowitz family had been enjoyable. But what if they knew our secret?

The Landlord's Game box

The Landlord's Game board

Aspinwall Equestrian Center   *Aspinwall Equestrian Center resident*

Horse stalls at Aspinwall Equestrian Center

Step Twenty-Nine ❖ *Transitions*
Monday, August 14, 1911

Deborah and Miriam were sad to leave these sweet people and their magic turret room. They lamented living in separate homes for Miriam's last days in the Berkshires.

On this final morning, they arrived downstairs for breakfast to find another decadent meal of sweetened pancakes. The children, enamored with the strawberry shortcake pancake, had begged the cook to make them again.

After breakfast, everyone loaded their belongings, including Deborah's gifts, into the buggy. The Berkowitz children kissed Deborah and Miriam each many times but Deborah was certain Miriam got more than her share of wet smacks. The children handed all their guests apples for the trip and, as the buggy departed, waved until it was out of sight.

Mr. Levine could sense the air of sadness surrounding everyone in the buggy. To cheer the family, he suggested, "Let's go home the long way. Milton has been especially tolerant, enduring a houseful of women for several days, so I want to do something special for him. I know he loves trains, so let's ride home along the Housatonic Railroad. The almost five-mile Housatonic Tunnel, one of the largest tunnels ever built, is far north on the Deerfield River, much too far for us to travel. But they built a trestle under the road, creating a smaller tunnel. I looked up the train schedule and, if we time it right, we can watch the train as it exits."

Milton yelled out in joy. It was lovely to see his zeal and so nice his father acknowledged his patience with all the females.

Everyone enjoyed the excitement of watching for the train. Even though it was a twenty-minute wait, everyone remained enthusiastic, lifting their somber mood. Anna yelped as the train exited the tunnel and everyone enjoyed the five-minute event.

When the Levine's dropped Miriam off at the Gold's home, she was sad to be separated from the family. Everyone wished her well and invited her to visit often during the rest of the summer.

Deborah helped her into the house with her things. Deborah whispered, "I love you," into her ear. Miriam noticed Deborah's eyes glistening as they parted.

As the buggy pulled away, Deborah's mood plummeted and she immediately started plotting when she could take leave of her family to visit Miriam. Would they think it odd if she headed to the ice cream parlor just an hour after arriving home? Deborah assumed Miriam would be there, especially since she seemed to be alone at the Gold's house. Deborah hoped her mother would think she missed her friends and could not wait to see them. That was a reasonable assumption but so untrue. Deborah only cared for Miriam.

At the Gold's home, Miriam headed up the stairs to change into fresh clothing. It was strange to be there alone; even the servants were missing. They knew Miriam was due back this afternoon but there was not even a note. She assumed Ruth was with the horses or with Michael, but where were the others? Not wanting to be alone, Miriam headed to the ice cream parlor, hoping Deborah would arrive soon.

As Miriam walked in, one of Ruth's friends hurried to her, exclaiming in a loud rush of words, "Ruth had an accident on her horse this afternoon and broke her leg. Michael was with her. He rushed to get the doctor and then stopped here to tell us before running back to Ruth. The family and the doctor are with her right now on a path not far from the house."

Miriam was unsure what to do. Luckily, Deborah arrived moments later and the two of them decided to walk back to the Gold's to wait for Ruth.

It was over an hour before the family and house staff returned. Ruth was in a lot of pain and everyone was quite upset. The doctor had created a splint for her leg. They brought Ruth back to the house, where he would set the bone and put on a cast. Mrs. Gold was pleased Deborah and Miriam were there, so they could take Beth and David away during this painful procedure. Miriam was relieved to be absent.

Deborah and Miriam walked Beth and David the short distance to the ice cream parlor and found Ruth's friends still there. The young people began to tell tales of others who had broken bones but Miriam stopped them. Beth and David did not need to hear the awful details and Miriam's stomach lurched as they began their stories. After the others left, Deborah and Miriam bought ice cream for all four of them, to settle everyone's nerves.

Deborah and Miriam sat with Ruth's siblings for over an hour, offering them cream soda as well as ice cream. It was difficult to entertain them, since they seemed to have nothing in common with each other or with the girls. Miriam described their trip to Lenox, getting the youngsters to smile at the story about the apples for the horses. They were interested to hear of the long wait for the train to exit the tunnel but then Miriam ran out of things to say. Beth and David soon asked to go home.

Everything was calm when they returned. Once Ruth was settled in her bed, Mrs. Gold came downstairs, wringing her hands and saying, "Ruth was given Barbital for sedation, so she is sleeping. I had someone send a telegram to my husband, telling him of the accident and asking him to return to Great Barrington immediately. The doctor told us it was a simple break but Ruth will need to stay off her leg for several weeks. The doctor contacted a local nurse for us, who will stay with her. This woman will need to stay in your room, Miriam, because it is right next to Ruth's. Deborah, would it be possible for Miriam to move back to your house?"

Deborah took a gulp of air, trying to remain calm, "I am certain my parents would welcome Miriam."

After Mrs. Gold turned away, Deborah whispered to Miriam, "I never heard a more wonderful request!"

Feeling a bit guilty, as it is not good to wish anyone ill, Deborah could not help but be pleased. Ruth would be convalescing at home for the next few weeks. Right after Mrs. Gold asked if Miriam could stay with her, Deborah rushed home to tell her parents of the situation. They were happy to welcome Miriam back. Both Anna and Milton cheered when they heard Miriam was returning.

Within the hour, Miriam settled back into the room right next to Deborah's. She had barely unpacked when Milton was at the door, asking if she would like to play "The Landlord's Game." Since the game was his sister's, he invited her too. He ran downstairs to set up the board and deal the play money.

Miriam could not be happier. Two more weeks with her Deborah! And so much better than spending time in the Gold household. Miriam recognized she no longer valued Ruth's friendship. They had grown further apart, rather than closer. Miriam understood that her love for Deborah exaggerated her feelings.

Housatonic Tunnel

Step Thirty ❧ *Comfort*
Monday, August 14, 1911

It seemed a miracle Deborah and Miriam did not have to spend a single night separately. After everyone headed to bed, Deborah brazenly went directly to Miriam's bed. It felt so wonderful to have Miriam in her arms, something Deborah wished she could do every night for the rest of her life.

Both Deborah and Miriam spoke quietly of how they wished they could tell everyone they were in love. They also talked of wishing they could find other girls who love each other. They could not be the only ones. They fell asleep, still wrapped together.

Suddenly it was morning and past time to get up. Deborah heard her brother's voice and panicked because they were still in bed together. She kissed Miriam to wake her and quickly rushed to her own room, shutting the adjoining door quietly behind her. She was just in time. Deborah's mother opened the bedroom door and walked in, wondering if Deborah was awake. Luckily, she was looking for her slippers and not still in Miriam's bed. Her mother had no reason to think anything was amiss.

I need to be a little more careful, Deborah thought.

As soon as they finished eating, Deborah and Miriam went down the street to check on Ruth's condition. Her mother greeted them, explaining that Ruth had a rough night. She was vomiting this morning because of so much pain but now she had fallen back to sleep. Mrs. Gold asked if the girls would check on Ruth's horse because she was sure Ruth would be more concerned about the horse than her own health. Deborah was less sure. Mrs. Gold suggested they come back afterwards, when Ruth would be anxious for their company.

As soon as Deborah and Miriam arrived in her room, Ruth explained the whole scenario, "My horse was stung on his nose by a bee and became very agitated. He alternated between digging his nose in the ground and rearing up on his hindquarters. I held on as long as I could but eventually I flipped right over his head. I landed very awkwardly and immediately knew my leg was broken. Michael ran for help. I was screaming but that was not the worst of it. When the doctor arrived, he had to splint my leg in order to move me. I was in excruciating pain as he moved the leg. The ride back to the house was horrible; I felt every bump. It was even worse when the doctor had to set the bone."

As Ruth described her agony in detail, she hesitated regularly for Deborah and Miriam's expressions of horror. It was as if Ruth had practiced this story for maximum sympathy. She told them how the doctor wrapped her leg in plaster of paris, admitting it felt better when held firm.

Once her story was over, Ruth told them her mother had asked about the young man who ran for help. Luckily, Mrs. Gold was so concerned with Ruth's broken leg she left her questions unanswered. Ruth knew she was going to have to tell her parents Michael was her boyfriend, yet she worried that might make her mother monitor them closely.

"This was the worst part of this whole crisis," said Ruth.

As Ruth talked endlessly about how wonderful Michael was, Deborah understood some of Miriam's attitude about Ruth. It was boring listening to her rattle on about him.

Deborah and Miriam realized they would need to be Ruth's liaison with Michael and the rest of her friends. They would report on her condition daily and help Ruth find ways to sneak Michael into the house when her parents were not home. Ruth promised she would tell her parents about him, but it was clear she would not admit this right away. She would only tell them she had a boyfriend when it was absolutely necessary. Deborah reminded Miriam they were in no position to judge Ruth, since they too withheld a trove of information from their parents.

The two of them resigned themselves to their new role as information runners. They knew they would tire of delivering Ruth's messages but they remembered to be appreciative every night when they climbed into bed together.

So it went for the next two weeks. Deborah and Miriam were messengers, delivering Ruth's notes to her friends and running to find Michael every time Ruth's parents left the house. Ruth's nurse was a shy older woman who would never report any of Ruth's behavior to the Gold's. Deborah and Miriam felt bad that Ruth was hurt but were a bit disgusted with the way Ruth pushed everyone around to meet her needs. Ruth also had a stomach ailment; she was constantly nauseous, which made things even worse.

During the last two weeks of Miriam's summer visit, Mr. and Mrs. Levine left the girls to their own devices. They had successfully entertained Miriam during her first weeks. Deborah and Miriam were thrilled to find their own activities, spending days with the horses and evenings playing games with Anna and Milton. In between, they found plenty of time for loving pleasures.

Deborah and Miriam had much opportunity to discuss their relationship, their plans for the future, and the impact their connection could have on their lives. They talked of how to best hide their love and what might happen if they were discovered. They were certain Miriam's parents would be less accepting than Deborah's, due to the conservative and religious nature of the entire Cohen family. The girls expected Miriam's sister Hannah to be their biggest challenge. As for Deborah, her friends would be stunned to find she had a girlfriend instead of a boyfriend, yet she hoped they would be welcoming, even if they could not understand the joy of Deborah and Miriam's connection.

They hoped and prayed no one would ever find out their secret.

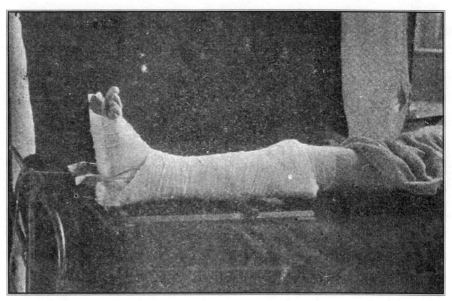

Miriam's fractured leg with splint

Step Thirty-One ❖ *Arrangements*
Thursday, August 24, 1911

Deborah and Miriam spent lots of time planning ways to see each other before next summer. The thought of spending time apart was wrenching but having a goal of visiting one another eased their pain. Their plans included a trip to Boston for Deborah and a trip to New York for Miriam. They worked their schedules around the Jewish Holidays in the fall and spring, so they could each be with their own families. In-between, there would be lots of bad weather, making traveling difficult.

With wide eyes, Miriam declared, "I think you should come to Boston during the changing seasons in the fall, when your train ride will include a view of the splendid fall foliage. After *Yom Kippur* and *Sukkos* I hope there will still be some colorful autumn leaves."

"Tell me how your family celebrates *Sukkos*. My family is lax about the minor holidays, though we all love creating the *Sukkah* at the temple," said Deborah. "I bet you have your own *Sukkah* in your back yard."

"You are right. There are several Sukkot on our street and ours is always the nicest. It is delightful to celebrate the harvest season inside the open wooden shelter my father builds each year. Hannah and I string all the fruit from the sticks at the top. We eat all our meals there, though Mother won't let us sleep outside, as her parents did in their *Sukkah*," declared Miriam.

Deborah moved quickly to the next holiday. "Your trip to New York needs to be in mid-March. That way you will be home in time to help your mother prepare for Passover, which begins April 1 this year. Hopefully the snow will have passed."

Miriam made strong eye contact with Deborah as she said, "And about next summer..."

"I want you to stay with us, rather than the Golds," Deborah said, leaning forward. "I will ask my parents, but not until summer approaches."

Miriam furrowed her brows. "It is great fun planning fall and spring vacations to see one another. It is so much better to focus on the time we will spend together than all the months we will be apart. But we do need to face our time away from each other."

"You are right, as usual," replied Deborah with a nod.

"I have written my family long letters each week," Miriam said, "telling them of my adventures in western Massachusetts and about you, Deborah. They might question why I want to spend such extended time in your company.

I have never had a close friend before, other than my sister Hannah and my neighbor Marjorie. I am sure my parents will be pleased, though they might not understand our need to see each other so frequently. We had better tell them of one plan at a time."

"That is a good thought. I don't want them to question our visits," Deborah said fidgeting. "I am less worried about my own family, since they have seen our friendship develop this summer. I am certain they will support our plans."

Deborah spent a few moments in silent thought, then said, "My life in New York is fun, but suddenly my friends do not interest me anymore. What can I say to them about my summer? There is no one I trust to confide in."

"I understand," Miriam conceded, biting her lip. "We are alone in the world now."

"I wonder how we can find other girls like us. There must be others, but I have no idea where to start. Who can I talk to? There is a man in the bookstore near us who everyone talks about as "strange." I think it is because his voice and mannerisms are quite feminine. Maybe he likes men, as people have said. He is the only person I know who I can imagine like that."

"Would you try to get to know him?" asked Miriam as she wrinkled her nose.

Deborah answered, with a sour expression, "Maybe I will frequent the bookstore. He seems an odd choice for a 19-year-old girl to befriend, but I feel desperate to find like-minded people. Maybe he could offer some information."

Miriam shared, "I have only one thought about how we could meet others. I heard people say disparaging things about the women who are Suffragettes, those fighting for the vote for women. I heard mention of a Suffragette from Boston, Lucy Stone, who died a few years ago. She was married, so she was not like us, but maybe the things they say about her followers are correct. They said some of them like to wear pants and they don't want anything to do with men. I will try to find out more when I get back to Boston. Maybe I can find where those women gather. I have no other clues where to find girls like us."

Miriam thought a moment, then said, "I keep returning to thoughts about my sister Hannah. I wonder if she might be jealous of our relationship. She would never consider that I had fallen in love with a girl, as she is as naïve as I was before I met you. I would love to share my good news with her, but she would be shocked. Hannah has never had any intimacies herself and her opinions are quite conservative. Hannah and I have always had a special relationship, so it is difficult, though necessary, to withhold from her the most important experience of my life. If I did try and share with her, how could

I approach her? Maybe I could bring up the question of girls together. Or maybe I could make it even less personal, by talking of men, the ones called homosexual. Is that even the correct word? I do not know how I could say anything, really."

Trying to be helpful, Deborah added, "She would have heard of Oscar Wilde. Maybe you could engage her in a conversation of his life to gauge her feelings."

"Perhaps, but I think I should wait until after she meets you to bring up this topic. I am certain she will like you a lot, so maybe that would make it easier to broach. Oh, that pin I bought for you might be a clue!"

They both smiled. Deborah said, "That brooch really was a big statement of how much you care for me. You know how special it is to me."

"It should be, after what I paid for it!" Miriam exclaimed, smiling.

Sukhah

Step Thirty-Two ✤ *Reflections*
Friday, August 25, 1911

Miriam's Diary, August 25, 1911

My heart hurts. My eyes are swollen and my face is flushed. I have been unable to control my tears during my first hour of the train ride taking me away from Deborah. As I sit with my large pink bear in my arms, I feel I am heading back to an unfamiliar home. Nothing will be the same in Boston as when I left. I am a different person than the innocent young girl who boarded the train for a summer in the country.

I will forever remember the summer of my 18th year, when my heart was opened. Deborah's love has given me purpose, direction, and a deeper understanding of my own needs. I have never cared so deeply for anyone. I have never experienced love outside my family, an experience that has added richness to my life.

All that really matters to me now is Deborah. I will miss her determination, kindness, self-assuredness, inner strength, and certainly her kisses. I will miss the way she runs her hands along my back, caressing me so gently and lovingly. She has awakened me to physical delights I never imagined before. I long for the day I am back in her embrace.

Thanks to Deborah and my country experience, I am more attuned to the natural world. I loved awakening to the sound of birds instead of city noises, seeing flowers bloom in meadows instead of flowerpots, and appreciating trees growing naturally, instead of being planted in even rows. Just months ago, Boston was an exciting place, with constant action and throngs of people. Now the serenity of the countryside has entranced me.

I don't know how I will fit back into my old life. Will everyone know I have changed? Will they see love on my face or excitement in my body? Will they know I am no longer satisfied with the old ways? I will be returning to parents who love me but no longer know me. Hannah will think I am the same person she has always known yet I cannot tell her who I have become without risking her rejection. I am different than that silly child who left Boston in July. To my surprise, I am now a young woman in love.

Deborah's Journal, August 25, 1911

Our parting was so difficult. When I helped Miriam onto the train, I felt I was sending half of myself off to a different life. I worry she will become re-entrenched with her old ways in Boston and miss me less than I miss her.

I know Miriam loves me and she appreciated every moment we spent together. I trust her feelings were genuine. For her, it was all new and exciting. But her former world was different from mine. She was not struggling for inner peace as I was. One of the many things I love about her is her innocence. She marvels at the little things I never noticed. She sees grace in the butterfly and industriousness in the ant. She sees the goodness in every person and she brings out people's best qualities. Children are drawn to her. Both my family and the Berkowitzes were enchanted by her sweetness.

I never imagined the joy a girl's body could bring to me. In my wildest dreams, I never thought I could experience passion, but now that I felt it, I want more.

I still have another month in the country. What will I do with my-self? Will I continue to be Ruth's accomplice? I can go to the ice cream parlor but there is nothing there for me. No one there is my friend. No one understands my heart is broken.

Stuffed bear

How can my parents possibly understand? They know I valued Miriam's friendship but they cannot understand why I am unengaged in life without her. They will try to cheer me but there is no way to sooth my ills. Anna, Milton and I will play "The Landlord's Game" day after day, filling my hours with their quest for monopolies and luxury apartments. Their silly games will please me and bring small smiles to my days.

When I return to New York, I will find new activities to occupy my mind. I will head to the bookstore, to search out that strange man who may provide advice for me. I hope to find other people who will understand me. I will find new books to read and maybe some will give me insight into this new person I have become. Most of my days will be spent reminiscing about my wonderful summer and dreaming of the days to come when I am reunited with my Miriam. I have fallen in love and a new world awaits me.

Stages in Romance

Stage I ✤ *Introduction to Boston*
Monday, October 16, 1911

"There she is, Mother! I see her!" exclaimed Miriam standing on her tiptoes on the platform at South Station. She sounded like a 12-year-old girl rather than an 18-year-old young lady.

As soon as Deborah disembarked after her long trip from New York to Boston, Miriam bounded to the train. "Deborah! Deborah! You're here!" Miriam shouted, fighting lines of passengers heading in the opposite direction.

As they met, Miriam placed a huge kiss right on Deborah's lips. Embarrassed, Deborah spoke formally, hoping to calm Miriam. "It is so good to see you, Miriam."

Completely unaware of Deborah's embarrassment, Miriam said, "It is wonderful to finally have you in Boston. It is so lovely here in October."

Mrs. Cohen, a casually dressed non-descript woman, greeted Deborah with a warm handshake and a pleasant, "How nice to finally meet you. We have heard so much about you."

"It is nice to meet you too," Deborah said, pleased for a warm greeting from Miriam's mother.

As soon as they were out of Mrs. Cohen's earshot, Deborah moved close to Miriam, shook her head, and whispered, "I wonder how your mother reacted to that kiss. A public kiss might not be the best start. I wanted to make a good first impression on your family and I am afraid she will think me a bad influence on you."

Miriam spoke in a slightly elevated tone, "Don't be so worried. Mother knew I was excited to see you. After all, it has been two months since I left Great Barrington."

As soon as Deborah recovered from the dramatic introduction, she took a closer look at Miriam's parents, who were a striking contrast from the sophisticated people who inhabited her New York world. Mrs. Cohen's face was soft, with no distinct characteristics, and her clothing was simple, no adornments or concern for fashion. She piled her graying hair atop her head with no design, as if to get it out of her way. More noteworthy than her appearance, was the warmth and sweetness Mrs. Cohen exuded, much like her dear Miriam.

Mr. Cohen, significantly older than his wife, presented the image of a learned man. His worn three-piece suit fit comfortably on his ample body. His equally casual hat sat on his head of coarse white hair. His untailored pure white beard framed his pleasant face and his glasses faded from notice as he spoke in a pronounced Yiddish accent.

"Nice to meet you," Mr. Cohen said as he strapped Deborah's two large suitcases onto their Model T Ford. Her valises barely fit.

"Hannah was right," Mr. Cohen said as he turned to Deborah. "Miriam's older sister stayed at home because she was concerned there wouldn't be enough room in the car."

Miriam bubbled to her mother, "Now you finally get to meet my good friend, Deborah. I have told you a lot about her, but now you will get to see for yourself what a wonderful person she is."

Deborah blushed. "Miriam," she said, embarrassed by the accolades.

In the car, Mr. Cohen spoke, in enormous detail, of the meeting he had attended that morning of the temple Brotherhood. "... and then Mr. Glaser asked everyone to consider adding a blessing at the beginning of each meeting. It was..."

Mrs. Cohen called to the front seat to interrupt her husband when he finally took a breath. "Dear. Would you describe your meeting when we get home? Miriam and I want to tell Deborah about our city and I cannot describe things while you are talking. We are just about to reach Copley Square and our incredible public library."

"Oh. How impolite of me," Mr. Cohen said. "I am certain Deborah would be more interested in our fine buildings than the ramblings of old men from the *Shul*. Please excuse my thoughtlessness, Deborah."

Mrs. Cohen then began a monologue of her own, "Here we are in Copley Square, named for the painter, John Singleton Copley. Straight ahead is the Boston Public Library, the first public library in the world. There are 21 neighborhood branches, bringing books to all classes of people. This empty spot next to the library was the site of the Museum of Fine Arts until just two years ago; it was torn down when they built the new museum nearby. They moved the art in horse-drawn carts, one or two pieces at a time."

"Mother. I want to take Deborah to the museum while she is visiting. I would love to show her my favorite Degas sculpture."

"Certainly, Miriam. We will put that on our list of places to visit. I am sure Hannah would like to visit the museum too."

As Miriam's father drove through Copley Square, Miriam just wanted to rush home to get Deborah settled in to their room together. More than anything Miriam craved giving Deborah another huge kiss. It had been forming on her lips for the past thirty minutes.

As the car reached Miriam's street, in the Roxbury section of Boston, Deborah looked out the window, commenting, "These homes are lovely."

"I am glad you see the charm of my neighborhood," said a gleeful Miriam.

She knew the homes were less grand than the estates belonging to Deborah and her friends. There were no stables or servants. She wondered if Deborah really found these homes attractive, or whether she was just being polite. Or maybe Deborah noticed the rest of the neighborhood featured triple-deckers for which Boston was famous, and she was impressed the Cohens lived on one of the few streets of single-family homes. She could not wait to show Deborah her home. And her bedroom.

Model T Ford

South Station, Boston

Stage II ❦ *Cohen Family*
Monday, October 16, 1911

Arriving home, Miriam felt anxious. This would be Hannah's first view of the young woman who Miriam chatted about endlessly since returning from her summer holiday in the Berkshire Mountains. Would Hannah like Deborah? More importantly, would Hannah guess Deborah had stolen her little sister's heart? And her innocence?

"Hannah. We are home," Miriam called, opening the front door. "Deborah is here."

A slender, small, and somewhat plain girl descended the stairs. Hannah, four years Miriam's senior, resembled her sister, though without the sparkle and vigor in Miriam's countenance. Hannah had soft, unblemished skin, dark blonde hair arranged casually, and a distant expression. Her eyes, though resembling Miriam's in shape, held no secrets and expressed no joy. Deborah was surprised. Miriam frequently extolled her sister, so Deborah expected Hannah to have a more impressive presence. Hannah quietly introduced herself and shook Deborah's hand.

"Nice to meet you," Deborah and Hannah said simultaneously. Deborah smiled. Hannah did not.

Miriam interrupted with, "Come meet my Bubbie. She is always in the kitchen cooking. Her specialties are *tsimmes* for the holidays, loaded with carrots, sweet potatoes, and prunes, and her special poppy seed *munn* cookies, which everyone requests as soon as they walk into the house. Bubbie's first language is Yiddish, so we have all learned. Do you speak Yiddish?"

"Some," said Deborah. "My parents speak it when they do not want us to understand what they are saying. Through the years, I have learned a lot of phrases. My grandmother calls me *gezunt in deyn kepele*, which translates to 'good health in your head,' but my grandmother says it means 'crazy in the head'!"

"Bubbie calls me *meshuggina*, which is the same thing! I guess we are both crazy!"

Deborah greeted Bubbie with her best, "*Sholom alaichem,* meaning "Peace be upon you" and "*a gutn-tag*" for "good day."

Bubbie responded "*Alaichem sholom, Kumen. Hobn epes tsu esen.*"

She's saying, "Upon you peace. Come in and have something to eat!" Miriam translated.

"*Ahdank.* Thank you," said Deborah to Bubbie, a short elderly lady with unkempt white hair piled on her head and a wide smile that showed her crooked teeth. She hugged Deborah warmly, beginning their relationship in a wonderful way.

With Bubbie's famous poppy seed cookies in both her hands, Miriam said, "Now, I will take you on a tour of the house."

"On the first floor, we have a double parlor and our dining room," Miriam announced as they walked through the average-sized rooms. Miriam was acutely aware her tour was much shorter and less impressive than the journey through Stonegate.

In a complimentary style, which Miriam soon recognized as typical, Deborah commented, "I love the ornate wooden plant stand with the intricate carvings on the base and your mother's collection of chocolate pots is delightful."

Miriam smiled at the compliments. Her mother suggested she show her guest upstairs. The three girls headed up ahead of Mr. Cohen, who dragged the heavy suitcases up the staircase.

"Come to my bedroom," Miriam said. "As I explained in my letters, we will share one room."

"This is so very charming," Deborah said, gazing around the small room. "I love the bedspreads and this porcelain lamp is adorable. I am not surprised everything is blue!" Deborah knew everything was much less elegant than at her family's home. And she noticed Miriam watching her reaction.

Miriam's mother arrived in time to hear Deborah's comments and she smiled in appreciation. Hannah said nothing.

Mrs. Cohen backed out of the room, saying, "Deborah. I am sure you want to unpack and freshen up."

Miriam turned, as if she too was exiting the room, but Deborah implored, "Miriam. Can you stay and show me where my things go?"

"Dinner will be in an hour," Mrs. Cohen announced. "Why don't you girls get reacquainted? We'll see you downstairs for dinnertime."

Miriam quietly shut the door and even before the sound of footsteps faded from the stairwell, Deborah and Miriam fell into a tight embrace, kissing each other with ardor.

"I love you," murmured Deborah between kisses.

"I missed you so very much," said Miriam, fondling Deborah with enthusiasm.

"Serious intimacies will have to wait," Deborah said coyly, as she eagerly touched Miriam.

"I have missed your caresses more than you know," Miriam answered, as Deborah began to remove her travel clothes to change for dinner.

"I know exactly how much," Deborah chuckled, as she stroked Miriam's breasts through her clothing. "I think you need to change for dinner as well," she snickered, helping Miriam out of her dress.

At dinner, the family chatted easily, though Deborah found it hard to warm up to Hannah. She was aware Miriam adored her sister, so it felt important they get along. She wondered whether Hannah's aloofness was typical or was she being especially cautious? Was she jealous Miriam showed so much interest in someone else? She hoped time would tell.

After dinner everyone sat in the parlor except Bubbie who said, "*Gay Shlafen* in Yiddish, which translates literally to "Go to sleep." In thickly accented English she said, "I am going to bed."

Before heading into the parlor, Miriam led Deborah onto the porch, where Deborah immediately picked up the scent of chocolate drifting from the Baker's Chocolate Factory, a short distance away. The breeze was just right this night, with Deborah noticing a number of neighbors on their porches for their evening sniff.

After indulging in a piece of the chocolate candy always kept in a covered bowl inside the porch, they settled in for their evening activities. Miriam's dad read, her mom did needlework, and Hannah played games with Deborah and Miriam. They alternated between gin rummy, whist, and Parcheesi.

Deborah, attempting to engage Hannah asked, "Who is your favorite author?" "Which museums do you like best?" "Where is a good place to take a walk?" Her answers were curt and simple, baffling Deborah.

Hanna did not speak of friends or interests. Knowing of Hannah and Miriam's long talks, Deborah believed she must have some opinions. She remained determined to learn more about this timid woman. But first, a long-anticipated night with Miriam.

Chocolate pots, Bubbie's stove, Baker's Chocolate Factory

Stage III ❧ *Privacy*
Monday, October 16, 1911

Deborah and Miriam retired to their room, keenly aware they were within earshot of everyone except Bubbie, who was quite hard-of-hearing. They shut their door and fell into a long embrace.

Deborah cleared her throat repeatedly, whispering, "I worry your family will wonder why we are so quiet."

After readying for bed, each snuggled in their own small bed, under their own soft blankets. Mrs. Cohen came to the door, opened it and peeked in. "Good night. Sleep well."

As soon as Mrs. Cohen left, Miriam climbed out of her bed and cuddled next to Deborah. Deborah stiffened. "I am uncomfortable with you in my bed. It would be disastrous if your mother found us together and I am scared we will be discovered. I love being here with you, but I am uncomfortable having your parents and your sister so close. I had dreamed of privacy, but this does not feel private."

Miriam reassured her with a gentle hand on her arm. "Don't be so worried. My mother just came in to say goodnight. She will not come back."

"How do you know for sure? What if she forgot to tell you something? What if she has a question? And what if she hears us? I am afraid your parents will hear our conversations, so even talking does not feel private. And I am certain they could hear any intimate sounds. And the door does not lock!"

"Shh," whispered Miriam.

"See. I can't even talk with you. You are afraid they will hear us." Deborah said tearfully.

"No, I was just trying to calm you down," said Miriam, reaching out to touch Deborah.

Deborah withdrew. "I am not calm. I am worried. How can I sleep by your side for three weeks without privacy? There are no woods to wander off to like in the Berkshires. What will we do?"

Miriam tried soothing Deborah with a hug, but she was too agitated to be comforted and did not want to be held. Miriam sat in her bed, watched tears stream down Deborah's cheeks, then got out of bed, and went to her top drawer to fetch a handkerchief.

As she handed her the hankie, Miriam quietly said, "I love you."

Miriam's words brought on more tears and a couple of sobs which Miriam was certain her family could hear. She went back to her bed to let Deborah relax, pained to see her tears. When Miriam returned to her side, Deborah did not want her.

Miriam, not expecting to be shunned, lay in her bed, hugging herself and feeling devastated. She had anticipated their reunion for so long and now it had gone poorly. Deborah was not only upset but she had rejected Miriam's comfort. Miriam worried, Maybe Deborah does not love me anymore. Or Deborah does not like Hannah. Maybe we will not have any opportunity for intimacy.

Miriam lay there, eyes open, thinking and agonizing. After about a half hour, Miriam realized Deborah had cried herself to sleep. Then Miriam noticed sleep sounds from the other rooms. She was awake and alone.

After an hour, sleep seeming impossible, Miriam climbed out of bed. She quietly approached Deborah's bed and climbed into the spot she had vacated before. Then she dared reach out to Deborah. Miriam's touch woke Deborah, who moved closer as Miriam caressed her back and she responded with a purr.

Very quietly Miriam whispered, "I love you. It will all be okay," as she held on tighter. Deborah released the hold, then noticing the fear on Miriam's face, quickly apologized. "I am sorry. I did not mean to worry you further. I just wanted to flip around to face you."

Miriam released the breath she had been holding, "Everyone is asleep. Touch me. It is safe."

Convinced, Deborah kissed Miriam gently, ran her hand up and down Miriam's body, caressing her through the softness of her nightdress. Deborah slowly moved her hands beneath the thick cotton cloth, saving the best for last. When she reached Miriam's special spot, Miriam was ready. Deborah caressed her gently and lovingly and Miriam responded with rhythmic movements, making her appreciation clear. Suddenly Miriam's body shook with a familiar satisfaction. There had been no noises to awaken anyone.

They lay quietly in each other's arms for a few minutes before Deborah drew Miriam's arm beneath her nightdress. She began with a caress of Deborah's breasts and soon Deborah made soft sounds and pulled Miriam's hand lower. Miriam was pleased to rub Deborah's private area, enjoying the slippery wetness. She quickened her pace, as Deborah's heartbeat raced. Soon they were both lying back in satisfaction.

"Welcome to my home. I love you," whispered Miriam.

"I love you too. Thank you for loving me and for proving me wrong," With a chuckle, Deborah added, "Now get back to your bed, before I get anxious all over again."

Stage IV ❖ *Adjustment*
Tuesday, October 17, 1911

In the morning, all was calm, so Deborah asked, "Could I take a bath? I would like to get rid of the dust from my long trip."

After Miriam set up Deborah's bath, she went downstairs to where her mother sat in the dining room. Mrs. Cohen signaled for Miriam to sit next to her. "I am pleased to have some time alone to talk. I heard weeping last night, after the two of you went to bed. Is everything okay with Deborah?"

Miriam struggled a minute with what to say. "Deborah has a lot on her mind. Thank you for asking. I tried to talk with her but she was afraid she would keep everyone awake if she talked with me."

"I have an idea," said Mrs. Cohen, making eye contact with her daughter. "I know you two wanted to stay together in your room but what if she takes the small room on the third floor? That way you can go upstairs for your long chats and she won't have to worry about waking anyone. The room is not as nice as yours but maybe she will like the privacy. We can move a second wingback chair into the room."

"Oh mother. What a perfect idea. When we were in the Berkshires we often stayed up late into the night talking. I will tell Deborah and I am certain she will not mind the smaller room. I promise I will come down the stairs quietly after our gabbing sessions are over so we won't bother anyone."

Miriam hugged her mother in appreciation – how much appreciation, Mrs. Cohen would not know. She then greeted Hannah, who had just joined them. "Good morning, Sister. Did you hear our plans to move Deborah to the third-floor bedroom?

"Yes."

Miriam thought, I often wish Hannah showed more emotions, but she is a wonderful older sister, guiding me when I have a decision to make and encouraging me in everything I do.

Later, after discussing the pleasing turn of events, the girls moved Deborah's things upstairs. Then, Miriam, Deborah, and Hannah took a walk around the block, stopping to visit Miriam's good friend Marjorie.

Marjorie was a pleasant young woman with a perpetual smile and a cheerful manner. Unlike Miriam's friend Ruth, she was neither self-absorbed, nor boy-obsessed. Miriam and Marjorie chatted easily, speaking of the recent High Holiday services and of mutual friends, including Deborah in their conversation as much as possible.

"How does your life in New York City differ from the way we live here in Boston, Deborah?" Marjorie asked. "I have never been there but often imagined the excitement it would offer."

Deborah chuckled. "That is a huge question and hard to answer since this is only my first day in Boston. My guess is New York is more cosmopolitan, crowded, and bustling. But Boston seems more welcoming. New York has a wealth of cultural and artistic venues. Miriam tells me Boston has enough choices to satisfy most anyone."

Continuing their conversation, Deborah noted Hannah was no more talkative with Marjorie, which pleased Deborah. Perhaps Hannah's behavior toward Deborah is not an expression of dislike.

Back at the house, the Cohens discussed upcoming adventures Deborah might enjoy. Mrs. Cohen, Hannah, Deborah, and Miriam sat at the kitchen table chatting with Bubbie. They made plans to travel the city by streetcar since Mr. Cohen would not be available to join them. His publishing shop in downtown Boston occupied his daylight hours.

Bubbie haltingly explained she found it tiring to travel. "I only go temple, funerals, and Shiva calls when my friends die."

Smiling lovingly at Bubbie, the four females went back to planning their time together. For Deborah's first full day they would eat lunch, then venture to the Museum of Fine Arts.

Marjorie

Third floor bedroom

Stage V ❧ *Museum*
Tuesday, October 17, 1911

Their trip on the subway heading towards the Museum of Fine Arts proved uneventful, but Deborah paid lots of attention as she traveled through this unfamiliar city. She commented on everything she saw, including the subway stations, which seemed to fascinate her. There was well-publicized competition between the New York and Boston for the finest transit system.

"I am used to going to The Metropolitan Museum of Art on Fifth Avenue," Deborah explained, as the four of them left on their adventure. "The Metropolitan is the most visited museum in the United States. It is vast and often overwhelming, even to a New Yorker. The Boston museum sounds more manageable. I look forward to exploring."

When they got to there, Miriam led the way, saying, "Come see the Impressionists. The works of the late 1800's intrigue me. I especially love the soft, graceful works of Claude Monet and Pierre-Auguste Renoir."

At Miriam's favorite gallery, Deborah instantly understood Miriam's attraction. Everything was bright, light, and cheerful, much like her young girlfriend.

Miriam guided the group to a corner of the gallery to view her very favorite piece, the Edgar Degas sculpture of a fourteen-year-old dancer she mentioned when Deborah first arrived. I have always been entranced by this bronze sculpture, *La Petite Danseuse de Quatoze Ans.* When I was younger, I imagined myself as this lovely young dancer. I adore the contrast of the bronze sculpture and the soft fabric ribbon in her hair."

"I can tell you of Miriam's early interest in this stature," Mrs. Cohen said sweetly. "Every time I brought her to this museum when she was a child, we had to stop for her to visit the dancer."

Deborah smiled, "We have the very same statue at the Metropolitan and it has been one of my favorites since I was fourteen. I had no idea there was more than one."

"Me either!" Then Miriam turned to her mother. "Next let's visit those teapots and fancy plates for you and the Sargent paintings Hannah treasures."

Deborah thought, I am intrigued with Miriam's passion for art. My perspective on all forms of art is likely to expand as I view things through her eyes. This is such a joy.

When they got home from their wonderful day, all four of them spoke animatedly about their museum experience, sharing differing comments and tastes. As Miriam noted, Mrs. Cohen did indeed enjoy the porcelain collection and Deborah loved the huge tapestries filling the large walls in the grand hall near the rotunda. Even Hannah spoke up, commenting on the art of Europe, and then leading everyone to see her favorite paintings. It was most interesting to hear her become talkative and describe the paintings of her favorite artist, John Singer Sargent, Deborah thought.

Over dinner, Mr. Cohen heard stories of their museum trip, an animated discussion with voices often talking over one another. Mr. Cohen questioned his eldest. "What did you like best today, Hannah?" he asked.

"I always enjoy the local artist John Singer Sargent the most, though today I saw the gallery of tapestries in a new way. I was glad Deborah described how they were made."

"Tell me, Deborah," Mr. Cohen requested.

"I imagine many skilled hands weaving each huge masterpiece," she said slowly, pleased to share her perspective. "They construct each warp separately, creating a series of grids. It is fascinating they can have a vision of the whole piece while working on one small part at a time."

"Your description makes them so much more fascinating," Mrs. Cohen chimed in. Then she continued, "I especially liked the white Limoges bowls. The hand-painted floral designs, gilt edges, and perforated designs along the rolled rim are unique and delicate."

"Likewise, your description of those bowls makes them more interesting to me," responded Deborah.

Stories of art, sculpture and elegant china continued until Bubbie called them in to dinner, a time to show off Bubbie's kitchen artistry.

Gallery of Tapestries, MFA, Boston

The Museum of Fine Arts Gallery, Boston

La Petite Danseuse de Quartorze

Painting by John Singer Sargent

Stage VI ❧ *Intolerance*
Tuesday, October 17, 1911

After a dinner of meat-filled cabbage rolls, Mr. Cohen's favorite meal, and continued conversation about art, Deborah and Miriam excused themselves early. Miriam climbed the extra flight to join Deborah, and as soon as they were alone, they embraced and kissed tenderly. Miriam spoke first.

"I have wanted to tell you something which happened last week," Miriam said with a quiet voice and her head bent downward. "It was very disturbing. May I discuss this with you now?"

"Certainly. Sit down so I can hear what has been on your mind."

"I am upset about something that happened following High Holiday services a couple weeks ago. Yom Kippur services are always meaningful to me, but this year the Day of Atonement had a special significance. Rabbi Feldman talked of forgiveness, saying G-d will forgive all. He spoke of how it is important to cast away all wrongs, so we can all be written into the Book of Life for another year. I hear these words each year, but this was the first year they had such personal meaning for me. "

She paused, took a deep breath, and then continued. "Does G-d see our love as sin? Can we be forgiven? I was so moved by the rabbi's promise of forgiveness for all that I asked to discuss this with him privately, at another time."

Deborah listened intently, somewhat taken aback, but wondering what Miriam would reveal.

"Last Thursday, before the Sabbath," she continued, "We had our meeting. Fearful to tell Rabbi Feldman I was concerned about religious views regarding my own behavior, I told him I wanted to talk about a friend who had fallen in love with someone of the same sex. I barely had the words out of my mouth when the rabbi began a tirade. 'This friend is committing a sin against G-d,'" he shouted.

Then the rabbi quoted Leviticus, saying, 'Thou shall not lie with mankind, as with womankind.' He told me I should tell my friend he must stop his evil ways. The *Torah* forbids such action. There was not one bit of forgiveness in the rabbi's heart. He said 'he.' He could not even imagine my friend was a woman. I was relieved he did not suspect I was talking about myself, about us."

Deborah, wide-eyed, cleared her throat, but said nothing.

"Deborah, it was awful," Miriam continued, her voice cracking a bit. "I felt cast away from Judaism, being told we cannot love each other in the eyes of G-d. How can this be? How can my love for you be anything but pure? I thought he was the ally we have been seeking, but instead he is our enemy."

"Oh, Miriam. I love your innocence but I am pained you experienced this. I knew the rabbi would reject us. And I would expect him to be harsh, which he certainly was. The world can be very cruel. I am afraid there is no one to whom we can turn for compassion, certainly not anyone Jewish. This just makes me more anxious to find others who are like us."

Miriam nodded and said, "Yes."

"Does this make you fearful to bring me to your temple this Sabbath?" Deborah asked with shakiness to her voice.

"No. I want you there. I am excited for you to come to my temple with my family. It is still a place I love and I do not believe G-d will reject us. The rabbi is not G-d."

"I look forward to being there. We will pray together, despite the rejection from the rabbi. What matters is our love for one another and no religion can take that away."

"Hold me tight," begged Miriam. "I am worried."

They climbed into their third-floor bed together, held each other, both feeling somber. This evening Miriam's needs seemed desperate, rather than tender.

Deborah noticed the tenseness Miriam's of body, so she soothed Miriam's furrowed brow, then moved to her neck and back. Her muscles relaxed some under the pressure of Deborah's hands yet the tension quickly returned. As Deborah moved lower, Miriam grabbed her hand and pushed it hard against her special parts, moving her hand back and forth with significant pressure.

Deborah always began with gentle strokes down there, so this was very different. As she moved Deborah's hand faster and harder, Miriam gasped several times. Once satisfied, she made Deborah start rubbing again. Again and again she released more tension and it would build. The last time, Deborah had to muffle Miriam's moans with her other hand. Miriam's eyes were wet when she lay back in a puddle of sweat.

Deborah was a bit nervous Miriam would want to give her the same treatment but instead Miriam caressed her calmly and lovingly. She gently touched Deborah, making circles with her fingers until they were coated in Deborah's sweetness. She slid her fingers in and out of Deborah slowly then circled the outer parts before reentering her. It was delightful.

After an hour of secret loving, both girls sighed quietly; Miriam descended their hideaway stairs.

Stage VII ✤ *Exploring Boston*
Wednesday, October 18, 1911

They began Deborah's second day in Boston window-shopping along Newbury Street, passing several new stores of high-fashion clothing. They stopped to look in the windows, but as the Cohen's tastes were simple, they were not tempted to go inside. Next, Mrs. Cohen and the three girls walked along the parallel street, Commonwealth Avenue, with rows of elegant four-story Brownstone homes. Well-dressed locals strolled in small groups down the wide walking path they called the Commonwealth Avenue Mall, in the middle of this beautiful tree-lined street. Their feet crunched through the colorful fall leaves as they walked.

"Let's return to Copley Square," suggested Mrs. Cohen. "Deborah, do you remember my telling you about the magnificent Boston Public Library the first day you arrived?"

Before they walked inside, they stood on the huge steps, gazing silently at the impressive building which had been called "a palace of the people" when it opened sixteen years earlier. Together they walked into the decorative vestibule, with architecture as varied and striking as any building Deborah had ever seen. The walls, ceiling, and floors were inlaid in various patterns of imported colored marble. Before them stood three massive bronze doors, depicting stunning representations of women.

"Let me tell you about these doors," Mrs. Levine said excitedly. "The left one represents music and poetry, the middle door is knowledge and wisdom, and the one on the right depicts truth and romance. I find them breathtaking."

The entrance hall was equally dramatic, with a vaulted ceiling with mosaics naming prominent Bostonians. Next, Mrs. Cohen led them up the grand marble staircase, flanked by great twin lions and into a myriad of rooms, each with artwork more bold and unique than the last. On the third floor, they marveled at the extensive work of muralist John Singer Sargent, with the paint still fresh from his most recent addition to his sequence of panels, "The Triumph of Religion", following Paganism, Judaism, and Christianity.

Hannah, though usually silent, questioned Sargent's depiction of the Jewish panels, displeased with Sargent's interpretation. Sargent contrasted the steadfast church with a collapsing synagogue, which she viewed as endorsing past discrimination. After Mrs. Cohen's informative tour, they sat serenely in the library's open-air courtyard. It replicated a sixteenth century Italian plaza, with a magnificent fountain and tall, arched columns. "It feels like we are visiting Italy," Deborah said, marveling at the design.

Later, Deborah said, "I was most impressed with the vast Bates reading room, with its' many rows of dark, rich wooden desks, each with small reading lamps. It felt cavernous! The tall arched windows brought bright light into the room for the scholars, young students, and adults sharing their love of books."

To Mrs. Cohen's delight, she continued, "Most of the library rooms are decorated with art as outstanding as that in the museum. This library is so much more than a collection of books; it is a showplace of Boston's fine arts."

Miriam added, "I don't know if you or my mother are more excited you were finally able to see the library."

Before heading home, the foursome walked by many other beautiful buildings in Copley Square, ending at the magnificent Trinity Church. The building had been reconstructed after the Great Boston Fire of 1872 and was quite impressive. Since observant Jews, like the Cohen's, may not enter churches, they viewed the structure from the outside.

Deborah whispered to Miriam, "I wish we could see the beautiful inside. I wonder whether the G-d of this church would be any more forgiving of us."

When they got home, they were surprised Mr. Cohen had arrived from work early, greeting his guest, "What did you like best today, Deborah?"

"I was most impressed by the Boston Public Library, with its incredible architecture and artwork," answered Deborah. "It is very exciting this city has brought knowledge and art to people of all means. I loved seeing the wide variety of people appreciating the library, everyone from the young and old, rich and poor."

After talk of museums and libraries, Mr. Cohen added a story of his temple brotherhood meeting, which seemed his only personal activity. Then he surprised everyone, suggesting, "Let's go for a ride to the North End."

"That usually means a trip to get Italian pastry!" Miriam responded gleefully.

"But we have not had dinner yet!" Mrs. Cohen called out, somewhat shocked.

"It won't hurt any of us to miss one healthy meal!" Mr. Cohen said, going in search of his hat.

"I will warn Bubbie we will be late for dinner and will just want a light meal, said Miriam's mother.

After climbing into the buggy, Mrs. Cohen explained to Deborah, "The North End was Irish, then Jewish, and is now becoming Italian. There is still one Jewish bakery and, addressing her husband, "I would like to stop for some pumpernickel bread."

In a short time, the sweet smell of cannoli and biscotti filled the car as everyone ate their decadent desserts right then, as bringing non-*kosher* food home was not permissible. They agreed not to tell Bubbie about their treats, but later, when Bubbie served vegetable soup with the fresh pumpernickel bread, little was consumed. Bubbie surely guessed their secret.

To their delight, Mother encouraged Deborah and Miriam to head upstairs early, to have plenty of time to talk about their day. Eager for their supposed chat, it did not take them long to excuse themselves. Actually, chat is what they did for quite a while. They talked again of the problem with the rabbi, and discussed how their lives would be different if, in the future, they were not allowed to practice their beloved Judaism.

"Being Jewish is a part of who I am," said Miriam frowning. "My friends are all Jewish; our food and customs are Jewish. It is so much more than a religion for me."

"For me also," said Deborah, nestled in the wingchair. "Being Jewish is my culture too and why I worried what life would be like in Great Barrington. Hearing there were only four other Jewish families worried me. I am not used to having non-Jewish friends."

Miriam thought for a moment. "I have always valued being Jewish too, but will I continue to be comfortable? Knowing the rabbis cannot approve of us means other Jews might never accept us either."

They spoke of Miriam's other friends, who Deborah would meet at temple this weekend. Deborah took this opportunity to discuss Hannah. "I am not sure if Hannah likes me," she said softly, with a sigh.

"Certainly she does," Miriam said. "She just does not show it easily. Hannah is quite shy and does not always know how to interact with others. She is a good person but often ill at ease."

"I noticed she was not comfortable with your friend Marjorie either."

"She likes Marjorie a lot. She just does not know what to say to people. I am certain she will warm up to you over time."

The conversation made Miriam wonder if Deborah was judging her sister, family, home, or friends. Deborah never said anything disapproving, but Miriam worried anyway. It often seemed Deborah was unaware or unconcerned about the difference in their financial status, though it still worried Miriam.

The girls continued to talk until all the noises in the house quieted. Then it was time for them. Deborah reached over to Miriam and brought her closer.

As soon as they touched, magic happened, as they pulled at each other's clothing. Remaining quiet became a true challenge as they undressed and lay on Deborah's bed. Miriam rose to lock the door to assure privacy, and they reverted to their passionate ways.

Boston Public Library doors

Bates Hall doors

Boston Public Library stairs

Bates Hall

October 19, 1911

During Deborah's third day in Boston, the whole group visited Beacon Hill. As they climbed the steep streets, they came upon Louisburg Square, where many of Boston's aristocratic families lived. The Greek rival homes, with wrought-iron fences and tiny city gardens, were among the most expensive properties in Boston, despite their close proximity to one another and to ordinary rooming houses.

They walked through Boston Common, the oldest public park in the United States, viewing the Massachusetts State House, a masterpiece of Federal Architecture, with its shiny gold leaf dome. They walked past the Old South Meeting House, site of protest meetings before the American Revolution. At the Granary Burial Grounds they found the graves of Paul Revere, Samuel Adams, John Hancock, and the victims of the Boston Massacre. While the girls wanted to visit everything in one day, Mrs. Cohen soon tired from all the walking.

When they got home, Mrs. Cohen and Hannah headed to freshen up for dinner. Still energetic, Miriam asked Deborah, "Would you like to go to visit Leah, the little neighborhood girl I visit weekly? It is Wednesday, the day I usually visit. I told her I might not see her while you are here and she was very disappointed. It would excite her if I were to show up and it would be especially nice if I brought someone new into her world."

"I would love to join you. I enjoyed reading about Leah in your letters over the winter. It would be wonderful to meet her, as you have certainly become important to her."

Deborah and Miriam walked to Leah's house where Leah's mother, a disheveled lady with her smallest child on perched her hip, greeted them enthusiastically. Deborah glanced around the comfortable home, with crocheted antimacassars over the backs and arms of each chair and handmade afghans slung over each couch and lying in puddles on the floor. There were signs of children everywhere, with paths in the middle of each room for Leah's wheelchair.

After quick introductions, Miriam and Deborah were escorted into the den, Leah's bedroom, so the family would not have to carry her up the stairs. Leah was singing to herself as she played with a homemade doll. A look of glee covered Leah's face when she spotted Miriam, lighting up the whole room. She was thrilled to meet Deborah, who Miriam had talked about repeatedly.

They visited, with the girls telling Leah of all their adventures and Leah asking about Deborah's life in New York City. "Did you ever go to the big park in the middle of the city? Does it hurt your neck to look up at the tall buildings? Did you ever get to go on the boat that takes people to see the Statue of Liberty?"

Although Deborah claimed to have minimal experience with children, and none with a child who could not walk, she adapted easily. Leah was thrilled to have a new playmate. Deborah loved meeting Leah and she admired Miriam for making such a huge difference in the child's life."

Louisburg Square

Stage VIII ❧ *Discovered*
Thursday, October 19, 1911

After a lovely dinner, Deborah and Miriam went upstairs to Deborah's room. Their conversation ended early, since they could not resist touching each other's bodies. Quietly, they undressed and headed to bed, although they could still hear the rest of the family downstairs.

As they touched each other lovingly, they became caught up in passion and never noticed the sound of footsteps on the stairwell. Nor did they hear the door open and Hannah walk in. Sensing something, they looked up in shock, to find her standing there, staring at their nakedness. Most certainly Hannah had seen Deborah sucking on Miriam's breasts. Their shock was nothing compared to that of wide-eyed Hannah who turned away and rapidly left the room.

"Hannah!" Miriam called out frantically.

There was no response.

"We were so distracted, we forgot to lock the door!" Miriam said, to herself and to an equally shocked Deborah.

Panicking, Miriam dressed quickly and headed to Hannah's room, where she found her door tightly locked. There was no answer to her insistent knocking, so Miriam retreated, afraid her continued banging would alert their parents to something amiss. Distraught, Miriam returned to the third floor.

"What have we done? Will my sister talk with me? Will she still love me? Will she tell my parents?" Miriam rattled on with one frantic worry after another.

Deborah could hardly speak, but tried to console Miriam, who was weeping openly in her embrace. She could not be comforted. There were no words to calm her, so Deborah just held her. After the tears subsided, Miriam retreated downstairs to her own room and remained there all night.

Miriam's Diary, October 19, 1911

What have I done? How could I have shocked Hannah so? I have alienated my sister. It was so foolish to forget to lock the door and get caught. Why did Hannah come upstairs? Was she lonely and wanting our company? Did she want to ask something? I will never know.

Will things ever be the same between us? How can they be? I am ashamed I withheld the truth that Deborah and I are more than friends. I betrayed Hannah by not sharing the most important thing ever to happen in my life. Hannah has shared every confidence with me. Or has she? Does she, too, have secret thoughts?

What does she think of what she saw? How does she feel about my being with a girl? Did it disgust her? Would she be equally upset if she found me sharing my body with a boy? Will she ever be my best friend again?

Deborah's Journal, October 19, 1911

What a horrid night. I am worried. Miriam is understandably distraught and Hannah looked so shocked. I am concerned for Hannah and especially worried about what will happen to us. Will Hannah tell her parents? Will they send me home? Will they forbid us to see one another? Will Miriam retreat from me following this horrible event? Life has just taken a disastrous turn and I am overwhelmed.

Stage IX ✣ *Discord*
Friday, October 20, 1911

The next morning was hideously awkward. No one talked to one another, a significant change from typical morning breakfast banter. Mrs. Cohen noticed something amiss and she asked, "Is everyone okay this morning?"

When Deborah feigned a headache, Mrs. Cohen offered a solution, "I just got a new drug for headaches. It is called Bayer aspirin. Would you like to try it?"

"No thank you," Deborah said, hoping she did not seem ungrateful. "I am certain I will be fine soon."

If Mrs. Cohen had looked closely she would have noticed the absence of glee in all three girls' eyes, the corners of every mouth downturned. But she prattled on about the day. "Today we will go to the Public Gardens to ride the Swan Boats. The weather is perfect for this adventure."

Deborah, trying to sound enthusiastic responded, "That sounds marvelous." But it did not. Nothing sounded marvelous to her at all.

Deborah and Miriam unhappily gathered their belongings, while Hannah wandered off aimlessly. Mrs. Cohen placed all the breadcrumbs she had been saving for days into small satchels and took a small pile of coins from the jar in the cupboard, to pay for their travels and boat ride. Miriam feared being by her sister's side all day, not knowing if anything would be said.

The four females traveled by streetcar to the Public Commons, one of the two downtown parks. Each carried some of the stale bread to the feed birds and ducks. Despite their moods, everyone was amused by crowds of animals surrounding them as they attempted to serve the tiniest birds. Pigeons ate the food meant for sparrows, squirrels took whatever they wanted, and chipmunks gathered the miniscule leftovers. Everyone saved a few scraps to feed the ducks while on the boat.

Mrs. Cohen cheerfully explained why they should all be excited, not stopping to notice the continued quiet of all three girls. "When we cross Charles Street, we will be in the Public Gardens and you will get your first glimpse of the Swan Boats, which circle a small lagoon. The large boats appear to be driven by a huge swan. The young drivers are concealed between the wings and propel the pontoon boats by foot pedals. The newest boat was added this year, but they were designed over twenty years ago."

"I can hardly wait," said Deborah, the only one who could manage a response.

Mrs. Cohen went on. "The concept for the swans came from the Wagner opera Lohengrin, in which a knight crosses the river in a boat drawn by a swan." No one responded.

Although they could see a small lake in the background, their attention was riveted on the formal gardens. The vibrant fall flowers in hues of orange, red and gold made a striking picture. Then the swan boats came into view.

After handing in their pennies, everyone carefully chose a seat in the first two rows of the boat, gathering their skirts in their hands as they made the short leap from land to boat. They set out on the leisurely cruise, passing under a small bridge in the middle of the pond. As a pair of swans appeared just ahead, squawking and confusion erupted. One of the swans took off after a small, dark duck. The swan flapped his wings loudly, as the little duck tried to scurry off as fast as he could. The swan was a close match for the duck and he almost caught it several times.

Deborah turned to the young man peddling the boat and asked loudly, "Has this ever happened before?

"The ducks are usually able to get away," he said.

"Usually is not good enough!" answered Deborah excitedly. "Stop! Get away!" she yelled loudly at the swan, to everyone's amusement. Even Hannah's.

Happily, the duck escaped and they were able to complete their boat ride with no further crisis. Surprisingly, the rest of the day was calm, with no mention at all of the night before.

At home, Miriam tried to talk with Hannah. "Would you take a walk with me, so we can talk?"

Hannah's only response was, "I don't wish to discuss it."

After dinner, Deborah and Miriam joined the family for their usual evening of games. Hannah played with them, though she did not talk at all. She usually made some comments, so this was slightly atypical, though not pronounced enough to arouse suspicion from Miriam's parents. Later than was usual, the two girls retreated to the third floor.

"What do you think I should do?" asked Miriam. "Hannah still won't talk with me about finding us together."

"Nothing at all." said Deborah. "She will come to you when she is ready to talk."

"I just want to make certain she talks to me, not my mother."

Deborah looked at Miriam with sadness. "I understand you are upset about Hannah and what happened. But things feel different between you and me today as well. I feel you are distant."

"It is hard to think about you when I am so worried about what Hannah saw and how she will proceed. Every time I start to relax, something reminds me of Hannah's face when she discovered us. That is all I can see. Over and over. It haunts me."

Although Deborah and Miriam had no worries Hannah would again show up unannounced, they did not engage in any physical intimacies. Miriam claimed they needed to make up for lost sleep, while Deborah assumed Miriam was just too distracted by her worries to feel connected. They quietly parted for the night, each unsure of what the next day might hold.

Boston Garden

Swan Boats

Stage X ❖ *Jewish Practices*
Friday, October 20, 1911

The Cohens set out as a group on their two-block walk to temple, as they did every Friday evening and again Saturday morning. Bubbie found the walk difficult, so she usually stayed home Friday nights and only joined the family for Saturday services. Mr. and Mrs. Cohen talked with one another, seemingly unaware of the strain in their home.

Miriam whispered to Deborah, "Notice, Hannah is walking by herself, rather than with us."

"I was aware of this. I just hope your parents don't figure out there is something is amiss."

Before arriving at the *shul*, Mrs. Cohen began one of her teacher-like lectures. "Our Temple, Mishkan Tefila, was the first Conservative temple in New England. Immigrants from Prussia and Poland, like our ancestors, established it in 1858. A few years ago, the temple moved from the South End to the neighborhood of Roxbury, and it is now near our house. We were fortunate to find an English-speaking Rabbi with an appreciation for tradition."

Mr. Cohen added, "Our whole family was deported in an ethnic cleansing of Prussians in 1887. This was an inhumane expulsion of people of Austrian or Russian descent, as the country of Poland was divided. At the time we embarked for America, I was about 20 years old and married to your mother, who was with child during our voyage. Before that time, there were only about 3,000 Jews in Boston, but due in large part to this deportation, the number reached almost 40,000 by the turn-of-the-century. Our community continues to grow."

Deborah listened to his words and was moved. "I am sorry your family suffered, but I appreciate that you shared this with me," Deborah said. "I wondered about the history of the Jewish population of Boston."

Deborah stopped still as she entered the vast sanctuary. The *Bimah*, the platform for the rabbi, cantor, and others participating in the service, was simple, yet elegant. The *Torahs*, housed in an extremely tall, mirrored cupboard, called the Ark, dramatically reflected the eternal light, the sanctuary lamp which continuously glows in every synagogue. What made the room spectacular were the extremely high ceilings and simple arched windows surrounding the room. Deborah gazed in awe as she took her place with the family.

The traditional service enabled Deborah to participate in all of the prayers, though a few were chanted in unfamiliar melodies. Miriam enjoyed having Deborah at her side.

After services, Miriam headed to a spot outside where her friend's congregated. She introduced Deborah as her friend from the Berkshires, whom she had spoken of so often. They were all warm and polite, though they seemed more interested in catching up with one another.

They arrived home to the wonderful aroma of *challah* and the meal Bubbie had prepared before Shabbos. Before the Friday Sabbath meal, as the Cohen's did every week, they lit candles, broke bread, and said blessings over the wine. Mr. Cohen said a special blessing for his daughters, with his hands over their heads. After dinner, the whole family recited the long version of the melodic Grace after Meals, called the *Birchas Hamozon*.

Retiring for the night, Miriam asked Deborah, "Did you notice Hannah's lovely voice was barely audible? She seems to have retreated further into herself."

Deborah had nothing to say, so she just pulled Miriam into her embrace and sighed audibly.

On Saturday, whole family, including Bubbie, headed for temple. After services ended, Miriam's friends all greeted Deborah warmly for a more leisurely conversation. Several of the girls asked Deborah questions about her temple in New York, their interests lying mostly in her religious practices. This was something none of her friends at home would have asked about.

Deborah was introduced to the father and daughters Miriam had been helping, though Miriam had explained she could not watch the children while Deborah was in town. The father had not been able to be inside the sanctuary in Miriam's absence but he said nothing to make her feel badly about this.

After services, Deborah and Miriam spent the day quietly, reading, talking, and taking walks. They met up with Marjorie for a while, and as seemed to be typical, Deborah warmed up to Miriam's amiable friend. When the first stars were visible in the sky, the family gathered in the living room for *Havdalah*, the ceremonial end of the Sabbath. By having this service at home, Bubbie could participate. During prayers, they lit a braided candle with multiple wicks, drank wine from the *Kiddush* cup, and smelled fragrant spices in the spice box. These comforting traditions provided calm to the girls.

"I enjoy your Shabbos rituals," said Deborah to Miriam. "At my home on Friday evening we go to services to welcome Shabbos, then have dinner together and light the Shabbos candles. That is all we usually do. When more observant neighbors stop by, we bring out the Havdalah candle but otherwise Saturday feels almost like any other day. My father does not work or drive on the Sabbath, in the same fashion as his parents, but otherwise, we do not have a day of observance, like with your family."

"We have always lived this way. I would not know how else to be," Miriam said.

"My family does attend all the High Holidays services," continued Deborah, hoping she was not being judged for her family's lack of observance.

Miriam chuckled, "I think we are at our temple more than we are at home during some parts of the year. We don't miss any holidays, including the minor ones. All of my friends, as well as all of my parents' friends are members of our temple. This is how it has always been. I know your family is less observant, but it is for each of us to worship as we please," Miriam said, holding Deborah's hand.

Deborah's Journal, October 21, 1911

I was pleased to see Marjorie again, finding her optimistic and enthusiastic. Miriam's other friends, all young women her same age, were also sweet, but while I found them easy, I did not sense much spirit in any of them. I could not help but compare them to my friends in New York. Mine are more varied in interests and more apt to strike out on their own paths. None of my friends would be considered rebels, but at some future date, it would not surprise me if one or more had accomplished things not befitting young women of the upper class. I could not imagine any of Miriam's friends breaking with tradition.

Mishkan Tefila. Top: *Sign,* Above: *Interior,* Below: *Exterior*

Stage XI ❖ *Boston History Lesson*
Monday, October 23, 1911

As they sat around the breakfast table, Deborah spoke to Mr. and Mrs. Cohen sincerely. "Thank you for planning a whole week of tours to historical sites. I am excited to visit places I read about in my school books."

Mrs. Cohen described the route they would take. "We will begin with a trip to the north end of town, where we got pastries the other night. But this time, we will point out the Old North Church, where lanterns were hung to warn Bostonians of the coming of the Redcoats, on the night of Paul Revere's ride."

"Like every schoolgirl," said Deborah, "I read the Henry Wadsworth Longfellow poem telling of this journey. How interesting it will be to see the actual places."

"Let's all recite as much as we can remember of the poem," Miriam challenged. "Listen my children and we shall hear, the midnight ride of Paul Revere…"

Hannah's voice droned on long after the others, recalling the complete poem.

In addition to visiting the North Church and the site of Paul Revere's ride, Deborah's last week in Boston was indeed a history lesson. On Sunday, Mr. Cohen took everyone to the towns of Concord and Lexington, where the first military engagement of the American Revolution began. They stood on the Lexington town green, imagining it was 1775, when the first shots of the war were fired. Just a few months earlier, the Daughters of the American Revolution installed a bronze plaque commemorating the battle.

Their tour included a visit to Breed's Hill, with its tall monument, built in 1843, to commemorate the battle of Bunker Hill, one of the first battles between the British and the Patriots.

Deborah and Miriam delighted in these visits, spending time together, sharing their thoughts and views of the historic events. They also shared time at the Museum of Fine Arts, and the magnificent Isabella Stewart Gardner Museum, which opened several years before. It was a cross between a historic Italian palace and a world-class showplace for art. Every corner sparkled with objets d'art from the massive private collection Mrs. Gardner had gathered during her extensive world travels.

In the center of the multi-leveled structure, a huge courtyard, containing marble statues, large trees, and water features anchored the museum. They even caught a glimpse of Mrs. Gardner herself, a true patron of the arts, as she entered the private section of her residence. She generously opened her home to Bostonians and visitors, sharing her massive private collection of masterpieces and decorative arts.

"You will have so many stories to tell your New York friends," Miriam exclaimed.

"Ah, but not the best story of all, "Deborah teased, squeezing Miriam's hand.

At Symphony Hall one evening, the group heard the Boston Symphony Orchestra, perform Bruch's *Kol Nidrei* for Violoncello and Orchestra.

"The Jewish prayer is also known as All Vows, which is the meaning of Kol Nidrei in Aramaic," Miriam whispered. It's such a beautiful melody."

"This building was built in 1900, as the first to be constructed with scientific acoustic principles and it is acclaimed as one of the finest concert halls in the world," said Mr. Cohen proudly. "The orchestra, conducted by Max Feidler, will play pieces by and Liszt and Tchaikovsky and then the *Kol Nidrei*, the piece we have come to hear." The family listened, mesmerized by the music, especially the haunting Jewish melody.

"Boston may be smaller than New York and have fewer venues," Deborah said with wide eyes, "but the quality of music here is equal to anything I have heard at Carnegie Hall."

"Oh," said Miriam, "we have yet to go to a concert at Jordan hall, where the New England Conservatory of Music students perform. The hall is said to be acoustically perfect, and has over 1,000 seats, each with a perfect view of the stage!"

The family adventures continued. One of Deborah's favorite Boston experiences was simply taking the streetcar. There had always been competition between New York and Boston for the first streetcar and subway systems in the country. Deborah found Boston's system less complex than New York's, but quite appealing, like much of Boston.

While the girls filled their days with exploration of the city, their recurring horror that Hannah had found them together continued to plague them. Even while traveling the streetcar, Deborah worried if anyone sensed their turmoil. She worried constantly about Miriam, who often seemed distracted. She could not stop worrying that Hannah would tell all and ruin everything.

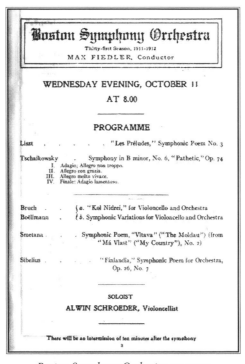

Boston Symphony Orchestra program

Courtyard at the Gardner Museum

Stage XII ❖ *Birthday Celebration*
Wednesday, November 1, 1911

During their three weeks together, Miriam would celebrate her nineteenth birthday. If it were not for their constant worries about Hannah, Deborah and Miriam could have focused on this celebration. But each day, each hour, their thoughts, together and separately, turned to the crisis that was threatening their happiness.

To celebrate Miriam's birthday, the family ordered a meal to be brought to their home from the local delicatessen. The family did not eat out, as restaurants did not follow their religion's strict dietary laws. Even though this birthday was a special occasion, no one was willing to relax their adherence to the *kosher* laws. But food from the delicatessen was *kosher* and could be enjoyed at home. It was delicious and plentiful and the nicest part was having Bubbie at the table, not in the kitchen.

After dinner, Mr. and Mrs. Cohen quietly handed Miriam a birthday gift - a beautiful strand of pearls with a pearl and gold clasp. "What a lovely gift. I always wanted pearls. I will cherish this," said Miriam with a warm smile.

Bubbie handed Miriam a small package, saying "*A bisl epes*," then haltingly explained to Deborah, "A little sumting for my Miriam." And to Miriam she said, "*Trog gezunterhait*. Wear it in good health." Inside was a light blue shawl she had crocheted.

Miriam wrapped it around her shoulders and kissed her Bubbie on her cheek. "I love it Bubbie. *Dank*. Thanks."

Hannah handed a box to Miriam.

"Pearl earrings with the same setting as in the clasp!" Miriam said with as much enthusiasm as she could muster towards her sister. "What a thoughtful gift." Miriam reflected. What a thoughtful gift, given our recently strained relationship.

Deborah handed Miriam a package and waited to see her reaction. She slowly opened the box, finding a delicate silver and sapphire bracelet inside. Miriam smiled in a wide grin, "This is beautiful. I love it. You have found something with sapphires, my favorite stone because they are blue. I am really touched with your thoughtfulness. I will wear it every day." She smiled at Deborah, then turned to thank everyone for the celebration.

Deborah and Miriam headed upstairs to the third floor, hoping they could banish their fears for the evening. After locking the door, Deborah undressed Miriam and positioned her on the bed. "I want to give you the rest of your birthday gift." Miriam smiled. Then Deborah ran her hands along Miriam's entire body, not missing a single spot. She began with the top of Miriam's head, blew into her sensitive ears, and ran her fingers across her lips and down her neck. Deborah massaged Miriam's shoulders with heavy pressure but lightened her touch as she caressed her front side. Miriam's belly and hips were her favorite places to linger. Deborah carefully tickled the hairs on her lower regions but left that area, promising to return shortly.

After gliding along her inner thighs, Deborah noticed Miriam wiggling, but Deborah did not give in to Miriam's desires. She thoroughly touched every inch of Miriam's feet, squeezing the instep and pulling at the toes. Deborah brought her tongue down to the toes, and carefully licked them lightly. Miriam squirmed and giggled, but as Deborah continued, Miriam's laughter turned to sighs of pleasure. Deborah sucked her toes, until Miriam's panting became insistent.

But Deborah did not stop there. She covered every bit of Miriam's back, listening to Miriam's ragged breathing. Deborah nuzzled her neck insistently, blowing in her ears again. When Deborah finally turned Miriam over, Miriam was ready to begin touching Deborah. But not yet! Deborah reminded Miriam her birthday gift included these luscious caresses of her body and Deborah was not done. Deborah began again, using her tongue to go directly to the spots that had aroused the greatest reactions. After more play, Miriam breathed hard and Deborah stopped at her nipples, alternately sucking and softly licking. Deborah moved lower. She circled Miriam's entire nether region with flicks of her tongue, getting closer and closer each time to the center of Miriam's excitement. Neither of them had ever experienced this before but both enjoyed the exploration immensely.

Finally, Deborah reached the secret spot she had so often touched with her fingers. Deborah found it wet and inviting. At first, Deborah darted her tongue and found sweet juices. Gradually, she lapped at her, creating more wetness. Miriam was writhing beneath Deborah's lips and tongue. After a short while, Miriam grabbed Deborah's head and pushed it harder against her. In just a few moments, Deborah could feel Miriam's private area shutter. Deborah kept licking and sucking and Miriam's shudders continued.

Miriam placed a pillow over her mouth and Deborah continued until Miriam pushed her head aside and brought her body up against Deborah's. Miriam lay limp in Deborah's arms.

When she could finally speak, Miriam just said, "Wow." Then she smiled a wide-eyed grin as she lay back.

It was quite a while before Miriam regained her composure. All she uttered was, "Your turn."

"But it is not my birthday," Deborah whispered.

"It will soon feel like it is," said Miriam as she lowered her head to Deborah's special place.

Miriam was right. Deborah felt like it was her birthday too! What a gift! Afterwards, they crawled into each other's arms and fell asleep. Luckily, at 4:00 am, Deborah awoke and sent Miriam to her own room.

Crocheted shawl

Miriam's birthday bracelet

Stage XIII ✤ *Lesbian Connections*
Thursday, November 2, 1911

Deborah agreed with Miriam that attending a meeting of Suffragists might be a good way to find like-minded girls.

"Let's began our search at Radcliff, the women's college of Harvard University," Miriam suggested.

They searched the campus for a long time before Deborah called out, "I found a poster for 'Boston Equal Suffrage Association for Good Government'. It says they are the largest women's voting rights organization in Boston and they are meeting this Saturday. Let's go."

"Look. Here are some posters about other Suffrage groups," Miriam said, completely ignoring Deborah's request. "One is a Christian group, so I am not interested. The other one tells of the organization but does not suggest any specific activities. Let's keep looking."

Deborah realized why Miriam had avoided answering her first suggestion. "Would you be willing to go to a meeting on a Saturday, on Shabbos?" asked Deborah.

After a gulp and a moment's hesitation, Miriam replied, "Yes. I believe so." She did not seem certain, but Deborah hoped it wouldn't be a problem between them.

November 4, 1911

Miriam's parents, however, were shocked the girls would be going somewhere on the Sabbath, a much bigger issue to them than it being a suffrage meeting. Mr. Cohen would not discuss this and left the room. Mrs. Cohen sat silently, with a glassy stare. Despite their reactions, Miriam decided this meeting was important enough to defy her parents for the first time in her life. Deborah hoped they did not think her a bad influence on their sweet daughter.

She was a bad influence. On Saturday, Deborah and Miriam headed to the meeting. They traveled by streetcar, something normally forbidden on Shabbos, heading for the luxury Hotel Somerset, on Commonwealth Avenue. They stopped for a moment as peered up at the huge white building, having little idea of what to expect. They fortified themselves with large gulps of air, as they entered the foyer of the bustling hotel. Many finely dressed middle-class and upper-class women filled the lobby. These must be the Suffragettes! Neither of them knew much about the work that had already been accomplished in the fight to gain the right for women to vote, nor had they known what type of women were part of this cause.

As they took seats in a large hall filled with females of varied age and status, they looked around, wondering how would they know who were like them. Shrugging at each other, they silently wondered what to do next. They listened attentively to the first speaker talk angrily about The National Association Opposed to Women Suffrage. It was made up of Catholic clergymen, southern congressmen, and others who opposed the right for women to vote. Deborah grimaced, unused to such hostility.

The second speaker, a frail older woman, spoke of the success of Washington State in adopting women's voting privilege. Miriam peered at her, quite entranced with her enthusiasm. There was a huge burst of applause each time she mentioned Washington's accomplishment. The last speaker talked about New York City's suffrage parade in 1910 and plans to hold a larger parade this year. There was a great deal of enthusiasm during this last speech.

When Deborah noticed a lot of attractive younger women showing interest in this parade, she said, "Let's find out more. Maybe this is how we will meet others."

Miriam teased, "I do not see anyone wearing pants. And no one talked of hating men. Maybe we are stilly to think this is where we will find girls like ourselves."

"Maybe we won't, but it is delightful to be in the presence of so many articulate women fighting for a cause I believe in," Deborah said. "Let's sign the paper they are sending around, agreeing to participate in the parade planning. Unfortunately, I will be doing this back home in New York, but I still want to sign."

"Okay," agreed Miriam hesitantly.

As they left the large auditorium, they passed tables set up with varied propaganda. Miriam noticed something of interest and said, "Deborah, Deborah! Come look at what I found."

Reaching the display and picking up a pamphlet, Deborah said excitedly, "Literature about Emma Goldman. And here is her paper about Oscar Wilde and homosexual rights!"

"Oh my. Someone who is willing to support Oscar Wilde's rights. And she is even Jewish!" Miriam exclaimed.

Deborah grinned, "I have rarely seen you so eager!"

At that moment, a pretty young girl in a dark-colored dress approached the table with the Emma Goldman material and sat down behind it. Deborah and

Miriam looked at each other in amazement. Could this actually be someone like them? Do they even call women homosexuals? Miriam mused.

"Hello", the young woman said, looking at the two women by her table. Then she boldly asked, "Are you two interested in Emma Goldman, in Oscar Wilde, or are you lesbians?"

Deborah and Miriam blushed in unison, amazed this woman could be so blunt. Miriam's mouth hung open a bit and Deborah was certain she had an equally stunned look on her face.

"Okay. I can tell this is all new to you. Sometimes I can be too forthright. My name is Abigail. Pleased to meet you both." She stuck out her hand for each of them to shake.

Deborah, tongue-tied for the second time in her life, just as she had been when she first met Miriam, stood silent. Miriam said, "I am Miriam and this is Deborah. I am not sure about that word you used but I think it may describe us."

"Oh my! You never heard the word 'lesbian'? You really are new to this. Let me get my girlfriend and the four of us can talk." Then Abigail whispered, "She was new at woman love until last year, when I seduced her right from her daddy and mommy's house."

As Abigail went in search of her girlfriend, Deborah and Miriam looked at each other, stunned by Abigail's openness and shocking language. Hopefully Abigail could not read their wide eyes and flushed faces as well as they could read each other's expressions. Both were not sure whether to be excited or fearful that they had actually found other girls who were together. Should they leave before Abigail returned or stay and find out more?

It was only a moment later when Abigail returned, having found her girlfriend, Margaret. She made introductions then said, "Let's go into the lounge, where we can have some privacy."

Miriam and Deborah, dazed, followed the women. Margaret seemed shy and sweet, which put them a bit at ease. As Margaret offered to get a round of drinks, Deborah and Miriam looked at each other in amazement.

Miriam admitted, "I have only had tastes of wine for the Sabbath and Passover. I have never had an alcoholic drink other than that."

"Me either," admitted Deborah. She was relieved when Margaret suggested a bottle of wine for everyone to share.

They settled at a round table in a corner and Abigail ordered the wine. Abigail and Margaret broke the ice by telling their story of falling in love. Margaret, like Miriam, had never considered being with another girl. Abigail had always considered herself homosexual, "a lesbian," she announced proudly, and was thrilled to have found a girlfriend. They were both 20.

When the wine arrived, Deborah insisted on paying for it. Miriam's face puckered from her first swallow, expecting it to be syrupy sweet like the Manischewitz wine she knew. Everyone giggled at her silly expression. Deborah, having been warned by Miriam's reaction, took a tiny sip with slightly more elegance. Before long, they had accustomed themselves to this strange taste, and each finished her glass of wine. Miriam's delicate skin turned quite red and Deborah noticed she felt a bit dazed. They both politely refused the offer of a second glass.

Drinking wine made it easier for Deborah and Miriam to tell their story, something neither of them had ever explained out loud. They did not offer many details but they managed to tell of their meeting in the Berkshires. They were happy to learn Abigail and Margaret knew two more couples and promised introductions.

There in the lounge, all four delighted in having found each other. Deborah and Miriam, quite overwhelmed with these chatty friends, mostly listened. To Deborah and Miriam's surprise, they talked of developing their physical relationship. The two innocents, already flushed from the wine, blushed even more.

An hour into their conversation, Miriam realized her parents would worry that she and Deborah were gone so long. As they began to take their leave, they exchanged full names and agreed to meet again at the next Suffrage meeting.

All the way back home, Deborah and Miriam talked excitedly of their good fortune. It was a real advance, discovering new friends and being able to call themselves by this exotic new word, lesbian. They said it out loud to each other several times. Suddenly they did not feel so alone.

Back at home, happily in time for Havdalah, Miriam's parents wanted to hear all about their adventure. They did not seem cross about the girls being gone for most of Sabbath, which was a relief.

Deborah and Miriam talked about the beautiful hotel, the suffragist meeting, and the speakers, never mentioning Emma Goldman or their new friends, Abigail and Margaret. Miriam's mother seemed genuinely pleased they had experienced such a good day.

Mrs. Cohen said, "I hope this new interest of yours will not take you away on the Sabbath again."

Although Miriam answered, "I hope not," she assumed her mother knew in her heart it was not to be.

After dinner, Miriam turned quietly to Deborah and said, "With our new adventures, it seems I am finding my own way in life. I believe I will take a different path than what Mother had hoped for me. I was a sweet, obedient child but I am becoming a slightly feisty young woman."

Deborah smiled adoringly.

During the evening Deborah and Miriam talked and chattered happily, while Hannah was her regular sullen self, so the contrast appeared quite remarkable. They played games, as they did every evening, with Deborah and Miriam the big winners. Somehow, the winning in their hearts transferred to their winning at the game table. Luck was with them.

As the girls returned to "their" room upstairs, they talked eagerly. "We have new friends, the first we made together. Abigail and Margaret are like the rebels I am drawn to," Deborah said, sitting on the bed. "How do you feel about them?"

"They may be like your New York friends but they are not at all like my Boston friends," Miriam said, seated comfortably in the wingback chair. "In some way, I found them more exciting than my regular friends. They have spunk, self-determination, and the bravery necessary to be themselves. These are characteristics I admire in you, Deborah."

"I am pleased you like them," Deborah said glowing. What she did not say out loud was, Miriam's attitude gives me renewed assurance that she has an independent streak. Possibly Miriam's safe, sweet friendships would no longer be enough for her. Deborah hoped Miriam could be moving towards taking greater risks in her life. Choosing to be with a girl was the first of Miriam's great risks and it was working out just fine, except for Hannah having caught them together. That memory was never far from either of their minds.

Upstairs, Miriam locked the door. She approached Deborah with a glint in her eyes and a smirk on her face.

After a period of breast play, Miriam began undressing Deborah. Then she pushed Deborah toward the bed, being much more assertive than was typical.

The next action was even more unexpected. Miriam produced a jar of Pond's Vanishing Cream and rubbed it on Deborah's body. Once her breasts were fully covered, she moved directly to Deborah's lower region, taking no time to warm her up. Before Deborah knew it, Miriam put several fingers inside her, finding her wet but adding cream to her fingers and inserting a large amount inside. Miriam then moved her fingers very quickly and firmly, taking great pleasure in Deborah's excitement. Deborah was sweating and smiling, looking at Miriam and whispering "lesbian!"

Miriam was ready for the same treatment and she loaded Deborah's fingers with the cream. It was not long until Miriam was stifling her own screams, and the two, totally spent, fell asleep in each other's arms.

Abigail and Margaret

Hotel Somerset lounge

Stage XIV ✤ *Ruth's News*
Tuesday, November 7, 1911

November 7, 1911

Dear Miriam,

I am writing with lots of news. Some of it is good but some of it is very disturbing. You can probably tell since my stationary is tear-stained. My whole life is tear-stained these days.

Excuse my impropriety for being so bold, but I must tell you I am going to have a baby. It was a shock for Michael and me but even more so for my mother, who noticed my swollen belly and morning illness before I dared to tell her my fear.

The good news is that Michael has asked me to marry him. Mother and I are searching for a place for the wedding on short notice. I have begun shopping for a dress, though I am afraid I will look awful in anything. I hope you will come to the wedding, which we are planning for January.

Ruth

Miriam stared at the letter then went to tell Deborah. "Ruth has written to me she is pregnant and Michael has asked her to marry him. The letter was focused on her wedding plans and her worry about finding a dress to hide her stomach."

Deborah digested this interesting news. "It is no surprise, given what we heard in the woods that day," said Deborah. "As I have come to expect, Ruth's concerns are with her clothing rather than the upcoming birth."

"I am learning to see Ruth through your eyes and you are right," agreed Miriam.

Deborah piped up loudly, with a wide-eyed expression, "Miriam. Now you have an excuse to come to New York to visit me in January for the wedding! I am certain my parents will be thrilled to have you as a visitor. Hopefully, your parents will be equally pleased to let you travel to the wedding of your friend."

"Yes," said Miriam, failing to match Deborah's enthusiasm. "I would love to visit you, but I am concerned about Hannah. She has hardly talked with me since she found us together. I wonder if things will ever be the same between us. I feel like I am losing my best friend."

"I know how upsetting this is to you, Miriam. Hopefully she will come around and be willing to talk with you as soon as I am gone."

"I don't know if that will happen. And I worry she will tell my parents what she saw. They can usually pull information from her, but they would be devastated if she talks. It is surely against their morals, especially since it is against our religion."

Deborah tried to comfort Miriam. "We have to take things one day at a time. First, let's be glad we have a good excuse to get together again so soon. I don't think I could spend any longer than that without you."

The next day, Miriam questioned the plans for Ruth's wedding, hoping they really would have an excuse to get together. "I wonder if Ruth's parents will put on lavish affair, as Ruth seems to expect. I have never heard of a Jewish family making a huge wedding for an obvious marriage of necessity. Most families arrange a private wedding when there is a pregnancy."

"You are right Miriam. A few times I heard of a quick private wedding, followed soon by a baby. I wonder if Ruth will beg them for this event or whether they, like Ruth, would welcome any excuse for a party."

Despite their upcoming separation, Deborah and Miriam had a happy last week together. They saw their new friends Abigail and Margaret at a suffrage meeting, and a second time at the girls' apartment in the South End of Boston. All of Miriam's friends lived in large homes in her neighborhood, so this apartment intrigued her. It was sparsely furnished, since they had to pay for everything themselves. Neither of their families approved of their relationship, so they supported themselves with jobs at Filene's, a large downtown Boston department store. Miriam knew of the store as it was owned by a Jewish merchant and her family shopped there. The visit to Abigail and Margaret's small apartment gave Miriam a new view of future possibilities.

Deborah and Miriam also made time to visit with Leah, the homebound little girl. Each time they stopped by, Leah's face lit up as she gifted the girls with a drawing or a song. It was unclear who was having the best time during their visits.

Deborah and Miriam cheerfully planned their reunion in New York. They did not know the exact date of Ruth's wedding, yet hoped Miriam could arrive in New York in time for the Central Park New Year's Eve Festival. It would be wonderful to celebrate the arrival of 1912 together as they anticipated an exciting year ahead. Just how exciting, they could not know.

Stage XV ❧ *Exploring New York*
Monday, December 18, 1911

Miriam boarded the 11:22am train to New York City and was due at Grand Central Station at 5:39pm, shortly after sunset. It was a long, yet fascinating trip. Looking out the train window mid-afternoon, Miriam spotted a huge marble dome as they passed through Providence, Rhode Island. The conductor announced that this building was the new State House, showplace of the city. As the train rumbled along, Miriam watched the magnificent countryside, blanketed in new fallen snow. The last leg of her journey took the train along the Mystic, Connecticut coast, where she observed huge steamers, cargo ships, and whalers along the waterways. Miriam could hardly wait to arrive in New York and see her darling Deborah.

As the train lumbered into the station, Miriam smiled and gathered all her belongings, excited to see Deborah in just a few minutes. She had no image in her mind of the vastness of Grand Central Station and no knowledge of the 19 different platforms where her train might disembark. Not knowing of the maze of tracks and throngs of people ahead, she innocently assumed Deborah would be waiting there to greet her and did not worry. Luckily, Deborah was near the correct gate.

As she battled her way through the crowds, Miriam's travel-weary face lit up upon seeing Deborah and her parents on the platform. Deborah said loudly, "I have missed you. Welcome to New York." Then she whispered in Miriam's ear, "I love you."

Miriam, responding loud enough for the Levines to hear, said, "It is so wonderful to finally be here. I have always wanted to see New York. And it is pleasant to see all of you again." Then she whispered. "I love you too, my sweet."

Miriam hardly noticed the magnificent building she had just entered, since her eyes were only on Deborah. She glanced up at the steel and glass ceiling, enough to entrance any newcomer to this city, but she only saw Deborah's smile.

As they climbed into the Levine's shiny new car, Mr. Levine proudly described it, hoping to impress Miriam. "This is a Cadillac Model Thirty, a new body style for the Touring Car. It can travel up to 60 miles-per-hour and has an electric, no-crank starter." While she did not care at all, she politely expressed interest.

They drove through city streets from the train station at 42nd Street, to the Levine's apartment on the Upper West Side. Mrs. Levine provided a travelogue along the way, much like Miriam's own mother would have done. She described this area of New York, pointing out Times Square, Central Park, the city's first elevated railway, and finally, Columbia University, very near their home.

Miriam paid partial attention to Mrs. Levine's tour, as she marveled at the wonders of this bustling city. She stared out the window with her eyes jumping from one amazing detail to another. People rushed along the streets past more tall buildings in this short ride than she had seen in her whole life. Each seemed more ornate than the last. There were shops of every type along each street, with many people selling their wares outside, even though it was December. When the car turned onto Riverside Drive, the scenery shifted. To her left was a long, carefully tended park, while on her right she saw rows of stately homes. She wondered how many people lived in each of these multi-floored buildings.

Mrs. Levine continued. "Our family moved to this area in 1905, just after the subway linked it to Uptown and Lower Manhattan. Mr. Levine's law practice is Downtown and he chose this as a convenient place to live. A growing number of Jewish families have made the same move from the Lower East Side. When they opened this building in 1910, we were one of the first families to move in."

As they pulled up to their building, Miriam marveled at the imposing twelve-story apartment building at 410 Riverside Drive. It had an impressive arched granite vestibule at the street level, but as she entered its shelter, the stained-glass awning dazzled her. Inside the marble-walled foyer, she noticed a huge grandfather clock, then tipped her eyes up to stare at the decorative, pure white ceiling. Her head spun from one beautiful adornment to the next and she was barely able to follow the small group to the elevator without tripping over her feet.

A white-gloved doorman greeted them as they approached the filigreed iron cage surrounding the elevator. He directed them into the equally ornate elevator, with mahogany walls and gold trimmings, for a trip up nine flights. A servant escorted Miriam into the grand foyer of the Levine's apartment. Everything was sumptuous, including elaborate moldings, exquisite brocade draperies, and glistening chandeliers. Miriam's mouth opened in awe, but she quickly closed it to hide her wonder. The spacious and beautifully furnished rooms were much like the Levine's home in the Berkshires, planned with luxury in mind. The biggest difference between this home and Stonegate was the view from every room of the city's excitement, instead of mountains and pastoral land.

Miriam's suitcases showed up in Deborah's room, though Miriam was not certain who brought them there. She was confused by such a large household staff. Deborah told her family they preferred to talk late into the night, so they were sharing one room. Talking was not all they planned!

As Miriam entered the large bedroom, the crimson walls and gold embellishments dazzled her. The rich wooden furniture was covered with decorative carvings and the vanity had an assortment of bottles and brushes carefully laid out. Most impressive was the pair of large beds, with rich, fluffy comforters in gold and maroon paisley with matching pillows scattered decoratively. Miriam almost swooned in anticipation.

After peering quickly at their room, Deborah escorted Miriam downstairs for dinner. There was lively conversation, with youngsters Anna and Milton telling stories of everything they had been doing since they were last together. After dinner, the family lit the *Chanukah* candles and sang a traditional holiday song, *Ma'oz Tzur*. It was the fifth night of *Chanukah*, so Miriam gave Anna and Milton each five candies she brought from Boston, along with five pennies. "That's Chanukah *gelt*," Miriam said, knowing that the youngsters probably knew the term for the money. Miriam had packed little trinkets for them for each night of the holiday.

In their letters, Deborah and Miriam had agreed to give each other only one small gift to be shared on the last night. The best gift was Miriam's decision to add extra days to her trip in order to spend part of *Chanukah* with Deborah.

After her tiring trip, Miriam excused herself early from the family games, with Deborah following. "I want to help Miriam get settled in," she said. As soon as they were in their room together, Deborah locked the door.

They rushed to each other's arms, kissing, hugging, and quietly reconnecting. It did not take long for them to be undressed and in Deborah's bed together, for a quick physical connection before Miriam fell asleep. Deborah quietly got out of bed, redressed, and headed back downstairs to join the family until an appropriate bedtime.

Later, Deborah went to sleep in her own bed, letting Miriam get some rest.

During the night, Miriam awoke to find herself quite disoriented and tried to find her dressing gown so she could make her way to the toilet. Deborah woke and turned on a small light to help her find her way. Once Miriam returned, Deborah invited her to join her in bed. Everyone in the house slept as they took advantage of the private time by slowly and quietly reacquainting themselves with each other's bodies. Door tightly locked, they were safe in their shared chamber.

Above: *Cadillac Model Thirty,* Below: *Train dining car*

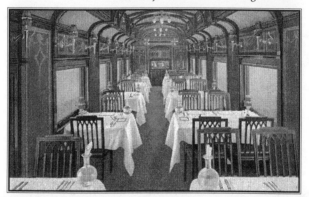

410 Riverside Drive interior

December 19, 1911

Monday was busy with sightseeing for the girls. At Miriam's request, the first stop was the Statue of Liberty. Many times Bubbie had described her experience of finally reaching New York's harbor after a treacherous ride in a huge, overcrowded boat filled with anxious and ill immigrants. Those still able to stand gathered in silence as they neared land.

Bubbie's eyes filled each time she told Miriam and Hannah of the thunderous applause which erupted as they watched Lady Liberty emerge from the horizon. Entering port, passengers feared they would be turned away, as they had been told it was an overcrowded America. The throng endured long lines at Ellis Island, awaiting the dreaded physical inspection, where, according to Bubbie, inspectors lifted her eyelids using a crotchet hook. Those who passed the examination waited for hours to board the barge to bring them to this land of opportunity. Miriam thought of these stories as she readied herself for her first look at The Lady.

The family bundled up for their trip on the Staten Island Ferry. Mr. Levine drove from the Upper West Side to the lower tip of Manhattan, so Miriam could see more of city life. She watched each neighborhood with amazement. It was not at all like Boston! This city was more crowded with buildings and people and it appeared much larger and more confusing than her beloved hometown. There were skyscrapers everywhere and by the time they arrived at the dock her neck was sore from glancing upward.

As the family climbed onto one of the five Staten Island ferries, Miriam was a bit fearful. She had heard from other passengers about two major accidents that had occurred before the city seized management of the ferry line.

Once on the water, Miriam watched the Statue of Liberty come into view, imagining Bubbie's first look. After an emotional view of the statue and a chilly ferry ride on choppy water, she was glad to be back on solid land. Miriam could hardly wait to tell Bubbie how she relived her experience.

Everyone was tired, but Deborah was especially anxious to show Miriam Times Square, at the junction of 42nd Street and 7th Avenue. This was the heart of the entertainment and commercial district, boasting the extremely tall New York Times headquarters and the Broadway theater district. Miriam noticed "The Little Millionaire," was showing at the brand-new George M. Cohan Theater and wondered if they would be going to see that show during her visit. They took a quick peek, enjoying the marquee, but were too cold and weary to linger.

When they arrived home, Deborah said, "It was definitely too cold for me today. I don't remember it ever being this cold, and certainly not for so many days in a row. Sorry you arrived for such awful weather."

Statue of Liberty

Program from the
George M. Cohan theater

Metropolitan Museum of Art, New York City

December 20, 1911

Despite the cold, Deborah could hardly wait to bring Miriam to the Metropolitan Museum the next day to see her favorite collections through Miriam's eyes. No one else wanted to leave the house again in the frigid weather, so they ventured by themselves, taking the subway to 5th Avenue.

"I love my family but I am thrilled to share this adventure with just you, Miriam," Deborah said.

From the moment they walked up to the massive entrance, Miriam was quite dazzled by The Metropolitan. Additions had been built in 1910, making the brick and stone building many blocks in length. Before they ventured out, Mrs. Levine explained that some critics had dubbed this high-Victorian gothic building 'The Mausoleum," and, as Miriam glared at the enormous structure, the title seemed apt.

They spent hours exploring a tiny portion of the two million works of art, with Deborah leading the way to all her favorite exhibits, including the museum's new Renoir and other Impressionists' paintings. Visiting the European paintings could have filled their whole day. For Miriam, it was exciting to see unfamiliar works by familiar artists and she thought of how excited Hannah would be to explore this museum.

For Deborah, it was a treat to show Miriam the Degas statue, which matched her favorite from home.

December 21, 1911

"Today's trip to the Jewish quarter on the Lower East Side was my favorite part of our sight-seeing thus far," Miriam said.

"My father calls it 'The capital of Jewish America," Deborah said.

"I observed a strange combination of poverty and happiness in that densely populated neighborhood. I believed it when your mother told me there were as many as fifteen people living in three rooms, but as over-crowded as it is, they seem to make do. I felt a sense of community and the spirit of the people, making me proud to be of the same heritage as many of them."

"It really is a community," said Deborah. "I got that feeling walking through the crowded rows of stalls, with the immigrants proudly selling their wares. Few of them spoke enough English to describe their items. I am glad we were only looking for treats at the pushcarts, because I would not know how to ask for anything else. And it was too cold to linger for long."

"Deborah," said Miriam changing her tone. "When I have a great experience like I did today, I wish I could share it with Hannah. If I send her a letter, she might never read it. It is so painful she is still so distant."

"I know how difficult this is for you. I wish I could fix your heartache," said Deborah, putting her arms around a tearful Miriam.

December 22, 1911

Deborah and Miriam talked frequently about the differences between Boston and New York, noting how New York City is very active in the evening. Boston is not; it has only occasional shows at any of the three major theaters."

"I am excited we are going out again tonight," said Miriam. "At home, I rarely leave the house in the evening, except to go to temple or for a shiva call. Once or twice a year we go to theater, but it is always a matinee."

"Tonight's performance is an adaptation of the operetta 'Vera Violetta,' written by Jewish composers," Deborah said. "This show has two famous new stars, Al Jolson and Mae West, who I am anxious to see. But what excites me the most is that the performance is at the new Winter Garden Theater. I have not yet been there."

Miriam smiled. "I have enjoyed everywhere your family has taken me. I love our evenings playing games, but I will remember our nighttime adventures as a highlight of my trip. My favorite so far is the new Russian ballet star, Anna Pavlova, who was breathtaking to watch."

At sundown on Friday night, the family lit seven candles on the Menorah, one for each day of *Chanukah*, followed by the lighting of the Shabbos candles. Then they headed to the Levine's shul, B'Nai Jeshurun, on the Upper West Side.

Deborah's temple was quite beautiful, with a decorative *Bimah* up front, colorful, patterned walls, and a high, ornate ceiling. It was smaller and older than Miriam's Boston shul, but was quite comfortable. Miriam enjoyed being there, feeling quite at home in this synagogue. During the services Miriam's mind wandered as she thought of her own family, picturing them without her, on these last nights of the holiday. Was Hannah missing her? Did she ever think of her?

On Saturday, Deborah and Miriam exchanged gifts at the end of the day, since it was the last night of Chanukah. In a delightful coincidence, Deborah had bought Miriam a book about New York and Miriam bought Deborah a book about Boston! Later, in their bedroom, they sat, looking at the books, comparing their hometowns. They enjoyed each other's company more than ever.

Lower East Side

Anna Pavlova

Chanukah menorah

Stage XVI ❧ *Christian Holiday Season*
Saturday, December 23, 1911

Over dinner, Miriam said, "I have seen many Christmas decorations. I saw an advertisement for the first public Christmas tree on display. Might I see it? I can hardly believe a nice Jewish girl like me is interested!"

"Let's go!" said Mrs. Levine eagerly. "Tomorrow is Christmas Eve. We can travel to Madison Square Park to view the tree lighting."

On the way to see the tree, Miriam admitted, "I am certain Boston also decorates for the Christian holidays but I never see decorations because I spend almost all my time in our Jewish neighborhood. Here in New York, Christmas holiday decorations are all over the city, even though you tell me there are over a million Jews here."

"There are many, many Jews, but also many Christians. Christmas decorations have always been popular, though they seem more prolific in the past few years."

"Look! There it is," exclaimed Milton.

"It looks like any other green tree," said Anna.

"The tree will not seem like every other tree after they light it." Mrs. Levine explained, "First we will listen to several choruses sing Christmas songs, so you will need to be patient."

"Are we the only Jewish people here?" Milton quietly asked.

"Maybe," replied Mr. Levine. "Though I doubt it. We can watch to see if there are others who do not sing along with the Christmas hymns. The Jews and some foreigners will be the only folks not singing."

The children looked around, watching official looking men in waistcoats and top hats surrounding the tree. They were not attentively listening to the music, interested only in finding those who were not singing, wondering if they were the Jews.

As the sky darkened and the music ended, Mrs. Levine whispered to her children, "We are about to see why they call this 'The Tree of Light.'"

Suddenly the tree lit up with over two thousand colored lights. Anna and Milton let out excited squeals, along with the thousands of other people. All the clapping sounded muffled, due to the mittens on everyone's hands.

"I appreciate you all for braving this cold night to bring me here. This has been special. I thank you all," Miriam said, shivering, but delighted.

December 24, 1911

Dear Bubbie,

I am thinking of you during my wonderful holiday in New York. It is very different here than in Boston. This city is larger, much busier, and more Christian. Tonight we saw people light a huge tree and listened to people singing Christmas songs.

I thought of you lighting our menorah on the last three nights of Chanukah without me. I have never missed lighting candles with you before. While I am sad to miss my family, I will have lots of tales to tell you when I get home. I hope you are well.

Much Love,

Miriam

Christmas tree at Madison Square Park

December 27, 1911

Miriam considered going to visit Ruth on Christmas Day as she was probably home because of the weather, her pregnancy, and her wedding planning but Miriam decided it was just too cold to go out.

After two days at home, keeping warm and sharing time together, Deborah and Miriam discussed their plans. "New Year's Eve is a much-celebrated time in our city," Deborah said. "There is a huge event in Times Square, created seven years ago by the Jewish owner of the New York Times. There are also special events in each of the city parks, so we will go to our local park, Riverside, along the Hudson River."

"I heard your father say this year there had been threats of cancellations of the celebrations," said Miriam.

"Yes, due to financial concerns. Luckily some prominent citizens, including John D. Rockefeller and Andrew Carnegie, saved the event. We have not missed a single New Year's celebration in the past nine years, so we are glad it is continuing. I am excited to share this with you."

When New Year's Eve arrived on a bitterly cold Sunday, Mrs. Levine announced, "The weather is down to the low 20's, so everyone needs to bundle up."

They put on layers of wool clothing, including scarves and hats, helping each other into two pairs of mittens. In their bulky outfits, they could hardly move. Their doorman had to assist each of them as they awkwardly climbed into the car for the short ride.

Huddling together for warmth, Deborah and Miriam delighted in an excuse to lean against one another without attracting attention. Deborah felt a thrill run through her whole body, despite the cold.

Everyone enjoyed the brass bands, singing groups, and even the parade. Milton was pleased his parents agreed to stay long enough for the canon firing, his favorite part of the festivities. Just after midnight they headed to the warmth of home, with Deborah and Miriam delighted to have welcomed the New Year together.

Stage XVII ❧ *The Letter*

Monday, January 1, 1912

The days leading up to Ruth's wedding stayed dangerously cold, with no end in sight, with the temperature predicted to be below zero all week. The freeze kept everyone at home except Father, who had to work. Anna and Milton missed school due to the bitter weather, so the family enjoyed a marathon of board games.

On Wednesday, Miriam suggested, "Let's go to Ruth's house to check wedding preparations."

"We have been enjoying our time together so much, I almost forgot Ruth and Michael's wedding is next Sunday," Deborah said.

After the girls trudged through the cold streets, Ruth opened her door, ushered them inside and, whined, "I am so unhappy. I am almost in my sixth month and I am still experiencing nausea daily. And I look so pregnant everyone will notice my belly instead of my beautiful dress. Oh no. I am going to be sick again," moaned Ruth, running off to the bathroom with a hand covering her mouth.

While Ruth ran off, Deborah turned to Miriam. "It would have been nice if she had thanked us for traveling through the horrible weather to visit her."

"You are being too harsh, Deborah. Every bride is entirely focused on herself the week before her wedding. Being pregnant and sick are certainly additional reasons to be unhappy."

"You are right. I think I am in the habit of complaining about Ruth's self-absorption. I will be more forgiving, given the circumstances."

Despite her awareness, Miriam added, "It is sad Ruth is much more focused on her appearance than her upcoming marriage and child."

"No amount of kindness will take Ruth out of her misery," Deborah concluded. But they were both glad they had come to see her.

January 5, 1912

Two days before the wedding, it began to snow. That day's mail contained a letter from Miriam's mother. Grinning, Miriam quickly opened the letter and began to read. Just two sentences into the letter, her face fell and her jaw dropped.

January 1, 1912

My Dear Daughter,

I am writing this letter with utmost regret and concern. Your sister Hannah has just told us what she witnessed in our home when your friend Deborah was visiting. She has been beside herself with worry since that time and noticing her sadness, we made her tell us why. We now understand her shock. You have defied your family and your religion with your unnatural behavior.

Your father has made it very clear you are no longer considered part of our family. He has declared you are dead. He has torn his clothing in mourning for the daughter he once had and he is sitting a private shiva, reposing alone in our home for the seven-day mourning period. He said the Kaddish, the prayer for the dead. He will never allow you back in our home.

I too am ravaged by this news. I cannot believe that my very own flesh and blood has committed such a grievous sin against her faith, her sister, and us.

Unlike your father, I have it in my heart to wish you well. I wonder if you understood the consequences of your behavior when you acted so recklessly. Much like a common woman, you have let the temptations of the flesh ruin your life. Yet your sin is even more egregious. You have chosen a difficult way to live your life.

If this is your choice, I wonder what I did wrong. I thought I taught you good values and prepared you to have a wonderful Jewish home. I guess my love for you was not enough to keep you from this wanton, immoral path.

But as you have chosen this disreputable way forward, I hope you find some happiness in your new life.

Mother

Miriam dropped the letter and burst into hysterical sobs, running upstairs to the bedroom and throwing herself on the bed. Deborah picked up the letter and hurriedly followed. Luckily, none of the family was witness to this extreme display of emotions.

Deborah, unable to console Miriam, read the letter. She, too, burst into tears and wrapped her arms around Miriam as tightly as she could. They cried and rocked together for a long time.

By the time they stopped sobbing, the family had gathered for dinner. Deborah went downstairs with her tear-stained face to tell the family Miriam had just suffered a considerable shock. She told them only that she must stay with Miriam for the time being and neither of them would be downstairs for dinner. To Deborah's great relief Mother offered to have a dinner brought upstairs for the both of them and did not pry.

When Deborah returned upstairs, Miriam stopped sobbing long enough to say, "I am frightened and heartbroken. I have no family now. What will I do? Where will I live?"

"You can stay with us until you figure out where you can go. I am certain my parents will welcome you," Deborah said quietly.

"But what if my mother reaches out to your mother, telling her of our sins?"

Deborah paused to think. "Maybe I should tell my mother now, before your mother says something."

"No wait. I could not stand to have her reject me too. Where would I turn?"

Again, Deborah tried to formulate an answer, though nothing came easily. "Is there anyone you can turn to?" Deborah said softly. "I think you need someone to talk to, other than me."

"I can't think of anyone. I would usually turn to my sister or Marjorie. Now I just turn to you."

The enormity of the situation struck both girls into a sad silence.

After more tears and further conversation, they concluded Deborah would eventually have to tell her mother because Miriam would be unable to go home next week at the appointed time. They agreed not to tell Deborah's father, in fear he would react the same way Mr. Cohen had.

They eventually each took a few mouthfuls of food, but neither had an appetite. After more tears, they climbed into bed and held each other. Even this closeness was unsatisfying, so they parted for the night, uneasy and exhausted.

January 6, 1912

It was too stormy to travel to temple on Friday night, so everyone stayed home. Deborah and Miriam welcomed a quiet day on the Sabbath, staying upstairs all day. Deborah made excuses for their absence, saying that Miriam was still feeling too upset to be sociable. Worried, Mrs. Levine asked more questions, then offered to talk with Miriam, ready to give her motherly advice, but Deborah refused her offer. She hoped her mother would not feel offended, but she knew Miriam would be unable to welcome the support without explaining the whole situation.

With Ruth's wedding the next day, the girls realized they had to face the family. Would they be able to keep themselves calm enough to attend the ceremony? Two sniffling friends making a commotion would upset Ruth and call attention to their sad moods. They vowed to put on happier faces and joined the family downstairs. Mrs. Levine was relieved the crisis appeared to have ended.

Mrs. Chaim Cohen

January 1, 1912

My Dear Daughter,

I am writing this letter with utmost regret and concern. Your sister Hannah has just told us what she witnessed in our home when your friend Deborah was visiting. She has been beside herself with worry since that time and noticing her sadness, we made her tell us her concern. We now understand her shock. You have defied your family and your religion with your unnatural behavior.

Your father has made it very clear you are no longer part of the family. He has declared you are dead. He has torn his clothing in mourning for the daughter he once had and he is sitting a private shiva, reposing alone in our home for the seven-day mourning period. He said the Kaddish, the prayer for the dead. He will never allow you back in our home.

I too am ravaged by this news. I cannot believe that my very own flesh and blood has committed such a grievous sin against her faith, her sister, and us.

Stage XVIII ⚜ *Wedding*
Sunday, January 7, 1912

A break in the weather allowed the family to leave the house and reach the wedding venue safely. Everyone was impressed as they peered up at the extravagant Hotel Knickerbocker, a luxury Times Square hotel in the dramatic Beaux-Arts style with red brick and exaggerated terra cotta details. The hotel, built by John Jacob Astor IV, a prominent New York businessman and part of the famously wealthy Astor family, was a place of refined extravagance. The hotel boasted several famous long-term residents, George M. Cohan, Enrico Caruso, and Mary Pickford, so everyone agreed to keep their eyes peeled for a glimpse of celebrities.

Miriam brightened when she entered the foyer, dazzled by everything in view. The hotel was grand, richly decorated with elegant upholstered chairs, dramatic chandeliers, and intricately patterned rugs. She was in a world of opulence, surrounded by elegantly dressed families being attended to by finely costumed bellmen.

They were guided to elevators bringing them to the lower level where they entered the charming room selected for the wedding. The family chose to have the ceremony at a hotel, rather than at their temple, because of the bride's advanced pregnancy. This was far from the private wedding the girls had speculated the parents might choose.

Everyone in attendance was dressed in his or her finery. Deborah and Miriam looked attractive, except for the red rings around their eyes. Deborah's mother must have said something to the family to keep them from asking too many questions about what was going on with Miriam.

"We are quite early so let's go find the Old King Cole painting by Maxfield Parrish while we wait for others to arrive," Mrs. Levine implored. "I have heard it is quite impressive."

"I learned it is in the bar," said Mr. Levine. "Let's bring in the youngsters quietly."

They arrived in the bar, clearly a man's area. It was dark, reserved, with simple wooden tables and chairs and little else. The oak bar stretched 30 feet, and above it was the equally large painting they had come to see. Though it depicted the fabled story character Old King Cole, it was not childish. The monarch was seated among his distracted followers, who the bartender explained was frowning because the king had just "passed wind". Anna and Milton found this very funny and giggled quite loudly. The adults gazed at the artwork with as much enthusiasm as they could muster, then quickly departed, hoping to calm the children down. When they returned to the wedding area, they found many others had arrived.

Miriam spotted the Berkowitz girls and the youngsters waved wildly from their seats towards the front of the temporary sanctuary. Seeing them in their pretty dresses put a smile on Miriam's face, practically the first since the shock of her mother's letter.

Miriam was able to ignore her woes during the service and focus on Ruth and Michael. Before they entered the sanctuary, the bride, groom, and two witnesses signed the *ketubah*, the wedding contract, which detailed their obligations to one another. Then Michael veiled his bride. Even though the ceremony was at the hotel, rather than in the synagogue, they completed many traditional Jewish wedding rituals.

"Look Mother. Ruth is fat," Anna whispered as Ruth walked down the aisle on her father's arm. It was clear from Anna's comment that neither Ruth's magnificent off-white beaded dress with a full skirt, nor the large bouquet she held in front her large stomach, had adequately hidden her secret.

Ruth and Michael stood under the marriage canopy, as the seven blessings were recited. The bride circled the groom, denoting perfection. As she walked, it was obvious to anyone who had not yet noticed, that Ruth's profile included a very large bump across her belly.

After exchanging rings, the Rabbi placed a glass under Michael's right foot. He raised his foot and stomped down, breaking the glass, reminding everyone that joy must be tempered. Everyone shouted "*Mazel Tov*", then broke into the traditional song, *Simin Tov U'Mazel Tov*, a wish of good luck, as the couple came down the aisle.

After the ceremony, the newly married couple was ushered into an adjoining room for *yichud*, a period of privacy. The guests headed into the lavish reception outside the ballroom. Martini's, the signature drink of the hotel, flowed freely. The Golds had hired a *kosher* caterer to accommodate their guests. There were bountiful tables of Jewish foods: meat *knishes*, chopped liver, chopped herring, *kishke*, and platters of lox.

"What is *kishke*, Mother?" asked Anna when she spotted the unfamiliar food.

"It's a Jewish sausage," replied Mrs. Levine, avoiding the more accurate description of stuffed intestine. "Have a *knish*, that egg-shaped pastry over there. You will like it. You have tried *knishes* filled with potatoes but this one is filled with meat, which is even more delicious."

After the appetizers, white-gloved men escorted everyone into the lavish banquet hall. Miriam's eves were first drawn to the elegant gold plates and huge flower centerpieces. The wooden pillars and multiple chandeliers provided an opulent yet warm setting.

As Miriam approached their table, all four of the Berkowitz daughters greeted her with cheers. She was able to put aside her personal grief for long enough to hug each girl, finding comfort in the children and all the familiar foods. By the time everyone sat down for the meal, they were almost full, with most guests picking at the delicious food. Deborah was glad to see Miriam finally eating something.

Mrs. Berkowitz approached Miriam and looked at her, gaunt from all the crying and lack of food. Miriam burst into tears when Mrs. Berkowitz put an arm around her shoulder. Miriam tried to pull away but Mrs. Berkowitz held on tight. Deborah had tears in her eyes as well, which did not go beyond Mrs. Berkowitz's notice.

After a few moments, Mrs. Berkowitz asked Deborah's mother, "Would you mind if I took Miriam away for a short time to help her freshen up?"

When Deborah attempted to join them, Mrs. Berkowitz begged, "Please leave us alone for a few minutes. If we have not returned within ten minutes, you can come find us."

As Deborah continually glanced in the direction they had gone, her mother asked Deborah directly, "Will you tell me what is going on?"

"Mother, this is Miriam's issue. I am not free to explain her problems."

Reluctantly, Deborah's mother retreated and they all waited quietly for Miriam and Mrs. Berkowitz to return. When there was no sign of them after ten minutes, Deborah excused herself and went to find them.

Entering the ladies lounge, Deborah spotted the two of them huddled in a corner. Miriam was no longer crying inconsolably and Mrs. Berkowitz actually had a quiet smile on her face as she held Miriam's hand and spoke to her with a gentle voice.

As Deborah approached them, Mrs. Berkowitz softly explained, "Miriam has told me your dilemma. I understand how overwhelmed you must be. I have a plan that might help."

"What could possibly make things better?" Deborah asked, tears running down her cheeks.

"I have asked Miriam to come live with my family. I will need to spend extended time in Queens over the next year because my mother is quite ill. The children adore Miriam and they will be excited to spend lots of time with her. The four girls are quite a handful for the governess, so this arrangement will be a great help to us all."

Deborah began crying, this time from relief, and soon both girls sobbed loudly. Mrs. Berkowitz placed her arms around the two them, making it possible for them to hug each other while embracing her, too. Others in the lounge looked over at them, but they could not stop the hugging and tears.

It took a few moments for them to calm down enough to begin to thank Mrs. Berkowitz, then repeat their thanks over and over. Miriam, with eyes glowing, said "You have come up with a remarkable solution. You have saved me! You are the sweetest person in the world."

Mrs. Berkowitz was glad when the cries of the two distraught girls had turned to tears of relief. She certainly had her own concerns about their relationship and the troubles it might bring, but she looked first for a solution to their distress. She knew she would need to explain her feelings to them later. She and her husband had discussed this type of situation many times and she had serious questions regarding their future happiness. But for now, she knew Miriam needed shelter and support.

Mrs. Berkowitz took a deep breath, "No thanks are needed. Tonight, we have a party to attend and several children are waiting for you both."

The girls remained astounded and relieved at the good turn of their fortune. After Mrs. Berkowitz returned to her family, Deborah and Miriam talked together for a few minutes while drying their tears.

"Why do you think she is doing this for us, Deborah? Do you think she has thought about what she and her husband would suffer if someone were to figure us out?"

"I think she is just a kind person, who saw how distraught we both were. I doubt she thought about the consequences for her family. We must be very careful not to arouse suspicions."

"I think it is more than that, though we may never know why. I am just so grateful."

After a long embrace and more tears, Deborah and Miriam returned to the reception with renewed hope. The Levine family was left to wonder what miracle cure Mrs. Berkowitz had provided for the two previously weepy girls.

Mrs. Berkowitz asked Deborah and Miriam to watch the children while she talked to her husband. Deborah watched the adults deep in conversation in a distant corner, nervously clearing her throat, afraid he might not approve of the plans. Deborah looked at Miriam, who was obviously worrying too.

When their conversation had been completed, Mrs. Berkowitz asked Deborah and Miriam to join her for a few minutes, and both their faces fell. Back in the ladies lounge, Mrs. Berkowitz began with, "Mr. Berkowitz approves of our plans."

Both girls wept all over again as Mrs. Berkowitz continued, "My husband actually had another idea to add. He thinks it would be wonderful if you would move into our house too, Deborah."

"What?" was all Deborah could manage to say.

"You heard me right. He would like you both to move into our home. Our New York apartment is not as expansive as our Lenox home but there is one private room you two could share. During the summer, you could both join us in Lenox. It would be our pleasure to welcome you into our family."

"But why?" Deborah still found it hard to believe, "Does he understand we are together? How could he approve when even the rabbis don't?" Deborah asked.

"I will explain," Mrs. Berkowitz began quietly. "When Mr. Berkowitz was a young man, one of his closest friends admitted to him he was homosexual. His friend tried to hide this from his family, but when his parents confronted him he confirmed their suspicions. The next day he was banished from his home. My husband tried to stay in touch with his friend, but it was not possible. Within two years, he got word this young man had taken his own life. He never knew what happened, but it was one of the saddest experiences of his youth. He was reminded of this story when I told him of your situation. He was not able to save his friend, but he would be very pleased to help the two of you. He is the one who suggested you both live with us to help with the children."

Astounded and trying to grasp the enormity of this acceptance, Miriam could only think to ask, tearfully, "May I thank him?"

"You certainly may," replied Mrs. Berkowitz. "But more important right now is to decide what Deborah will say to her parents, now that they have witnessed all this commotion between us. For now, I will tell Mrs. Levine we have been helping you solve a very big problem with your family, Miriam."

Deborah and Miriam went directly to Mr. Berkowitz to thank him, but they were still too overcome with emotion to say more than "Thank you."

The four little girls looked very upset, so Miriam told them, "Your parents are the nicest people in the whole world."

Ruth's wedding dress

Knickerbocker Hotel

Stage XIX ✤ *Explanations*
Tuesday, January 9, 1912

During the week following Ruth and Michael's wedding, snow fell and fell, blanketing the streets and buildings. It did not stop for ten days, dropping a total of 13 inches on the city. The bad weather provided the perfect excuse why Miriam was unable to return home to Boston on the appointed date.

Mrs. Levine told Miriam, "This is one of the worst snowfalls on record. It has not rivaled the 1888 storm but this blizzard shut down most everything. Following such extreme cold makes this one of the most horrible winters in the city of New York. It is too bad you are here for this."

"I have not enjoyed the weather, but I have thoroughly enjoyed your city." Miriam said, happy for no more questions about her recent angst.

Anna and Milton enjoyed being home from school for so many days, especially since their playmate, Miriam, was with them. Together they played every board game multiple times and Miriam taught them every card game she knew. Miriam's sadness softened considerably with their new plans. She saved her tears for the evenings.

During the blizzard, Deborah and Miriam ventured outside twice, each time to take the Berkowitz children out to play in the snow. They talked with Mrs. B. on several occasions.

How would Deborah explain things to her parents? They debated many possible stories to tell them but, in the end, the truth won.

Deborah would tell her mother exactly what was happening. Her father, like Miriam's, would be less apt to manage the information comfortably, so they decided to keep the facts from him. Deborah would tell him they were needed to assist the governess in minding the children when Mrs. B. left town to care for her sick mother. Hopefully he would accept this partial truth.

But Deborah worried. "How can I describe this to my mother? What words can I say which won't cause her to dismiss me from her life, as Miriam's mother has done?"

Mrs. B. provided reassurance. "You will find a way to tell her. I will be there to support you if you wish. Remember, you are safe and loved here with us."

Miriam's response to these discussions was mostly tears. Her pain was so acute that everything seemed to trigger her sadness. Miriam worried, "How will Hannah manage in life without me? I was her strength. I am as worried about my sister, as I am about my own misfortunes."

"She will manage," Deborah assured her, unsuccessfully.

"And what about Bubbie?" Miriam said with tear-stained eyes. "I cannot imagine what she is thinking. Did my parents tell her the whole story? She is old and frail. It would be a horrid shock and I would be responsible if anything happened to her."

"You mustn't fret so," Deborah said kindly, knowing she had no answers to Miriam's concerns.

Once the snow finally stopped falling, Deborah and Miriam knew it was time to tell Mrs. Levine the truth. They practiced what to say over and over, deciding they would wait for a day when Mrs. B. could be there for support.

In the meantime, Mrs. Levine remained worried and could not keep from asking the girls what happened. "The Cohen's are very angry with Miriam," Deborah said. When Mrs. Levine asked Miriam directly, Miriam burst into tears and retreated to her room. Mrs. Levine bit her tongue, trying not to meddle, feeling helpless.

January 15, 1912

The day finally arrived for explanations. After Mrs. B. arrived, they all had tea and cookies in the parlor. Mrs. B. and Miriam found an excuse to retreat to the dining room. Deborah told her mother she had something very important to tell her and she hoped Mother did not notice her shaking hands. With a dry mouth and unsteady voice, Deborah said, "Mother. I am finally ready to tell you why Miriam has been so upset. I have some information that might upset you, too. Please know that I love you and I am really hoping you will continue to love me and care for Miriam, too."

"What could this possibly have to do with you? Nothing could ever affect my love for you," Mrs. Levine promised, though a white pallor crossed her face.

"I certainly hope so." Deborah took a deep breath and said, "The problem with Miriam is love. She has fallen deeply in love and the Cohen's do not approve. They have rejected her because of her choice." Deborah's voice faltered at 'for her choice.'

"I don't understand how parents could reject their own daughter."

"I so badly hope that is true… The fact is - the person Miriam has fallen in love with is me."

There was a deafening silence as Deborah's mother took in those words. She stared at Deborah, then looked away. They sat in silence for about half a minute, though it felt like hours. Mrs. Levine rose from her chair, with Deborah fearing she would walk away, never to speak to her again. But her mother walked towards Deborah, holding out her arms, as Deborah leapt to her feet and ran into her embrace. They stood entangled silently for several moments, tears running down both their faces.

"I love you, Deborah. I love you no matter what choices you make in your life. I could never stop loving you."

Mrs. Levine paused, thinking. With a change in her tone she said, "I fear you have chosen a very difficult path in your life, but I will always be a support for you. I am your mother and I will always be your mother."

"I love you, Mother. This was the most difficult thing I ever had to tell you. I hope someday you will learn to be happy for me. I have found great love and I am happier than I ever thought I would be."

Mrs. Levine smiled softly at her daughter. "Now go get that wonderful girl, Miriam, who I am sure is waiting with great fear in her heart. Go get her and bring her to me."

Deborah raced to find Miriam and Mrs. B. in the next room. Deborah looked at them both and smiled. Then she took Miriam's hand and walked her to where her mother was waiting for them in the parlor.

Miriam did not know what to expect, but there was Mrs. Levine, arms outstretched, reaching towards Miriam.

"You poor girl," Deborah's mother said as Miriam entered her warm embrace.

For a moment, Miriam thought Deborah had only explained that Miriam's parents had rejected her. She understood when Mrs. Levine said, "We love you Miriam. I will find a way to accept you and Deborah together."

She smiled and continued, "It is not actually a terrible surprise for me, since I noticed Deborah never really liked the company of boys, as other girls her age did. You, my sweet miss, are more of a surprise. But I understand it would be hard to resist loving my wonderful Deborah. She has a heart of gold and a will almost as strong."

Miriam could only muster, "Thank you," before she sank into another bout of tears.

Once they all gained control of their emotions, they called for Mrs. B. She, too, had tears in her eyes. They talked for a long time, with Deborah's mother agreeing it was unwise to tell Mr. Levine anything. They all feared he would reject Deborah for her religious betrayal. They made a pact to keep the truth of the girls' relationship from him.

They also promised one another, that someday, the two mothers would reach out to Miriam's mother to see if there was a soft spot in her heart that could be mended. Maybe someday she could accept Miriam back into her life. For now, this was her new family.

When the topic turned to Deborah and Miriam moving into the Berkowitz home, Deborah's mother fretted. "I don't want to lose you," she said to her daughter.

"You will not," Deborah said with confidence. "But we could not keep this secret from Father if we were to continue to live together in the same home. Eventually he would figure it out."

"You are right," said Mrs. Levine, resigned to letting her daughter go. "I am incredibly thankful to you, Mrs. Berkowitz, for your offer to shelter the girls."

Deborah quickly added, "Miriam and I promise to visit regularly. What if we spend every Friday evening Shabbos with you? We both want to maintain our closeness with you and Father, Anna, and Milton."

Mrs. Levine looked at her daughter, as if for the first time in a long while. "You are certainly growing up, Deborah. You have thought of everything. I think your plan is a good one. I don't have to lose you. Instead, I will gain one more daughter."

"I love your family so much," Miriam said shyly. "We will be happy to spend lots of time with you and Mr. Levine, as well as Anna and Milton. You have all been so gracious and welcoming to me. It will be a pleasure to be part of your family."

With a long sigh of relief, Deborah added, "This discussion, which I approached with so much fear and trepidation, has turned out better than I could have ever imagined."

From that moment on, Deborah, Miriam, and both families worked to figure out what to tell Deborah's siblings, when the move would take place, and how excited they all were to be one big extended family.

Deborah and Miriam could live together and love each other. All six children would be in their lives, Miriam had a new set of chosen parents, and there might be a tiny bit of hope that in time, Miriam's mother would welcome her child back into her life.

There was finally peace in all their hearts. But each, in their own way, worried about what the future might bring for two young girls choosing a dangerous life.

Romance to Relationship

Peyrek (Chapter) A ❧ *New York Adjustment*
Sunday, January 21, 1912

After dinner, for the first time during their hectic moving day, Deborah and Miriam were alone. Sitting on comfortable chairs in their new bedroom in the Berkowitz home, they both emitted deep sighs at the same moment and laughed a bit. They were both too tired for full grins.

Miriam glanced at the spacious room and their piles of their possessions and said, "Well, my unpacking will not take long, since I only have those things I brought for my visit to New York."

Deborah looked at Miriam with a bit of sadness.

Miriam managed a full smile, saying, "I can hardly believe we are living together, from this moment forward."

"I could not be more pleased," Deborah said, standing by Miriam's chair, squeezing her shoulders. I am glad my father was easily persuaded that I am living with this family so we can both care for the children."

"I thought your father was going to cry when the doorman packed your suitcases into his car. Did you feel bad we did not tell him the whole truth?"

"Not really. I love Father but I think it was kind to tell him a partial story. He would have been upset if he knew you and I were choosing a life together."

"I am happy, which I did not think possible after my family disowned me."

"Oh Miriam, I am so glad to hear those words. I worried you would never feel cheerful again."

"I am surprised myself," Miriam said, holding Deborah's hands in hers. "The Berkowitz family is exceptionally sweet. And so generous to let us move into their home as part of their family. Do you recall the first day we stayed with them in Lenox? We talked about wishing we could live with them forever. I can hardly believe our wishes came true. It is still beyond my imagination."

Deborah's Journal, January 23, 1912

My life has taken many sudden and wonderful turns. I have not only found the girl of my dreams, but we can live together. Miriam is every-thing I ever imagined. She has showed me her strengths and ability to cope with horrible adversity. I want to make her happy, which feels like a huge job, as I must make up for the loss of her whole family.

I still worry we will be isolated. I have my friends but I have not yet told them about my relationship with Miriam. Will they be accepting? If they reject me, I will be almost as alone as Miriam. Will they be comfortable with the two of us? When they marry and begin their own families, will they include us in their social circles? There is so much unknown.

Meeting Margaret and Abigail helped me believe there are other couples like us, though I am still unsure where we will find them. After the weather clears and we settle into our new home, we will search for friends.

Miriam's Diary, January 23, 1912

All at once, I lost my parents, my sister, and even my Bubbie, so my heart is heavy with emptiness. Yet, I have incredible blessings, which help dispel the pain. I now live with my love and sleep next to her every night. We are fortunate for the generosity of her parents and the Berkowitzs, my new family.

Mrs. B. may be the kindest person I know. Mr. B. is easy, calm, and very loving too. When Mrs. B. travels, their wonderful children will be our charges, which feels like an enormous responsibility. I am greatly relieved their governess, Bridget, will share the child care duties with us.

It is uncomfortable living in New York, a city I know little about. I have no friends here other than Deborah and Ruth, though Ruth's new life as a wife and mother will distance us further. I am not certain what will occupy us when we are not caring for the children. We can visit the museums, theater and concerts, but that is not enough. My world has gotten very small. Surely, we will find other girls like us.

Peyrek B ✤ *First Steps*
Monday, February 19, 1912

Deborah nodded to Miriam as she sat down at the small desk the Berkowitzes had provided. Miriam sat in the second chair and pulled out her own paper and a pen. The two of them sat scribbling, lost in their own thoughts.

Miriam's Diary, February 19, 1912

Although Deborah and I share everything, I do not want to upset her with my deepest feelings, so I turn to my diary for comfort.

I am so very lonely. I have been in New York for almost a month, but it does not feel like home. I love Deborah, though I find a loving relationship is not enough. The Berkowitz family is exceptional, but I miss my family and my community. I think of my parents and Hannah all the time. And what does Bubbie think happened to me? I have written a few letters to my friends but I have not yet risked telling anyone the truth. I really want to tell Marjorie, but what will I do if she rejects me? I could not stand being even more alone. Will any of them keep a place in their heart for me? Will I ever see any of them again?

And this is a secular life. The Berkowitz family hardly acknowledges the Sabbath, so I am pleased to spend each Shabbos with the Levines, who are not as observant as my family, but it is enough.

Deborah's friends have not been coming around. They are so different than the sweet girls I spent my whole life with. They are city girls, independent and adventurous. Although I love those qualities in Deborah, I have not warmed to any of her friends yet. No one has questioned our friendship, but I wonder if they are uncomfortable with us.

Deborah's Journal, February 19, 1912

The past month has gone by quickly. It has been wonderful to spend every day with Miriam and I cherish holding her in my arms every night. Being near my family, my friends, and everything familiar has made my move to the Berkowitz home relatively easy.

But Miriam has neither friends nor family here. Nothing is familiar to her. I can sense loneliness in her downturned glance when I talk of my connections. I want so badly to see the sparkle back in her eyes.

*How will we find friends who are like-minded? We can try going
to Suffrage meetings, as we did in Boston and maybe that will lead to
friendships. Yet Margaret and Abigail would never become true friends
as we have few similarities, other than our mutual love of girls. Are
there other Jewish girls like us to understand Miriam's dilemma?*

After Deborah put her pen down, she turned to Miriam. "How are
you managing?"

"I have been missing all of my family, but especially my Bubbie," said
Miriam, with sadness. "It feels so unfair that my grandmother has gotten
caught up in this tangled mess. I don't know if she too has dismissed me from
her life. I doubt she knows why my parents consider me dead to them. But
I cannot help wondering what terrible thing she thinks I might have done. I
have written, then discarded many letters to her, but I have decided to mail
my latest one. May I read it to you?"

"Oh Miriam. Certainly you can read it to me. I also wonder what your
Bubbie must be thinking. Did she sit Shiva for you? Or maybe she has a loving
heart, as you have always said, and she forgives you. Do you really want to
know?"

"I do. I feel I owe it to her to explain the actual situation."

"Then read me the letter."

February 20, 1912

Dear Bubbie,

*I miss you terribly. I am situated with a wonderful family in New
York, but it is not home and they are not my family. I miss my real family
desperately, especially you, my sweet Bubbie. I miss your warm kisses
and hugs. I miss your munn cookies and your wonderful meals. But
mostly, I miss your sweetness and your kindness.*

*I do not know what Mother and Father have told you, but I want
you to know the truth. My crime against the family and against Judaism
is that I have fallen in love with the wrong person. My sin is far worse
than loving someone outside our faith. Loving a non-Jewish man, a goy,
is not as bad as what I have done. I have found a girl to love.*

*You met Deborah when she visited in the fall. Hopefully you saw
her strength and gentle heart. She has added much richness to my life.
This would be my happiest time were it not for our family's rejection,
causing me constant pain.*

My one hope, dear Bubbie, is that you can still love me, even if the rest of them do not. I still love you. You will always be my wonderful grandmother, my Bubbie.
With Love,
Miriam

Deborah stayed quiet for a moment. "It is a lovely letter, but I am scared for you. You have been bereft since your separation from your family and what if you get another rejection? It is brave, but, hopefully, not foolish, to reach out to your Bubbie. I don't what will happen, but I promise to dry your tears."

Desk

Peyrek C ✤ *New Endeavors*
Wednesday, February 21, 1912

Deborah believed the best thing she could do for Miriam was help her feel connected with other girls in New York. She looked to Barnard College, a women's college much like Radcliff, to find a Suffrage meeting. The day they chose to go was windy and blustery, so they dressed in their warmest clothing, with scarves and hats to protect them on their walk. When the Berkowitz's driver saw them bundled up, he offered them a ride, which they accepted even though Barnard was just a few blocks away.

As they arrived at the ornate gate, they both stopped to marvel. The gold letters read "Barnard College of Columbia University." Just beyond the gate they stepped into an impressive brick building, with four huge and beautiful pillars. "Look Deborah," said Miriam, excitedly pointing to a bulletin board. "The girls who attend this school have many wonderful activities to fill their days. Here is an advertisement for a lecture on impressionist art and another on careers for young women. And there is a violin concert soon and an invitation to join the choral group."

"No Suffrage groups? Let's check other bulletin boards," said Deborah.

A tall, attractive woman approached. "Excuse me," she said. "My name is Susan. I overheard you asking for information about Suffrage meetings. Although I have never attended one, I have been thinking about going so I have been asking around. My friend told me there is a meeting today in the new building on 116th. I am headed that way, and you are welcome to join me. It is just a short walk."

"That would be wonderful. I am Miriam and this is Deborah. It is nice to meet you, Susan. We will be happy to follow you."

Susan led them out the building, deeper into campus, passing several other large brick buildings. Miriam cocked her head from side to side, fascinated with groups of girls engaged in lively conversations.

"It is fortunate you overheard us," said Deborah. "Are you a student here?"

"Yes I am. I am in my third year, studying English and working on the school newspaper, The Bulletin. I am learning how to set type so we can print copies for everyone who wants one."

"My father is a publisher," added Miriam quickly, then painfully remembering she no longer had a father who is a publisher.

"Oh! Have you ever set type? I could really use some help," Susan said as they walked toward the new building.

"My father rarely lets me do anything at his publishing shop, but once his assistant was sick and he let me fill in for a week. I learned a lot in a short time. Since then, he has only called on me a couple of times to help out." And now, no more, she thought.

"You know more than I do, so I would love any pointers you could offer. Would you be willing to stop by the college newspaper office and give me some guidance?"

"Certainly," Miriam said, "but first I want to find out about this meeting."

They quickly discovered the meeting was to be held on the lower level in just over an hour. Before Deborah had a chance to suggest it, Miriam and Susan decided to use this time to go to the college newspaper office. Deborah followed with a smile on her face, glad to detect some added lightness in Miriam's step.

While Miriam and Susan talked of typesetting, Deborah made herself at home by talking to the other girls. By the time they left The Bulletin office for their suffrage meeting, Miriam had promised to return the next day. The girls had also enticed Deborah to assist them with a special section about the European paintings at the Metropolitan Museum, something Deborah knew a lot about. It was hard to pull themselves away from these exciting connections, but off to the lecture they headed.

A handful of women sat around a large wooden table with upright chairs, giving the meeting an air of importance. Both Deborah and Miriam were able to report about the Boston gathering they attended. Though their experience was limited, they were more versed in this movement than most of the other girls, making them a valuable addition to the group. By the time they left, they had offered to help coordinate the college participation in the huge Suffrage parade planned for May 6. Over 3,000 women were expected! Deborah and Miriam promised to return in three days for the next meeting.

After leaving Susan, they found their way back to the main building.

"Deborah, in just one afternoon we have met girls our age, discovered this wonderful college, and gotten involved with both the student newspaper and the Suffrage parade. My head is full of new ideas."

Deborah grinned. "I am excited too and glad to be appreciated. Not that the Berkowitzes don't appreciate us, but this is different. It is nice to have other girls to talk with. I am hopeful we can make some friends together. And the best part of all is seeing pleasure on your face, my dear Miriam."

"The truth is, I have been so very lonely. I love you a great deal, but you, your family, and the Berkowitzes are the only people I have been with in over a month. Now that I have some new connections, I can hardly stop smiling."

"I think today is a new beginning." Deborah announced, "We now know how to meet other girls and I am hopeful we can do something meaningful with our lives. I am so excited to use my writing skills on the student newspaper and to benefit the suffrage movement. I am happy to begin our shared life on such an uplifting note."

Filled with enthusiasm, they bundled up in their hats, scarves and mittens, ready to brave the elements on their walk home. Walking under the sign that had welcomed them to the college, the girls felt the cold wind lashing against their faces. They walked quickly, without further conversation but with stimulating thoughts swirling. When they arrived home, the doorman opened the door quickly, commenting on how brave they were to venture out in this terrible weather. Their frozen lashes and reddened cheeks had been a small price to pay for the warmth in their hearts.

After a cup of hot tea, followed by a hearty evening meal and family conversation, they headed to their room. Though they had all the privacy they could want, Deborah and Miriam had been less enthusiastic in bed lately. Miriam was sad and found it hard to put her feelings aside when touching Deborah. They satisfied one another physically but most sessions ended with Miriam crying. Deborah was sad she could not satisfy Miriam's deepest needs, which had nothing to do with her body.

But this night, Miriam approached Deborah with a flirtatious smile, something Deborah had not seen recently. Miriam undressed and moved around the room in a tantalizing way, finally getting into bed, and touching Deborah with zeal. She took care of Deborah's needs first, which was not often the case these days. Usually Deborah had to work hard to excite Miriam but today they were equally excited, with joy in their loving and no tears at all. Their intimacy reflected their wondrous day.

Barnard College students

Barnard College publication

Barnard College gate

Peyrek D ✤ *Bubbie*
Thursday, February 22, 1912

The next morning, the girls still glowed from their exciting day and romantic evening, though everyone's attention turned to the extreme wind rattling the windows throughout the apartment. The whole family gathered in the large parlor, watching in amazement as the tall buildings within their view swayed! Mr. B., home in celebration of President Washington's 180th Birthday, tried to guide them away from the windows, though everyone held steadfast.

Mr. B. ventured onto the street below to collect the morning paper but was quite shaken when he returned. He explained that the young "Newsie" who sold him the paper had a gash across his face from being thrown against a building. The morning Times warned of the huge storm arriving from the Midwest, which they now watched from their windows as the winds hurled people across the streets and sent debris into the air. Watching huge buildings moving side-to-side frightened them all.

Following an especially forceful gust, young Minnie moved close to her mother. With a detectable tremble in her voice, she asked, "Are we going to get blown away?"

Mrs. B. comforted Minnie, telling them all, "This building is reinforced to withstand high winds and storms, standards required after the terrible Blizzard of 1888 which killed more than 400 people." They all hoped Mrs. B. was correct.

On Friday, the following day, the New York Times headlines read, "The Big Wind of 1912: New York skyscrapers in peril, as monster gales hurl men and women down city streets". City dwellers awoke to find overnight winds of 70 miles per hour had shattered windows, thrown telephone poles across streets, turned carts upside down, and toppled the 200-foot electric sign outside the Hotel Knickerbocker. There was a huge fire in Brooklyn, but luckily only one life was lost during this horrific storm.

During the afternoon, Miriam went downstairs to see if the postman was able to deliver the mail to their building. Her eyes opened wide when she saw a letter addressed to her in unfamiliar and unsteady penmanship. Miriam tore open the envelope, read it, and burst into tears. She ran upstairs. "Deborah. Come see the letter I just got from my Bubbie. She still loves me! She wishes me to write her! I am so happy! Come read this!"

"Read it to me," said Deborah, sitting on the edge of the bed and patting the spot next to her. Miriam joined her, leaned against Deborah, and began to read.

February 16, 1912

> *My Miriam,*
> *Mis Zetterbaum my friend. Her dahter Sadie. Sadie learn English.*
> *She red you letter. Now rite lettr.*
>
> *I happy yu send letter. I miss yu. Yu mama and yu Tate not tell me*
> *what wrong. Sat Shiva for yu. Everyone verclempt, all choke up. I tat you*
> *find gentile boy. No think be sweet girl Debora. I happy yu found her.*
> *Glad she not shiksa.*
> *Write me more.*
> *I love yu.*
> *Bubbie*

"A *shiksa*?" Deborah asked, as she wiped away the tears running down Miriam's cheeks.

"Yes, a non-Jewish girl," Miriam laughed. "Imagine her thinking that would be worse!" The girls thought about Bubbie's reaction and laughed until they were weak.

"Everything is happening at once! I am so thrilled for you." Deborah exclaimed. "We will enter *Shabbos* this week with gladness in our hearts."

"This is a day of blessings," said Miriam. "I can hardly wait to write Bubbie back, to have her in my life again." Miriam added, "I am thinking of writing to Marjorie, too. I want to tell her what is really happening to me, as I did with Bubbie. She must wonder why I never came back. I am certain my parents would not tell her. I wonder how Marjorie will feel knowing the truth. But I really need a friend right now."

"I know you are excited about Bubbie's response to your letter, but I want you to think hard about writing to Marjorie with the truth. She may not be as accepting as your Bubbie."

Miriam paused a moment. "This letter from Bubbie gives me a little hope Marjorie will not be lost to me forever. She has been my friend since we were little children. I don't want to wait another day to reach out to her. I will write letters to both Marjorie and Bubbie tonight. I know you are worried for me, but I need to do this."

That evening, after dinner, Deborah stayed downstairs while Miriam headed to their room to compose her letters. Miriam sat at their small desk, a sheet of Crane's stationary on the table, a Waterman fountain pen in her hand, and a tear running down her cheek. She began with her letter to Bubbie.

February 22, 1912

Dear Bubbie,

It warmed my heart to hear from you. When I read your words, it felt like you were right here with me. I imagined I could smell your wonderful cooking aromas on the stationary! No one cooks as well as you do, Bubbie. I miss you so very much.

My life here is good. I am living with a wonderful family, the Berkowitzes. They have four adorable girls who range in age from four to ten. The youngest are twins. Mrs. Berkowitz needs to visit her ailing mother for a week or more at a time, so we are here to help the governess when she is gone. They are very sweet children so they add joy to my days.

Deborah is living with me at the Berkowitz home too. It makes me very happy to have her with me all the time. Deborah's mother has been very kind to us but we are afraid to tell Deborah's father about us being together because he might react like Father did.

I am hoping someday I can see you again. I will always love you, Bubbie.

With lots of love,
Miriam

Then, with nervousness and careful wording, Miriam began her letter to Marjorie.

February 22, 1912

Dear Marjorie,

I miss you. I have been afraid to explain why I did not return after my trip to New York for Ruth's wedding. I am certain my parents have not explained anything to you, even if you asked. They sat shiva for me and consider me dead. I am not allowed back into their home or their lives.

The sin I have committed, in their eyes, is to fall in love. You are probably thinking it is with a non-Jewish boy, but that is not the case. I have fallen in love with Deborah, the wonderful girl who came to visit me in Boston in the fall. I love her very much. I wanted so badly to tell you but I was afraid, fearing you would reject me, just like my mother and father have done.

I worry about how you will feel about my loving a girl. I know the rabbis do not accept this, but I hope you can be more understanding. I have been so happy with Deborah. Love is better than we ever imagined in all our talks about finding the perfect boy and getting married. I hope you can be happy for me and not cast me out as a sinner. I want so badly for you to be understanding and be pleased for me. I so want us to continue to be friends.

I have been desperately lonely in New York. I miss my parents, my sister, my Bubbie, and you. I wrote to my Bubbie and she had her friend read my letter and write back to me. In her broken-English, she says she still loves me! Her letter gave me the courage to write to you.

I hope you will write back, and if you do, please let me know how my sister Hannah is doing. I worry about her. I was her only friend and now she is really alone. If you can find it in your heart to speak with her when you see her, it would be wonderful. I know she likes you a lot, yet I fear she will never reach out to you or anyone else. Even if you cannot accept me, maybe you could do this one kindness for me and reach out to Hannah. She needs a friend. I will be forever grateful.

I will continue to consider you a true friend Marjorie, no matter what you decide to do.

Miriam

More than an hour after Miriam went upstairs, Deborah quietly entered the room and asked her swollen-eyed girlfriend, "Is this a good time for me to hear what you have been writing?"

"Yes. Please come in. Thank you for giving some time to gather my thoughts and write these letters. It was exciting to write to Bubbie, but the letter to Marjorie was quite difficult. Here, read my letter to her," Miriam said with a sigh, as she handed it to Deborah.

After reading the letter, Deborah said, "Oh Miriam, that is so like you, worrying about your sister when you are experiencing so much pain and loss yourself. I love you for your concern for others."

"She is my sister. Certainly I am concerned for her. You would care greatly if something were to happen to Anna or Milton, would you not?"

"Yes, but I still love you for your overwhelming compassion in the face of your own adversity. I hope this letter brings Marjorie back into your life. I know she matters a great deal to you and there is almost nothing as important as friends."

They sat together on the edge of the bed for a few minutes, holding hands and each reflecting on their conversation, their friendships, and the risk

Miriam was about to take. Miriam looked directly into her eyes and broke the silence. "I was thinking about friends. When are we going to get together with your girlfriends again, Deborah? We have not seen much of them since we moved here."

"I have been neglectful." Deborah said, clearing her throat. "I have been so worried about you, I have not even thought of them. I will make plans to get together with several of my city friends. Just because we may have found some new friends, I don't want to abandon those already in my life."

Miriam said, "I am certain Mrs. B. would be happy to have you invite them here."

"What a wonderful idea. Do you think we should invite Ruth?"

With some hesitation, Miriam said, "No. I have barely thought of Ruth since the wedding. I think we should go visit her; she is now too pregnant to go out. Thank you for suggesting we connect with her. I have not been to see their new apartment. I assume that either her parents or Michael's family are paying for it, so it must be huge and nicely decorated. We can both put up with her long stories and complaints for one afternoon!"

March 4, 1912

"I am glad we went to see Ruth this morning," said Miriam and she slid onto a chair in their room and let out an audible sigh. "It makes me feel fortunate. Despite everything I have been through, I can experience happiness. I am not sure if Ruth will ever be content. She spent our whole visit complaining."

"She certainly did - About being fat, being uncomfortable, unable to wear pretty clothes, and being stuck in the house," replied Deborah with a sarcastic tone. "And then she complained about her wedding. She did not like the chopped liver, she overheard someone saying she was fat, and Michael did not stay at her side every moment. It just went on and on."

"I can understand complaining about being uncomfortable," Miriam said, shaking her head. "She is really huge and must feel terrible. But everything else felt like whining. I don't know how Michael handles it."

"I wonder about him. I never heard Michael mention the baby. I wonder if he is excited; or maybe he feels trapped," said Deborah.

"I have thought about that myself. He seems quite sullen these days. Not that I ever found him exciting, but he seems more drab than usual. Maybe I should never have encouraged Ruth to get close to him."

"It is not your fault they got together. I assume that she would have acted as she did without your praise of him."

"Enough about Ruth. I don't want us to complain about her. Then we are as bad as Ruth with all her whining."

Miriam's Diary, March 5, 1912

Having new interests and speaking with new people has brought me happiness recently. I have even been more interested in our nighttime activities. For so long I did what I thought Deborah wanted, but my heart was too broken to care. My satisfaction felt like an attempt at relief, rather than the joy we had before.

Tonight I was more enthusiastic. I wanted to touch Deborah's whole body like she did for me on my birthday but she insisted I move right to her special place. She guided my head to exactly the right spot and told me how she wanted me to touch her with my lips and my tongue.

Her reaction was intense. When I was done giving her pleasure, she wanted more. I thought I would never get my turn! Again and again she was satisfied and then insisted I continue. When it was my turn, I was less insistent on repeated pleasures but she would not stop. Each time I felt satisfied, she continued. There were multiple times she brought me to the explosive feelings I have come to expect. I want to repeat this again soon, if I am not too sore!

Peyrek E ✦ *Friends*
Wednesday, March 6, 1912

"I can hardly wait to go to Barnard today," Deborah said with glee, as she and Miriam dressed warmly for the day.

The girls had been going to Barnard for the past several weeks, helping to put the newspaper together and engaging with the student staff. Deborah wrote several articles, including one they chose as the feature piece regarding the Metropolitan Museum. Deborah was thrilled to see her first story in print!

"The Bulletin, has changed us both," Miriam said. "We wake up excited these days. It is really pleasant to be with others our own age and I especially like Susan."

Deborah hesitated, then asked a question which had been on her mind for several days. "Does it bother you when the other girls talk about their boyfriends? Does it make you scared they will figure us out?"

"I don't think of that at all. I just think about the tasks we are doing. Do you worry about that Deborah?"

"I always worry about being different than everyone else. That is how I have always been, concerned people will reject me if they know the truth about me. I want to be more trusting. And, by the way, have you noticed Susan is the one person who never talks about boys?"

"No, I had not noticed. Are you thinking that she might be like us?" Miriam asked.

"I had not thought of that, but maybe we are comfortable with her because she is not one of those girls who is silly about boys. Would you be okay if we told Susan about us?" Deborah asked, cocking her head, waiting for an answer.

"No! She might be offended if we tell her."

"But think of how wonderful we would feel if she was supportive. Or even a girl like us."

On their walk to the school, Deborah thought more about telling Susan of their relationship. While she hesitated to tell old friends, she wanted their new friendships to be based on the truth. As she trudged through the snow, Miriam worried about whether Deborah would tell Susan and worried it would risk their growing friendship.

When they got to the newspaper office, they found several girls sitting around a large table, talking about their classes. Deborah was envious, wishing she could join in their chatter, but instead headed to a quiet corner to plan her next article, "The Suffrage Movement on Campus". Miriam and Susan began typesetting an article Deborah had just finished which compared the Met to Boston's Museum of Fine Arts.

Suddenly, something surprising happened. A tall, stately girl neither Deborah nor Miriam had seen before walked into the office. As she approached, she put her hand on Susan's waist in a way that was quite familiar. Susan looked up at this lovely girl with a warm smile, clearly pleased to see her.

"Miriam," Susan said, "I want you to meet my girlfriend, Helen."

Deborah and Miriam greeted Helen warmly, but dared not look at each other, concerned that their interest in this couple would spark concerns. Susan and Helen began talking excitedly with one another and Miriam tried to concentrate on the papers in front of her, though she could not help glancing frequently at the two of them. Shortly, Helen bid everyone goodbye and Susan turned back to her typesetting, unaware of the focus directed at her. Deborah and Miriam stole a quiet look at one another, smiling and shrugging their shoulders at the same time.

The minute they were away from the office, Miriam chuckled, "I wonder what kind of girlfriends Helen and Susan are? Is it just our wish, or could they be together, like we are? Or maybe they are just good friends. I could tell they really liked each other. How can we figure it out?"

Deborah thought about this for a moment and suggested inviting Susan to go somewhere with them to see if she brings Helen along.

"Great idea," Miriam said. "Let's bring her with us to the Suffrage meeting. She had come with us when we first met her, but she has not been attending. This will be our secret plan," she said, clearly enjoying the intrigue of it all.

March 8, 1912

When Deborah and Miriam arrived at Friday's suffrage meeting they took their places at the table and waited for Susan. Miriam looked up, seeing Susan in the doorway, and feeling a jolt of disappointment. Not one second later, Helen appeared. As they walked into the room arm in arm, glancing at each other with a familiarity, their manner seemed to answer Miriam's question.

Deborah and Miriam exchanged barely perceptible glances as Deborah began her report on the progress she made in getting parade details from some off-campus organizers. The parade was set for 5 pm, with the line up at 4:30. Other area schools were sending representatives too, with all students marching together. Deborah spoke of signs to be made, with slogans like: "President Wilson. How long must women wait for liberty?"; "New York State denies the vote to criminals, lunatics, idiots, and women"; and simply, "Votes for Women." Susan suggested each student wear a blue banner with "Barnard" printed boldly in white, the school colors, to be worn across their chests. Helen offered to create them.

After the meeting, the four young women chatted for over an hour in a nearby lounge, discussing the parade, their lives, their interests. At one point, Susan leaned back in her chair, asking, "How did you two meet?"

After explaining about their mutual friend, Ruth, and the visit to the Berkshires, Deborah asked, "And what about you two? What is your story?"

"We met on campus. We were both taking the same English class and we were assigned to write a story together. We have been friends ever since." It was a safe, unrevealing answer.

The four agreed to meet again on Monday, following another meeting about the May Suffrage parade.

"Susan and Helen are both bright," began Deborah after they left, "and they seem to get along well, no matter what their relationship."

"Does it matter if they are like us? Can't we be their friends anyway?"

"Certainly. I really like them both. But how can I feel open with them if they don't know about me? About the two of us?"

It was Miriam's turn to soothe Deborah's concerns. "I can see how this has been an issue for you for many years, Deborah. Do any of your other friends know about your feelings?"

"No. I never told any of them. But they all knew about the episode with Judith when I was in school. Although we never discussed it, they probably guessed. None of them ever asked me about boys. As a matter of fact, none of them has ever discussed boys either. Now that I think about it, their lack of chatter about boys may have been part of what drew me to them."

Miriam smiled warmly. "I will always love you." She put her hand over Deborah's, but withdrew it quickly, even though there was no one else around.

Susan and Helen

Peyrek F ✤ *Reconnection*
Monday, March 17, 1912

March 10, 1912

Dear Miriam,

I am sorry it has taken me a while to get back to you but I must admit your last letter was quite a shock. I have never known any homosexuals. Well, I guess I knew one, you, but I was never aware. Did you always feel this way about girls? Was this a secret you were hiding from me? Did you have those feelings towards any of our friends?

I am very sorry about your family; you don't deserve being shunned. As you requested, I reached out to Hannah and asked her to take a walk with me. She was awkward and slow to warm up. She is so quiet I never got to know her before. When the two of us were alone, I found her extremely bright, as you have mentioned, with amazing knowledge about art. This interests me also, so it has been fun to talk with her. We have arranged to go to the Museum of Fine Arts next Tuesday. I started by doing this for you, but now I am really enjoying her company. I know that will please you.

As for our friendship, I will always be your friend. I feel a bit awkward. I always thought of us being close but I worry I did not really know you.
Marjorie

March 14, 1912

Dear Marjorie,

I just received your letter. First, I want to tell you how incredibly pleased I am you are still willing to be my friend. I have missed you so much.

Secondly, I want you to know I never had any desire for girls before I met Deborah. It was not something I ever considered. Actually, I did not know love between women existed. I was drawn to Deborah from the moment I met her. I missed her during the winter we were apart and I was thrilled to be back in her company last summer. But I still did not understand my feelings.

Deborah did nothing to rob my innocence. We got acquainted while spending time together. It was entirely surprising and thrilling when we became closer than just friends. Our connection was absolutely mutual. I do not want you to think that Deborah behaved badly. We just fell in love.

Deborah is the most wonderful person I have ever met. She has helped me to be more self-assured, both by example and through guidance. She is strong, yet sensitive. She has supported me through this horrible ordeal with my family in such a loving manner. I feel very fortunate to have met her. I am certain you would like her if you got to know her better.

Please be assured I never kept anything from you when I was growing up. The only time I kept information from you was this fall. I now wish I had been open with you, but I was quite overwhelmed. I should have trusted my secret with you.

I will never be allowed back in my parents' home, so I am not sure if or when I will be back in Boston. I cherish our friendship and I hope to remain in touch with you. It may just have to be through our letters.

Chag Same'ach. Have a wonderful Passover.

With Love,

Miriam

March 20, 1912

Dear Miriam,

It was wonderful to get your letter. I am relieved you have not been keeping secrets from me all these years. I am sorry you did not feel safe telling me about your closeness to Deborah when I last saw you. But I completely understand. I am not sure, if I were in the same situation, I would have behaved any differently.

I had a wonderful day at the museum with Hannah. Her knowledge about art is outstanding. Now that she is comfortable with me, she has become quite talkative. I have invited her to come to my house this week for tea, though I doubt she will talk much with the rest of my family. I will let you know how that goes.

I have been thinking differently since our correspondence. I have been looking at people who are not like me and I now realize they have a right to live as they wish. I don't think I have ever met women like the two of you, but maybe I am wrong. You have opened up my eyes, and I thank you for that.

Chag Same'ach. I will write again soon.

With Love,

Marjorie

Peyrek G ✤ *Next Steps*
Thursday, March 21, 1912

One evening, after dinner, Deborah and Miriam sat in the comfortable chairs in the corner of their room and Deborah asked, "Have you ever thought of going to college, Miriam?"

"I never considered it until we started spending time at Barnard. The girls we meet there love their courses."

"I have been thinking about it a great deal lately. I miss going to school and being exposed to so many new ideas. I wonder if I could take an English class in the fall. What about you, Miriam?"

She thought for a moment, "I don't know if school is right for me. I have other thoughts. I would love to make a difference for people who are less fortunate than me. Yesterday I talked with two girls at The Bulletin who plan to be social workers. They have already started to work with people in need and find it satisfying to be of assistance.

The girls told me about the 'Bread and Roses Strike' which has been going on for the past couple months in Lawrence, Massachusetts, not far from Boston. The textile mill workers are striking to keep current work hours so that their pay will not be cut. They need the money to support their families. It is making world news."

Miriam continued, "They also talked of the horrible fire here last week at the Triangle Shirtwaist Factory when over 140 garment workers were trapped in the building and died. Most of them were young Jewish girls."

"Reading about it in the newspaper made me weep," Deborah said.

A disturbed look overtook Miriam's face. "I like how these students are helping others. That's what I want to do!"

Deborah encouraged Miriam to look into this further, since college is not a requirement to do this type of work. "I heard Susan mention she was going to volunteer at a settlement house, helping young women down on their luck. Why don't you ask her about it?"

"I will ask when we get together with Susan and Helen this afternoon. I would love to do something meaningful with my days. Not that the work on the student newspaper and the Suffrage parade is not important, but I want to do even more," said Miriam.

Deborah mentioned that Miriam no longer had the youngsters at her temple or the little girl in her old neighborhood to care for, so it would be wise to find some other outlets.

Miriam scowled a bit and said, "I miss Leah. I feel badly that her world is small again, yet I am certain there are other children here I could help."

"I am thrilled that we both found new interests that will add meaning to our lives," Deborah said with wide eyes and a large grin. "I am going to find out about enrolling in school. I am certain my parents will pay the class fees."

The more Deborah thought about it, the more she was intrigued with the idea of being a college student. She always loved to write and an English degree would be the perfect direction for her. She thought how she would love to be on the campus officially, rather than as a visitor.

The girls stopped at the Levine's on their way home so Deborah could talk with her parents. As she expected, her mother was pleased with her college plan, and, without hesitation, her father agreed to pay for her schooling. She would sign up for classes the very next day.

Saying out loud that she would like to work with people less fortunate than herself, excited Miriam. She discussed this with the other girls and they told her lots about the settlement house movement. She loved the idea of working with poor women and children, in hopes she could help them change their lives.

Susan decided to work with the University Settlement Society and Miriam decided to explore the Henry Street Settlement, both on the Lower East Side. Miriam chose Henry Street because it was developed by a Jewish woman, Lillian Wald, who was related to someone at her temple in Boston. She made plans to go to Henry Street after Passover to see if they could use some help.

Bread and Roses strike

April 1, 1912

The Berkowitzes were away, so Deborah and Miriam headed to the Levines for Passover. As they dressed in their nicest holiday clothing, Deborah said, "My parents will have 17 people coming to our Passover Seder tonight, including distant relatives, Ruth's whole family, and a couple of local college students who were unable to get home to be with their families. I love the practice of inviting people to our table who have no Seder of their own."

"We are always inviting people to our Seder too," said Miriam, with a tinge of sadness.

Before the guests arrived, the girls came downstairs to admire the table, set with the special Passover dishes that had been stored away since last year. As Miriam focused on the Seder plate, containing the symbolic foods for the upcoming ritual meal, tears came to her eyes. She recalled the lovely Seder plate her family used every year, the care that Bubbie took to roast the shank bone and the egg, and how Bubbie's eyes watered as she cut up the horseradish. Miriam helped make the *charoses* with its mixture of chopped apples, walnuts, and honey. Although all these traditional dishes would be at the Levine's Seder, she knew it would not be the same.

Deborah saw Miriam's tears, saying, "I am so sorry that you are not able to be with your own family during this holiday. I know how difficult it must be for you." She touched Miriam's hand and looked at her lovingly.

Triangle Shirtwaist Factory fire

"I am sad, but I look forward to making new traditions with you and your family."

Deborah tried to lighten Miriam's mood by saying, "Luckily, the reading of the prayer book does not last five hours, as at my parents' Seder when they were children. We learned to serve many foods to snack on during the service, so no one is overly hungry by the time the meal is served. And our four cups of wine are very small, so no one falls asleep before the end of the meal, as my father's uncle often did."

Miriam smiled, "My Bubbie is often asleep before dessert, even though she only has four sips of wine when everyone else has their four small cups. She rarely is awake for the continuation of the service after the dinner. I never saw her eat the *afikomen*, the piece of *matzoh* that ends the meal."

Mrs. Levine came into the room for a last-minute inspection of the table, and Mr. Levine could be heard in the next room, practicing the prayers. Although it was the same service every year, he wanted to make certain his voice was ready for many hours of chanting.

"Everything looks lovely," said Miriam, attempting a smile.

"Why thank you," said Mrs. Levine. "I hope that you enjoy our service."

Then Deborah led Miriam back upstairs to their room. She wanted to have some time to talk to Miriam before everything got hectic. "How are you doing?" Deborah asked.

"I have mixed feelings. I love your family but I miss my family and our traditions. We have a long service, with my father reading the Hebrew so quickly no one can keep up. He mumbles for a long time then reveals the page on which he is reading. My Bubbie leaves the kitchen several times to ask if it is time to peel the hard-boiled eggs. We all laugh and ask her what prayer is said with the eggs, knowing perfectly well there is no prayer, even though the salted eggs are part of the service. Hannah always tells a story of the eggs being the only food which gets harder the longer they cook. She compares this to the Jews, who got stronger as they toiled harder. I will miss all these things."

What Miriam did not say is how worried she is about Passover with the Levine family. She knows they change all their plates and their pots and pans and they only buy food that is kosher for Passover, but she is not sure if their spiritual focus is as strong as she is used to. It will be hard to be somewhere new for this special holiday, which has so much meaning for her.

It was a delightful night, with their Barnard friends, Deborah's cousins, and Ruth, whose belly was quite large. She was calmer than usual, which was a pleasant change. The rest of the Gold family was also easier to tolerate, especially since Mr. Gold kept his booming voice down. During the meal, Miriam noticed that Ruth did not eat much and that she left the table several times to go to the water closet. Michael did not follow her.

Mr. Levine created a lovely service, skipping enough pages in the Passover book, the *Haggadah*, so they were not stuck silent for hours while he recited prayer after prayer. He included the children several times, and he encouraged all the youth to ask "The Four Questions," instead of just the youngest child, as is the tradition. During the meal, everyone took part in lively conversation, so animated it could have been heard in the next apartment. It was quite late when everyone departed, full from the plentiful meal and the spirit of the Passover holiday.

Miriam got through it and even enjoyed it, and the girls had passed another milestone together.

Seder plate

Peyrek H ❀ *College*
Thursday, April 4, 1912

"I have registered for two classes for next semester," said Deborah, rushing into the Berkowitz home. Miriam was the only person near the door when she bounded in, so she got an earful. Deborah was so excited she would have told the cook, if she had been the first person she saw!

"I have begun filling out forms, asking for formal acceptance. Did you know Fredrick Barnard, the President of Columbia College, tried to admit women starting 14 years ago? When he was unsuccessful, he created this separate women's college on the west side of the Columbia campus. The new Dean, Miss Gildersleve, hopes to enable married women and mothers to teach there, though they cannot even teach in the New York Public Schools. That's progress!"

"I love your animation, but slow down Deborah, so I can hear it all!"

"There is so much I want to tell you. I looked through the Mortarboard, the college yearbook. The Equal Suffrage League of New York State was listed as one club and I already belong to that one without even being a student! I would need to join a fraternity, since that is a requirement of all students."

"Whoa," Miriam piped in. "Your enthusiasm is overwhelming. You cannot do it all. You won't have any time for me! And the children will miss you if you are gone all the time."

"I know I can't do everything, but I am so excited by what the school offers. I can imagine myself as a student and I can even picture myself walking in the procession for graduation."

"How about trying one semester at a time? You are already busy graduating!" said Miriam with a full grin.

"You are laughing at me! I am so happy. I wonder why I never thought of this before. I have always been a good student, but I never imagined going to college."

Deborah tried to slow down, but it was like corralling a horse, which had other things on its mind. Realizing she was focused only on her good news, she said, "And after Passover ends, please look into the settlement house movement for yourself. I want you to be as excited as I am."

"I promise I will do that," said Miriam. "Now, how about some *matzoh brie*?"

Peyrek I ❧ *Henry Street Settlement*
Tuesday, April 9, 1912

Now it was Miriam's turn for excitement, telling Deborah and Mrs. B. about her experience during her first day volunteering at the settlement house. "From the moment I walked into the Henry Street Settlement House, I knew I belonged there. It is a like a village, with many separate buildings and a new gymnasium. They built a large public playground, the first anywhere, so the neighborhood children can play outdoors safely. There are so many services for poor, immigrant women and children."

She explained how Lillian Wald, the woman who founded Henry Street, was the only nurse there for a long time. During the winters, when navigating the snowy streets was difficult, she would travel from house to house by jumping from one roof to another!

"It is wonderful you feel at ease there," Mrs. B. said. "Tell us what you will be doing."

"I don't know yet, but my work will focus on the Jewish children." She told them of the children running up to her, grabbing her skirt, many of them speaking only Yiddish.

Deborah said, "Children will love you, whether you know their language or not. You have a natural way with all youngsters."

"I certainly hope so," Miriam replied, smiling.

Two days later, Miriam and Deborah sat in their bedroom, with Miriam telling of her first days at Henry Street. "I met one ten-year-old girl who has been coming to the Settlement House for the past year, so her command of English was quite good. She told me of her home in a three-room tenement apartment with her parents, an aunt, an uncle, her older brother, and baby sister. The family manages the rent by taking in borders, so five adults and three children live there. Can you imagine? In that tiny space? But the government now has rules to make sure there are two bathrooms for the four families living on each floor. And every surface becomes a bed at night. In the daytime, their apartment becomes a workspace, run by her father and uncle, with three girls arriving by 7:00am to do piecework. Every day the girls make just enough to put food on their family dinner table, so if a worker is sick, her family may not eat that evening. It is such a difficult life."

"It is hard to imagine living that way," Deborah said, glancing around at her own comfortable surroundings.

Just then, Mrs. B. arrived with the twins Margie and Minnie, who ran inside.

"Please sit with us," Deborah said to Mrs. B, pointing to the other rocker. "Miriam was telling me about the children she met."

Miriam looked directly at Mrs. B and said, "This experience makes me grateful for everything I have. If it were not for the generous nature of your family, I might be at this settlement house as a client, not as a volunteer."

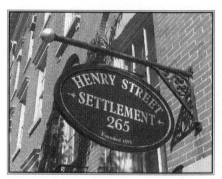

The Henry Street Settlement sign

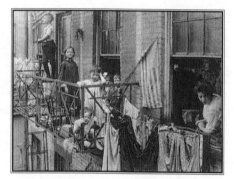

Lillian Wald with children

The Henry Street Settlement House

Peyrek J ❀ *Governess Duties*
Friday, April 12, 1912

After Passover, Deborah and Miriam settled into a regular routine, with Miriam heading to Henry Street two days each week and Deborah writing articles and preparing for school in the fall. The girls also worked on the upcoming Suffrage Parade. The attendance estimates kept growing, with more than 5,000 women now expected to march.

"Things are about to get very hectic for us," Miriam announced as Deborah walked into the house. "Mrs. B. got a telegram. Her mother is not doing well and she is upstairs, packing to head to Queens right away. We are in charge of the girls, along with Bridget."

"But how will we take care of the children and also do our work?" Deborah asked. "The Suffrage parade is only a few weeks away and I have articles to write."

"Stop. Don't get all worked up. We must care for the girls. If you stay calm, we can figure it all out," Miriam said.

"But how will we manage…"

"Stop saying 'but'. We will figure it out," Miriam said forcefully, with frustration in her tone. "Calm down. We have to think of Mrs. B.'s needs right now."

"You are right, of course. You are always right. I will calm down and let you do the thinking."

"Thank you, Deborah. I appreciate your willingness to put this family first. They are sweet, well-behaved children, but each with different needs. If I had not been there to stop the twins, they would have built a tower of rocks right underneath a hornets' nest in the park. Minnie is a young seven-year-old, asking for help with practically everything. Sometimes she seems younger than the twins. I am grateful for Fannie. She is a grownup ten-year-old. She talks back a little, so I fear adolescence will come early for her."

Over the next few days, Deborah was grateful Miriam and Bridget took over the majority of the child-minding duties. Bridget, a freckle-faced, red-haired Irish girl of 16, was at ease and easily in charge.

Miriam encouraged Deborah to go to the college on her regular two days. And though Deborah offered to mind the girls so Miriam could go to Henry Street, she was relieved when Miriam refused. Bridget watched all four girls so they could both attend a Suffrage meeting; the parade was only three weeks away. In the midst of all their duties, they also thought of Ruth, who was due to have her baby any day. They were almost too busy to think about the future.

Peyrek K ✣ *Extra! Extra!*
Tuesday, April 16, 1912

As everyone sat quietly in the parlor, Deborah rushed into the house. "The Titanic sank!"

"What do you mean? It's supposed to be unsinkable," Miriam called out, wide-eyed.

"Bridget!" they both exclaimed, looking directly at the distraught girl.

"'Tis impossible," Bridget said, tears rolling down her face. "It cannot be true. My aunt and uncle were steerage passengers on that boat, coming from Ireland with my four little cousins for a better life. They sold everything they had to come here to get rich," Bridget muttered, weeping.

Miriam put her arms around the sobbing girl, asking Deborah, "Was anyone saved?"

"The newspaper said the lifeboats saved some of the women and children."

"Oh, I pray the little ones were saved and my aunt. How do I find out?" she asked with a wail.

"You must go be with your parents, Bridget," Miriam offered. "They may get information. Do you need me to go with you?"

"I am sure she can get home okay," said Deborah, panicking. Miriam immediately read Deborah's fear: she would be alone with the four girls.

"Thank you, but I will take leave of you on my own. That is my mother's sister on the ship and I need to be with her. Can you manage with the children?"

"We will be fine," Miriam said, looking towards Deborah.

"I will be off right away then," said Bridget, gathering her things and heading out the door.

Turning to the children, who had been listening, Miriam explained, "There was a very large boat. One of the biggest boats ever. It sank last night and many people were killed. Bridget had cousins from Ireland coming to America on that boat. She is going home to see if her relatives have been saved."

"What are lifeboats?" asked Fannie. "Do they keep people alive and give them a new life?"

Miriam almost smiled at the innocent question but somberly answered, "They are small boats to carry people to safety. Right now, we need to hope Bridget's family and many others were saved."

Deborah explained, "I was not able to get my own copy of the newspaper. Lots of us looked over the shoulders of anyone holding a paper. I read the boat hit an iceberg."

"What is a iceberg?" asked Minnie. "Is it like a big ice cube?"

"I think it is," said Miriam. "The ship was out at sea, so it must be a giant ice cube on the water."

"Later I will fill you in on what I know," Deborah whispered to Miriam.

The girls went to bed without a fuss, but they each had questions about the death of the passengers, with Miriam answering their questions as best she could. She wished their parents were home to discuss these difficult issues with them. But they would be long asleep by the time Mr. B. returned for the night.

Alone finally, Deborah said, "I heard 1,200 people may have perished. There were famous people in first class listed in the paper. One of those who probably perished was John Jacob Astor, IV, the owner of the Knickerbocker Hotel, where we were for Ruth and Michael's wedding."

"How very sad. So many lost lives." Miriam said softly.

"Possibly as many as 800 people were saved, most probably all from first class. Nothing was said of those in steerage. It is likely all of Bridget's family has died. April 15, 1912 will be remembered in history for this horrible tragedy."

Deborah changed the subject. "What are we going to do about watching the children? Do you think we can manage on our own until Mrs. B. or Bridget return? I am nervous about having full responsibility," Deborah said sheepishly.

"We will do just fine. I am not worried. But we will have to give up all our other activities, even the parade. There is nothing we can do about this horrid situation."

"We need to give up things," echoed Deborah, "but not the parade! We have worked so hard. Maybe we can find someone to watch the children for that one day."

"We still have three weeks. Hopefully Bridget or Mrs. B. will return by that time. In the meantime, we must focus on the children. I am just grateful the cook is here and Mr. B. returns each evening. I can't imagine what it would be like if they were not available."

Deborah laughed, "It would be as if we had four daughters! All of a sudden, Deborah stopped speaking. Then, slowly, she spoke words she had never said before, "I never had a desire for children. What about you? You are so wonderful with them. Did you always dream of having a houseful of your own?"

"I always wanted two children. But now we have the Berkowitz family and your sister and brother, so I have children in my life. I do ache to have some of my own, but you satisfy my need to be loved."

"You have filled my life too, Miriam. I know we are exhausted but let's try to stay awake for a while tonight so I can show you how much I love you."

New York Times and Yiddish newspaper cover sinking of the Titanic

Peyrek L ❖ *Baby Sylvia*
Wednesday, April 17, 1912

Deborah was busy feeding the children afternoon snacks when Miriam came into the room and said, "I need to talk with you privately for a moment."

Miriam quietly said, "I just got a telegram from Mrs. Gold. Ruth had her baby yesterday, a little girl she named Sylvia. But things are not right. There is something wrong with the baby."

"What did she say?" Deborah asked.

Miriam read, "April 17: Ruth had baby yesterday. Girl. Sylvia. Baby not healthy."

"What could be wrong? Do you think Ruth can manage a child who is not perfect?" asked Deborah.

"I cannot imagine. I would head to the hospital right now, if I could. Once Mrs. B or Bridget returns, I will go there directly."

Miriam turned to the little girls. "Our friend Ruth just had her baby. She named her Sylvia, a pretty name."

Two days later, Bridget returned to work, grieving for the loss of her family, but providing relief for the girls. She needed her salary, despite the tragedy of the Titanic.

"I know she needs the money," Miriam said, "She told me so. But how awful to leave her grieving mother so soon. She looks horrible today, like she cried all night."

"I am sure she did. Just think how sad she must be, losing her family," Deborah said without thinking.

"I know," Miriam said, "She is probably as sad as I have been, losing my whole family." Miriam grimaced but did not fault Deborah for her comment.

Deborah said softly, "Sorry. That was insensitive of me."

"It is okay, "Miriam replied. Then, with an upbeat change in her tone, she said, "Let's go see Ruth at the hospital."

That afternoon, Deborah and Miriam headed to Mt. Sinai Hospital on Lexington Avenue and 66th to visit Ruth and her new baby. This hospital, once called "Jews Hospital" because of its mission to serve poor Jewish immigrants, was now the finest Jewish hospital in the city. They entered the large multi-building complex, glad the woman at the front desk gave clear directions.

In the maternity ward, they found Ruth, a sad new mother, but no baby with her. They asked the nurse to bring Sylvia to the room, assuming Ruth would want to show off her infant. When Sylvia was brought in, Miriam picked up the little bundle and held onto her for their whole visit.

Sylvia was quite pretty, with wisps of light colored hair and a round face, yet the baby was clearly not normal. Her eyes had a slightly unusual slant and her mouth gaped open. This was not the perfect child Ruth anticipated and Miriam was surprised Ruth never held the baby the whole time. Even when Sylvia cried, Ruth just watched as Miriam comforted her.

Little Sylvia was a tiny, sweet baby. Miriam, mesmerized, had never held a brand-new baby before. Sylvia was so small she barely fit into the crook of her arm. Miriam smelled the sweet infant smell and listened to her coo. She could not help but think she would never have the opportunity to hold her own baby in her arms. Miriam looked to Ruth, wishing the new mother would show some interest. She feared that was not to be.

Deborah and Miriam left the hospital silent but shaken. The visit had been as emotional as the rest of their recent experiences. It was sad to see Ruth so upset and to sense her disinterest in her own baby. The girls felt helpless.

Sylvia

Peyrek M ✷ *Crisis in Boston*
Friday, April 19, 1912

April 19, 1912

> *My Miriam;*
> *Sadie help me rite agan. I need tell you Tate, you fatha very sick.*
> *He hav harts attak. He in hospitol. he be ok. So much tsoriss, sufering.*
> *Hannah to print shop to help Wilam.*
> *We al scare. Wish you be here. But plez no come.*
> *Love, Bubbie*

April 24, 1912

> *Dear Bubbie,*
> *Thank you so much for writing to me. I am upset my father is ill and I cannot be there. I know it would not be good for him if I were to show up so I would never do that. I hope that his worry about me did not have anything to do with his heart attack.*
> *I love you and I wish the whole family well. Please write me again to tell me how he is.*
> *Love,*
> *Miriam*

"Deborah. So much has happened today," Miriam called out before Deborah had gotten through the doorway. "My Bubbie wrote to tell me my father had a heart attack. I am scared and sad I cannot be there. I wrote a letter back to Bubbie and I was just about to leave to post it."

"I am so sorry," replied Deborah. "I will go with you to the Post Office but let's talk first. Do you know how bad it is?"

"Bubbie wrote he will be okay, but I do not know for sure. She also said Hannah is going to the publishing shop to help out. Father has just one employee, William, who is very bright but a bit odd. I cannot quite picture the two of them, Hannah and William, running the shop!"

"They will be an odd pair for sure. Hopefully your father will recover quickly and get back to work soon."

Miriam smiled at Deborah, thought for a moment, then bit her lips. She took a deep breath, saying, "I want to talk to you about something else. I have been thinking of writing to Hannah. I wonder if this is the right time."

"You certainly are a brave girl. You know she is unlikely to write back. What if she writes you a note which condemns you for your behavior?"

"Hannah would never do that," Miriam said emphatically.

"I certainly hope not," Deborah said, as they walked out the door, heading for the post office. "If you do write this letter, may I please read it before you post it?"

"Absolutely. Thank you, my love. I will write as soon as we get back."

April 24, 1912

Dear Hannah;

I have missed you so much, my sweet sister. I think of you all the time. I have started to write many times but thought it kinder to stay out of your life. But I felt I had to write to you now, since I just heard from Bubbie about Father's heart attack. I want you to know you are not alone in being scared. I am so very upset about Father.

I hope that anger about me has not caused him to have this heart attack. I know how stressful this has been for me and I am sure it is equally upsetting to all of you. I promise I will not try to contact him or see him because I do not want to add any tension to the family. I love you all too much to cause you any more pain.

Bubbie also tells me you have been going to the publishing shop. I know you have not spent much time there, so that must be hard. Is William teaching you things so you can be helpful? I am sure you are learning quickly, but it must be hard. This is a terrible time.

I know you have tried to put me out of your mind. I have tried to do the same but I still cry almost every day. I miss you all so very much. I know how upset you were after finding me with Deborah that day. She did not force me into anything. We fell in love, to the surprise of both of us. I hope you find love someday. Love is the most wonderful feeling I have ever experienced.

I would happily tell you more about my life but I am not sure if you want to know. If you do, please write back, and I will tell you all the things that have happened over these past four months. For now, I will just tell you I am safe and happy.

I love you.

Miriam

Peyrek N ❖ *Suffrage Parade*
Monday, May 6, 1912

The past weeks had been difficult. Miriam and Deborah faced being alone with the four girls, the death of Bridget's family, sadness about Ruth's baby, and the letter from Boston. Somehow, they put aside their woes and looked forward to the Suffrage parade.

This day was about getting the vote for women. Spending time with all the brilliant students at Barnard taught Deborah and Miriam about the power of women together. Both were convinced females should have their fair say in politics, adding a practical perspective to governmental decisions. They hoped to convince others that the women's vote would make the country stronger.

Deborah called out loudly, over the roar of voices, "Miriam. Our group is gathering near the beginning of the parade route. Let's find our way through the crowds to find the other students."

Miriam watched the huge crowd with great excitement, thrilled to see so many women risking their safety to ask for the right to vote. After just a few minutes in this crowd of women, Miriam shouted, "I see our group. I see my sign, 'BARNARD GIRLS FIGHT FOR WOMEN'S VOTING RIGHTS'. I will be so proud to carry it."

Deborah, then, saw her own sign, held aloft by a student who was waiting for her, 'IT IS UNJUST FOR HALF THE COUNTRY TO BE DENIED THE RIGHT TO VOTE!' "Oh," Deborah said. "There are Susan and Helen."

The enthusiasm of the crowds was enormous. Most delegations of women wore white, with banners draped across their chests, creating a vision of brightness as far as the eye could see. Others were dressed in their long darks coats and wide-brimmed hats, as if strolling in Central Park. There were some supportive men in the parade and many clapping wildly along the route. The marchers were students, teachers, mothers, doctors, lawyers, nurses, musicians, clerks, and factory workers, who came together to fight for women's right to vote.

Miriam and Deborah, Helen and Susan, all felt it was a privilege to march. They walked proudly, convinced they were fighting for a just cause. It was orderly and somewhat festive, surprising since the right for women to vote was a serious concern.

The foursome walked arm in arm, feeling a strong kinship. None of them had yet to describe their relationships to one another but their connections were apparent.

The parade was wondrous, without incident. Riding home on the subway, they chatted excitedly with all the strangers around them, sharing a bond with everyone who experienced this magnificent day. None of the girls had experienced camaraderie like this before. They were so proud of what they had done, hoping they had accomplished their goal of gaining voting rights for the women of New York.

When they got home, they found Mrs. B. waiting anxiously. They never considered that she had feared for their safety. As they tried to explain their feelings to her, their words tumbled out and each could barely catch her breath. Mrs. B. smiled broadly, enjoying their excitement. Although she was in favor of women voting, neither Deborah nor Miriam felt she understood the power so many women could express.

Deborah, energized about the parade, spent the rest of the evening writing a piece for the school newspaper. When she shared it with Miriam before they went to bed, both girls grinned and had tears of happiness in their eyes. That night, there was excitement streaming through both their bodies, expressed in passionate loving.

The next morning, the newspapers claimed the parade was historic, with more demonstrators gathered in New York City than for any previous rally. Both girls marveled at estimates of tens of thousands of participants and up to 100,000 spectators.

Suffrage Parade

I have never done anything as significant as participating in the march for Women's Suffrage. I looked at the sea of mostly women, estimated to be up to 60,000 strong, and I felt a connection with each and every person. The power of these masses was enormous.

We are making progress in our fight for equality. In October, California became the sixth state to add voting rights for women and it nearly doubled the number of women with the right to vote in this country. I am convinced that the show of solidarity today, on the day before President Woodrow Wilson's inauguration, will have the needed impact to encourage our legislature to pass the Suffrage Act in New York. Harriet Stanton Blatch and the Women's Political Union have made this Suffrage Parade a land-mark event. The journalists can no longer avoid the power of women. The right to vote must become a statewide referendum. It is time for economic and political justice and for the full rights of women.

When Deborah saw her words in print a couple of days later, tears came to her eyes. She was proud she had captured the intensity of the day. Miriam felt pride for her girlfriend's accomplishment. They were certain the New York referendum would pass.

Suffragists march for women's right to vote

Peyrek O ✤ *Baby Love*
Wednesday, May 8, 1912

It was nearing time for the Berkowitz family to move back to the Berkshires. Mrs. B.'s mother had improved enough to join them in Lenox for the summer. The family began planning for their belongings to be sent ahead.

Deborah and Miriam visited Ruth's home together twice during the week after the parade. Both times they found Ruth in bed; the infant with the baby nurse. They found the situation disturbing, and they cut each visit shorter than they would have, had she been more engaged.

May 13, 1912

After a third troubling visit to Ruth and Sylvia, Deborah pulled the baby nurse aside, asking, "Does Ruth spend much time with the baby?"

"No Mam. Practically no time. Ruth sleeps all day and does not care to see the baby except when she needs to be fed."

Deborah and Miriam tried to talk to Ruth about her role as a mother, but she seemed distracted. It was hard to know if it was because of her blue mood or because she did not want to deal with a child who was imperfect. Either way, it was not a good situation. Miriam was especially concerned, stopping by Ruth's house almost every weekday on her way home from the settlement house, even though it was not convenient.

Miriam told Deborah, "I am very concerned for little Sylvia's welfare. Ruth's baby needs love and attention as much as any baby, if not more. I have not seen Ruth hold the baby a single time. It is almost as if the baby disgusts her. Don't you think it would affect such a tiny a child to be unloved by her own mother?"

Deborah shook her head sadly. "Perhaps we should talk with Mrs. B. With four children of her own, she knows about babies."

Mrs. B. was helpful. She shared Miriam's concerns and suggested they bring the baby home for a visit. The girls would fuss over the newborn and make her feel loved. Miriam suspected Mrs. B. missed having a tiny baby in her arms.

To Miriam and Deborah's delight, Ruth was willing to let them bring tiny Sylvia to the Berkowitz home for regular visits. Miriam admitted she enjoyed visiting with the baby more than visiting a very sad Ruth. Miriam actually found Ruth less offensive in this condition but it was upsetting to see her with no life in her eyes. She had been like this for the entire month since the baby was born.

Deborah and Miriam also talked about the lack of involvement of Sylvia's grandparents. Neither could understand why both Ruth's and Michael's families seemed uninterested in their first grandchild. Were they ashamed of the premarital pregnancy? Now that Ruth and Michael were married, that seemed less relevant. The girls sadly concluded they were probably ashamed of having a special child who they could not brag about. This was not a baby who would go on to achieve great things in life. It was unfortunate that they could not embrace this child for her sweetness.

May 14, 1912

Over breakfast, when Miriam announced she was going to pick up Sylvia for a visit, Bridget came to Miriam, "I was thinking. I would love to care for the babe. I love the babies and it helps so much to hold her. My family has been so unhappy since the loss of my aunt and her little ones," said Bridget with a downturned glance. "I love to have a baby in my arms, and Sylvia is very easy. She rarely cries and I will welcome time with the little one."

May 17, 1912

In the weeks before their return to the Berkshires, Deborah and Miriam saw Sylvia daily. Deborah had never spent much time with an infant before and she had to learn the basics of feeding, dressing, changing, and washing. She thought they just ate, messed their diapers, and cried. When Sylvia responded to Deborah's voice as well as Miriam's, Deborah's heart was tugged. Over time, when Miriam was occupied, she spent periods alone with the baby. Both girls found Sylvia to be an easy baby to love.

"Miriam! I am in the living room with Sylvia. Come see what she is doing!" Deborah called loudly.

Deborah could hardly contain her enthusiasm. "She held her head up by herself! I know you said newborns often do that, but she has not done that before."

"She did it again!" Miriam said, as she kissed Deborah on the head and reached for the baby.

The two of them sat on the couch, discussing the move back to Great Barrington. Miriam admitted she was worried about Sylvia being left alone with just Ruth and the baby nurse. Michael was not much help, as he was studying at the University. They could not leave town with the rest of the family because of his upcoming graduation. Mrs. Gold remained surprisingly uninvolved with the infant, so she would be of no assistance either.

Miriam said, "It will only be a few weeks until Michael's graduation. What if baby Sylvia travels with us to the Berkshires and we can watch her until her family arrives?"

"That is a wonderful idea," said Deborah, smiling, "But would that be alright with Mrs. B. and of course, Ruth?"

Once the girls got Mrs. B.'s approval, Miriam was ready to make the suggestion to Ruth. She would explain they could care for the baby for the two weeks until she and Michael arrived. Miriam thought this plan would give Ruth an opportunity to gather her strength, as she had been quite weak since the birth. She also thought it would give the baby constant love and attention during these formative weeks.

Miriam tried to imagine what Ruth was thinking. Did she feel inadequate to care for a baby with such special needs? Did she think Miriam could do better? Did she think having a damaged child was her just-reward for getting pregnant out of wedlock? Did she feel guilty she was not being a caring mother? Was she worried she had disappointed her family, first with the pregnancy and then with a child who was not normal? Was she upset she was no longer carefree? Was she unhappy with her marriage? Thoughts swirled in Miriam's head as she practiced what she would say to Ruth.

Miriam went to Ruth's house alone. Since she and Ruth were friends first, she felt she should make such a personal suggestion herself. Deborah agreed Miriam should go alone but was worried that Ruth would be offended by the offer, and more worried about Miriam's reaction if Ruth refused. Deborah knew how unhappy Miriam would be to be apart from Sylvia for two weeks.

Miriam arrived at the Gold's midafternoon and was quickly led into Ruth's bedroom. As she expected, the baby was not there. She approached Ruth timidly, not wanting to make Ruth feel worse than she was already feeling. "Hello Ruth. How are you today?"

"The same," was the unemotional answer she received from Ruth.

"I worry about you, Ruth. You have not been your cheerful self since Sylvia was born." She paused, but Ruth said nothing, then continued, "We've been spending time with the baby to help you regain your strength. We hope it gives you time to heal. Has that been helping?

Ruth muttered, "I guess so."

"Oh, Ruth, you are so sad. Are you getting any pleasure at all from your baby?

"Not really."

Miriam blew out a couple short breaths, then proceeded. "Deborah and I have been thinking. Would it be helpful for us to take the baby for a couple weeks while you recover from the birth? We could take her to the Berkshires with us. You could reunite when you and Michael move to Great Barrington and you are feeling stronger."

"That would be fine," Ruth said, flatly.

"Really? I don't want to upset you further, but we hope you might get past this blue mood without the baby to care for right now."

"I just don't care about anything."

Heartsick and worrying about Ruth, Miriam offered her a hug, but Ruth sat stiffly, not able to take in the warmth Miriam offered. "Do you need to ask Michael or your parents?"

"No. You can take her. I will tell Michael. He does not seem to care much for the baby anyway."

Ruth called the nurse from Sylvia's room and suggested she pack the baby supplies for a trip next week. She told the nurse she would not be needed for two weeks but offered to pay her wages during this time. Miriam noticed Ruth never mentioned Sylvia by name.

Miriam, shaken and with nothing else to say to Ruth, visited with Sylvia instead. Miriam's eyes welled up when she saw the baby and, picking her up from her bassinet, she held her especially tight. She did not know if her tears were for the joy of having two whole weeks together or whether it was sadness that Ruth did not love her baby.

When Miriam walked in the door at home, she found Deborah, shoulders hunched, waiting in the living room. Miriam's nod told Deborah everything she needed to know and her shoulder's relaxed immediately. They held each other tightly, though it was atypical for them to display physical affection in public. No one was around to witness this, but they separated when they heard little feet approaching.

They took this opportunity to tell the four girls about their plans to bring Sylvia to the Berkshires. The children were tremendously excited, jumping up and down and offering hugs to both Deborah and Miriam. Everyone had become attached to Sylvia's sweet smile.

May 20, 1912

The New York referendum for the voting rights of women failed.

Peyrek P ❧ *Return to the Berkshires*
Wednesday, May 29, 1912

"We are here!" shouted Ethel from the bright red Oldsmobile "limited" Tournabout, the fancy six-cylinder automobile the Berkowitzes had purchased for their Lenox home. The flashy car made heads turn as they drove down the country roads.

"Shhh. The baby is sleeping," Miriam said as she covered Sylvia's ears from the shouting nine-year-old.

Their staff greeted them warmly. Some travelled ahead by train from New York and others were locals joining them for the summer. The servants helped everyone out of the car, rushed the little girls to the toilet, and brought the others to the porch, where they had a variety of drinks and snacks waiting.

As Miriam headed up the stairs with the wonderful extra bundle of sweetness in her arms, she had a strange feeling of coming home. Deborah was at her side and there would now be a baby in their lives, even if just temporarily. They smiled at the bassinet awaiting Sylvia in their familiar turret room and Miriam placed the infant in her bed, careful not wake her.

Miriam thought, if I had fallen for a boy instead of Deborah, things might be so very different. This could be our own baby and she would be able to stay with us forever. Instead, she is just our borrowed child, soon to return to Ruth and Michael.

The first few days back in the turret room in Lenox were delightful and having Sylvia day and night was a special treat. She was an easy child, sometimes sleeping through the night even though she was just six weeks old. The little girls treated her like a doll and Mrs. B. lit up every time she set eyes on her. She and Deborah were happy, despite all the losses they faced.

Deborah and Miriam's intimacies were curtailed once Sylvia came into their lives. Miriam said she was worried about the noise but Deborah thought she was just exhausted from the baby care. Even though the baby was easy, the hours were still difficult. Sylvia woke most days before the birds began to sing, but that slight inconvenience was worth the joy on Miriam's face – and Deborah's!

June 5, 1912

Their first week back in the Berkshires passed quickly. Deborah and Miriam spent much of their time caring for Sylvia.

"Deborah," Miriam yelled out as she bounded up the stairs. "I just got a letter from Hannah. It went to New York and then came here. Please sit with me in while I read this."

"Miriam. Are you ready for this? You know it could be very upsetting. Hannah was very disturbed when she saw us together. She may never have it in her heart to forgive you."

"I know that. But the fact that she wrote gives me a little hope. This might be an angry, scathing letter or it might be one filled with love and understanding. I need to find out."

She carefully opened the envelope with trembling fingers and a pounding heart. As they sat close to one another on the edge of their bed, Deborah rubbed Miriam's shoulder. Miriam began to read aloud.

May 25, 1912

Dear Miriam;

I took a long time to write back to you because I have been uncertain what to say. This has been a very difficult time for me, as you imagined. First was the shock of discovering you with Deborah. I was disgusted at first. Then I was worried. Then I was envious you had found someone to love. Then I was angry you had not shared with me about your relationship. I thought we shared everything.

Mother pressured me to tell her why I was so upset and, one day, I gave into her demands. I was feeling spiteful because I was so angry with you. After I told her what I saw, I immediately felt regretful. When I heard Father's reaction, I felt guilty I caused you to be thrown out of the family. I felt you deserved it, yet I missed you desperately. As you can tell, my feelings have swayed one way and then the other. You always were my best and actually, my only friend.

Now things have changed a little in my life. Your friend Marjorie and I have become friends, too. We have gone to the Museum of Fine Arts together several times and we have gotten together for tea three times. It is nice to have a friend to do things with.

Since Father got sick, I have been going to the shop daily. I am glad to have somewhere to go every day. It is good to do something meaningful. Nothing in my life mattered before. Now I feel needed.

William has been helping me learn new things about the business.
He has been very kind to me, even when I make mistakes. The other
day I spilled ink all over a large pile of newspapers we had just printed.
Another day I used the wrong glue on the book I was putting together.
And once, I gave someone the wrong order. William never gets angry,
as I think Father would have done. William tells me everyone
makes mistakes.

Father is doing much better. He came home from the hospital two
days ago, after a full month. He is not pleased he cannot go to work yet.
He dislikes staying quietly in his bed or on his favorite chair in the parlor.
Mother gets exasperated with him when he gets up too much or he walks
the stairs too quickly. She got really scared when he had his heart attack
and now she is working very hard to keep him from having another.
Sometimes I think her fretting makes things worse for him. If she would
stop picking on him, I bet he would recover more quickly.

Bubbie has also been very worried about Father. She told me she gets
Mrs. Zetterbaum's daughter to write to you. Mrs. Zetterbaum's daughter
is just learning to read and write English, so I don't know if you can even
read what she writes. I would be happy to help Bubbie with her letters.

That is all for now.
Love,
Hannah

Miriam had been weeping since the first sentence but managed to get through the whole letter. After she finished sobbing on Deborah's shoulder, they spoke of the newsy note. It was like Hannah to avoid talking directly about the fact they had not spoken or written in five months.

"Let's go find Mrs. B. to tell her about my letter," Miriam said. "When your parents come to spend Shabbos with us this weekend, I will tell your mother as well. I will write Hannah back soon."

June 9, 1912

The visit with Deborah's parents was lovely. Anna and Milton were visiting their cousins, so the adults had uninterrupted conversations about life, politics, and little Sylvia. The Levine's made a huge fuss over the baby, saying she had grown, though she was actually much the same as when they saw her a couple of weeks earlier. In fact, there had been little change in Sylvia's size since her birth, something which concerned Miriam a great deal.

Peyrek Q ❧ *Ruth's Choice*
Friday, June 14, 1912

With mixed emotions, Miriam faced the day when Ruth and Michael were to come to get Sylvia. She hoped this time apart had helped Ruth recover.

"Deborah, I am nervous about whether she has missed her baby during these weeks apart. It is extremely sad she is not as excited about Sylvia as we are. I will miss the baby terribly."

As soon as Ruth and Michael pulled up at the house, Miriam could see things were not good. Ruth had no color in her cheeks and no glee in her eyes. She walked in slowly, barely noticing anyone who had come to greet her. And most tellingly, there was no baby nurse with them. Miriam tried to hand Sylvia to Ruth, but she refused.

There was an awkward silence, and then Ruth said, "No. You keep her."

"Yes, but... she is your daughter, your child. I am certain she will be glad to see you," Miriam stammered.

"Not really. I am sure she had a better time with you."

Miriam and Deborah, shocked, glanced at each other and neither could find words. They took the baby into the dining room to escape from this upsetting reunion. Miriam held tightly to the baby, glad Sylvia was not old enough to understand her mother's words.

Deborah whispered, "This must be the sadness I have heard happens to some women after giving birth. I certainly hope this ends soon. It is not good for Ruth, nor is this good for her baby."

Miriam nodded and took a deep breath. "I agree. This is horrid."

"And Michael said nothing. Nor did he attempt to hold the baby. Deborah said with narrowed eyes, "Men! They just leave the baby care to their wives. How hard this must be for Ruth; he clearly has no idea how to support her."

Miriam responded softly, while rocking the baby, "I really wonder about him. He does not seem pleased to be a father. I also wonder if Ruth still cares for him."

Deborah shrugged, hugged them both, and suggested she take the baby for a walk while Miriam visited with Ruth.

Miriam walked back into the parlor and found Ruth sitting on a chair, staring ahead vacantly. Just then Mrs. B. asked Ruth to come into the kitchen to help her with something. Miriam was certain Mrs. B. was about to give Ruth one of her pep talks, the kind that had helped them so often, so Miriam went outside in search of Deborah and the baby.

After about fifteen minutes, Miriam and Deborah returned to the parlor, hoping that after a few tears, Ruth would come to her senses. Despite what Miriam assumed was Mrs. B.'s greatest effort, Ruth returned to Michael, unchanged. Ruth had sadness in her eyes as she departed.

Next, Mrs. B. called Miriam and Deborah into the kitchen. With an expressionless face she said, "Ruth asked me to tell you she wishes you would continue to care for Sylvia. She does not feel up to giving Sylvia the loving attention you two can provide."

"What?" asked Miriam with crunched brows, "What do you mean she wants us to provide care for her baby? Is she unable or unwilling to provide love to Sylvia? I don't know what to say."

"I have no idea how to respond to you. That is what she told me. She wants you to continue to be the guardians of her daughter."

Miriam glanced at Deborah. "I love this baby with all my heart. But I desperately want her own mother to love her just as much. How can she sit there and not even touch her?"

Deborah was so startled by this news she could only stare at Mrs. B., then glance to Miriam.

Mrs. B. looked sadly at the two baffled girls. "I don't have any answers for you. Ruth is not able to stop the sadness she feels. She does not think she can provide for her daughter."

"And what does Michael say about this?" Miriam asked.

"Nothing," Mrs. B. practically whispered. "I assume he never wanted a baby. Nor do I think he has any skills to provide care for a special child. Right now, they do not feel they can be Sylvia's parents."

Finally, Deborah spoke up. "This, this is shocking. I have never heard of a parent rejecting her own child."

"Unfortunately, I have," said Miriam. "This happens sometimes with a family at the settlement house. The workers have told me of mothers who give up their children. I cannot understand it."

"Do you think this is because Sylvia is not healthy?" Deborah asked Mrs. B.

"It certainly might be," she said. "Maybe Ruth cannot cope with having a sick child. Most babies like Sylvia get put into institutions."

Miriam's eyes grew wide. "No. That cannot happen. I will never let that happen. Sylvia deserves a loving family!"

"This is not your decision, Miriam," said Mrs. B. as gently as possible.

"This is so very sad." Miriam whispered. "I will take Sylvia upstairs."

I will go with you," Deborah said softly, as they walked up the stairs.

Peyrek R ❋ *Sylvia's Fate*
Monday, June 16, 1912

"We can't let Sylvia be put in an institution," Miriam said with clenched hands, which she banged forcefully on her legs.

"I agree," Deborah said, sitting up straight and taking a deep breath. "But Mrs. B. says that is what Ruth wants. Parents have the right to decide what is best for their child."

Miriam looked at the baby resting comfortably in her bassinet and continued insistently, "But they have never spent any time with her. They don't know how sweet she is. How can they make a choice for a child they do not know?" Miriam walked across the room, lowered herself into a chair slowly, and let out her breath.

"They can make any decision they choose," Deborah said, sitting at their bedroom desk. She put her fisted hand under the side of her chin, propping up her head, and looking at the sweet baby lying comfortably on her back, gazing at the ceiling. Deborah thought, This baby is so easy. She does not require much other than food, diaper changes, sleep, and love.

"Do you think Ruth would let us care for her a while longer? Maybe, when her sadness lifts she will not feel the same way," said Miriam leaning forward in the chair.

"That may be the case. But how will you feel if this baby is suddenly taken from us? We are already so attached to her," Deborah softly asked.

Miriam looked directly into Deborah's eyes and asked, "Do you think there is any chance we could keep Sylvia?" Deborah's eyes grew huge with the question. "Oh, that is a terrible thing for me to ask of you," Miriam said as she glanced downwards.

Deborah reacted quickly, "It is not at all terrible. I have learned to love that little girl too. I would love to keep her."

With tears in her eyes, Miriam said, "That is a serious statement you are making. Are you really ready to have a child in your life? This is something we cannot say casually. You and I need to have lots of conversations about this if you are sincere."

"I agree we need to talk. But I am thinking about how this will make us a real family: you, me, and Sylvia."

"Oh Deborah. While that does sound wonderful, we must think of all the consequences of such a huge decision."

Miriam spoke so quickly she could hardly catch her breath. "How can we afford to take on a child? And where will we live? How will we support ourselves? Are we really ready to be parents? And will Sylvia's grandparents approve?"

Deborah moved toward her, placing a hand gently on Miriam's heart, hoping to slow her down. Miriam responded by taking a few deep breaths, gaining some control.

Deborah moved back to the writing table, sat, and continued to stare at Miriam, hand on her own forehead. "There is so much to think about. I am afraid Ruth may make a quick decision to abandon her child to an institution, so we must discuss this immediately. And we should include Mrs. B. in our decision. We would need to stay with the Berkowitz family for now."

"And we would need to talk with your family too," said Miriam, grappling for words, "Your parents offered to support you while you were in college, but would they also support a child? Can we manage with your school and everything else? Maybe I could get a job at Henry Street, but who will watch Sylvia? It is complicated."

"And she will not always be a baby. When she gets older she will have lots of needs, especially if she isn't healthy. How can we afford her care?"

"But," concluded Miriam, "We both love this little girl. And we are clearly trying to think of ways we can be her parents. I am glad we are both in favor of trying. I love you so much."

"I love you too, "Deborah said with great relief. "I sincerely hope this will work and we can be a complete family. It is more than I ever dared to dream."

Miriam's Diary, June 16, 1912

Sylvia. I think of her constantly. Her tiny little fingers, her soft sounds, her baby smell. I love her so much. It already feels like she is our baby.

Yet I am so very worried. There are many significant issues we need to face before making this gigantic decision. And it all feels so rushed. I fear that Ruth is anxious to get rid of the baby and she will quickly abandon her to an institution.

I can hardly imagine I might be a mother. It is something I always wanted. I was willing to give up that dream to be with Deborah, but over time I might be left with a huge hole in my heart. If Ruth agrees to let us be the baby's parents, my life will be fulfilled.

Deborah's Journal, June 16, 1912

I am overwhelmed with the thought of having a child. This is not something I ever considered and I never thought I would have any skills at childcare. But I never had a baby in my life before and I have quickly learned to love little Sylvia. She is so precious, and Miriam is a wonderful model for me. And it is comforting to have Mrs. B. to turn to when we have questions. She makes it easier for me to know what to do. Suddenly, the idea of having a child is real and very exciting.

I am fearful about what will happen as Sylvia grows up. My sweet Miriam only sees the good side of things, but I am a worrier. My biggest concern, which I have not yet voiced to Miriam, is what it will be like for Sylvia to have two mothers. No one else in her school or her life will be like us. How will she explain us to her friends?

Sylvia will not grow up like other children. But that is probably the case whether she has two mothers or a mother and a father. Because of her special needs, she will be different than the others anyway. But she deserves to have parents who love her and I hope it will work for us to keep her.

June 17, 1912

In the morning, while lying in bed, Miriam asked Deborah tentatively, "How do you feel today about Sylvia? Did you become fearful overnight?"

"I had a dream of us walking down the street pushing her carriage and showing her off to everyone who passed us. I was so proud to be her mother and to share our joy."

"You surprise me, Deborah. I thought you were the one who would have thought of a million reasons that it would be a bad decision. Instead, it was me, waking up many times during the night with my heart beating very fast, worrying about taking this huge step."

"What worried you?"

"Everything. How will we manage financially, whether people would accept us, how we would care for her special needs, and whether we would be good parents."

"I understand all your concerns except the last one. You will be the best mother any little girl could have. I see how gentle and understanding you are with her and how every child adores you, including Leah, Anna, Milton, and all four Berkowitz girls."

"I don't think Beth or David would have anything good to say about me!"

"I doubt they would have anything good to say about anyone!" Deborah said with sarcasm.

Ignoring Deborah's comment, Miriam said, "I have another concern. How would it be for her if people did not accept the two of us as her mothers?"

The color drained from Miriam's face and she turned serious. "I hope we are not being foolish. It is a huge commitment to take on the care of a child who will have unique needs for her whole life. How will we deal with her lifelong limitations, her education, and her medical care? How will we react if other children tease her or if she is upset because she cannot learn as quickly as other children? Or, as you say, what if people cannot accept two women caring for her?"

Deborah walked to Miriam and put her hands on her shoulders, rubbing gently. "We will handle things as every parent does- one issue at a time. Maybe we can find some books to read, but least we will have each other."

Miriam said, "I feel badly for Ruth. She has been very alone in dealing with this baby. I don't think I could be considering this if I did not have you to share parenthood."

"And I trust that we will be in this together forever."

"Yes, forever."

June 18, 1912

"I thought of another issue," said Miriam as soon as they awoke the next morning.

"Good morning to you, too," Deborah said with a yawn and a simultaneous smile. "I guess you have been up again during the night."

"Not so many worries last night, just thoughts of how we would manage this. What if one of us gets sick? Then the other would need to care for her full-time. And what if you had an exam or I had something special at Henry Street I just had to attend?"

Deborah shook her head. "I would call that worrying. We would just have to make decisions as things come up like every family does."

"Family is such a wonderful word, especially if there is a baby included," said Miriam as her chest heaved, then fell.

"And we might have to limit some of our outside activities, especially while she is small. We might be too tired to do anything except care for her for the next few months. Having her full-time every day is a big change in our lives.

It will not be the same as when she came to visit or even like having her for these past few weeks. We will need to put her needs ahead of ours."

"And another thing, what if we disagree on something about her care, or if Mrs. B. disagrees, or if the baby starts waking the other girls during the night, or…"

"Hold on. Here you go again, getting worked up," interrupted Deborah as she gathered Miriam into her arms. "Let's talk about one concern at a time. No need to get riled up. And your rant has woken the baby, so we will have to curtail more conversation so that we can take care of her."

"Thank you for calming me down," said Miriam as she left the bed and gathered the weeping child in her arms.

"I love you Sylvia," Deborah said as she stood by them and stroked the infant's head.

"Deborah", Miriam asked, "What would happen if Ruth changed her mind. What if she came out of her blue mood and decided she wanted the baby back? Or what would happen if five years from now she saw what a wonderful little daughter we have and she decided to be her mother?"

"Oh my. More things to discuss. These are all reasonable concerns and I am glad we are thinking about them now, rather than when it is too late. But I don't like these apprehensions keeping you awake at night. You need to be rested to care for the baby and to think clearly. Let's take a long walk after breakfast to discuss your latest worries. And I think we should ask Mrs. B. to sit with us later today to talk things over. She has left us to our own thinking until now, but I bet she has many of her own thoughts about this. I feel ready to find out her concerns."

"I am sorry to be such a worrier all of a sudden. I have never made a major decision in my life before and it is hard to have only you with whom to review the situation. I would have talked this over with my mother. I have been missing her lately."

"I am sure you would have discussed this with Hannah also. What about Marjorie?"

"Her too. I have not written her lately, but that is a good idea. By the time I hear back from her it will probably be after we have made the decision but writing down all my feelings and concerns might help."

June 19, 1912

Dear Marjorie,

I am writing to tell you of the biggest decision I have ever faced. Ruth and Michael decided they cannot be Sylvia's parents because she is not healthy, and they are planning to send her to an institution. Deborah and I have been talking about taking Sylvia permanently!

I have been overcome with worry but also with excitement about being Sylvia's mother. It would make my life with Deborah complete. This is more than I ever dreamed possible. But dealing with a special child, or actually any child, is a huge decision. And because Ruth is ready to give her up soon, this major decision must be made immediately. Ruth and Michael will be back to discuss this in a few days, so, by the time you receive this letter, there will be a resolution.

I am fortunate to have Deborah to share this decision with. She is able to calm me when I become overwhelmed and she offers so many helpful perspectives. I could not decide independently and I certainly could not take on motherhood on my own. I will let you know what we decide.

Love,
Miriam

June 20, 1912

The conversation with Mrs. B. went well. She shared their concerns and also their eagerness. She promised to be there for support if they took on the lifelong task of motherhood.

"The quickness of our decision has played into the frantic feelings we both have," said Deborah, as she and Miriam talked in bed.

"I don't see you being frantic, Deborah."

"I hide it well. Your worry is so obvious that I figured I better disguise my own or no one would consider letting two nervous girls take on motherhood."

"I like the sound of that word – motherhood."

"So do I. And after getting Mrs. B.'s blessing, I feel it really may happen. "*Zal es zayn azoy*, May it be so."

Deborah's Journal, June 19, 1912

Everything has moved so quickly. We have engaged Mrs. B. and my mother in the conversation and to my surprise everyone is in agreement. My family has pledged financial support. I am confident this is the right decision!

Our last hurdle is Ruth. When she arrives this weekend, we will tell her we are ready to take Sylvia, rather than sending her to an institution. I hope, for once, Ruth makes the right choice. How could any mother refuse a loving home for her child, rather than an institution? I pray she says yes and we can begin our family life.

June 21, 1912

Ruth and Michael arrived in Great Barrington. A couple of hours later, two incredibly nervous girls sat in the parlor at Ruth's parent's house, waiting to talk with Ruth. The girls had left Sylvia in Mrs. Levine's care while they went next door for this important meeting. Deborah's leg jiggled and Miriam kept clearing her throat. When Ruth entered the room they both stood and hugged her somewhat awkwardly.

Miriam spoke up, getting right to the point. "Ruth, Deborah and I have been talking a great deal about Sylvia. We know that you and Michael are not comfortable being her parents. We love her and we want to keep her permanently. We don't want her to be placed in an institution."

All Ruth said, in her non-emotional style, was "Fine".

They all sat quietly for a few minutes, then Ruth asked, "Are you certain you could provide for her? You know she is not normal."

Both girls assured her they had discussed this at length and were very excited to be Sylvia's parents. They tried to involve Ruth in a conversation about the child, but it was obvious Ruth wasn't the least bit interested.

Ruth said, "I will talk this over with Michael and my parents. Thank you for offering. I will let you know by the end of the weekend."

Deborah and Miriam, encouraged, were unsure what would happen when Ruth told her family.

As it happened, Ruth's parents had many concerns about anyone being able to take care of an ill baby. Mrs. Gold was not in favor of the girls taking Sylvia, thinking the baby would be better cared for in an institution. She had never heard of a special child being raised by a family and did not want to be party to this unusual request.

When Ruth approached her grandparents, who were visiting for the weekend, she was met with more significant opposition. When her grandmother was appalled that two girls wanted to be parents together, Ruth came out of her sullen state long enough to disagree with her. She argued, "Miriam and Deborah have already proven themselves as capable caretakers. They have provided better care for my daughter than I could provide for her myself. They would do a wonderful job with her."

This sudden emotional response quieted her grandmother, who did not continue to argue.

Ruth left her grandmother to find Michael, who was perfectly amenable to this idea. Ruth was not surprised, since he had not shown interest in anything else.

Later, Mrs. Gold and her mother, each arguing her own position, hardly noticed they were on the same side of the debate. Beth spoke up, saying she wanted Deborah and Miriam to be the baby's parents. David surprised everyone when he talked, even though all he said was, "Me too."

Surprisingly, Ruth participated as well, saying, "I think it is wonderful that Deborah and Miriam will give the baby a chance for a happy life."

Both the Golds and Levines talked of little else over the weekend. On Sunday afternoon, there was a knock at the Gold's door. They were surprised to see Mrs. B., who had come all the way from Lenox to Great Barrington. When Ruth and her parents welcomed Mrs. B. into the parlor, she did not wait for a lot of small talk. "I have come to discuss the issue of Deborah and Miriam becoming parents to Sylvia."

Mrs. Gold and her mother looked at one another. Mrs. Gold spoke first. "We are not pleased. The child belongs in an institution where she may receive proper care."

"And I do not think that two girls can be parents. I have never heard of two mothers for one child," added Mrs. Gold's mother. "It is just not right."

Quietly, but firmly, Mrs. Berkowitz said, "I disagree. I think these girls are the perfect parents for little Sylvia. They will provide great love and care for Sylvia, which an institution could never provide."

Ruth unexpectedly interrupted. "Wait. This is our decision to make, mine and Michaels. We have talked it over and we have decided to let Miriam and Deborah take the baby."

"You are not making sense," Ruth's mother said.

"I certainly am. I am making more sense than I ever have before. I know I cannot be a good mother to this baby. I am not able to provide her with a loving home, but those two girls have proven they can do just that. I want them to be the baby's parents."

Mrs. Berkowitz got up from her chair and hugged Ruth. There were tears in her eyes, partially because she was pleased to see Ruth speaking up and also because she was hopeful that Ruth's decision would be honored.

The discussion ended quickly, and Mrs. Berkowitz headed back to Stonegate with directions to send Deborah and Miriam over in an hour for the decision.

Deborah and Miriam had been distraught since observing Mrs. B going into the Gold's home. Deborah paced across the parlor, while Miriam sat quietly, with a despondent expression etched on her face. As the door opened, Miriam rushed to greet Mrs. B., with Deborah close behind.

"Hello. I just talked with the Gold's and they are close to a decision. They need just one more hour. This is a difficult decision, and the three Gold women are fighting over whether Sylvia belongs in an institution or with you two."

With anguish, Miriam said, "How can that be? Why don't they see that Sylvia would be better off with us?"

"You will be pleased to know that Ruth agrees with you. She was very vocal, saying you should be Sylvia's parents. But her mother and grandmother put up quite a fuss. We will see if Ruth is strong enough to stand her ground. She was surprisingly strong while I was there."

Miriam's stomach gurgled and she put her hand to her mouth as she rushed to the water closet.

For the next hour, the three of them sat on the divan in tense silence. When the clock struck the hour, the girls glanced at each other and headed out the door. Half way across the lawn, they spotted Ruth walking towards them and they each feared bad news. Had she come outside so there would be no scene inside the Gold home? But as they got closer, Miriam was the first to note something she had not seen in a very long time. Ruth was smiling.

Ruth approached them, coming closer, then hugging both girls at once. With tears, she said, "I won the argument. You can have the baby. You can be Sylvia's parents. This makes me very happy."

It was difficult for any of them to speak, but through her sobs, Deborah eked out, "Thank you."

Peyrek S ✤ *Family*
Monday, July 1, 1912

Deborah's and Miriam's dreams had come true.

Miriam would be the legal guardian of the child, though both the girls were equally committed to her. They worried about financial matters, even though the Levines had offered assistance. In the end, both Ruth's and Michael's families agreed to share in the cost of Sylvia's care until she reached age 20, telling each other this damaged child would certainly not live that long.

Elated, Deborah and Miriam could not believe their good fortune, excitedly telling the Berkowitz children that Sylvia would live with them forever. The children applauded and shouted gleefully.

The next weekend Ruth and Michael arrived with the remaining baby supplies. Everything went into the room the Berkowitzes provided for Sylvia's nursery. For the time being, her bassinet would remain in Deborah and Miriam's room in Lenox, but, as she grew, she would be moved to the room right below them. The children made a sign for the door, 'Sylvia's Room'. Miriam suspected it would always be filled with the girls' drawings and love.

In the privacy of their room, Deborah said to Miriam, "The time has come to be practical. Everything is easy here in Lenox but we need to figure out our lives in the fall. We must find a New York doctor who will understand Sylvia's condition and offer us advice. We need to arrange our schedules so I can go to school and you can go to Henry Street."

"I disagree. We need to pay attention to Sylvia's needs right now, not in the fall. We need to get a local doctor to examine her now. We need to know what to expect and what she needs."

"But it is silly to have two doctors, one in New York and another one here. They might have different ideas. I think we should wait."

"I will not wait. She is our baby right now. Her needs are immediate," Miriam said, voice raised defiantly.

Deborah was displeased she and Miriam were arguing. She had wanted Miriam to be more self-assured but now that she was, Deborah found it difficult. She thought Miriam was not being sensible because she was so caught up in this baby's life. Waiting a couple of months could not hurt. Nothing would change in that amount of time.

"I will stop arguing. Let's ask Mrs. B. for her opinion," conceded Deborah.

Mrs. B. and Miriam thought the doctor should come see Sylvia now. Deborah agreed, though Miriam could still hear reluctance in her voice.

After the doctor's visit, Miriam explained to Mrs. B., "Now we know what Sylvia's problem is. The doctor was certain she is a 'Mongoloid Imbecile'. He says most babies like this are placed in institutions. If we choose to raise her at home, we should know she will be very slow to do everything. She will probably learn to walk and she might be able to talk but she will never be more than an eight-year-old in her mind. People will call her 'feeble-minded'," she said sadly.

"I am so sad for little Sylvia," began Deborah. "I am sorry she will not be like other children. But the doctor says there is nothing special we can do for her except love her."

"Love her we will," added Miriam. "I want to tell the whole world we have a wonderful little daughter and you and I are filled with love for her."

"I do love her. Almost as much as I love you."

July 1, 1912

Dear Hannah;

So much is going on in my life that I want to tell you about. Deborah and I have moved with the Berkowitz family to Lenox for the summer. It is so lovely to be in the Berkshires again.

Ruth and Michael had a baby, Sylvia, in April, and things did not go well for them. The baby is not normal. And Ruth has been very despondent since having the child. Nothing interests her, including the baby. We began taking Sylvia to our house for periods of time so she could have some loving attention. As summer arrived, Ruth let us take the baby to Lenox with us. It was shocking when Ruth was not even interested in visiting. So quite simply, she has asked Deborah and me to take over the parenting of her child. It was a surprise - but a wonderful one. We are now to be parents!!!

Sylvia is a very easy baby but very slow at learning. The doctor told us will probably never grow mentally to be more than a young child. I am certain Sylvia's condition is one of the reasons Ruth was not able to provide love to her, which I find very sad. But Deborah and I adore her and are happy to be Sylvia's parents.

I hope all is well with you and the rest of the family. I hope Father is improving and you are still able to help out at the shop because you seem to be enjoying that.

I love you and I miss you.

Love,

Miriam

July 4, 1912

For the holiday, Deborah and Miriam packed picnic lunches and headed into Lenox. They excitedly joined the towns-folk for a special celebration of the raising of the brand new 48-star American Flag. Although a town of just over 3,000 people, Lenox hosted huge throngs of visitors for this celebration, with patriotic speeches on the town square proclaiming the flag the great symbol of the United States.

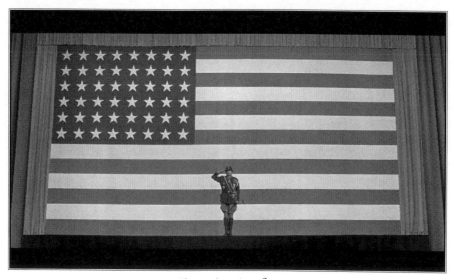

48-star American flag

Peyrek T ✤ *Heartache*
Monday, July 8, 1912

July 1, 1912

Dear Miriam,

I rite to tell you Tate had mor harts attk. He in hopital. No do good. Oy Vez mear. Oh, woe is me. I lov yu.

Bubbie

July 8, 1912

Dear Hannah;

I just heard from Bubbie. She told me Father is back in the hospital after another heart attack. She said he is not doing well. Can you please write to me to give me an update on his health?

Please know I am there with you in spirit. I love you all. I hope he recovers soon.

Love, Miriam

July 18, 1912

Dear Miriam;

Father is not doing well at all. He is still in the hospital and he seems to be getting weaker. This was a much more serious heart attack than the first one. Bubbie is frantic. Mother and I go to the hospital each day and bring him kosher food. His appetite is very poor. He looks horrible.

I also go to the shop each day. William is doing a wonderful job of keeping everything going but it is too much for him. It is actually too much for the two of us. We have gotten some new work and it is quite demanding. I am not certain if we can keep up with it. I don't know what will happen if Father cannot return.

William is very organized so he gets more work done than anyone could imagine, but he is staying very late each day. I found him asleep in the office a couple of times when I arrived in the morning. I think he spent the whole night. Sometimes I suspect he only goes home for Shabbos. I don't know what we would do without him. He has been very helpful.

I am anxious to hear more about your baby. I am happy for you.

Love,

Hannah

WESTERN UNION
TELEGRAM

NEWCOMB CARLTON, PRESIDENT   GEORGE W. E. ATKINS, FIRST VICE-PRESIDENT

Form 1204

WESTERN UNION TELEGRAM
RECEIVED AT GREAT BARRINGTON, MASS   JULY 22, 1912

MIRIAM COHEN
FATHER DIED. FUNERAL TOMORROW. COME SIT SHIVA.
MOTHER SAID OK.
HANNAH

WESTERN UNION
TELEGRAM

NEWCOMB CARLTON, PRESIDENT   GEORGE W. E. ATKINS, FIRST VICE-PRESIDENT

Form 1204

WESTERN UNION TELEGRAM
RECEIVED AT BOSTON, MASS   JULY 23, 1912

HANNAH COHEN
ARRIVING SOUTH STATION TOMORROW 5:15 P.M.
BOSTON AND ALBANY RAILROAD.
MIRIAM

Peyrek U ✣ *Reunion*
Tuesday, July 24, 1912

The train ride to Boston was horrible. Miriam cried off and on the whole six hours, missing Deborah and Sylvia already and feeling grief-stricken over her father's death. Plus, she was extremely nervous about seeing Hannah and Mother again.

Would Hannah come to the train station or would she send a driver? Would Hannah hug her? Would Mother greet her warmly or would she just tolerate her being there? Would she tell her she missed her? Or that she loves her?

"Hannah! I am here!" Miriam shouted from the platform when she saw her sister. As Hannah rushed to her, Miriam could see tears rolling down Hannah's face too. Were they tears of relief Miriam was there or shared sadness over their father's death?

As they embraced, Hannah squeaked out, "I am so glad you are here. I could not face this alone."

To Miriam's surprise, she saw William waiting at the end of the platform, ready to carry her suitcase. "Hello," he said in a shaky voice.

"Thank you for bringing Hannah," Miriam said to the unexpected member of her welcoming party. She looked at William, a short man in his mid-thirties, with slicked back dark hair, a square face, and large ears. He was clean and well mannered. The few times Miriam met him at her father's shop, he made no impression at all. If it were not for Hannah's continuous mention of him, Miriam might not have recognized him.

The trio walked quickly to the car, and climbed in as Hannah began talking non-stop, "It has been so awful. Father was really sick after his second heart attack. Every time I arrived at the hospital I worried I would find him dead. Whenever he fell asleep, I worried he would not wake up. Mother stayed with him most of the day, but I had to go to the shop. I don't know how I would have managed if it were not for William. He has worked so hard. We have barely kept up with the orders."

"How is Bubbie?" Miriam asked, "And what should I expect from Mother when I walk in the door? Will she talk to me?

"Bubbie is very sad. No mother should lose her child. That is the wrong order. He should be here to help her with her declining years."

Miriam shook her head sadly. "And Mother?"

"She is distraught, hardly sleeping at all during the past month. Since the funeral, she cannot stop crying."

"And how do you think she will be with me? Will she let me stay at the house?"

"She said it was fine to telegram you that he died. She said I could invite you for the Shiva. Certainly you will stay at the house. Where else would you go?"

"I am sure I could stay with Marjorie, if Mother prefers."

"No. She already put fresh sheets on your bed. Not that anyone slept in them since you left."

With an audible sigh Miriam said, "Baruch Hashem, Thank G-d! This is a great relief to me. Hannah, I was afraid I would never see you or Mother or Bubbie again. I am so glad to be home."

Hannah babbled for the rest of the ride, occasionally turning to William to ask a question. As they pulled onto their street, Miriam's stomach was in knots and the hairs on her arms stood up.

"Hello, Mother," Miriam said, walking into the parlor filled with friends sitting shiva with the family. The visitors left Mrs. Cohen's side, letting Miriam and her mother have a private reunion.

Mrs. Cohen turned to Miriam, crying out loud as she lifted herself from the chair and looked at Miriam with arms outstretched. "Thank you for coming," she said, with warmth and sincerity.

"I have missed you so much Mother," said Miriam between sobs.

"I am glad you have come home. It all feels wrong. You were gone and now your father is gone. It is so sad."

"I wanted so badly to be here for the funeral but it was too late to get a train yesterday after I got the telegram."

"Don't worry. You are here now."

"Where is Bubbie?"

"In the kitchen. Where else?"

As Miriam ran toward the kitchen, she shouted "Bubbie. I am home," with a new surge of tears.

"*Meyn shayner maidel*, my beautiful girl," said Bubbie, first in Yiddish, then in English. "*Kinahora*, praises. You home."

They embraced in a long, tight hug, with Bubbie's warm arms and wet apron adding sweetness to their connection. Both wept openly, then talked, both at the same time, about how wonderful it was to be together again.

After reconnecting with Bubbie, Miriam rejoined the other relatives and neighbors, who greeted her kindly, giving their condolences, avoiding asking where she had been all these months. Miriam moved from group to group, never staying long enough for lengthy conversation. Soon there were ten men,

the required number to hold their nightly service. Together they recited the
Mourner's Kaddish, *Yit'gadal v'yit'kadash sh'mei raba*, which does not mention
death but rather affirms the steadfast faith of the mourners in G-d's goodness.
Then they chanted the melodic *El Maleh Rachamim*, a prayer for the rest of
the departed. Once the service ended, everyone left, including William, leaving
just the immediate family standing together in a suddenly silent house.

"It is wonderful to have you home," Mother said to Miriam, holding her
face in her hands.

Miriam sniffled. "It is good to be here."

Mother and Miriam embraced for a long time, then parted with just a
quiet, "Good night".

In her old room, Miriam felt strange seeing the blue flowered bedspreads
and little blue lamp, the things Deborah had admired, sitting in place just as
they had always been. It seemed such a very long time ago. Everything was
the same as it was when she left for her summer vacation in New York over
six months ago. She could hardly believe all that had happened since.

Despite her racing thoughts, sleep came easily for Miriam. She was
exhausted. And when she awoke, it almost felt like the past year had been a
dream. She dressed and headed down stairs.

"Good morning Miriam," said Hannah as if it was just another day.

"Good morning Hannah. It is good to be home."

"William is heading to the shop," Hannah said in a matter-of-fact manner.
Then her eyes narrowed as she said, "I don't know how he will manage alone
during the week of mourning, since I cannot join him. There is so much to
do. He will be back here before most of the people arrive for the evening
service tonight."

"I am certain people will understand if he falls behind at work. I would
like to go with you to the shop when shiva is over. Would that be okay?"
asked Miriam.

"Certainly. That would be nice," responded Hannah.

Miriam looked around Bubbie's kitchen, which had not changed at all.
The stove was polished perfectly, the pots hanging from hooks on the wall
were worn but clean, and the wood floors shined. The delightful aromas
lingered.

"I like being here. I am so pleased Mother let me come," Miriam said,
sitting on the chair next to Bubbie.

"You belong here. Where else you go? You mother, she want you come.
But you Tate say no."

"I understand she had to follow his decision. I am glad she let me back into the family now that he passed away. But I keep expecting him to come home from the shop."

After they both shed tears, Miriam excused herself to find her mother. As she expected, Mother was sitting in her favorite chair in the parlor, reading the newspaper. Beside her was the latest Jewish Advocate and a shawl, in case she got cold. Next to her was Father's empty chair.

"Good morning Miriam. I am so glad you are here."

After a grand hug, Miriam said, "Mother, I want to tell you about my life since I saw you last."

"Sit here and we will talk." Mother pointed to Father's chair. Miriam never sat in that chair before and she was a bit uncomfortable. After biting her lips and raising her eyebrows she asked, "In Father's chair?"

Her mother saw her discomfort, so she patted the arm of her own chair, and Miriam happily perched on it. Mother held Miriam's hand or ran her fingers through Miriam's hair as she asked many questions, especially about Sylvia. She was genuinely interested in everything Miriam had to tell her. They talked about Father, and Bubbie interrupted their conversation several times, always about food people brought to the house. Some things never change, Miriam thought.

William appeared, as promised, just as a large number folks arrived for the evening service. That night, the third night of *shiva*, brought a new crowd of mourners, all with plates of food. It did not take long for the required ten men to arrive for the *minyan*, signaling it was time for prayers.

Hannah spent the evening sitting by William, talking easily with him and with Marjorie, though she engaged in few other conversations.

As she walked Marjorie to the door, Miriam asked, "What is the story with Hannah and William? She seems so comfortable with him."

"She has not said a word about their relationship but she talks about little else. It is 'William this' and 'William that'. I think your shy sister has a boyfriend but I am not sure she knows it."

A few days later, after all the guests had left, Miriam looked around, as if making certain there was no one to hear, and asked Hannah, "So what is your relationship with William?"

Miriam noticed a slight blush on Hannah's face. "What do you mean? We work well together. We get along well," answered Hannah, clearly surprised by the question.

"I don't think I have ever seen you so comfortable with anyone, Hannah. You seem to be in good spirits when you are with him and he seems to be equally comfortable with you."

"Well, we work together all day so we have gotten used to each other."

"Hannah. I think you have feelings towards him."

"I like him and I am grateful for his hard work. He treats it like his own business." The blush on Hannah's face grew to a bright red and she turned away to hide it from her sister.

"I think he likes you more than just as a business partner."

"Oh, Miriam. You are so silly." Hannah's leg began to shake back and forth, though she seemed unaware of it.

"We will see. I think he is a nice man and I think he is good for you."

Hannah suggested it was bedtime, so they turned off the downstairs lights and both headed upstairs for the night.

Sitting Shiva

Peyrek V ❧ *Publishing Shop*
Wednesday, July 30, 1912

As the week of mourning was coming to an end, Miriam thought of Deborah and Sylvia constantly. She had planned to return to them soon after this period ended. When she brought it up sitting around the breakfast table, her mother and Hannah reacted in shock.

"I thought you were coming home for good," announced Mrs. Cohen with concern on her face.

"We need you at the shop," Hannah said.

"But I have a family waiting for me. I am aching for my little girl and I have never been apart from Deborah this long."

"When will you be back?" asked Mrs. Cohen.

"I would love to return with Deborah and Sylvia," Miriam said hopefully and without hesitation.

After taking a gulp of air, Mrs. Cohen conceded, "They would be welcome here as well."

"Thank you, Mother. I would love you to meet my little girl."

Hannah added, "And we sure could use your help in the shop."

"Deborah has skills that would help. She has been working at The Bulletin at Barnard College. She does lots of editing, providing skills I do not have."

"We can put her to work too," said Hannah.

"One of us needs to stay home with the baby, so you only get one of us at a time," Miriam said, smiling.

"What about me?" asked Mrs. Cohen with wide eyes. "Couldn't I take care of the baby?"

Miriam could not believe she heard her mother say those words. "What a wonderful idea, Mother," Miriam said with a huge grin.

After the last night of *Shiva*, as they cleaned the last of the dirty plates, Miriam reminded Hannah she would like to go to the shop with her the next day.

"You will need to be ready at 8:00am, when William will pick us up."

"Then I will go to bed now," said Miriam. "I want to be fresh in the morning so I can be of assistance to you."

By mid-morning, at the shop, Hannah told Miriam she was pleased she came to work, not just to watch. As they worked side-by-side, Miriam shared some of the shortcuts she learned at the student newspaper office, which thrilled Hannah. When the conversation turned to Miriam's relationship with

Deborah, Hannah fidgeted a bit, but Miriam kept talking. When Miriam talked about Ruth and baby Sylvia, Hannah was comfortable again.

William worked extremely hard all day, organizing orders, ordering supplies, dealing with customers, and a myriad of other tasks, just as Hannah had described. He talked very little. Miriam was not sure if this was because he was focused on his work or because he was feeling awkward with her. When they headed back to the house, he answered Miriam's questions, offering little else. It was clear to Miriam that Hannah and William were seriously overworked.

"I will be glad to come the next couple days, before I leave."

In unison, Hannah and William said "Thank you."

Before leaving Boston, Miriam knew there was one more thing she needed to do, visit the cemetery. Hannah agreed to join her and quickly enlisted William to drive them. Mother refused to go and Miriam was afraid her mother was ashamed to face Father, since she had defied his wishes by welcoming Miriam back to the family.

They walked up a small hill to find his burial spot, passing simple headstones, many with small stones atop them. As Jewish families visit departed relatives, they place small stones instead of flowers. There would be no headstone on Father's grave until next year, when they would have a ceremony for the unveiling of the stone. Miriam hoped to be back for that ritual.

Miriam thought of her Father with the same love she always had for him; she held no resentment. He had done what he believed was right. He rejected Miriam for her behavior, but Miriam knew he loved her. She stood at the gravesite, tenderly reciting the Mourner's Kaddish. Her tears were genuine.

1910 Yiddish book

Top: *Large printing press,* Above: *Printing press,* Below: *Type case with fonts for presses*

Peyrek W ❧ *Readjustment*
Thursday, July 31, 1912

"It is wonderful to have you home," Deborah said as soon as she saw Miriam at the train station in Lenox.

"I missed you both so much," Miriam said, reaching out her arms for the baby and paying no attention to the other people. She only saw her little family.

Sylvia made no noise and did not smile but cuddled comfortably against Miriam's shoulder. Deborah said, "She is so happy to see her mama."

As they walked to the waiting car, Miriam said, "It is time we come up with different names for each of us. One of us can be Mama. What do you want her to call you, Deborah?"

Deborah, with a twinkle in her eye, said, "How about she calls me Mama and she calls you *Ima* (eem-ma), the Hebrew name for mother?"

Miriam smiled, absorbing the decision. "That sounds perfect. From now on, I am *Ima*."

"It is so nice to have our little family back together. You are more relaxed than I have seen you in a long time. You have your sparkle back, my love."

On the way home, Miriam talked eagerly about Boston, all the while stroking baby Sylvia. When the baby fell asleep, she reached out to touch Deborah. They held hands as Miriam talked about Bubbie, Mother, Hannah, and William. It was apparent how very much she had missed her family.

That evening, once the baby was down for the night, Deborah and Miriam had a long-awaited opportunity for intimacy. Miriam touched Deborah softly, stroking her whole body with a sensual touch. Deborah practically purred. Even though it had been a while since they had been together, their loving was languid. They caressed each other slowly; once they were both satisfied, they started all over again. Their second round was more intense, but still loving.

Miriam had missed having Deborah at her side in bed. She missed her caresses and the excitement she was able to create in her body. Miriam hoped they would rarely need to be apart for as many as those long nine days. She wished she could sleep in Deborah's arms every night for the rest of her life.

In the morning, Deborah asked, "So you want the three of us to travel to Boston together?" "Your mother is willing to see me, despite my corrupting her daughter?" Deborah said suggestively.

Miriam teased, "Don't be silly. It is just Sylvia she wants to see. She is willing to put up with having you."

"I think there is a little bit of truth in your joke," said Deborah smiling.

"Maybe an itsy-bitsy bit," Miriam said with a laugh. "But Mother was not the one who rejected us in the first place; it was my father. He could never accept anything outside of the Talmudic teachings. But we are fortunate that Mother now wants us both to be part of the family."

"And what about Hannah? Has she gotten over the shock of what she saw?"

"Truthfully, I think she is so busy with the publishing shop and with William, she hardly notices anything else. She is really smitten."

"Do you think he feels the same way?"

"Oh yes. He watches her with the same intensity. It is charming that two misfits have found each other."

"Miriam! I never heard you talk of your sister that way!"

"I guess I never said it out loud before but I have thought it to myself many times. It is so good to see her enjoying life."

August 6, 1912

One relatively cool day, soon after Miriam's return, the girls took a stroll with the baby. "Miriam," Deborah said after taking a deep breath. "I have a difficult question to ask you and I want you to answer it honestly. Do you wish you were living in Boston with your family?"

"Oh Deborah. You are my family, you and little Sylvia."

"I know that. But what I am asking is whether you want to move back, now that you have reconciled with your family?"

"Certainly, I have missed them all. But we have begun to make a life for ourselves, the three of us. I do hope I will be able to visit them but I can adjust to living wherever we are, as long as we are together."

"That is very sweet to hear," said Deborah, with a sigh.

She felt relieved Miriam said she was not anxious to move back there, yet Deborah did not feel the conversation was done. Later in the day, they discussed traveling to Boston in early August, prior to the start of classes at Barnard and before celebrating the Jewish New Year, Rosh Hashanah. All the pieces were coming together for them. With Mrs. B.'s mother living with them, they were free to travel to Boston.

Peyrek X ✤ *Boston*
Thursday, August 21, 1912

In Boston, the family of three was welcomed graciously. Mrs. Cohen treated Deborah with more kindness than Miriam expected, almost as if she was another daughter. Hannah responded affectionately to their little girl and Miriam thought that perhaps Hannah's relationship with William had softened her. Both of them wondered when Hannah and William would finally acknowledge their feelings towards one another.

Sweet Bubbie held Sylvia most of the day, telling everyone repeatedly what *naches*, pride and joy, the baby brought her. Often Miriam had to pry Sylvia from her to spend time with her own child! Mrs. Cohen barely got her turn.

There was a difficult side to their visit as well. Hannah and William worked very hard to keep the shop running well but it was more than they could manage. Miriam wondered how Father and William had managed.

Mrs. Cohen, who had no head for numbers, was floundering, trying to keep the books straight. Deborah tried to help but it was difficult. Deborah and Miriam took turns working in the shop, but even that was not enough. Although she did not say it, Miriam wondered if her mother was thinking of closing the business.

It was Deborah who thought a great deal about the situation, realizing that she and Miriam might be the only answer to saving the business. Quietly, without mentioning it to Miriam, she began entertaining the idea of moving to Boston. Deborah had already gotten used to living separately from her parents, and, although she would miss them desperately, she was certain Anna and Milton would assure regular visits.

Deborah did not share these thoughts. It would mean giving up Barnard College, Henry Street and everything they planned for their future in New York in the winters and Berkshires in the summers. Yet living in Boston would make Miriam incredibly happy and they would be welcomed into a loving family. The Berkowitzes had been their saviors, but the pull towards family was equally strong.

After finishing a lovely dinner of brisket and kasha, buckwheat grouts, Mrs. Cohen began to speak. "I have gathered you all together tonight for a reason other than to say goodbye to Miriam and Deborah. And I have included you, William, because I want to talk with you all about the publishing shop. As you all know, we are all struggling to keep it going. I am not good with the books and Hannah and William are having a difficult time keeping up with the orders. It was wonderful to have Miriam and Deborah to help out but they are leaving tomorrow and we will be back to where we were before. One of your father's friends has approached me about buying the business. He has watched us struggling and he has made a generous offer to take it off our hands."

"No Mother. You can't do that," Hannah said loudly. "Father would never want that. He worked his whole life to build up the business and would be heartbroken to hear of this. *Zikhrono livrakha*, may his memory be a blessing." Hannah stared at her mother.

"Hannah is right," Miriam said. "Father put his heart and soul into growing the shop. There must be another answer."

Deborah looked around at the stricken looks on everyone's faces and spoke, despite not having said a word to Miriam. "I have an idea. Miriam and I have lots of skills that could help. Miriam is a strong worker and I have a good business head and editing skills."

All heads focused on Deborah until Miriam spoke. "But we don't live here Deborah. How can we help them?"

"We could move to Boston. Mother and Bubbie could watch the baby while we work at the shop," Deborah said to a roomful of wide-eyed family.

"But where would we live?" asked Miriam, stunned by the course this conversation had taken.

"Right here," said Mrs. Cohen. "We would make do."

Miriam stared at her mother. "But there is just one room for Deborah and Sylvia and me. As Sylvia grows, that will not be enough space," she said, half statement, half question.

To everyone's complete surprise, William stood up and stammered, "Hannah and I could get married and live on our own. Then there would be plenty of room for the baby."

Everyone stared at William and there was total silence.

"That sounds like a marriage proposal," Miriam said, eyes riveted on William.

"I guess it is," said William, walking towards Hannah. He stood by her chair, then got down on one knee and asked, "Will you marry me, Hannah?"

"Yes, yes, I will," Hannah answered softly, with no hesitation and with tears in her eyes.

Hannah rose and William awkwardly embraced his new fiancé as everyone clapped and cheered. After the applause died down, Mrs. Cohen said, "This is time for celebration. May I offer you an engagement gift?"

Everyone watched as Mrs. Cohen slowly took her husband's simple gold band off her right hand, where she had placed it after his death. She handed it to William. "Mr. Cohen would be glad to welcome you to the family, William. He would want you to have this to give to your bride."

After a few tears and hugs, the room quieted and Deborah spoke again. "I will move to Boston if Miriam agrees to this plan."

Miriam openly cried. "I love you Deborah Levine." Everyone cheered and there were more tears. Miriam blushed a bit, embarrassed she had been so forthright in front of everyone, but all knew the sentiment was genuine.

"We need to go wake Bubbie, with this good news," said Miriam, leading the whole group on a parade to Bubbie's room.

Mr. Cohen's ring

Peyrek Y ❖ *The Move*
Monday, August 25, 1912

Back in New York, Miriam stood sorting the large pile of mail awaiting the Berkowitz family.

"Deborah! Look! It is a letter from Barnard. I am certain it is an acceptance letter," exclaimed Miriam, quite out of breath after running up the long stairway to their bedroom.

"It would be nice to think they want me but I will be pleased to tell them I will not be coming because my family is moving to Boston. We are making the right decision," said Deborah.

"I hope so. I feel badly, uprooting you from everything familiar. You are giving up so much to help my family."

"You are not forcing me to do anything. If you were, I would probably be resisting – on principal! I want to move to Boston with you and Sylvia. I am excited about this."

Deborah looked at the letter, still in Miriam's hand. "We don't even know if it is an acceptance letter. But even if it is, it does not matter as much as coming to Boston. And if I got into Barnard, perhaps I can also get into Radcliff. But right now, that is the last thing on my mind. All I want is to settle Sylvia into her new home and settle you into your old home. Please don't worry about me."

"But…"

Deborah interrupted, "No 'buts'. That is what you always say. This is the right decision. I am sure of it."

Deborah looked lovingly at Miriam. "I am glad I dared to mention this move. If I had remained quiet, your sister Hannah might have been a spinster." Deborah grinned.

"Oh, Deborah. You are right. That was very brave of you. How wonderful that William said his piece. I doubt he would have had the courage to invite her on a date. Instead he invited her to be his wife!"

"It was not bravery on my part. It was my impulsivity. You have been too kind to me, accepting this bad habit of mine."

With a glint in her eyes, Miriam looked directly into Deborah's lovely face, "I love you. I love you just the way you are, Deborah Levine."

As an adoring look crossed her face, Deborah said, "And I will always choose to see you as the most accepting, loving girl I have ever met. I love you too, Miriam."

Peyrek Z ✣ *Success*
Tuesday, September 23, 1912

Miriam was thrilled when Mrs. Cohen offered half the business to William as a wedding gift so he would have an adequate way to support his new wife. She was even more elated when her mother offered Miriam and Deborah the other half.

Over many meals and discussions in the Cohen parlor, the family planned how to manage the business. Hannah and Miriam would run the printing presses. William would make the decisions about the back room, where he was well versed in keeping the machines working. William, Hannah, and Miriam would translate from Yiddish to English, as needed. Deborah would communicate with the customers and also offer editing services to increase the profits.

They clearly needed additional assistance, so they hired Marjorie, Miriam's friend, to keep the books. Marjorie's younger brother, Aaron, a bright boy who asked to apprentice in the shop after finishing school next year, would run errands on his bicycle. Mrs. Cohen was put in charge of bringing in new business. This role made her feel important, even though she would probably do it anyway.

Bubbie was also noted as a key player, caring for Sylvia while everyone else was at the shop. Deborah and Miriam decided it would be fine if their little girl spoke Yiddish before English. No one could provide for her better than Bubbie.

December 16, 1912

"Miriam, you know I wrote to Susan and Helen. I have thought of them often and I have wondered how they are doing. They have written me back. Wait until you read what they wrote! They have answered our questions about their relationship."

December 10, 1913

Dear Deborah and Miriam,

We want to tell you how much we like you, too, and how much we have admired your bravery in being true to yourselves. We learned a lot from you. Your openness helped us realize it is possible to love another woman. We had not been involved with each other physically before knowing you, though we are now a couple, like you! Thank you both for giving us the strength to be true to one another.

Wishing you happy holidays.
Fondly,
Susan and Helen

Miriam said, "I am glad our openness has allowed them to be together."

"I am so glad they admitted their feelings to one another. I hope they are able to live their new life together without the rejections we had to face. Let's continue to be in touch with them."

Mrs. Chaim M. Cohen

Requests your presence at
the marriage of her daughter

Hannah L. Cohen

To

William S. Goldman

On Sunday evening June fifteenth
Nineteen hundred and Thirteen
at three o'clock

Temple Mishkan Tefila
206 Seaver Street, Roxbury, Massachusetts

Reception to follow

January 13, 1913

"It is wonderful to be surrounded by love," said Miriam as she and Deborah settled into their room one night.

"Yes. These past months have been wonderful. We are in love. Hannah and William are in love. Your mother and Bubbie are in love with Sylvia. Even your friend Marjorie has a new beau."

"I hope she doesn't get married before Hannah and William," Miriam said. "I am thrilled Hannah finally set the date. It was difficult because it is auspicious to be married on the first of the Jewish month, on the new moon, but they had to avoid all the Jewish holidays and the time between Passover and Shavuos. They also needed to avoid the winter months, since they wanted to include your family, Ruth and her family, and the Berkowitz family. It was very complicated!"

"I thought it was sweet of Hannah to invite them all," said Deborah. "She seems so much more aware of others. Falling in love seems to have changed her."

"Hannah was always sensitive in her own way. It was just that she was afraid to show it before," Miriam said a bit defensively.

"I am sure." Deborah said, changing the subject so Miriam would relax. "I am so very glad my family is coming. I especially miss Anna and Milton. Even though we have frequent visits, they change a great deal each time we see them."

"They are certainly growing up. When we went to New York for Chanukah, Anna was more interested in her friends than us. Milton was much more involved in his studies than I have seen before," Miriam said. "Your mother was the one most glad to see us. It was wonderful to spend time with her. I found it a little unsettling that your father had very little to do with us. I wonder if he suspects the true nature of our relationship."

"I wondered that also, though he has said nothing. I fear he is a little uncomfortable with the two of us."

January 21, 1913

"Miriam, I just received an exciting letter from one of the Barnard professors. I did not know I had a fan until just now." Deborah waved the letter in her hand as she approached Miriam and Sylvia.

"Read me the letter while I feed the baby."

January 15, 1913

Dear Deborah Levine,

I have read several articles you wrote for 'The Bulletin' and I have found your writing style to be exemplary.

I would be pleased to assist you with publishing the article you wrote entitled, "Parents of Young Women" in a women's magazine. I would also like to include it in a book of essays I am writing. I think your talent should be used to benefit other young women. Please let me know if you would like to pursue this.

Sincerely,

Grace A. Hubbard

Associate Professor of English, Barnard College

"I am so excited for you, Deborah. You do have a fan! And an opportunity to be published! I am pleased you will have an outlet for your creative expression and maybe you can have a small income of your own."

"Let's not count the pennies yet! I am glad you are not the only person to think my thoughts are worthy. Thank you for your encouragement."

They sat in the parlor, holding hands. Deborah said, "We have become important support for each other. I am less impulsive than I was when I met you, thanks to your guidance."

"And I am more self-assured," said Miriam with a sigh. "I did not think I would ever find a way out of the predictable life that was set out for me."

"You are the girl of my dreams!"

Love

Part 1 ❦ *Valentine's Day*

Friday, February 14, 1913

My Dear Deborah,

Happy Valentine's Day, My Sweet. I love you. You are the best thing that has ever happened to me.

A couple of years ago, I was feeling unfulfilled. I feared I would only be the sum of my parent's wishes. I did not see a path out of the uninspired life I was facing. Now, my life is enriched by you, our baby, and a career. It is more than I imagined and I am so very happy.

Because of you I am learning to accept who I am, with less fear. I feel much stronger, thanks to your support and encouragement.

I will love you forever,

Miriam

Happy Valentine's Day, Miriam,

Thanks to you, my life feels complete and I am no longer hiding who I am. When I met you, I ached with my hidden desires to find a girl to love and now that I have found you, I feel whole.

Your love has given me the patience to control my impulsive nature by taking a deep breath and talking things through with you. I can also resist the temptation to run away from uncomfortable situations! It is amazing you love me despite my faults.

You are more wonderful than the girl of my dreams. You are kind, loving, supportive, tender, and the best mother! Our little Sylvia is very lucky to have you as a parent. Our daughter has your appreciation of the beautiful, small things in the world which I learn through both of you.

My dreams have all come true and I look forward to creating new dreams with you. I have discovered happiness is possible and I am filled with love for you both.

Deborah

Part 2 ❊ *Shanda/Shame*
Monday, February 17, 1913

On their second day in New York, Deborah and Miriam brought Sylvia to the Berkowitz apartment. While they were waiting for the family to greet them, there was a knock on the door. The doorman handed Deborah a sealed note, addressed to her.

> *Father found your Valentine. Do not come home.*
> Mother

"What have you done? Did you bring your Valentine's Day card to my parents' home?" Deborah asked through clenched teeth.

"Oh no. I put in my pocket so I could re-read it. It must have slipped out," Miriam said with tears in her eyes.

"Well, you have ruined everything. Now my father is rejecting me, just like your father did." Deborah turned away.

Their first vacation since taking over the publishing shop had turned disastrous. They had gone to the Berkowitz home for a visit and now they would need to remain there, with Mr. and Mrs. B. being their saviors for the second time. Soon, Deborah stopped lashing out at Miriam and the two of them discussed their newest difficulty. And they discussed it. And discussed it.

Two days later, after many tears and little sleep, Deborah and Miriam were startled by another knock at the Berkowitz home. This time, instead of a note, a tearful Mrs. Levine stood in the doorway. She immediately spread her arms, enfolding her weeping daughter. Mrs. B. whisked the children away, so Mrs. Levine, Deborah, and Miriam could talk privately.

"Mother, I am so glad you have come. Please tell me what Father has decided," Deborah said, wringing her hands. She had a bit of hope he had changed his mind.

With a shaky voice, Mrs. Levine said, "You are not going to be pleased. I begged him to be more understanding than Mr. Cohen, but he refused. I acknowledged that most Jewish fathers would behave in this same manner but I encouraged him to be more accepting. He would not listen. Despite my best effort, he wanted to tear his clothing and announce he was in mourning for the daughter he used to have. I persuaded him not to do this, because then he would have to explain the whole situation to Anna and Milton."

Hysterical crying followed, with deep, loud sobs. Miriam's cried with equal distress, her grief triggered by Deborah's devastation. Mrs. Levine seemed as distraught as the two girls, though her tears were silent. Then Mrs. B. entered.

Both girls ran to her open arms. As they had learned to expect, she had an idea. She turned to Mrs. Levine and said, "Rebecca, I think your husband may respond to my husband's story about his best friend who died after being rejected by his family. Maybe he will fear for Deborah's welfare and forgive." In desperation, Mrs. Levine agreed to share the story, though the reminder of this story increased her own worry about the potential outcome of his rejection of Deborah.

After two more days, Mrs. Levine returned to report her progress in persuading her husband to relent. She was sorrowful as she reported that he remained steadfast, refusing to accept them, repeatedly describing his disapproval of their lifestyle. Mr. Levine demanded they remain silent about this situation, especially with Anna and Milton. The girls agreed to this requirement, though Mrs. Levine was fully aware that she would need to offer some explanation to her two other children about why Deborah and Miriam disappeared to the Berkowitzes.

It was a relief for the girls to return to Boston. For Mrs. Levine there was no reprieve; she had nowhere to escape.

During the next few months, Mrs. Levine worked relentlessly to soften her husband's attitude. Each time she received another distraught letter from Deborah, she became agitated and unable to sleep. She felt torn between her daughter and her husband. She was aware he was shamed by his daughter's life choice, yet she reminded him how much he loved her. Worried about seeing Deborah at Hannah and William's upcoming wedding, she was beside herself. The week before the wedding. Mrs. Levine took a huge, dishonest step in hopes she could calm Deborah and bring her some peace. She sent the following telegram:

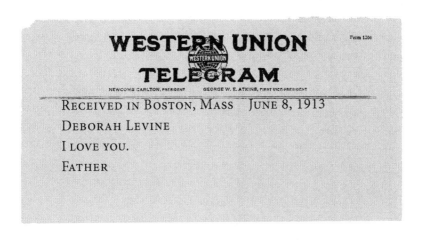

WESTERN UNION
TELEGRAM

NEWCOMB CARLTON, PRESIDENT   GEORGE W. E. ATKINS, FIRST VICE-PRESIDENT

RECEIVED IN BOSTON, MASS   JUNE 8, 1913

DEBORAH LEVINE

I LOVE YOU.

FATHER

Part 3 ❦ *Wedding Preparations*
Sunday, June 15, 1913

It is Hannah and William's wedding day.

1:00pm

Deborah and Miriam sat in their bedroom, looking forlorn, as they talked of how they both wished Hannah would allow them to help her get ready for the 3:00pm ceremony. They had no responsibilities other than getting themselves and Sylvia dressed. It felt wrong. Miriam should be at Hannah's side, helping her prepare for the upcoming event. While Mother helped Hannah fix her hair and attach her veil, and Bubbie fussed over the bride, the two girls were banished from the wedding preparations.

Hannah told Miriam she was anxious about being the center of attention and having Miriam nearby would make it worse. It made no sense. Miriam wished she could be there to calm her sister but felt she needed to respect Hannah's wishes on her special day.

Miriam's only jobs as bridesmaid had been to help Hannah choose her dress and pick up the flowers. The dress shopping had been difficult, with Hannah rejecting most dresses presented to her at the bridal shop. She finally relaxed when a very simple ankle length silk dress was offered. The loose top was embellished with a simple lace overlay and an almost invisible white rose. The sleeves were pinched above the elbow, the only detail to an otherwise undistinguishable dress. Hannah selected a simple, long veil with a headband of small flowers. Miriam would have chosen something more special, but Hannah was pleased with the unpretentious outfit.

Now, Miriam sat on a chair in her room, next to the huge box, which held the very large bouquet of white and pink roses with long ribbons hanging almost to the ground. Miriam worried Hannah would trip over one of these ribbons, but she would not mention it to the very nervous bride.

"I never thought this would happen for her. I am thrilled for both of them and I believe they will be good for each other," Miriam said, trying to take her mind off her disappointment.

Deborah, who was by her side, smiled warmly as she readjusted the baby in her lap, "They are a perfect pair."

"Look how adorable our little girl is, all dressed up in her new pink dress," Miriam cooed.

"You are *kveling*, bursting with pride, as any mother should be. I feel the same way. The Berkowitz girls will be so surprised to see how Sylvia is growing. She is still pretty small for her age but bigger than the last time they saw her. I cannot believe it has been nine months since we last saw the little girls," Deborah reflected.

"I am excited to see them and to see Mr. and Mrs. B. They really saved us when things were most dire. I will always be grateful for their kindness."

"We have not seen them since before Mrs. B.'s mother died. I was so sorry to be unable to attend the funeral."

"Deborah, on another subject... I am really relieved that your father chose not to come today. Despite his telegram to you, you have still not been in touch, nor have you seen each other. It would have been very difficult to have him here."

"I hope that I will see him again soon, but I agree that this would not have been the right place. I wonder what excuse he gave to Anna and Milton."

"We may never know," Miriam said with a shake of her head.

Before the girls had the opportunity to dress, there was a knock on the door. Mrs. Cohen stood there with tears running down her cheeks. "Miriam, I need you to help me with Hannah."

Miriam looked to Deborah, who nodded in agreement. In response to Miriam's confused look, Mrs. Cohen explained, "Hannah is so nervous, I am worried she will be sick." Miriam left quickly.

Upon entering Hannah's room, Miriam took one look at the pale, sickly-looking bride and suggested everyone clear out. "Hannah," she said softly, standing at her side.

"I am so scared, Miriam. I am afraid I will trip or faint as I walk down the aisle. I want to be married, but I don't want to go through this awful ceremony."

Miriam sat on the arm of Hannah's chair and put her arm on her sister's back. "I will help you. I can walk you down the aisle, so you won't fall."

"Would you do that? I am glad Uncle Abraham will be there to walk with me, but I would feel so much better with you there too."

"Wipe your tears. I want everyone to see what a beautiful bride you are. We will walk together and I will stand by your side until William takes over. I am certain you will be comfortable once he is near you. It will be my pleasure to be your support on this very special day."

Miriam thought, I am so much happier now that I am able to provide comfort to my sister, rather than sitting idly in my bedroom.

Hannah relaxed considerably knowing she would have Miriam by her side. The two even joked about her getting sick all over the rabbi. As they talked about the ceremony, Hannah got nervous again so Miriam suggested that William could circle the bride, instead of the ritual of the bride circling the groom. "No chance to trip and fall," Miriam said.

Hannah let out a huge sigh.

Miriam also suggested it would be fine for Hannah to repeat her vows softly, so only William could hear. She did not have to say anything loud enough for the guest's ears.

At the knock on the door to tell her it was time to leave, Hannah blanched and announced she was not ready. Miriam sent the others away and told them to return in ten more minutes.

"What else are you worried about Hannah?" asked Miriam, scrunching her brows. Hannah hesitated, then began panting. Miriam put her hand on Hannah's shoulder, until her breathing became normal again.

When Hannah whispered, almost inaudibly, "Tonight." Miriam understood.

"Are you worried about your wedding night?" asked Miriam very quietly.

"Yes," was all that Hannah could say.

"Do you know what married people do on their wedding night?"

"Oh, Miriam. I don't know anything. I am just scared that I will have to get undressed in front of William. How can I get into my new nightdress with him in the same room? I don't want him to look at me. And what if he tries to touch me? I am really scared."

"Hannah, this sounds like too much for one day. Just the wedding is enough."

"It is. Would you talk to William and ask him to go very slowly with me? If he gives me privacy to change and does not try to touch me, it would make me feel better."

"Certainly. I will do anything to make this a wonderful day that you will remember with joy."

"I cannot promise that, but if you talk with him, it would be better."

"Another day we can talk about more about what married people do. I can only guess what men want, but I think I know more than you about how people show their love to one another."

"I do love him, Miriam."

"I know you do. Wipe those tears and let's make this an agreeable day for you, with no worries about tonight. I promise I will talk with William."

"Thank you," said Hannah, some color returning to her cheeks.

"Now I will tell Mother and Bubbie you are ready to leave."

2:00pm

As soon as Hannah was ready, Miriam returned to her bedroom to find Deborah and Sylvia. She told Deborah she had calmed her sister, but she did not offer details about what was wrong. She commented on how beautiful Deborah looked in her dramatic off-white, two-piece tailored dress with multiple pleats. A black and beige ribbon along the collar and down the slope of the dresss, added contrast and allure.

Miriam quickly donned her bridesmaid dress, a simple white costume, similar in fabric and style to Hannah's wedding dress. It was not very pleasing to Miriam, but Hannah had chosen it. Deborah made a fuss, just the same.

At the synagogue, she found Mother and Bubbie had whisked Hannah off to the vestry, which was used as the Bridal Room. Miriam entered and whispered to Hannah that she would return after she had spoken with William.

Miriam found William looking quite dapper in his dark suit, white shirt, white bow tie, neatly trimmed moustache and hair. After complimenting him on his appearance, she asked to have a moment alone with him. The two found a quiet spot in the back of the sanctuary.

Miriam began awkwardly. "I need to talk with you. Well, Hannah needs me to talk with you. Actually, I offered to talk to you for Hannah. Let me start again."

"What is wrong? Has Hannah changed her mind?"

"No, William. Not at all. She is very excited about marrying you. But she is very nervous about the ceremony and, well, everything else."

"What can I do to help? Should I go talk with her?"

"No. You must not see your bride yet. But she was so nervous I came up with some ways to calm her down. I offered to walk her down the aisle, along with our uncle. Then I will turn her over to you, where she will feel very safe."

After explaining to William about the need for him to circle her during the ceremony and about how Hannah would repeat the vows softly, to just him, William thought he had heard all the news.

"William. There is one more thing." Miriam gulped several times, her voice becoming shaky as she mentioned their wedding night. She explained how Hannah needed to undress in privacy and needed him to be very slow in trying to touch her. He sighed loudly, smiling awkwardly, seemingly pleased the pressure was off him to perform his duties as a husband. He promised to be sensitive to his new bride's needs.

Miriam returned to Hannah and nodded, trusting Hannah knew that her sister had taken care of the difficult conversation.

Miriam's dress   *Deborah's dress*

Chupah

William and Hannah

Part 4 ✤ *Nuptials*
Sunday, June 15, 1913

3:00pm

The wedding music began as the small wedding party lined up at the back of the sanctuary. Miriam noticed the sweat breaking out across Hannah's brow, but when she held on tightly, Hannah relaxed. They watched William's parents walk a little too briskly down the aisle, followed by Mother and Bubbie who walked exceedingly slowly.

Hannah linked her arms with Uncle Abraham on one side and Miriam on the other, and they slowly ambled down the aisle. Hannah faltered a bit when she looked out at the spectators but Miriam held firm and Hannah stood strong. When they got to the *Bimah*, Hannah's eyes locked onto William's and his presence calmed her. Miriam dropped her hold; in William's grasp, she was steady.

Gathering under the wedding canopy, the *chuppah*, the rituals began. Hannah did not trip, there was only minimal whispering when William circled her, and Hannah actually smiled slightly. At the end, their kiss was a bit awkward, obviously something they had not practiced much. It took William two tries to break the glass at his feet, since his first stomp missed the handkerchief-covered vessel completely, causing a bit of a chuckle by the congregation. To everyone's delight, they were man and wife!

4:00pm

While the bride and groom were sequestered for the period of *yichud*, a short seclusion, Miriam reunited with Deborah and Sylvia. The reception was simple, with homemade appetizers on a large table. After kissing the baby, Miriam said, "I think it went smoothly."

"I will be looking forward to hearing your stories later. I have a feeling you worked very hard to get Hannah through this experience. It looked like it was quite an ordeal for her."

"You are absolutely right. I will tell you later."

Just then the Berkowitz children pulled away from their parents and barreled towards Miriam. They almost knocked her over. Luckily, the baby was in Deborah's arms. All giggles and excitement, the younger girls patted the baby on the head, just like they would do to their dolls. Their oldest, Fanny had grown significantly, both in height and in attitude. Although she rushed to them with the others, she became quiet when faced with questions. Before long, the girl's parents caught up, hugged Deborah and Miriam warmly, as Deborah happily transferred her bundle to Mrs. B's waiting arms.

Mrs. Levine approached them, with Anna and Milton at her side. Deborah swallowed hard, not used to seeing her mother alone at an affair like this, though she knew ahead that her father would not be attending. She actually thought it better that their reunion be somewhere else, since today was all about the couple about to be wed.

Mrs. Levine, looking gaunt and uncomfortable, greeted them with hugs. Deborah whispered in her mother's ears, "Thank you for everything."

Mrs. Levine shuttered and whispered back, "I trust that someday Father will welcome you home. I will continue to try."

"Getting his telegram made such a huge difference. Someday he will be back in my life."

Mrs. Levine turned away, not wanting Deborah to see the tears rolling down her cheeks. She was feeling very out of control. Deborah's siblings were hovering, waiting for their greeting, so the conversation went no further. Anna and Milton seemed as happy to see Miriam and Sylvia as their sister. Anna opened her arms for the baby, but Miriam made her sit in a chair before receiving her. Mrs. Levine excused herself while she regained her composure while the rest of her family chatted happily.

After a few minutes, Marjorie approached, with her new boyfriend on her arm. The Berkowitzes took leave, and the girls were free to talk with this glowing new couple. Micah, a sweet looking young man with a lopsided hairdo, could hardly take his eyes off Marjorie. She talked freely with Deborah and Miriam, glancing repeatedly at his adoring eyes.

"What an exciting day," said Marjorie with glee. "Micah and I enjoyed the service."

"I am so happy," said Miriam. "Could you tell how desperately nervous Hannah was? I practically had to hold her up, coming down the aisle."

"She did look uncomfortable and really pale at the beginning but she seemed to relax as the service went on."

"Did people snicker when William circled her? Hannah was so afraid she would trip that I suggested they do it backwards."

"There was a bit of talk since this was unusual, but it died down quickly. Everyone who knows Hannah was just glad for this wedding day."

Just then Deborah spotted Ruth. Deborah offered to hold the baby and nudged Miriam to approach her old friend. Miriam noticed Michael was not by Ruth's side, but instead was quite animated, speaking with a group of attractive young girls.

"Hello Ruth," Miriam said in an overly cheerful voice.

"Nice to see you, Miriam. It has been a while."

"I am sorry. Since we moved to Boston, we have not been back to New York often. And we will not be able to return to the Berkshires this summer, because we are needed at the shop."

"I hear that you and Deborah saved the shop from being sold. That was wonderful of you."

"Thank you," was all Miriam said, thinking, it was something I needed to do for my father.

Miriam was acutely aware how stiff this conversation was. Neither of them discussed the baby, nor their prior friendship.

Ruth seemed equally awkward, with her eyes glancing around for an excuse to end their discussion. "It is time to go into the dinner. Let's go take our seats, which are near each other."

"Fine. Let's talk more later," Miriam said, relief in her voice.

When Miriam found Deborah, she whispered that the reunion had been uncomfortable and they had avoided discussing anything of significance. She said she would try to have a real conversation with Ruth later.

Micah

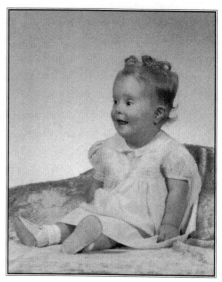

Sylvia

5:00pm

The table was set with the same linens and plates as every wedding and Bar Mitzvah celebrated in this room. Deborah and Miriam sat with the Berkowitzes, Mrs. Levine, Anna, and Milton, who jabbered with the four little girls, though Miriam noted that Fanny was again quiet. Only Milton's silly jokes got a rise out of her. Miriam sensed the beginning of a tough adolescence rapidly approaching.

At the next table sat Marjorie and Micah, Ruth and Michael. As Miriam planned her visit to this table, she hoped Marjorie's presence would make her more comfortable. She considered asking Marjorie to help her with the discussion with Ruth but realized this was her own challenge.

Finally, the bridal couple arrived. Everyone rose to welcome them, which made Hannah nervous all over again. She tripped as she entered the room, creating a syncopated gasp among all the partiers until William caught her. The couple sat at the head table, next to both their parents. Hannah tried her best to ignore the crowd, but it was not until wait staff began laying out the food on long tables that her tension lessened.

Dinner was an affable affair, with favorite dishes created by each of the Cohen's friends. The Prussian and Latvian food included potatoes with pickled fish, borscht, stroganoff with buckwheat and mushrooms, and pike cutlets. This was a Kosher meat meal, having been blessed by a rabbi according to Jewish law, with no dairy in any of the dishes. Everyone piled their plates high and ate with great fervor.

6:00pm

Once the plates were cleared, there was a pause before the arrival of the wedding cake. Miriam approached Ruth.

"Can we talk some more, Ruth?" Miriam said with a shaky voice.

Ruth rose, suggesting they take a little walk, finding a bench in the sanctuary for their conversation.

"Ruth, it is wonderful to see you more cheerful and acting more like yourself. I was really worried about you after the baby was born."

"I had a very tough time. I did not care about anything, including whether I lived or died."

"I know. I was not a very good friend. I did nothing to cheer you or to care for you."

"That is not true at all, Miriam. You were the only one to visit me and to try to cheer me up. I will be forever grateful to you for trying to help me."

"I am so glad you appreciated my visits. I could not tell. I worried that I was being more of a drain on your already sad mood."

There was a short silence, with both girls thinking of the topic they hesitated to approach. Finally, Miriam took a very large gulp of air, then bravely said, "And we must discuss the baby."

With downcast eyes, Ruth said. "Yes, we must." There was another silence.

Miriam grew pale and her eyes misted over. "I don't know if we did the right thing, offering to take your baby. I have often felt guilty we took your child, when you might have come to love her once your blue mood lifted."

"Oh Miriam. You should not fret. I am the one who should feel guilty, not you. I was unable to love my child. You and Deborah saved her from a life in an institution and I will always be grateful to you."

Large tears fell down Miriam's face and she could hardly talk. She managed, "I have been afraid of so many things. Afraid we acted too quickly, afraid we could not provide for her has well as the institution, and mostly, afraid that you would want her back."

"Do not worry. I could not accept her being different. I have heard you and Deborah have a wonderful way with her. That is all I could ever want for my child."

"Thank you so much for saying that, Ruth. You have given me such relief. I have been so afraid that you would want her back when you saw her."

"You do not have to worry any more. Just know that I appreciate the wonderful care you provide for her. You clearly love her, which is more than I could have done."

"Oh Ruth. Sylvia is the best thing that could have ever happened to me, other than Deborah."

"I am happy for you and Deborah."

Miriam paused and approached the next subject. "Did you know all along that we were together?"

"It is hard not to notice. You look at each other with such tenderness. I wish Michael and I shared feelings like that."

"You don't? Don't you and Michael love each other?"

"I am not sure we ever did. If it were not for my pregnancy, our relationship would never have ended in marriage. But we are making the best of it."

"I am sorry to hear that, Ruth. I had hoped you could share a happy life together, like Deborah and I do."

"That will never happen. He is not a bad person but there is no love between us."

Miriam dried her tears and moved closer to Ruth. She took her hands and held them firmly. "Ruth, at this moment you feel like the friend I had at camp. I remember the talks we had with such fondness. We grew apart in Great Barrington. I have missed the friendship."

"I became self-centered and very foolish. Getting married, having a baby, and learning how to live in a loveless marriage has changed me. I am finding my way back to being that girl you befriended at camp."

Miriam looked Ruth in the eye before continuing. "Do you think we can be friends again, even though I have Sylvia?"

"I think we can be friends again because you have Sylvia. She is your baby, Miriam. Yours and Deborah's."

The girls embraced, like old friends who had found each other after a long absence.

7:00pm

Marjorie and Micah wheeled out the wedding cake, which was made by Bubbie with great love. Everyone shouted praise as it reached the center of the ballroom. Miriam and Ruth looked at each other and smiled. Deborah caught this and was puzzled. Miriam whispered, "I will tell you about my new friend later."

As the Berkowitz family got ready to leave, Mrs. B. said to Deborah and Miriam, "You know you are welcome at our home anytime."

"I always feel welcomed by you," said Deborah.

Miriam squeezed Mrs. B. and said, "We will always love you and feel appreciative of everything you have done for us. Your support saved me and was more important than anything."

Deborah cocked her head and cleared her throat. "Well, more important than anything other than me and Sylvia! But you helped to make that happen."

After more hugs, they parted, knowing it would be a long while until they were together again.

9:00pm

Miriam and Deborah sat in their bedroom after putting Sylvia to sleep, reminiscing about the day. Miriam said, "The wedding was such a sweet affair. Hannah did not smile for the formal photographs but William was friendlier with the guests than I would have imagined."

"I agree. I think those two have cared a great deal about each other for a long time."

Deborah laughed, "My mother always said, 'As the Lord makes them, he matches them.' They are a great pair."

Deborah smiled as Miriam continued, "It was grand to see the Berkowitz family. They all made such a fuss over Sylvia; actually, everyone did. Our little girl was admired by every single person at the wedding."

"And everyone seems to accept we are both taking care of her," said Deborah.

Miriam nodded, "Not a soul asked questions. If they thought we were together, they might not be so accepting. I assume they don't think about it."

"Maybe they do, my innocent girl. Maybe they are just accepting us because they love you. They might talk behind our backs but no one has been unkind. As long as we don't make them uncomfortable, I think we will be alright."

"For Sylvia's sake, let's hope so."

"It was strange to see Ruth and her family," Deborah said, changing the subject. "I wondered how she felt seeing her daughter. And what happened with the two of you?"

Miriam explained, "Ruth is different. Having the baby and giving her away had a huge effect on her. She is not her former bubbly self, though happily she is past her blue mood. She talked about her feelings and seemed more like the girl I remember from camp."

"Might you be friends again? Deborah asked.

"Yes. I think she is very different," said Miriam, yawning. "She has been reflecting on all the changes in her life."

Deborah leaned forward, speaking softly, "And I noticed Michael paying lots of attention to the pretty young girls, even though he is married, but Ruth doesn't seem to care. I would not be so gracious if you were making such a fuss over other girls."

"Don't, worry, Deborah. I only care about you."

"How I love to hear those words."

"Mother and Bubbie looked lovely and were extremely happy for Hannah. I know they were missing Father but they both glowed throughout the evening."

"I don't think either of them thought this day would come. And Marjorie was so happy and thrilled to have her own boyfriend at her side. She has grown quite fond of Hannah."

Miriam said, "As the wedding took place, I was thinking of you Deborah. I love you as much as Hannah and William love one another."

"I love you equally," said Deborah wistfully. "As I watched Hannah and William under the chuppah, I wished we could announce our love to all our friends and family. That will never happen. But today everyone supported us, our family, and friends...."

"And hopefully they will forever. Maybe even your father someday. I love you, Deborah Levine."

"I love you, Miriam Cohen."

"Come here," Miriam said softly. "It is a wedding night."

The End

The wedding cake

GLOSSARY

HEBREW

Afikomen אֲפִיקוֹמָן
Half-piece of matzo which is set aside for dessert after the Passover meal

Ark/Aron Kodesh אָרוֹן קֹדֶשׁ
Torah Ark is an ornamental closet, which contains the synagogue's Torah scrolls

Bimah בִּימָה
Platform or pulpit

Birchas Hamozon ברכת המזון
(Blessing on Nourishment) Grace After Meals

Chag Same'ach חַג שָׂמֵחַ
Happy holiday

Challah חַלָּה
Special Jewish bread, usually braided

Chanukah חֲנֻכָּה
Jewish holiday commemorating the rededication of the Holy Temple
(the Second Temple) in Jerusalem

Charoses חֲרוֹסֶת
Sweet, dark-colored paste made of fruits and nuts eaten at the Passover Seder

Chuppah חוּפָּה
Canopy under which a Jewish couple stand during their wedding ceremony

G-d י ה ו ה
A way of avoiding writing the name of G-d, to avoid the risk of the sin of erasing
or defacing the Name

Haggadah הַגָּדָה
Jewish text setting the order of the Passover Seder

Havdalah הַבְדָּלָה
Jewish religious ceremony that marks the symbolic end of Sabbath and holidays

Ketubah כְּתוּבָּה
Special type of Jewish prenuptial agreement

Kiddush קידוש
Reciting kiddush prayer on the eve of Shabbat and holidays is a commandment
from the Torah

Kosher כָּשֵׁר
Foods that conform to the regulations of kashrut dietary law

Ma'oz Tzur מעוז צור
Liturgical sung on the holiday of Hanukkah

Matzo מַצָּה
Unleavened flatbread eaten during Passover

Matzo Brie מצה בריי
Ashkenazi Jewish dish made from matzo fried with eggs

Mazel Tov מזל טוב
Congratulations!

Mezuzah מְזוּזָה
Piece of parchment in a decorative case mounted on the doorframe of the house
and inscribed with specific Hebrew verses from the Torah

Minyan מִנְיָן
Quorum of ten Jewish adults required for certain religious obligations

Mitzvah מִצְוָה
Good deed done from religious duty

Kol Nidrei כָּל נִדְרֵי
Aramaic declaration recited in the synagogue at the beginning of the evening
service on Yom Kippur

Seder סֵדֶר
Ritual feast that marks the beginning of the Jewish holiday of Passover

Shabbos שַׁבָּת
Judaism's day of rest and seventh day of the week

Shema Yisrael שְׁמַע יִשְׂרָאֵל
First two words of the of the morning and evening Jewish prayer services

Shiva שבעה
Week-long mourning period following burial

Shul שול
Jewish house of prayer; Synagogue

Simin Tov U'Mazel Tov סימן טוב ומזל טוב
Two phrases: "good sign" and "good luck"

Sukkos סֻכּוֹת
Harvest holiday on the 15th day of the 7th month

Sukkah סוכה
Temporary hut constructed for use during the week-long Jewish festival of Sukkos

Talmud תַּלְמוּד
Central text of Rabbinic Judaism

Tisha B'Av תשעה באב
Annual fast day, on which a number of disasters in Jewish history occurred

Torah תּוֹרָה
Central reference of Judaism: the first five books of the Hebrew Bible and the
rabbinic commentaries

Yichud ייחוד
Ritual during an Ashkenazi Jewish wedding in which the newly married couple
spends a period secluded in a room by themselves

YIDDISH
(spoken language transliterated)

bisl epes	little thing
gutn-tag	good day
ahdank	thank you
bubbie	grandmother
gay shlafen	go to sleep
gelt	money
gezunt in deyn kepele	good health in your head
hobn epes tsu esen	have something to eat
kishke	intestines
kumen	come in
kvell, kvelling	great pleasure combined with pride
meshuggina	crazy
munn	poppy seed
naches	feeling of pride and/or gratification
shanda	shame
shiksa	young non-Jewish woman (often derogatory)
sholom alaichem	peace be upon you
trog gezunterhait	wear it in good health
tsimmes	Rosh Hashanah dish of carrots, sweet potatoes, honey, and meat
Zal es zayn azoy	may it be so

.

Made in the USA
Columbia, SC
23 September 2018